NO STONE UNTURNED

ALSO BY JAMES W. ZISKIN

Styx & Stone

james w. ziskin

NO
STONE
UNTURNED

An
ELLIE STONE
MYSTERY

SEVENTH STREET BOOKS®
AN IMPRINT OF PROMETHEUS BOOKS
59 JOHN GLENN DRIVE • AMHERST, NY 14228
www.seventhstreetbooks.com

Published 2014 by Seventh Street Books®, an imprint of Prometheus Books

Cover image © helene cyr/Media Bakery
Cover design by Jacqueline Nasso Cooke

Inquiries should be addressed to
Seventh Street Books
59 John Glenn Drive
Amherst, New York 14228
VOICE: 716–691–0133
FAX: 716–691–0137
WWW.SEVENTHSTREET BOOKS.COM

18 17 16 15 14   5 4 3 2 1

Library of Congress Cataloging-in-Publication Data

Ziskin, James W., 1960–
  No stone unturned : an Ellie Stone mystery / James W. Ziskin.
    pages cm
  ISBN 978-1-61614-883-6 (pbk.) — ISBN 978-1-61614-884-3 (ebook)
  1. Women journalists—Fiction. I. Title.

PS3626.I83N73 2014
813'.6—dc23

2013047666

Printed in the United States of America

To Lakshmi

CHAPTER ONE

SATURDAY, NOVEMBER 26, 1960

The story I heard was that Fast Jack Donovan was chasing a rabbit through the woods when he tripped in the wet leaves. As he fell on his shotgun, the muzzle peeked out from under him and blasted a volley of lead and powder past his right ear. He twisted on the ground for a while, kicking and swearing until the ringing in his ear had faded. Then he picked himself up, scraped a layer of muck off his brand-new hunting jacket, and saw the crop of blonde hair half-buried in the mud.

✥

It was just turning dark. I was driving myself home from a date: a Saturday matinee of *BUtterfield 8* with an eager young bank clerk of my acquaintance. For weeks, we'd been flirting through the teller's window as he scribbled entries into my passbook and dealt me my withdrawals with the panache of a seasoned croupier. He seemed fun, and I thought he might have potential. But I never imagined that an innocent movie (well, not so innocent) would lead to his pinning me on the sofa for a count of three. The wrestling was a disappointment, at least for me. As I buttoned my blouse, I swore to myself there would be no rematch. And of course I would have to change banks.

I turned north and started to climb Market Hill, just as one of those Mitch Miller sing-alongs came on the radio. I nearly broke the knob switching it off and turned up the police scanner instead. A dispatch was in progress: a body had been found in Wentworth's Woods, near Route 40, north of Wilkens Corners Road.

In all my time in New Holland—nearly three years—the most exciting event I had covered for the *Republic* was a mysterious trash-can fire in front of Tesoro's Pharmacy on East Main Street. The boredom had just about worn me down, and not even the odd afternoon of heavy breathing with bank clerks, lawyers, or junior editors made any of it seem worthwhile. My life was grinding by like a glacier inching down a mountainside. I was ready to leave the bars, bowling alleys, and empty knitting mills behind. Abandon this forsaken backwater like an unwanted child and go back to New York to prove my late father right once and for all—that I was wasting my time writing filler and shooting photographs for a small, upstate daily that didn't appreciate me.

My father's death in January was a recent wound, made all the more tragic by our long, unresolved estrangement, now fossilized and permanent. Abraham Stone, celebrated Dante scholar and professor of comparative literature, had challenged me to show him one significant piece I'd written for the paper, and when I couldn't, we essentially stopped speaking. We'd had little to share anyway, especially with my mother and brother gone. Elijah was killed on his motorcycle in June of 1957, and my mother succumbed to cancer three months later. My father and I were left alone, two survivors uncertain and unsympathetic of each other, thrown together without the option. And now he, too, was dead.

Furthermore, my position at the paper was going nowhere fast. Artie Short, publisher of the *New Holland Republic*, didn't like the idea of a girl reporter and hated the sight of me to boot. Yet, somehow, I hadn't found the words to tell Charlie Reese, my editor, that I couldn't stand one more day in New Holland. It was five thirty on a cold Saturday afternoon, two days after Thanksgiving, and I was getting the feeling I'd be sticking around just a bit longer.

꩜

The woods were crawling with cops: New Holland police, state troopers, and county deputies. Even Big Frank Olney, sheriff of Montgomery County, had managed to pry himself out of his swivel chair to investigate the biggest crime of his tenure. When I pushed through the cordon, Doc Peruso, the county coroner, was pulling a sheet over the naked body.

"Hey, Eleonora," called Olney. "Our guy's in Schenectady. Can you take the pictures?"

"Sure, Frank," I said, unsnapping my Leica, knowing he called me that just to gall me. Everyone knew I went by Ellie. "What happened here?"

"Murder," said Peruso. "Not sure how long she's been dead; maybe twenty-four hours. I'll know later if she's been raped. And here's your headline, young lady: that's Judge Shaw's girl under the sheet."

"Judge Shaw?" I gulped. "As in the Shaw Knitting Mills Shaws?"

"That's off the record," said Olney. "We don't have any positive ID."

"I've been their family physician for twenty-five years," said Peruso. "That's Jordan Shaw, all right."

"Off the record, please, Ellie," repeated the sheriff, nicer than he'd ever been in a nonelection year. "We haven't raised Judge Shaw yet."

"I'll hold off on the ID," I said, plugging a flashbulb into the reflector. "Can you move these guys back while I take the pictures? No need to put on a show."

Olney ordered the cordon to retreat twenty yards, and Fred Peruso turned back the sheet. I'd seen a few dead bodies before, but none so fresh or so young. I'd never met or even seen Jordan Shaw before, which I'm sure made photographing her corpse a little easier. They don't teach you this stuff at the Columbia School of Journalism.

"Pretty girl," I said to Peruso. That was an understatement, even with the mud smeared over her bare, white skin. "How old was she?"

"Twenty-one. Just back from school in Boston for the holiday."

"You said her name was Jordan?" I asked. "Kind of an unusual name for a girl, isn't it?"

"Family name," said Peruso, puffing on his pipe. "The judge's grandmother was one of the Saratoga Springs Jordans."

"Any idea of the cause of death?"

"Look at her," he said. "I'll give you three guesses, and the first two don't count."

Her neck was indeed twisted into a difficult and, apparently, fatal angle. I knelt down next to the body and snapped a tight shot of her colorless face.

"Can I touch her?" I asked. Peruso nodded, relighting his pipe in the cool breeze. Frank Olney had no objections. My boldness surprised me. "Doctor, what's this mark on her pelvis?"

Peruso joined me to examine her lower abdomen. "What the . . . ?" he said, brushing some dirt away and exposing a two-inch, horizontal gash in her skin on the left side, about an inch above the line of her pubic hair. Frank Olney joined us, peered over Doc Peruso's shoulder, and swore to himself.

I backed off to shoot the torso, pelvis, and legs.

"Is this how you found her?" I asked the sheriff, ejecting another spent bulb onto the wet earth, where it hissed for a brief moment before going cold and silent.

"No. Her face was in the mud, body twisted clear around. Buttocks almost flat against the ground."

"Not a comfortable position," I said, rewinding the first roll of film.

"You're gonna clean up them bulbs when you're done, ain't you, Ellie?" asked the sheriff to needle me.

I nodded yes. "I suppose she was already dead when she hit the ground?"

"Dead before she got here," clarified the doctor.

"What's the nearest road? Forty?"

"Route Forty's about two hundred yards back that way," said the sheriff, throwing a thumb over his shoulder. Then pointing past me, "There's a service road to the water tower about fifty yards over there."

"Paved?"

"Just mud." He squinted at the moon then nudged the wet ground with his toe.

"Are your boys checking for tracks over there?" I asked, loading the second roll.

He glared at me. "You want this job, Eleonora?"

"Take it easy, Frank," I said. "It's for my story."

Olney stared me down for a moment, hands on wide hips. It must have made him feel tough to push a girl around. A girl just trying to do her job. Then he lit a cigarette and took a deep draw.

"Halvey and Pulaski are over there now, looking for tracks," he said. "Why don't you see if there's anything worth shooting when you're done here?"

"Almost finished. I just want to get some tight shots of her neck."

"She ain't in no rush," he mumbled. "But remember, the paper doesn't use any of these. They're for my investigation. And black and white. I ain't paying for Kodachrome."

"I'll bill you for film and processing," I said, returning to the body. "And bulbs . . ."

Jordan Shaw's hair was matted with mud and wet leaves, making it impossible to tell if she'd been clubbed on the head. Peruso would know better in the morning. Her face showed no contusions or abrasions. The neck appeared to have been snapped neatly, with no sign of trauma anywhere on the skin, if you didn't count the gash in her pelvis. But that hadn't killed her. I finished off the second roll with some wide shots of the crime scene, picked up my exploded flashbulbs, then set off in search of Halvey and Pulaski.

I tramped through the woods toward the service road, wondering if I was following the murderer's route. The ground was saturated from the previous night's rainstorm, and the soggy earth tried to suck the shoes right off my feet. I wished I'd worn boots; my heels were ruined. If anyone had left Wentworth's Woods on foot the night before, there would surely be tracks left behind.

∞

"Jesus, Ellie!" cried Halvey. "You scared the hell out of me. Make some noise when you sneak up on a guy!" He put a hand on his heart and took a seat on a dead log.

I snapped a picture of the distressed deputy, blinding him for about ten seconds with the flash. "Check the bulletin board at the jail on Monday," I said.

Once he'd regained his sight, he leapt from his log and snatched the camera from my hands.

"I'm confiscating this film," he grinned.

"I've got shots of the body on that roll, you big bully," I lied. "Olney'll have your head."

Halvey frowned and gave me back the camera. "What are you doing over here anyway?"

"Frank sent me to take some pictures of tracks. Found any?"

"Just this mess here," he said, pointing to the deep ruts that cut through the middle of the road. "And those have been there for years."

"Where's Stan?"

"I don't know. The Polack's poking around somewhere. You go look for him; I'm beat."

I walked about a hundred yards in each direction, searching the ground with the flashlight Halvey had given me. I passed Stan Pulaski going and coming as he knelt in the mud to examine the ground. He said he was looking for tire tracks. The ruts seemed as old as the water tower itself, and I could find no evidence of footprints.

"Where does Judge Shaw live?" I asked Pat Halvey once I'd returned to the log.

"Market Hill," he said. "Big old mansion in the nice part of town."

"Any houses around here?"

"Nope. The Mohawk Motel's about a mile up Route Forty, and the Dew Drop Inn's just over there." He pointed through the woods.

"What do you make of all this, Pat?" I asked.

The deputy's eyes narrowed. "Something dirty, Ellie," he said. "Nice, pretty girl like that turns up dead, bare naked. I think she was raped and killed by a sexual pervert."

I murmured agreement as I snapped a few shots of the mud. Pat Halvey was the kind of fellow who would notice a puddle on the ground in the morning and deduce that it had rained the night before.

"Jordan Shaw was a nice girl?" I asked.

"Sure," he said. "Homecoming Queen her junior year."

"You knew her?"

"No, but you know how it is. Everyone kind of knows everyone else around here. At least by name."

⌘

Sheriff Olney and Doc Peruso were huddled over two cups of coffee from a thermos bottle, their hot breath puffing billows into the wet air. The body had been wrapped into a big, old Packard Henney ambulance and carted away to New Holland City Hospital on Franklin Avenue, where Peruso would spend a busy Sunday morning on the postmortem. Police officers were now combing the area, scanning the muddy landscape with bowed heads and long, black flashlights.

"Find anything?" Olney asked when he saw me approach.

"Nope. Scared the life out of Halvey, though."

The sheriff muttered something under his breath and took a sip of cooling coffee.

"So what do you think, Frank?" I asked. "What happened here?"

"Goddamn it, Ellie," he said, pitching the dregs of his coffee onto the muddy ground. "I got here an hour ago, and you expect an arrest?"

"I'm just asking where the investigation stands. I've got my job to do, too."

"I'm waiting for the coroner's report," he said, tossing his head in Peruso's direction. "Then I'll consider the physical evidence and go from there."

"*Is* there any physical evidence?" I asked. "Besides the body, I mean."

Olney glowered at his feet. "No. No tracks; nothing."

I nodded and made a mental note for my story. The sheriff took notice, and his face fell flat.

"What are you planning to write anyway, Ellie?"

"You haven't told me anything," I said. "Our next edition won't be out until Monday noon. I'm hoping you'll get something more by tomorrow night."

"I'll get the bastard who did this," he said, glaring at me. "You can put that in your damn story."

Olney trudged off to confer with the troopers and his deputies, leaving me and Doc Peruso behind.

"Would you mind giving me some information tomorrow once you've examined the body?" I asked.

"Sure," he said. "I should be finished around eleven."

"In the meantime, how about I buy you a coffee in a proper cup?"

Whitey's Luncheonette on East Main was crowded as usual for a Saturday night. The richer kids were home from college for the holiday, and the poorer kids were always around. Whitey's was a renowned late-night hangout for young and old, and it was busy even on the Saturday after Thanksgiving. Whitey Louis kicked some dawdling teenagers out of a booth and ushered us over personally. I thought this singular behavior, since the proprietor was a royal prick who rarely budged from his seat at the cash register, and even then only to call his bookie.

"Why the first-class treatment, Whitey?" asked Doc Peruso. "You need some free medical advice?"

Whitey laughed, took a seat with us—another first—and summoned Carmella, a slim waitress of a certain age, whose jet-black beehive belied the years she'd clocked on her odometer. Peruso eschewed his pipe and lit a green cigar instead. We ordered coffee. Whitey told Carmella to bring a large order of fries and gravy, and Peruso and I shrugged at each other. Tony Di Gregorio, the fruit wholesaler on West Main, once told me Whitey Louis was cheaper than a Scottish Jew living in Genoa. Italian humor, I gathered, my feelings none too hurt.

"I hear something happened up on Route Forty," Whitey said. Peruso and I exchanged glances.

"Maybe," I said, toying with one of the spoons on the table; Fred Peruso had to be more diplomatic than I did.

"Come on," said Whitey, lowering his voice as I lit a cigarette. "I hear someone was murdered. Ten minutes later, the coroner and Lois Lane stroll into my diner arm in arm. You two were out there, right? So what's the story?"

"Read the papers, Whitey," I said, payback for the Lois Lane crack.

"Come on, girlie. There ain't no paper tomorrow. Just give me a hint. I won't breathe a word to nobody."

"To tell you the truth, Frank Olney asked us to keep quiet until tomorrow."

"Screw him, the fat slob. I know something happened out there, so why don't you just tell me?"

Carmella returned with the coffee.

"Sorry, Whitey," I said, feeling a sudden chill from our host.

"Thanks loads," he said, rising from the booth. "Don't take too long; I got paying customers who want to sit down."

Whitey returned to his register, pausing at the kitchen window on the way to cancel our fries and gravy.

"I was wondering, Doctor, does Judge Shaw have any enemies?" I asked Peruso once we were alone.

"Call me Fred, will you?" he said. "You make me feel like an old man."

"Freddy sounds even younger," I smiled. Flirting is a habit of mine that I can't quite control.

"Fred is young enough, thanks. And, by the way, Eleonora doesn't exactly scream youth."

"Okay," I said. "I'll call you Fred if you'll call me Ellie."

"Deal. Now, what was the question again?"

"Do you think the judge has enemies?"

Peruso shrugged and sipped his coffee.

"That wasn't the judge under that sheet," he said.

"You think a twenty-one-year-old girl has that kind of enemies?"

"I think a pretty girl like Jordan gave fellows ideas. Maybe one of them didn't want to take no for an answer."

I stubbed out my cigarette in the tin ashtray.

I left Whitey's parking lot at the wheel of my company car: a two-toned, white-and-canary-yellow Plymouth Belvedere of a none-too-memorable recent vintage. The roads were slick from the persistent drizzle that had followed the downpour of the previous night. I was late for my usual evening appointment with a tumbler of whiskey and ice, but I wanted to drop in at the Dew Drop Inn and make some inquiries.

I had visited the Dew Drop only once, about a year and a half earlier. It was too dingy and sad to make a regular haunt of mine. At ten forty-five on a Saturday night, the regulars had all turned out for the merriment and were holding down their usual barstools in the dim, smoky light. The clientele consisted of old-timers, some of whom still worked in the last of the shops on the East End, at the bottom of Polack Hill. The others had been put out to pasture and were biding their time until the quitting whistle blew for the last time.

When I entered, the five gray men at the bar twisted as one on their stools. I gave a short wave and said hello. Their stony faces, creased and stubbly with white whiskers, showed little sign of cognition. They just stared at me blankly, their eyes barely visible in the low light, their rough hands flat on the bar as if they'd been ordered to place them there and not to move. From four tin ashtrays before them, smoldering cigarettes hissed a thick pall into the close air, like incense in some polluted sacrament for the dead. I thought they should change the sign outside to "Don't Drop Inn." After a moment, the men turned slowly back to the bar and bowed their heads in bleak silence over their Genesee drafts.

"What'll you have?" asked the bartender. He sounded like Lawrence Welk.

"Draft, please," I said, removing my gloves and taking a seat at the bar. I was sure there was no whiskey worth drinking. "How's business?"

He shrugged and pushed a glass under my nose. "Ten cents. And the gents would probably not appreciate any music you might want to hear on the jukebox."

"Thanks, friend, but I didn't come here for the ambiance. I wanted to know if you saw anything funny last night. Any strangers drop in?"

"Like you, you mean? Who are you, anyways?"

"Eleonora Stone, reporter," I said, offering my hand. "Ellie." He thought about it a moment, wiped his on his apron, then took my hand.

"Stosh Barczak, proprietor. How come I ain't seen you here in over a year? How do you think I make a living? Giving out tips to reporters?"

"Sorry about that," I said. "Quite a memory you've got there, Stosh."

"Yeah, well, it ain't often we see someone new in here. And it ain't often she's a girl, neither. I got a good memory for faces that don't look like a catcher's mitt," and he gave the subtlest tip of his head to his left and the five men at the bar.

"What about last night?" I asked. "Anyone worth remembering?"

He drew another beer for the man to my right. The guy hadn't moved so much as a finger, but Stosh knew his customers. Another of the regulars pushed off his stool silently, dropped four dimes on the bar one after the other, and shuffled toward the door.

"Drive slowly," called the bartender after him. "Don't slip on the ice."

"There was one fellow," he said, returning to me. "Never seen anyone like that around here before. Big and dark, with a turban and a funny way of talking. Some kind of foreigner. Kept shaking his head a funny way, too. Like one of those cat figurines with a wobbly head."

"Really? What was he doing here?"

"He didn't say. Just asked for a *pint*. I thought he wanted milk and I nearly threw him out. Then I figured out he wanted a beer, so I gave it to him. The membership committee here wasn't crazy about the idea, but I got to make a living, don't I? He turned out to be kind of friendly. A smiley kind of guy."

"What time was that?" I asked.

Stosh squinted at the bare bulb hanging from the ceiling over the pool table. "It was late. Close to midnight."

"Any idea where he was going or where he was from?"

Stosh pursed his lips and shook his head. "I don't know."

"What kind of car?"

"Looked like a light-blue sedan. Maybe a Chevy, but I couldn't be sure of the make in the dark."

"Did he have mud on his shoes?" I asked. "Or on the tires?"

"No, he was wearing city shoes, and they were clean. I don't know about the tires. The rain started later anyway. There wasn't any mud at that hour."

Once I'd finished a second glass of beer a while later, I slipped back into my coat, thanked Stosh for his help, and wished him and the regulars goodnight.

"Don't be a stranger," said the bartender as I turned the knob on the door. Then he smiled at me, "Drive slowly. Don't slip on the ice."

Finally heading home around midnight, I thought about the weather and Wentworth's Woods. No footprints in the mud; no tire tracks on the service road. Jordan Shaw's murderer had either dragged her to the shallow grave from Route 40 or lugged her corpse more than a quarter mile up the unpaved service road. What was certain was that he'd dumped her body before the rain started.

Once home, I switched on the light in my parlor, poured myself a drink, and fell into my armchair. I picked up the phone and dialed Charlie Reese, waking him from a sound sleep, and he growled his displeasure.

"I've got a big story, Charlie." I said, waiting for some kind of reaction.

"What? Did Mrs. Navona win the meatball-rolling contest down at the K of C?"

"Judge Shaw's daughter's been murdered," I announced with a glee reserved for bearers of bad news.

I could tell he'd sat up in bed. "Don't joke about things like that, Ellie." I'd broken the news of the Communist victory in Cuba to him nearly two years before, and he didn't believe me then either.

"It's no joke. Someone tripped over her body in Wentworth's Woods about four thirty this afternoon. I got there about an hour after she'd been found."

"Why didn't you call me right away?"

"Sorry, I had to get my story. And Frank Olney offered me the chance to take pictures at the scene."

"Pictures of the body?"

"Forget it. The sheriff won't let us use them. They're too grisly anyway."

I gave Charlie all the information on the murder I had, answering his questions for almost an hour.

"I've got to call Artie Short," he said before hanging up. "Be careful how you write it, and I'll try to convince Artie to let you have the story."

"Please, Charlie!" I said. "This is my story. You can't give it to George Walsh."

"I'll do what I can," he said. "But you're going to have to outwrite George at every turn, and even then I can't promise Artie will allow it."

"Go to the mat for me this one time, Charlie," I said. "You won't regret it, I promise."

There was silence down the line.

"I'll give you copy and pictures tomorrow night," I said. "I've got a lot to do before then."

The Shaw Knitting Mills had been the town's first and most important carpet manufacturer. Judge Shaw's grandfather, Sanford Shaw, built the first knitting mill on the banks of the Great Cayunda Creek in the late 1870s. By 1910, Shaw Knitting Mills had carpeted half of the Eastern Seaboard, and New Holland counted thirty-five thousand souls. With the boom that followed World War I, glove and button factories sprang up, and New Holland grew to a prosperous population of forty-two thousand, one-third of whom wove rugs for the Shaws. When Sanford Shaw died in 1925, his elder son, Joshua, assumed control of the mills and spent three-quarters of the family's fortune breeding racehorses, marrying then divorcing gold diggers, and building empty mansions in Florida. World War II might well have ruined the mills, as the nation mobilized to defeat the enemy, buying war bonds instead of carpets. But after the attack on Pearl Harbor, Joshua Shaw was replaced by his younger brother, Nathan, the judge's father, who put the idle looms back into service, producing blankets and canvas for the war effort. The mill flourished. After the Japanese surrender, as the town shifted back to carpet production, costs rose and profits fell. Nathan Shaw took Draconian steps to save the company and the family fortune. The most noteworthy of his measures was the migration of Shaw Knitting Mills to Georgia, where labor was nonunion and cheap. In 1954, the last looms were dismantled, destroyed, or shipped south. New Holland atrophied rapidly, losing a quarter of its population to old age and labor exodus in just five years.

Unwilling to abandon the town his family had built and then orphaned, Judge Harrison Shaw stayed behind after his father and brothers had left for greener pastures in New York and Atlanta. New Holland loved and respected him for having stayed and elected him to the municipal-court bench four times before he was appointed Appellate Division judge by Governor Harriman in 1955.

The story of Jordan Shaw's murder was daunting, but I knew it represented the biggest opportunity of my career. Hard work aside, this murder would demand great care and sensitivity, given the girl's name. I felt up to the challenge, eager to carve out some kind of mark for the last of the Stones and, at the same time, sweep away the lingering disapproval of my late father.

⁂

SUNDAY, NOVEMBER 27, 1960

Around four thirty in the morning, I awoke in the same armchair, my last drink still sitting untouched on the table next to me. The ice had melted and the watery Scotch was wasted.

I trudged to the bedroom, stripped out of my rumpled clothes, and showered. Twenty minutes later, I buttoned my blouse, stepped into a skirt, and tightened the belt, feeling thin and empty inside. I hadn't eaten since noon the day before. Popcorn.

The sun would come up soon, and I wanted to return to the murder scene before the crowds of gawkers had trampled any evidence missed by Frank Olney's bloodhounds. I pulled to a stop on the graveled shoulder of Route 40, just about the time the car's heater had finally kicked in. I was surprised to find Olney hadn't secured the crime scene. No use searching for clues along the road; the three-ring circus of the night before had certainly erased any footprints or tire tracks that may have been there. Remembering my ruined shoes from the night before, I had thought ahead. I slipped out of my heels and into a pair of rubber boots, popped the door open, and climbed out.

The sun rose slowly, throwing a gray, dishwater daybreak over the land. I left my car beside the road and entered the woods, camera loaded and strung over my shoulder.

The police had marched long and hard over the area adjacent to Route 40, leaving it cratered like a moonscape. I made my way to the crime scene where Jordan Shaw's shallow grave cut into the mud. It was little wonder Fast Jack had tripped over the body; the hole where she'd been buried was barely two and a half feet deep. Someone had been in a hurry to cover the girl and blow.

What kind of instrument had dug the pitiful excuse for a grave? As a girl in New York, I had watched my brother, Elijah, hack better holes using the worn heels of a pair of PF Flyers, and all he'd wanted to bury was the nose of a football to kick off a sandlot game. Jordan Shaw's grave wasn't much deeper.

I crouched down to touch the soggy ground, careful not to muddy my stockings in the process. The gash sliced into the earth cleanly, but at a weak angle. The hole deepened gradually as it grew longer, as if opened by one stroke of a large spade. Lengthwise, it was no more than five feet, and its width extended to about thirty inches where the fissure was deepest. The grave wouldn't have held a large dog.

Reaching into the hole, I ran a hand along the length of the wall, exploring the grainy mud and clammy leaves with my fingers. I dug a little deeper, raking the ground with my nails, until I unearthed a small, metallic object: a bottle cap. Strange place for garbage, I thought, wiping the bent cap with my thumbs, then on a lens cloth. It was maroon and white: "the friendly Pepper-Upper," Dr Pepper, 10, 2, and 4. It looked new.

I shot ten frames of the gravesite by day, then moved on to the service road. Only Deputies Halvey and Pulaski had examined the scene, so, unlike the gravesite, there had been no stampede of cops and there were few footprints left behind. The ancient ruts carved in the dirt had swallowed any recent tire tracks that might have been laid; it was possible someone had come up the road recently but unlikely that any evidence remained.

By daylight, the road took on a different mien. The mounds, curves, and depressions had shrugged off the night and now stood out prominently, painted in various shades of gray and brown. I retraced my steps of the night before, hunched over like a contemplative monk, examining the ground for anything out of the ordinary: footprints, tire tracks, a stray bottle of Dr Pepper minus its cap . . .

After stooping several times to examine small artifacts in the mud, I began to distinguish the old from the new. A spent shotgun shell— possibly one of Fast Jack's—was clearly a recent arrival, though not germane to my search. In the ditch beside the road, I found a nest of rusting Schaefer cans, relics of some furtive caucus of teenagers. There was a broken milk bottle from Stadler's Dairy; a battered hot water tank, buckled by what appeared to be a sharp kick to the groin; soggy, yellowed newspapers; and a muddy garbage can, crushed flat, a few yards into the woods. Fodder for future archeologists.

I marched up and down the service road twice, searching for enlightenment. Plopping myself onto the same log Pat Halvey had held down the night before, I surveyed the high trees, craning my neck to see the water tower fifty yards behind me. A cold breeze had been blowing since before dawn, whistling through the bare trees and drying the muddy road. A tawny color was spreading over the crests of the ruts in the road, except for one curious spot about ten feet in front of me. From my seat on the log, it looked like a blackish blotch, as if it was still wet. But on closer inspection, I saw the mark was actually three circles about an inch in diameter each, forming an isosceles triangle. A touch of my finger confirmed my first impression; it was motor oil. I shot a few frames of the oil then trudged back through the woods to my car. It wasn't yet eight: plenty of time before my meeting with Fred Peruso at City Hospital to make some prints of the film I'd shot the previous night.

I was renting the upstairs flat of a homey duplex on Lincoln Avenue, across the street from Fiorello's Home of the Hot Fudge. It was a friendly, middle-class neighborhood, quiet and respectable, at least until Friday night when the youngsters descended upon Fiorello's and Lincoln Avenue to hang out and cause trouble. Confrontations between residents and the teens boiled over every few years or so. The locals would enlist the police to arrest loiterers, and the youths practiced a guerilla war of retaliatory mischief and late-night noise. Kids' stuff. Lincoln Avenue always found its way back to serenity, usually when a troublesome group of teenagers outgrew its taste for malteds at Fiorello's and moved up to beer in any of New Holland's legion of taverns. Things had been relatively quiet on Lincoln Avenue since I'd arrived nearly three years earlier.

For want of space, I had set up my enlarger, smelly chemical baths, and clothesline in my bathroom, the only room besides the kitchen with running water. I was no expert developer, but sometimes I needed a quicker turnaround than the photo lab at the paper could provide. I ran three rolls of film through the processor and made two sets of prints of the murder scene, hanging them to dry in my darkened bathroom.

Over coffee and a slice of dry toast, I dropped the sheriff's prints and negatives into an envelope. Then I selected a five-by-eight shot of Jordan Shaw's lifeless face and slipped it into my purse—the sheriff didn't need to know—and I headed for City Hospital.

Fred Peruso was in the doctors' lounge, dressed in his usual blue scrubs, writing a report amid thick cigar smoke. He looked up from his paper and announced without preamble that there were no lesions in the vaginal wall, no sign of struggle or forced penetration.

"Good morning to you, too," I said. "So no rape? At least her honor was intact."

Peruso frowned. "Not quite. She may not have been raped, but there was semen in her vagina."

I took a seat next to Peruso, tossing the envelope of Olney's prints onto the table in front of him.

"No rape and no prophylactic?" (I congratulated myself for having resisted the temptation to say "rubber.") "She wasn't worried about birth control?"

Peruso shook his head. "Do you know what this is?" He placed a small, metallic coil on the table for my inspection.

I picked it up, turning it over again and again. "No idea," I said, tapping it on the tabletop.

Peruso peered over his reading glasses at the small coil in my hand. "It's an intrauterine device. IUD. It's one of the most effective contraceptives available."

"Oh, I've heard of those," I said. "Not very common, are they?"

"These copper ones are new. There's been some testing here and there, in Europe and in the Third World."

"How does it work?"

"It's implanted in the uterus and prevents a fertilized egg from attaching itself. Effective, worry-free birth control. No chemical manipulation like with those new pills."

"So, a girl doesn't get one of these on a lark. Jordan Shaw must have been getting regular action."

Peruso glared at me. A curtain of blue smoke hung in the air, surrounding his head and closely cropped white hair like an aura or a corona. "You didn't know Jordan, Ellie, so I can't expect you to feel too sorry for her. But she was a heck of a girl. I don't know what she was doing in Boston, but I don't like to judge people for what they do behind closed doors. I'd assume a girl like you would agree."

He was right. I was certainly in no position to cast stones. I apologized, conscious for the first time of my cavalier attitude toward the life and death of a twenty-one-year-old girl.

"Let's see if I can be more clinical," I said, placing the coil on the tabletop with delicate fingers. "The IUD prevents pregnancy without the use of other methods of contraception?"

Peruso nodded, picked up the coil, and dropped it into a pocket-sized envelope.

"Is it your professional judgment, then, that the presence of an IUD would indicate regular sexual relations?" I felt like a district attorney questioning an expert witness.

"Yes, but I intend to deny I ever found an IUD. And I know I can count on your discretion." His eyes stared me down, dead serious.

"Of course," I said after a moment. Then, wanting to rid myself of his eyes, I asked about the exact cause of death.

"Broken neck. Severe damage to the spinal cord between the second and third cervical vertebrae." He produced an x-ray from another, larger envelope, held it up to the light, and showed me the anatomy of Jordan Shaw's death. "Quick and painless. Some gorilla snapped her neck like cracking his knuckles. I've fixed the time of death between ten p.m. Friday and nine a.m. Saturday."

"I'd guess before one a.m.," I said.

"Why's that?"

"The rain. It started about one thirty, I think. That would explain the absence of tracks in the woods."

"I hadn't thought about tracks," said Peruso, picking up the envelope with my photographs inside. He chewed on his cigar, flipping through the entire set.

"How does one break a neck like that?" I asked. "From behind?"

"Most likely. Doesn't look like there was much of a struggle."

"What about the gash in her pelvis?"

Peruso shrugged his shoulders, eyes fixed on one of the photographs. "Certainly not fatal, but it would've hurt like all get-out . . . had she been alive at the time."

"So you think she was already dead?" I asked.

"I know she was," he said, tapping the ash from the end of his cigar into a paper coffee cup. "Not enough blood to indicate a pumping heart."

"What kind of a monster snaps a girl's neck and slices out a piece of skin for sport?"

"That's the sixty-four-thousand-dollar question," said Peruso, laying the photograph face down on the table.

"Some kind of deviant?"

"Maybe. Or a clumsy killer."

I picked up the pile of photos and shuffled through the tight shots of the victim's pelvis, focusing on the gruesome details of the wound.

"Why, indeed?"

I tried without success to imagine a plausible explanation.

"You said sport, Ellie. You think whoever did this did it for some kind of sadistic thrill?"

"I can't see any other reason," I mumbled, peering into the muddied space where two inches of Jordan Shaw's smooth, white skin had once been. "What kind of weapon do you think did this?"

"Just a knife, I guess. A large one. Maybe a hunting knife. There doesn't appear to be any serration in the blade."

We sat quietly for a moment, digesting the photograph together, then I asked if Jordan had had any marks there.

"A scar? Birthmark? Old hernia operation? Appendix?"

"The appendix is on the other side," he grumbled. "And I examined her about three months ago before she went back to school. There was nothing there then and nothing there this morning in the autopsy. No hernia, no C-section, if that's what you're driving at. I examined her uterus very carefully; there was no scarring anywhere."

"Oh," I said, disappointed that my theory had been sunk. "But her killer took the time to carve out a piece of her flesh; I'd like to know what was there before. Maybe it was some imperfection he wanted to remove, as if he was obsessed by her beauty."

Peruso grunted, still chewing on his cigar, but offered nothing.

The lounge door swung open, and Frank Olney stepped inside.

"What are you doing here?" he asked me, none too friendly. I didn't answer. "Those mine?" he asked, motioning to the photographs.

I nudged the set of prints across the table. He examined them closely, groaning with each eight-by-ten. Finally, he put them down and took a seat.

"I just spent the longest hour of my life over to Judge Shaw's," he said, removing his cap to rub his balding scalp. "Broke his heart. It was torture, I tell you. You ever have to stand there and tell a man his child is dead?"

Peruso sneered. "A few times; yes."

"Oh, sorry, Doc. Of course." He shook his head. "His only child. He took it hard. Real hard."

"Is he all right?" asked Peruso.

"He's just crushed, like I kicked him in the stomach telling him. We had to call Doc Terrell from next door to tranquilize Mrs. Shaw. She went ape."

"Does he have any idea who might have done this?"

"No. No clue anything was wrong. Said Jordan was like always when she got home from Boston Wednesday night. Had a nice Thanksgiving dinner Thursday, then the judge and the Mrs. were out of town Friday. Got back Saturday afternoon and just assumed Jordan took the car and went out that day."

"Where's the car now?" I asked, butting in.

"He doesn't know. I figure it was stolen by the shit who did this to her. State police are looking for it now."

"What's the make and model?"

Frank looked at me funny at first, then figured I needed it for my story. "Dark-gray, four-door Continental Mark Five. Brand new. Same car as Elvis Presley got. The judge just bought it two weeks ago."

Probably not leaking oil, I thought.

"Have you checked to see if it's been towed?" I asked, sure the question would rile him.

It did. But he kept the lid on his stew, ignoring me and turning to Doc Peruso instead for the results of the autopsy. Frank Olney was under the gun; he had to catch a killer and catch him fast. I had the feeling that even if he solved the case quickly, he would never be the same again, as if it were somehow his fault that such a tragedy had taken place on his watch.

"Do you have any statements for the press, Frank?" I asked, once he and Doc Peruso had finished. He didn't.

I left City Hospital, intent on finding Judge Shaw's Lincoln. My car had been towed out of a snowbank the previous winter, and I had claimed it at Phil's Garage on the West End. Phil Leone was the proud holder of the lucrative towing contract with the City of New Holland and Montgomery County. If the judge's Lincoln had been towed, it would be on Phil's back lot.

CHAPTER TWO

The chain-link fence rattled in the cool Sunday breeze. There were plenty of cars inside, most of them junkers Phil used for spare parts. But front and center sat a brand-new, gray Lincoln Continental, its four canted headlights gazing back at me from either side of a sparkling billet-and-chrome-wire grille.

"Looking for something?" a voice startled me from behind.

I hadn't been expecting to find anyone there on a Sunday, but here was a kid in grimy coveralls and a crew cut, wiping his hands on an oily rag.

"Was that Lincoln towed in here yesterday?" I asked, motioning over my shoulder.

The kid nodded. "It yours?"

"No, I'm from the paper. Ellie Stone." I extended a hand, but the kid chuckled, holding me off with a display of his dirty mitts.

"Billy Jenkins," he said. "Whose car is it, then?"

"I would guess it belongs to Judge Shaw," I answered, looking back through the fence. "Hey, Billy, do you think I could take a quick look under the chassis? I won't touch anything."

"What are you looking for?"

"Oil leak."

Billy laughed again, pulling a key ring from his belt. "She's brand new! But if you don't touch, I don't see the harm."

He unlocked the gate, and I knelt down carefully to look. Too dark. Billy shoved a flashlight under my nose. The ground under the car was oily enough, but none of it was fresh. I stood up, brushed off my knees, and handed the light back to Billy the kid.

"Do you know where it was towed from?" I asked.

"Ought to," he grinned. "Hooked her up myself. We got a call from the Mohawk Motel yesterday morning. Someone left the car out back, blocking the trash cans. Jean Trent was spitting mad." He giggled like

29

an idiot, then he blew his nose into the oily rag. "The garbage truck couldn't get in, now she's got to wait till next Saturday to have her trash collected."

"Was it locked?" I asked.

"What, the garbage?"

I rolled my eyes. "The car."

"Well, yeah, of course," and now it was Billy's turn to roll his eyes. "Look at her," he said, admiring the Lincoln. "Not a finer car in the city."

⌘

A forty-foot-high wooden Indian rose from the shoulder of Route 40, pointing a tired arm down a long, unpaved drive to the Mohawk Motel. The motel sat stubbornly on a patch of dirt amid the pines, surrounded by encroaching weeds and brush, fighting a losing battle against Nature's onslaught. After twenty years perched atop a gentle hill two miles north of the New Holland city limits, it had forged its own niche in the county: a discreet if seedy trysting spot. Its very survival depended on the itches adulterers had to scratch. The proprietress, Jean Trent, was a salt-and-pepper widow who asked few questions of her guests, demanding only that they pay for the room in advance. I knew the procedure; I had visited the Mohawk a couple of times with a junior editor. He lived at home with his parents, and we both feared discovery at my apartment in town.

I pulled into the graveled parking area and stopped in front of the registration office. There were no other cars in sight. The Mohawk Motel was a ten-unit, cinderblock alcazar of peeling paint and mildewed carpets. Lined up along a thirty-yard walk of crumbling concrete, the cells were identical: a double bed for the main event, a blaring television to cover the din of the rut, and a small bathroom for hosing off afterward. There was a phone booth next to the office door, just to the right of the metal-and-glass Dr Pepper machine. I nodded to myself, fingering the bottle cap in my coat pocket.

Jean Trent emerged from the office, eyeing me suspiciously. People usually came to the Mohawk for a room, not to take in the sights.

"You looking for something?" she asked, her voice gravelly from decades of cigarettes and drink. Her faded skin, stretched tight over her cheeks, sagged into gray jowls and a wrinkled neck. She might have been a looker once upon a time, but the bloom was long since off the rose.

"I'm from the paper," I said, walking toward her.

She nodded guardedly and repeated her question.

"I'd like to ask you about the car that was towed yesterday," I explained.

Now she was annoyed. "Was that yours?"

I shook my head. "I think it belongs to a girl who stayed here Friday night. Pretty blonde, about twenty-one . . ."

"I forget my guests as soon as they pay for their room. Long as they don't make no trouble, they're no concern of mine."

"This girl was murdered that night," I said to no great effect.

Jean Trent uttered an ambiguous "Oh," and scratched her neck.

I showed her the photo I'd stashed in my purse. "Is this the girl?" I asked.

Jean Trent studied the picture at arm's length. "Yeah, that's her all right. You weren't kidding about her being dead."

She handed the photo back and looked me up and down. Then she said she knew me.

"I thought you forget your guests once they've paid."

She grinned a naughty smile at me. "Well, that's the official line, you understand. You came in here a couple of times with a handsome young fellow. A suit-and-tie type, wasn't he?" I said nothing, and she just kept grinning. Then her smile disappeared. "You didn't come here with that dead girl, did you? Some kind of perverted orgy?"

"Never met her."

Jean cursed the cold, pulling her windbreaker tight, then motioned for me to follow her inside. The office was as spartan as the accommodations, just fake wood paneling and a flat green carpet. Her rooms were through a door behind the desk, but she didn't take me that far.

"Want some coffee?" she asked, pouring herself a cup from the urn sitting on the curling Textolite surface.

I declined, sensing she was about to volunteer some information she deemed important, and I didn't want to sidetrack her with details about how many lumps and creams.

"Weird night, Friday," she said, raising her cup to my health. "Could've sworn it was a full moon."

"Strange?" I asked. "Besides murder?"

She slurped. "They catch the guy?"

"I wouldn't be here if they had."

"The girl arrived alone about half past eight Friday, and I put her in number four," she announced suddenly, the niceties over.

"Any other units occupied that night?"

"It's not exactly my high season, but there was a trucker in number eight."

"Where was he from?"

"Who knows? You know those big diesels; license plates from every state in the Union . . ."

"Didn't he register?"

"He just paid for the room and disappeared into number eight. He was gone by morning; the key in the drop-off box. I don't make out a receipt unless someone asks. Otherwise I got to pay tax."

Could be the truck driver, I thought. Probably strong enough to snap her neck. But why? Fred Peruso, whose opinion I trusted, said no rape had taken place. Had Jordan Shaw gone to the motel to meet the mysterious trucker? It didn't seem likely; they surely came from different sides of the tracks. And then, too, why bother to take two rooms at the Mohawk? Jean Trent wasn't judging anyone.

"You think he did it?" asked Jean, lighting a mentholated cigarette.

"I can tell you don't," I said, playing along. "All right, what else?"

"About a quarter after nine, a car pulls in," she said, rising to the bait like a hungry trout. "That's when I notice the girl came on foot. Or so I thought. You say that was her car out by the garbage cans?" I nodded. "Well, this other car pulls in, and a guy slips into number four, nice as you please. I wait a few secs to see if the girl's going to scream, and of course she don't. I was kind of expecting a fellow to show up, if you know what I mean."

She sucked half the cigarette into her lungs. The ash grew before my eyes.

"What kind of car was it?"

"I don't know cars," she waved. "And I told you I don't pay no mind to my guests, long as they behave."

"You remembered me well enough."

She looked me up and down again, the same dissolute grin emerging from behind the smoke.

"I don't often see a girl like you here," she said. "Or like that girl Friday night, for that matter. You two don't quite fit the profile of my regular clientele."

"Did you notice anything at all about the car?" I asked, trying to steer the conversation away from myself and my association with her motel. I may be a modern thinker, with broad ideas on sex, but, in the light of day at least, I like to pretend to be a *nice girl*.

"Average, light color. I told you I don't know cars."

"Did you see the license plates?"

She shook her head, looking at the light. "Couldn't see. Didn't try."

"So then what?"

"Like I told you, I didn't pay no attention. I don't know how long the fellow was there. When I looked outside a couple of hours later, the car was gone."

I waited, sure she had something else to tell me.

"I was watching the late show," she continued, "'cause I don't sleep much. I didn't budge again till after midnight when I heard another car pull into the lot. So I go to the window, thinking it's the same guy come back for more. Maybe he went out to get some liquor or something. But this time a different guy gets out and ducks into number four, thank you very much."

"Notice anything about him?"

"It was too dark. But I could see he was taller. And the car was different. And I didn't notice no license plate or color this time, neither."

"How long did he stay?"

"Do you think I got nothing to do but spy on my guests? I didn't hear no scream, so I went back to my movie."

"Was that the end of it?" I asked.

"What, are you in a hurry? After my movie, I get up for a smoke. I take a look out the window to see the rain, 'cause it was really coming down just then, and I see another guy come out of number four. He jumps into his car and drives away. By now I figure the blonde's turning tricks in my motel, and I don't like that. The cops would close me down if I let stuff like that go on. But then, like I told you, she was gone in the morning."

"You're sure this was a different man?"

"Positive. And his car was a darker color."

Didn't match the bartender's description of the foreigner's car, but what about the second one? Jean hadn't noticed the color.

My witness settled down into a chair behind the counter and took a sip of her coffee. I knew her story was over.

"Will you show me around the place?"

We left the office, me first, while Jean Trent locked the door behind her. I hadn't seen much to steal, but she wasn't taking chances, even if we weren't going far. The first thing I wanted to know about was the soda machine. Did folks drink a lot of Dr Pepper? What did she do with the empties? Wasn't there a receptacle for the bottle caps? Jean shrugged her shoulders and said folks drank whatever soda was there; the distributor drove down from Gloversville every Thursday to stock the machine and take away the cash and the empties; no, this particular machine didn't seem to have a slot for the bottle caps, and folks just threw them into the garbage can.

"What garbage can?" I asked.

Jean made a double take to the left of the machine. "Can you beat that?" she said. "Someone stole my damn garbage can!"

Nothing remained of the receptacle that had once swallowed Dr Pepper bottle tops except a rusted ring on the concrete.

"I'm gonna kill that Julio," she said.

"Who's Julio?" I asked. "Garbage can thief?"

"Real clever, missy. He's my handyman. Just a kid, really, who helps me out."

"Where is he now? Maybe he saw something the other night."

Jean Trent waved a hand and set off for number 4. "He wasn't here Friday."

The room looked as I had expected: dingy, flat carpet, worn from door to bed and bed to bathroom. If my memory served, I had spent a Friday afternoon in that very room after the *Republic*'s Christmas party a year before. The junior editor.

"What did this look like Saturday morning?" I asked. "Anything out of the ordinary?"

"Rumpled sheets are par for the course around here," she said, lighting another cigarette. "She had a good roll Friday night, I can tell you that. I've been cleaning up after fornicators for twenty years. Julio calls me the Love Detective."

"Just where is this Julio?" I said, since she'd brought him up again. "I'd like to ask him a few questions."

"Most days he shines shoes and sweeps up hair at Pirfo's barbershop downstreet," she said. "But it's Sunday. Probably in church." She smirked. Then she returned to the state of number 4 on Saturday morning. "Covers were pulled back to the foot of the bed, sheets torn loose, not taut like when I put them on. And there were more than a few hairs—short ones, if you catch my drift—some dark, some light. You might say the room smelled of sex."

I cleared my throat. The Love Detective, indeed.

"You want to know something else about your pretty blonde?" she asked coyly. I was listening. "You remember I said I thought she was turning tricks in here? Well, Saturday morning, I figured out that she only slept with the first guy."

"How do you know that?" I asked. "Peeping through the window?"

Jean swore at me. "I don't peep through no windows, see? So if you want to know how I know, cut the crap."

"Sorry," I said, and she continued as if lecturing to a protégée.

"Garbage tells you more than you'd ever want to know about a person. What do people throw away? What don't they throw away? Sometimes what's missing is just as important as what's there."

"And what did you conclude from her garbage?"

"She was a virgin. At least when she got here."

I remembered the IUD and realized Jean Trent was as dim as she looked. I begged her to elaborate.

"Bloody tissue in the wastebasket," she announced as if dropping the bomb on Hiroshima. "And a bloody towel in the bathroom."

"That's it?" I asked. "Maybe she had a bloody nose."

Jean Trent rolled her eyes. "She wasn't sparring with Marciano. These were lovers. There was blood in the bed. Not too much; they probably tried to save the sheets once they noticed. So I figure no virgin would screw three guys her first night out. I'd bet the farm she only slept with the first guy."

"May I see the towel?"

"No," she said, looking properly disgusted by my request. "Cleaners picked it up yesterday afternoon."

I weighed Jean Trent's story. How many virgins went to the trouble of having an experimental contraceptive device implanted in their uterus for their first time? I remembered my first time—it was his, too—and we used a latex condom he'd bought from a vending machine in a men's room at the Port Authority Bus Terminal.

"You said the towel was in the bathroom?" I asked, putting her facts in order. "And the bloody tissue was in the wastebasket?"

"That's right," she said carefully.

"Why not flush the tissue down the toilet?"

"The wastebasket was handy."

"Maybe she had her period . . ." Doc Peruso would have mentioned it, wouldn't he?

"Nope," said Jean. "No unmentionable lady products, if you know what I mean. A girl her age knows when it's her time of the month. Don't you know yours? And she don't meet a sweetheart in a motel unprepared. I told you, what's missing is just as important as what's there."

She was right about that, but I still doubted Jordan Shaw had been a virgin when she arrived at the Mohawk Motel Friday night. The blood was hers, all right, but it had come from the wound in her pelvis.

"May I have a look at your trash?" I asked.

"Are you nuts?"

"The garbage collector couldn't pick it up yesterday, isn't that right? Her car was blocking the way. The trash from her room must still be there."

"You're a real sicko," said Jean Trent. "But if you want to pick through garbage, be my guest."

Flanked by a gutted, rusted-out junker on one end and the shell of a television set on the other, seven dented trash cans sat unemptied in a moldering wooden enclosure about twenty yards behind the motel. The pen was there to discourage raccoons from rummaging through the garbage, but I sensed the varmints were carrying the day. A blue Ford pickup truck was parked nearby on a worn patch of grass.

Jean described her cleaning routine: Going from room to room, she filled up large, brown bags she'd collected from her trips to the Grand Union. She always started from her own unit, situated in the middle of the complex, before cleaning the guest rooms. Her trash would be at the bottom, with number 4's at the top or close to it. Jean watched as I picked through the first can. I grabbed the two freshest-looking bags, pulled them out, and tossed them onto the ground behind me.

"Watch where you're throwing that!" yelled Jean. "And you're cleaning up this mess when you're through getting your jollies."

"I need you to tell me if you recognize any of this stuff," I said, brushing off my hands.

I began retrieving articles from the first wet bag, holding them up gingerly for her inspection. Jean shook her head and uttered "Nope, don't think so . . ." Then she found her bearings: "That foot powder was from number six. You're in Thursday's garbage."

I scooped up the trash I'd taken out and dropped it back into the bag.

"Missed something," said Jean, pointing to a wad of chewed gum and a brown banana peel. I threw her a glare, picked the ground clean, and moved on to bag number two.

"Yeah, you're getting closer," she said as I dug deeper. "That's the stuff the trucker threw out. Number four can't be far."

Indeed it was not. I soon uncovered a wad of white tissue paper, stained with brownish-red blood. I removed it from the bag carefully and showed it to Jean Trent with glee.

"Maybe I look at garbage," she said, shaking her head. "But I don't touch it."

A little larger than a golf ball, the wadded tissue was mostly soft, with crusty patches where the blood had dried. I unwrapped the package, peeling layers from its hide like leaves from an artichoke, expecting to find the missing skin—and the solution to the mystery—at the middle. But there was nothing.

"Are you some kind of weirdo or something?" she asked. "You get your kicks from the blood of virgins?"

I frowned. "I'd sure like to talk to this Julio fellow," I said. "Don't you know where he lives?"

Jean Trent's face kind of froze where it was. She didn't exactly scowl at me, but I could tell she was vexed.

"I told you he wasn't here Friday night. He's just an ignorant Puerto Rican kid that helps out around here. He don't know nothing. And now I got things to do, missy. Why don't you let yourself out?"

With that, she turned on her heel and tramped back toward the motel. I watched her disappear around the corner of the building, and I ducked under the pickup to look for oil. Nothing. Then my eyes fell on the back wall of the motel, mostly obscured by a thicket of high bushes. Overgrown with weeds, paint flaking off the cinderblocks, the rear of the Mohawk looked even shabbier than the front.

And it struck me that the killer might have come around to the back Friday night, that maybe Jordan Shaw's body had been carried out through a window. I approached the back of the Mohawk, pushed through a narrow opening in the shrubs, and picked my way through the brambles and overgrowth to the wall. A narrow pathway ran along the back of the motel, where little more than a stubble of muddied grass grew. There was no way the body could have been taken out the back way, as the only egress was through the louvered bathroom windows outside each unit. Too small for a body to pass through without broken glass and a whole lot of noise. I crouched down for a closer look at the worn trail. The ground was smooth, no prints, but obviously in frequent use. Rising to my feet, I reached out to touch one of the louvers on a window and found it swiveled freely on its hinge. In fact, virtually every louver on every window opened and shut from the outside, offering varying views inside. From some windows, I could see the entire bed, while others—number 4 for instance—showed only a portion. I stifled a gasp; the Mohawk Motel had a Peeping Tom.

I hacked my way out of the jungle, collecting some burrs on my coat and skirt in the process, then went around to the front and knocked on Jean Trent's door again.

"I thought you left," she said, standing behind the storm door.

"I had a thought. Do you think someone could have gone around back the other night?"

"What are you driving at?"

I explained about the peeper's paradise, that one could spy through the bathroom windows with little chance of discovery and that the bushes made for perfect cover, especially at night.

"I already told you; I mind my own business here," she said, her face tightening like a screw. "The only reason I'm still in business is because people know this place is discreet. You think I'd risk everything to peep through some windows?"

I assured her that I hadn't meant to imply she was the guilty party.

"Maybe it's a local kid," I said. "Have you ever noticed anyone hanging around?"

Jean's eyes clouded over. "If you start spreading rumors I got a Peeping Tom, you'll ruin me. So just keep your mouth shut!"

With that, she slammed the door in my face. I turned and walked to my car, eyes down, examining the ground for triangular oil spots. There were none.

From the Mohawk Motel, I drove to Sheriff Olney's office, where Pat Halvey told me Frank was in an important meeting.

"Who's he got in there?" I asked.

"George Walsh."

"What's he doing here?"

"They're talking about the murder. Imagine that: both you and Walsh working on the same story for the paper."

George Walsh was the scribbler considered—unofficially—the number-one reporter for the *Republic*. Everyone knew it was because he'd been there longer than anyone else—twenty-two years—and because he happened to be Artie Short's son-in-law.

"Well, they're expecting me," I said. It was a pitiful lie, but Halvey bought it and let me pass.

"What the hell do you want, Ellie?" whined Frank, packed into his usual swivel chair behind his desk. George Walsh was seated before him, pad and pencil in hand.

"Pat let me in," I said, taking a chair. "How are you doing, Georgie Porgie?"

My colleague cast a wicked look my way. "This is my story, Eleonora, so you can just clear out."

"Since when do you hand out City assignments?" I asked. "And aren't you still working on the Lindbergh baby kidnapping?"

George's smug grin ached to be slapped right off his face. He leaned back in his folding chair, as if he expected it to swivel like Frank Olney's. When it didn't move, he righted himself and told me Artie Short himself had put him on the story.

"Mr. Short didn't want an assignment this important handled by a greenhorn, and a girl besides. Why don't you go brew us a pot of coffee? Then you can buff your nails till suppertime."

"Sure thing, Georgie. Lend me your emery board?"

Greenhorn? Coffee? I remembered the time two years earlier when Mayor Simpson had suffered a heart attack. Crack reporter George

Walsh spent the night outside the Intensive Care Unit at City Hospital, waiting for a statement from Dr. Henderson, while the mayor was expiring in a bed across town at St. Joseph's.

"Frank, I've got to talk to you," I said, ignoring Walsh.

"You two better decide who's writing this story," said the sheriff. "I can't carry out an investigation if I'm constantly tripping over both of you."

"Why don't we call Mr. Short?" asked George, still smiling.

"Frank," my tone was urgent. "You know I'm always straight with you, so if I say I've got important information, you've got to talk to me."

George took up the offensive, bellyaching that it was his story, and the sheriff should call Mr. Short.

"All right, shut up, the both of you!" bellowed Olney. "George, I'll talk to whoever the hell I please, whether Artie Short likes it or not. And Ellie, you better settle with Charlie Reese and Artie Short who's writing this story. In the meantime, George, I want to talk to Ellie alone."

Walsh's scalp almost blew off his head, and he stormed out of Olney's office. I was sure he'd be crying to his father-in-law as soon as he could find a pay phone.

"The judge's car is at Phil's Garage," I said, once I was alone with the sheriff. "They towed it yesterday morning from the Mohawk Motel. Here's the license number." I handed him a page from my notebook for him to verify.

Olney flipped open a folder on his desk and compared my number to the one in his report. They matched. The sheriff punched the intercom on his desk and told Pat Halvey to send two men to Phil's immediately. "Call the state police and have them meet you there. They're gonna have to dust for prints and all the usual. And then I want that car brought back here on a flatbed—not a wrecker, you got that?" He switched off the intercom without a goodbye and folded his fat hands on his desk before him. Then he asked me to go on. "I'm sure you've been to the Mohawk already. Let's hear it."

"Jordan Shaw spent the night there Friday."

He sighed. His job was getting worse as the victim came into focus. "Are you sure?"

I told him everything Jean Trent had told me, about the three cars and the men who'd visited her room. Then I explained what I'd found in the trash, retrieving the tissue from my purse and placing it on the desk before him.

"Her blood," I announced. "From the gash in her pelvis. The skin wasn't there. You'll want to send that for blood-typing."

He eyed me briefly with annoyance. Men really didn't like me telling them what to do.

"So what do you make of it?" he asked after prodding it once or twice with the nib of a pencil.

I shook my head slowly as I looked through the window at the gray day outside. "I'm not sure. We could be dealing with a sadistic psychopath who gets his kicks dissecting his victims. But the girl didn't scream; Jean Trent would have heard."

"Go on."

"Fred Peruso thinks the murderer cut her after killing her; that explains why she didn't lose much blood. But why cut her at all and why there?" I circled around his desk, considering the bloody tissue. "The cut was made cleanly, about two inches long, an inch wide, and half an inch deep; you can see it in my pictures."

"We got a goddamn maniac running loose," said Frank, sobered by the sight of Jordan's blood. "There's no rhyme or reason to a crime like this."

It seemed Big Frank was right, but the order of events bothered me. If the evidence had pointed to a struggle, if there had been a scream, I might have believed it was the work of a sadist. But her pelvis had been cut after she was already dead, and a sadist couldn't get his kicks like that.

"Anything else for me?" asked Olney.

"Just this," I said with a half-hearted chuckle. "The Mohawk Motel has a Peeping Tom."

Olney pursed his lips, eyes darting between some invisible foci. I could hear gears churning inside his head.

"There's a beaten path along the wall behind the motel," I continued, thinking about my own visits to the Mohawk. "It looks like it's been in use for a while." God, when had I last spent an afternoon there?

"Any idea who?" asked Frank, almost licking his chops. He could taste an arrest.

"Yes, but I wouldn't like to say. It's just a hunch, and I don't think he's our man, anyhow. The voyeur has a good thing going, right? So why now, after all this time, would he decide to snap a girl's neck and take a gash out of her pelvis?"

"Maybe she caught him looking." Frank was convinced already.

"You don't kill for that."

"You might if you're a homicidal maniac. Look at Jack the Ripper."

I didn't quite get the comparison, but I let it pass.

The sheriff rose from his chair and lumbered across the room to retrieve his red-plaid hunting jacket from the rack. I didn't need to ask where he was going, and I already regretted having told him.

"I almost forgot," he said, stuffing his bearish arms into his coat. "Judge Shaw wants to see you tonight. About six."

"What?" I asked, a little spooked. "What's he want from me?"

"He thinks the paper might help find this killer. He wants you to know what he knows. Do me a favor, Ellie, and drop by his house around six."

"What about George Walsh?" I asked. "Why don't you ask him to go?"

Frank Olney stopped at the door and stared back at me across the room. He raised his hat to his head and yanked it on tight. "He asked for you by name."

Great.

"By the way," he said, smiling, "good one about George and the Lindbergh baby."

CHAPTER THREE

B ack at my place on Lincoln Avenue, I went to work on my story for the next edition. "Local Girl Found Murdered," I led. I had a jump on my competition and was confident I would score my first big story. Charlie Reese had tried to temper my expectations when I'd begged him for the assignment. I knew my best chance to get the byline was to write a better story than Georgie Porgie. That much, at least, I knew I could do.

My father was not far from my thoughts. He had never approved of my choice of career, and he considered New Holland an inbred hick town, undeserving of his child. His only surviving child. How I had longed to prove him wrong, serve him a helping of humble pie with a shovel, and watch him admit grudgingly that I hadn't failed him. It was an all-consuming desire that I had chronicled in a journal, pursued with vigor and singularity of purpose. Then, with the passing of the months, anesthetized by obscene quantities of whiskey and bad behavior, I had somehow lost the impetus and put the journal aside. The lack of urgency, the slow pace of life, the absence of intellectual challenge had lulled me into a personal and professional slumber. I squandered my days and wasted my nights in trifling pursuits, meaningless, passing diversions. And then my father died in January, leaving me no opportunity either to sweep up the shards of our shattered relationship or to salvage his respect. I wondered if it mattered now that he was gone, if I still had a chance at ultimate success and redemption in my own mind. If not, then what was there to do but drown myself outright, dissolute, in a pool of whiskey and decadence?

That's what I thought in my darker, drunker moments. But somehow, when the sun rises and the day calls, you answer the alarm and go on. Something beckons: a cup of coffee, a football game, a chat with Fadge. Or a murder. Each new day is a chance to reinvent yourself, after all.

None of the regional papers—not the *Albany Times-Union*, the

Knickerbocker News, or the *Schenectady Gazette*—had picked up on the story in time for their Sunday-morning editions. But I wasn't discounting their ability to catch up. And George Walsh was nipping at my heels. My piece was almost complete, lacking only some background on the victim: details about school, her future hopes and dreams, some personal anecdotes. I would get all that and a photograph of her for the front page when I met the judge at six.

I pulled the last page of copy out of the typewriter at half past four. Hoping to catch some of the Giants' game, I folded my story into my purse and scooted across the street to Fiorello's. Fadge was alone at the soda fountain, back to the door, eyes fixed on the flickering blue television screen behind the counter. Another quiet Sunday, he told me, typical for November.

"Business stinks after Labor Day," said the huge man, drawing me a Coke from the fountain. Ron "Fadge" Fiorello was in his late twenties, a few years older than I, but more than twice my size at six foot two and over three hundred pounds.

I asked how the Giants were doing without Gifford, and Fadge cursed Chuck Bednarik.

"They were winning seventeen to nothing, and now it's twenty-three to seventeen. Shaw keeps throwing it to the other team." He handed me my drink. "Hey, Ellie, speaking of Shaw, maybe you know something about this," he said, leaning over the counter. "I heard Judge Shaw's daughter was killed Friday night. Is that true?"

I took a straw from a nearby dispenser and nodded. Van Brocklin heaved the ball to Ted Dean, who scampered into the end zone to tie the score. Fadge groaned as the point after fluttered through the uprights to give Philadelphia the lead, 24 to 23.

"I was in Wentworth's Woods last night," I said. "I saw everything. Even took pictures."

"So what happened?"

I shrugged. "Nobody knows yet. They just found her murdered, buried in the mud, naked." I sipped my Coke. "Say, did Jordan Shaw ever hang out around here?"

"Now and then about six years ago," he said. "She used to go out with Tom Quint. You know Tommy. He worked here before he went to college."

"Tall? Dark hair? Yeah, I know him."

"A good kid. He's at RIT. Probably back in Rochester already, unless he heard the news."

I asked for Tom's local number, figuring it was worth a try, and secluded myself in the phone booth to dial. Tom's mother answered and said he'd taken the morning bus back to Rochester on Sunday. I told her I was a classmate from RIT and needed his dorm-hall number to ask him about a homework assignment. She gave it to me, and I made a note to phone him after my meeting with Judge Shaw.

At six sharp I lifted the heavy, brass knocker and clapped it twice against the door. The evening air was cool, with just a hint of burning firewood floating on the breeze. As I waited for someone to answer the door, I surveyed the surroundings. Tall, green pine trees and bare elms; a manicured lawn; a long, concrete driveway. The gardener had already planted wooden stakes on either side of the drive to guide the plow once the snows started. The house was a spacious redbrick mansion with green shutters and three chimneys. To my right, I noticed a blue Chrysler New Yorker parked in front of the two-door garage. A red-white-and-blue sticker on the rear bumper read "Experienced Leaders—Nixon-Lodge." Great; maybe we could talk politics. I could tell him how I had canvassed for Kennedy and spent election night celebrating the victory flat on my back with the local Democratic campaign manager.

Almost a minute later, a tall, thin man with graying temples answered the door. He looked like hell, as if he hadn't slept for two days, as if the world had crashed down on his shoulders. He looked like a man who'd just learned his only daughter had been murdered.

"Miss Stone?" he asked softly. I nodded. "Come in."

The neat house creaked under the ponderous grief that hung in the air, hushing every room. Clean and ordered, the Shaw residence discouraged the visitor from making himself at home. I followed the judge through the foyer and down a long hallway to his den. Despite efforts to quiet my step, my heels thumped over the carpet runner and the wooden floor underneath, emitting a hollow echo as I went. I felt like a plow horse on a putting green. Once in the study, he offered me a leather armchair.

"Please accept my condolences, sir," I said. "I'm sorry for your loss."

"Will you have a drink?" he asked, seemingly unwilling to acknowledge my sympathies.

"Scotch would be nice," I said, feeling as if I'd asked for the moon.

"You must be wondering why I've asked you here," he said, dropping three ice cubes into a tumbler with a pair of tongs. His voice was a measured baritone, thoughtful and precise. He looked off into the distance for a moment, as if he'd lost his train of thought. "We've never met," he continued, returning to the task at hand. "And I'm not familiar with your work at the paper."

I just stared at him, wishing I could find something to say.

"I spoke to Fred Peruso this afternoon," he explained, pouring the Scotch absently. A healthy two fingers. "He spoke highly of you."

"Dr. Peruso's very kind."

The judge handed me my glass, stared at me purposefully for several seconds, as if trying to understand what value Fred could possibly see in me, then turned away. He gazed at a wall of books, lined up from floor to ceiling on mahogany shelves. Law tomes and heavy, leather-bound volumes.

"I think Frank Olney is in over his head," he continued. "Fred says you're smart, creative, and tenacious. I have my doubts, of course. You seem rather young, and you're just a girl, after all."

"I can't help my sex," I said. "If you like, I can go."

The judge shook his head vaguely and took a seat on the divan. He wasn't drinking. Then he leaned forward, the muscles in his face gradually tightening beneath the pale skin.

"I need help," he said in a strangled whisper. "All the help I can get. I want you to find the monster who did this to Jordan."

"I don't understand. I've never investigated a murder before," I lied.

"Really?" he blurted out. "What about your father's? Fred Peruso told me all about it."

I was stunned. My face surely blanched, and I stammered something inadequate about that being different. Then I took a large swig of Scotch and choked a bit on the first sting.

"I apologize," he said. "That was wrong of me."

I tried to compose myself, drew a couple of long breaths through my nose, then sipped my drink. Judge Shaw rose suddenly and crossed the room, stopping above me. He reached down to hand me a handkerchief. I dabbed my eyes, then looked up at him.

"Thank you," I said, returning the handkerchief. "But my father's murder is something I prefer not to discuss."

"And I wish I didn't need to discuss my daughter's murder with you. But I do." He paused and drew a breath. His eyes were bone dry, staring sternly down at me. "I will pay you to find Jordan's murderer."

"I'm paid by the paper," I said. Had he just offered me a bribe?

"Just find him, Miss Stone." His body shook with a buried rage.

"Yes, sir." I downed half my drink, then cleared my throat, resolved to see this through. "I'll have to ask you a few questions. You might know some details that could prove useful."

He nodded stiffly. "Of course. Go ahead."

"Did she have a boyfriend?" I asked.

"I don't know. She always had suitors, if that's what you mean. Jordan didn't have to worry about finding a date for Saturday night. But she hadn't mentioned anyone in particular recently."

"What about Tom Quint?"

The judge seemed surprised that I knew about Tom. "No, they went steady in high school, but Jordan ended it before she went away to college."

"Where did she study? Boston, was it?"

"Yes, Tufts."

"Did she see anyone over the holiday?"

"Tommy called Jordan on Wednesday night," he said. "But I don't know if she went out that night. I'm not sure. And I don't know if they saw each other or not after that."

"Tell me about him."

"Tom never quite got over her." He weighed his words carefully. "The boy was crushed when she broke it off. He came by the house once three years ago to talk to me about it."

"Yes?" I thought it charming, if somewhat obsequious, that a spurned adolescent would turn to his beloved's father for solace.

"He's a good boy," said the judge. "Better than the others she went out with." He seemed to suppress a shudder. "Tommy got along with Mrs. Shaw and me. Happy to sit in my den, chatting on a Saturday night, as if auditioning to be my son-in-law. He loved Jordan. Probably tried too hard. Jordan was like any other girl her age: not especially keen on spending her evenings sitting on the couch between her dad and her boyfriend watching Red Skelton."

"I get the picture," I said, emptying my glass before realizing my haste; Judge Harrison Shaw was surely a slow, pensive drinker.

"Anyhow, I came to understand that Tommy wrote Jordan many letters that first year of college. He called her almost every week. He tied up the pay phone in her dorm. Finally she became annoyed, and they had a falling-out."

I asked the judge if Jordan had received any other phone calls. Maybe visitors? Letters?

"Some calls, I think," he said. "No visitors, I'm sure of that. That is, except Glenda. She stopped by on Wednesday. And they may have spoken by phone on Thanksgiving."

"Who's Glenda?"

"Jordan's oldest friend. A nice girl. A bit awkward. Never quite fit in with others, but Jordan was always friendly with her."

I asked for her name and address, and the judge wrote it down: Glenda Whalen, 23 Lombard Street, just a few minutes' walking distance from the Shaw home.

"Poor Glenda," said the judge. "She's rather a large girl, tall and heavyset. The kids made fun of her for her last name. They called her 'Glenda the Whale,' but Jordan always stood up for her. They've been fast friends since kindergarten. That's the kind of girl Jordan was: caring and loyal."

I waited while the judge savored some private memory of his daughter. He smiled gently, looking at nothing in particular.

"What about Friday night?" I asked finally, calling him back. "Did the phone ring before she went out?"

"Not that I recall."

"Did she say where she was going?"

"Just out. I didn't require explanations from her." He paused. "Perhaps I should have."

"Did she keep a diary?"

"I don't know."

"And what was she studying at Tufts?"

"French language and literature. But she was planning on pursuing a graduate degree in engineering next fall. Jordan was one of those rare girls who are whizzes in both language and science. Every subject, really. Unusual for a girl."

He stopped suddenly and stared at me.

"Aren't you writing any of this down?" he asked.

"I rarely take notes," I said. "Except numbers, name spellings, and puzzling questions. I always remember a narrative."

"Perhaps you're something of a whiz yourself," he observed.

"Did she live alone at school?" I asked, ignoring his comment. "Any close friends?"

"She shared an apartment with a roommate. Ginny something; I don't remember her last name. My wife will know if you need it."

"That would be helpful."

"Surely you don't think this has anything to do with school," he said, taking my glass to refill it.

"I don't know, but I'd like to talk to her roommate." I paused while the judge poured more whiskey. He handed me what was unmistakably a double, at least three fingers. "I have some difficult things to tell you, sir," I said, once he'd handed me my refill. "May I speak openly?"

The judge hesitated, clearly dreading what I had to say. "Of course," he said finally.

"My investigation has revealed that your daughter spent at least part of Friday night in room number four of the Mohawk Motel."

The judge's face was a stone, but his eyes betrayed the painful comprehension in his heart. He knew the Mohawk's reputation. "Go on," he said.

"It appears a man arrived at her room around nine fifteen or nine thirty that night. He was driving a light-colored sedan."

Judge Shaw ran a dry tongue around his lips, hesitated for a moment, then rose to pour himself a drink. Bourbon. Straight. A good belt, and he threw it back in one go.

"The man left about two hours later," I continued. "A second car arrived before midnight, and a tall man went into her room. Different car, different man. He left sometime before one thirty, when a third man was seen leaving her room."

The judge didn't move now, didn't speak.

"Do you have any idea who those men might have been?" I asked finally.

"Of course not. Don't you have a description of them?"

"You just heard it."

"Tell me something, Miss Stone," said the judge, turning his back to me. "Tell me honestly." He took several measured breaths before he continued. "Did those men rape my daughter?"

I was startled. "Didn't you speak to Dr. Peruso?"

"I couldn't bring myself to ask him that. I know Fred too well."

Too bad the judge didn't know me so well. Thanks a lot, Fred, for leaving the dirty work to me. I didn't know how to tell him delicately that his daughter had had "a good roll," to echo the words of Jean Trent, Love Detective.

"No," I said hoarsely. "She wasn't raped."

The judge seemed to find consolation in that. He heaved an audible and visible sigh, then poured himself another bourbon.

"She wasn't raped," I said again. "But that brings me to another difficult question."

I saw the skin tighten over his jaw, then he nodded; how could it get any worse? I cleared my throat and asked if he knew what an IUD was.

It was the most painful exchange I've ever had. The judge must have hated me for telling him the truth about his daughter. I hated myself for the body blows I delivered; no couching could soften what I said, and it made me sick to my stomach. A metallic taste coated my tongue like a glue, and I couldn't swallow another sip of the judge's Scotch for fear of spitting it on the ground in disgust and sorrow. I told him, all right. I gave it to him straight, as he had asked, and the result was a broken man staring me in the face. Damn Fred Peruso.

Before I left, I managed to choke out a request for a family photograph of Jordan, explaining that it might help some witness somewhere remember something. I don't think the judge bought it, but he produced an album of photographs from which I could choose.

"I'll get Ginny's surname from my wife," he said, leaving me alone in his den.

I held on my lap the record of Jordan Shaw's short life. From the very first picture, the requisite nude on a baby blanket, to the last—a stylish portrait signed by a Boston photographer named Paul Thibaudet, I was privy to moments shared only by her family and friends. Jordan in the middle row of her third grade class picture; Jordan dressed like a fairy for Halloween; Jordan in her cheerleading outfit; as Homecoming Queen; on skis; at the train depot; with a dog; in saddle shoes, leaning on the car . . . She was a cool beauty. Her scrubbed face and clear eyes revealed an inborn propriety and quiet dignity. She looked like a Protestant princess, too pure and too proud to indulge in the sweaty rut of intercourse, disinclined to sully her body with the sticky intimacies of physical passion. Who said you can't fool the camera?

I put the album down and thought with irony that the photographic record of Jordan Shaw's life ended as it had begun. My pictures of a muddied, naked corpse—as naked as the day she was born, as naked as the day she posed on a baby blanket—closed the book on her brief, privileged existence.

The judge returned, appearing suddenly behind me and giving me a good scare. "Virginia White is the roommate's name. Here's her number," he said, extending a square of paper to me. "Jordan and Ginny's phone number."

I took the paper and thanked him.

"How do you plan to proceed, Miss Stone?"

"There's someone from the motel I want to talk to," I said. "And Tommy Quint."

He saw me to the door, and I was happy to be getting out of there. As I walked down the path to my yellow Plymouth, he called to me. I stopped and turned. The judge came out into the cold in his shirt-sleeves, approached me slowly, and looked deep into my eyes. I wanted to get away, but his determined gaze held me.

"How," he began, "how did you . . ."

I wanted to ask for clarification, but couldn't get the words out. My throat had closed tight, and I fought an instant urge to burst into tears. As he stared at me, his steel eyes glistened behind their intense stare. I understood what he wanted to know. In that moment, my reluctance to engage with him evaporated. He was tortured by the same pain I had felt, and he wanted help.

"It's horrible," I said softly. "There is nothing anyone can say or do to fill the void. It's a cruel agony, which is something I think you already know."

He sighed in the night air, looked skyward, then nodded knowingly. "It's a nightmare from which I cannot awaken."

He stared at me for another minute, with God-knows-what misery twisting his thoughts. Then he stepped back and thanked me for my help. I drove away, slowly. He watched me go, then turned like a condemned man to face the pitiless grief waiting for him inside.

Glenda Whalen's home was a modest, brick traditional, about ten years old, with an attached garage and a small front yard. The lights were on in the front room, so I switched off the motor and climbed out of my car. The door banged shut with a thud in the cold evening air, then all went silent. I made my way up the walk to the front door, through two rows of bare shrubs, my shoes clacking on the cement, again shattering the cold stillness of the evening. The small, steel knocker was cold in my fingers, and its rap echoed high-pitched and hollow against the door.

"Yes? What is it?" asked the tall, hefty man who answered.

"I hope I'm not interrupting your supper," I said.

"We already ate. And, sorry, we don't want any cookies, miss."

"Oh, I'm not with the Girl Scouts," I said. "I'd like to speak with Glenda Whalen."

"Glenda!" he called over his shoulder. "Someone's here to see you." Then he invited me into the foyer.

A large girl in slacks and a sweater appeared, and the man left us. Her eyes were ringed with red, and her nose looked raw, as if she had a cold. She regarded me curiously, her brow furrowed slightly.

"Do I know you?" she asked softly.

I gave her my name and explained that I was a reporter for the *Republic*.

"You're a reporter?" she asked. "What do you want from me?"

"I'm investigating Jordan Shaw's murder," I began, and the girl's red eyes grew before me.

"What's that got to do with me?"

"You were her friend. I thought I might ask you some questions."

She stood back and looked me up and down. "What could I possibly tell you?"

"I wanted to ask you about her friends. Her boyfriends, what she liked to do, where she liked to go."

Glenda's face soured. "Are you kidding me? Are you some kind of ghoul?"

"I'm just trying to do my job," I answered. "And find her killer."

"You're pathetic," she sneered. "Have you no shame? Or respect for the dead? Or for yourself?"

"I'm just trying to help."

"I am mourning my oldest and dearest friend," she said, nearly sobbing. "And you come here nosing around, trying to dig up dirt on the most marvelous girl I've ever known."

"It's not like that. Someone broke her neck, murdered her. Don't you want to help me find out who?"

"You're just a girl. What can you possibly do? You're not trying to solve this murder. You just want to ruin her name."

"That's not true, Glenda. Judge Shaw asked for my help. I just came from his house."

"No you didn't," accused Glenda. "You've been drinking is more like it. I can smell it on your breath."

Then the tears gushed from her eyes, and she buried her face in her hands. I tried to comfort her, awkwardly, and she didn't resist.

"Will you answer some questions?" I asked, once she'd stopped crying.

"Get out of here," she said, almost in a whisper, and she turned away. When I didn't move immediately, she spun back around and roared at me: "Get out of here and leave me alone!"

I arrived home at seven thirty, opening radiator valves and flicking on lights as I went from room to room. Charlie Reese would be waiting for me downtown at eight, so I had just enough time to make a call to Rochester.

"Is Tom Quint there?" I asked the boy who answered the phone.

"Quint!" the voice called. "Is Quint here? Some girl wants to talk to Quint!"

I could hear the chatter and laughter of several young men in the background, and after two minutes, I wondered if the phone had been abandoned. Finally, though, a soft voice came on the line and confirmed I had reached my party. I introduced myself, excused the interruption, and asked if he'd heard the news about Jordan Shaw.

"Yeah," he said weakly into the receiver, his voice tight with grief.

"Would you mind if I asked you a few questions? It might help the investigation."

Tom said okay.

"Did you see Jordan this past week?" Right to the point; I didn't want to dance with him.

"Yeah, I saw her . . . Wednesday . . . and . . . um . . ."

"Friday night?" I prompted.

A long pause. Nothing but faint white noise coming down the line. "Yeah, Friday night."

So much for Judge Shaw knowing his daughter's comings and goings . . . Now it was my turn to weigh my words. "Where and when did you see her Friday?"

"I don't want to talk about this," he said, and I thought he was going to hang up. "I don't know who you are, and . . ."

I repeated my name and affiliation. "You know who I am, Tom. I'm a friend of Fadge's. I live across the street from Fiorello's. You waited on me a few times last summer when you were home from school."

"Are you that girl with the long curly hair? The crossword girl?"

"That's right."

"You're that girl Fadge is in love with."

"Um, yes, I suppose," I stammered. That came out of left field. "Now listen," I said, trying to regain my balance, "I'm not trying to dig up dirt or make a mess. I just think it's important to know. Sheriff Olney is sure to be talking to you soon, so why don't you tell me what you know?"

"Why should I tell *you*?" His tone was polite, but distrustful just the same.

I decided to play my trump. "Judge Shaw has asked me to help find out who did this. If it was you, Tom, you'll be in jail tomorrow, because I'm sure you left some fingerprints on her neck or in the car." I was bullying him, and it worked.

"I didn't do it!" he yelled, coming to life. "I loved Jordan. I would never hurt her!"

"All right, then help me."

There was another long silence. "Judge Shaw asked you to help?"

"I've just come from his house. He gave me two Scotches in his den."

"Okay," he said. "I met Jordan about eight on Friday night. She picked me up at my house in her dad's car."

"And?"

"We went for a drive."

"Tom, you're going to have to tell the story, so just do it."

He relented, explaining that he had phoned Jordan Wednesday, and they agreed to meet that night at Blue Diamond Bar, a popular hangout for the kids home from college for Thanksgiving recess. The two chatted over a beer, and things warmed up between them. Jordan let him kiss her a couple of times in the parking lot, and they parted on the friendliest terms in years. Tom apparently read more into the kisses than Jordan had intended. He was expecting a definitive reconciliation, leading to a short engagement, marriage, mortgage, and Saturday evenings on Judge Shaw's couch. He convinced her to see him again Friday, if only briefly, as she insisted she had plans.

They didn't drive anywhere in particular on Friday, just around on some of the country roads in the hills above the Mohawk River. Tom tried, without success, to convince Jordan to take him back. After about twenty minutes, she grew tired of the hard sell and dropped him off at his house. She drove away.

"Did she say if she was going to meet someone?" I asked.

"No, but I got the feeling she was. She was in a big hurry. Kept looking at her watch and smoothing her hair. Looked like she'd been at the beauty shop that day. Her hair was kind of teased up, you know?"

Not when I saw her.

"Did she have a steady? Was that why she wouldn't come back to you?"

"Jordan always had someone, but she wouldn't have told me. She knew it would upset me."

"Do you think she was meeting someone from New Holland?"

"I don't know. Maybe a fellow who was back from college."

"What did you do the rest of Friday night?" I asked, realizing I'd reached a dead end. He stumbled on his answer, tried to have me believe he'd watched a movie on TV, but he couldn't tell me what it was. He might have been lying, but I couldn't believe he'd killed her.

CHAPTER FOUR

The night air packed a sharp bite now. A cold front had crossed the border from Canada and was creeping south, its crisp Arctic air and high, frosty clouds advancing on light winds. As I pulled up to the *Republic*'s offices, the moon peeked over the New Holland Bank Building and cast a pale shadow over Main Street. A quiet Sunday night, eerier than most, and I felt relieved to get inside where it was warm and bright. Charlie Reese was working in his office on the second floor. He didn't smile when I came in.

"I've got George Walsh's piece on the murder right here," he said, waving some paper at me. "Artie wants me to run it."

"He's lucky if he spelled her name right," I said, reaching into my purse for my own copy. "I've got everyone scooped on this. Mr. Short can't take it away from me."

Charlie frowned. "Don't count on it. You know he doesn't like you. And after you showed up Walsh today at the sheriff's office, he's just looking for one good reason to fire you." Charlie pushed George's copy across the desk to me. "Read this, then tell me if you've got something better."

The article stated the facts: the twenty-one-year-old daughter of State Appellate Division Judge Harrison Shaw had been found dead Saturday in Wentworth's Woods, north of New Holland. The sheriff's department and state police were treating the case as a homicide. Walsh described the condition of the body and the pelvic gash, and he quoted the coroner on the cause of death. He made no mention of the IUD— neither had I—nor that the judge's missing car had been found.

"I've lapped him three times," I said, sitting on the corner of Charlie's desk. He glanced at my bare knee, and I pulled my skirt down to cover it.

"Like for instance?" he asked.

"I found Judge Shaw's Lincoln at Phil's Garage," I said. "And I traced it back to the Mohawk Motel where Jordan spent part of Friday night. She would have spent all of Friday night there, by the way, but she was murdered in room four."

Charlie raised an eyebrow. "What else?"

"I found the bloody tissue in the trash. From the gash in her pelvis. Then I spent an hour talking to her dad over a couple of cocktails, and I had a long chat with an old flame of hers who saw her minutes before she went to Mohawk Motel. One of the last people to see her alive. And I interviewed the innkeeper, who identified Jordan Shaw from a photo I showed her. I've got more than a full day on George. Read my story if you don't believe me."

Charlie took my copy and rifled through it. When he'd finished, he settled back into his chair, thinking about what I had written.

"We may have to hold back on some of the coroner's findings," he said. "I don't think we can get away with saying there was semen inside her unless we say she was raped. And we can't say that because it's not true. I want to tip-toe through this minefield, Ellie; Judge Shaw is an influential man."

"Charlie, I just came from his house. He knows what I know, that I'm from the paper, and he didn't ask me to hold back on anything. As it is, I promised Fred Peruso I would keep quiet on the IUD."

"The what?"

I had to explain to Charlie what it was and that it had been found in Jordan Shaw's uterus.

"It may have to come out later," I continued. "But for the time being, I don't see what purpose would be served by including it in the story."

Charlie conceded. "Okay, I'll back you up on this one, as you wrote it. But take the advice of an older hand, and have another look at what you wrote about Frank Olney. He won't give you the time of day once he reads that. You make him look like a bumpkin lost in his own cornfield. Granted, it's a fair depiction, but if I were you . . ."

I saw his point. I could blur the focus on a sentence or two, making it appear that the sheriff had found the car and the tissue, or that they had come into his possession, without ever saying so in explicit terms. At the least, the public would conclude that Frank Olney was in charge of his own investigation. I was sure I could benefit from that.

After doctoring my references to Sheriff Olney, Charlie and I selected eight photos for the story, three of which would anchor the front page: the crime scene; the sheriff looking grimly determined and capable, above a caption of "I'll get the guy who did this"; and the portrait of the victim herself. My headline stretched across the top of the page—two inches high—with my story and byline in tow. In deference to the judge's reputation, we buried the picture of the Mohawk Motel deep inside the paper, on page seventeen.

Once Charlie had settled on the layout and sent it off to Composition, he congratulated me on the work I had done and told me he was putting out a special morning edition.

"It may mean my job tomorrow," he said, "but you ran circles around George."

I thanked him, and he smiled. We both knew he was going to take the flak for my story.

∂⊙

At ten I sat down in the phone booth at Fiorello's and dialed the Boston number Judge Shaw had given me—Ginny White. No one answered. I hung up and joined Fadge at the counter. The place was empty of customers, as could be expected on a Sunday night in November, and we talked about football, the weather, and Jordan Shaw.

"I heard a rumor she was raped," said Fadge, leaning against the cash register behind the counter, his huge shoes propped up on the ice cream freezer. Not the most hygienic practice, but par for the course.

"You heard wrong," I said, proffering my glass for another Coke.

He motioned for me to fill it myself. I leaned over the counter to pump some Coke syrup into my glass, then topped it off with carbonated water from the spigot. Fadge flipped a long soda spoon at me. I caught it and stirred my drink. No one ever accused Ron Fiorello of overexertion.

"Tomorrow's paper is going to raise some eyebrows," I continued. "And not just because a local girl was murdered."

"What do you mean?"

"The way she died. Or rather, the way she lived. She wasn't exactly saving herself for marriage."

Fadge shrugged it off. "That's overrated."

"How would you know?" I asked.

He ignored me. "So you were there, Ellie. What do you think happened?"

I explained, without giving the most sensitive details; I trusted Fadge more than anyone else in New Holland, but Fred Peruso and I had an agreement about the IUD. It was one thing to presume that Jordan Shaw had slept with someone Friday night. It was another to imply that she was bouncing on the mattress like a trampolinist every time the sun went down. I told Fadge exactly what was in my article and gave him my gut feelings besides.

"If she'd been raped, I'd get it," I said. "If she hadn't been cut, or even if it had been accidental, I might buy it. But something doesn't add up here. I believe people do things for logical reasons, whether we find their actions abhorrent or not. This guy cut out a piece of her skin and took it with him. Why?"

"Maybe he wanted a souvenir." said Fadge.

We sat quietly for a few moments, mulling over the possible explanations. Neither of us could think of any.

"Hey, guess what I discovered today," I said to change the subject and brag a little at the same time. "The Mohawk Motel has a Peeping Tom."

"You just figured that out?" He laughed, and he told me a story. "Joey McIlhenny used to screw his sister-in-law up at the Mohawk. To hear him tell it, he was giving it to her eight or ten times a week, but everyone knows Joey's a talker. Anyway, after a couple of weeks, he starts to worry maybe his brother's wise to him, and he feels like someone's watching every time him and his sister-in-law hit the sheets. Then, one day, he catches that Puerto Rican kid peeping through the bathroom window."

I told Fadge about my discovery behind the Mohawk, but that Jean Trent seemed unwilling to help me find her handyman voyeur. Fadge pushed off the register and leaned toward me. His brown eyes, bulging from a thyroid condition, sparkled with amusement.

"She's not going to turn him in, Ellie. Not her young rooster."

"You're telling me this Julio guy is..." I searched for the right word, "romantic with Jean Trent? She said he was just a kid."

"About twenty-one," said Fadge, pulling back to his position against the register. "And, by the way, *romantic* isn't the right word."

"She must be fifty years old," I said, ignoring him. "What's he see in her?"

"Who can say? Every Saturday night I see the prettiest girls in high school swooning over the cheapest punks and greasers in town. Nice, smart girls. Even girls like Jordan Shaw."

"I thought she went out with Tom Quint," I said.

"She did, but there was a goon she took up with for a while that last summer before college. His name was Pukey Boyle. A hood, a loser who never graduated high school. I kicked him out of here about five years ago for stealing magazines. After that, he used to wait in his car while Jordan bought him cigarettes. Now he sews fingers into gloves at Fowler's Mill down by the river."

"Seems like a strange match," I said, recalling Judge Shaw's shudder earlier that evening. "What do you suppose she saw in him?"

Fadge shrugged his shoulders and explained that a lot of New Holland girls displayed similar poor judgment at about that age.

"Puerto Rican boys don't seem to be immune, either," I added.

Fadge smiled. "A young kid like that has a roll with an experienced lady ... I'm sure he was overwhelmed by the whole thing. Sex is pretty scary at first."

"Sure," I mumbled, "when you're doing it with Jean Trent."

MONDAY, NOVEMBER 28, 1960

I rose the next morning at about five thirty. After dressing, I ran downstairs to fetch the Schenectady and Albany papers from the stoop in front of Fiorello's. Fadge was always late, and people just took papers from the bundles left by the drivers. Back at my kitchen table, I found a two-column item on New Holland's murder in the second section of the *Gazette*. "BODY FOUND IN NEW HOLLAND WOOD," announced the headline. The article was thin. I couldn't believe my luck until I noticed the byline: Harvey Dunnolt, Montgomery County Bureau Chief. He obviously hadn't bothered to look into the story; he didn't even have the victim's name. Harvey lived in Schenectady and only ventured west to New Holland for county-board meetings once a month. Now he'd missed the biggest story in years.

The *Times-Union* featured a concise, accurate story on the murder, but the *Knickerbocker News* had nothing. I smiled to myself and turned on WSCC, the local radio station. There were news flashes, bulletins, and a general frenzy over Jordan Shaw. The Capital District stations picked up on the story as the hour wore on. By eight, WGY, flagship station of the General Electric Company in Schenectady, was transmitting news of the New Holland murder as far as Montreal, Boston, Philadelphia, and Cleveland—I may be embellishing, but the weather *was* clear. I blessed Charlie Reese under my breath for the early edition.

∂⊙

The gravel lot of the Mohawk Motel was empty when I arrived at quarter to nine. Jean Trent had said this wasn't her high season, but I wondered how she stayed in business.

"You again?" she said through the storm door. "You're going to ruin my business with your newspaper stories. What do you want now?"

"I'm still trying to find Julio," I said, unable to shake the vision of a fiftyish Jean Trent in bed with a teenager.

"You and the Royal Mounties. The sheriff was here yesterday looking for him. What did you tell him?"

"I never mentioned his name. May I come in?"

"No." She held the door fast, her eyes difficult to read in the shadows. "I ain't receiving visitors."

"Where does Julio live?" I asked as nicely as I knew how.

"Down on the East End. I don't know exactly."

"Well, what's his last name?"

"Some Rican name. How should I know?"

"You pay him, don't you?"

"Cash. Never had to write a guy's name on a dollar bill before. And I ain't telling you nothing else," she snapped. "You've already ruined me with your nosing around."

She slammed the door shut and bolted it tight. I walked back to my car, and Jean watched me through a window as I drove away. Not ready to throw in the towel, I pulled into the Sinclair station a half mile up the road and called Frank Olney from the phone booth.

The sheriff told me he had indeed tried to find Julio the day before but hadn't located him yet. He knew his last name, though, and gave it to me: Julio Hernandez, resident of 2 Hawk Street on the east end of town.

"He wasn't there yesterday," said Olney. "But we've got the city and state police looking for him."

"I heard a rumor he and Jean Trent were playing house." I can't help looking for confirmations.

Frank chuckled. "Everyone knows that, Ellie." He gloated over his small victory, and I let him.

"Have you asked for a warrant to search her place? You never know what you might find."

"Uh, yeah, we're working on that." I could almost hear him scribbling a note to get a warrant. It seemed a little late in the game; if Jean Trent had wanted to get rid of incriminating evidence, she could have done so Saturday or Sunday.

"Will you take me along when you get it?" I asked.

Olney thought for a moment, then said sure. Before I hung up, he referred to my article in the *Republic*.

"That was a nice piece you wrote, Ellie," he said, his tone conveying more gratitude than admiration. "You're not like some smart-aleck reporters, just trying to shoot me in the rear. I appreciate that."

Charlie Reese was a wise man.

"Just doing my job, Frank."

I hung up the phone, intending to return to the Mohawk to do some exploring behind the motel. I was sure Jean Trent knew a lot more than she was telling, and I wanted the chance to prove it.

☙

I left my car on the dirt path that led to the rear of the motel, and I approached on foot. The garbage cans, still flanked by the rusting junker and old television, anchored the clearing. The blue pickup was there, too, alongside a new arrival to the pastoral scene: a dark-green Pontiac station wagon woody, circa late forties. The massive chrome grill and bumpers were rusted, the fenders were dented, and the wood paneling had faded and blistered from neglect. But the car was sporting four new whitewall tires. I ducked my head under the chassis, looking for a triangular oil stain. The car was leaking oil, all right, but in steady drops, forming a tacky, black pool in the dirt. No triangle. I stood up, brushed the dirt from my hands and knees, then tested the car door. Open; this was New Holland, after all. No one locked doors. I slid in on the passenger side and tried the glove compartment, which opened on command. Inside, I found a crumpled package of Pall Malls, a broken flashlight, varicolored fuses, and one size D Ray-O-Vac battery. No registration or insurance papers. I noticed, however, that the inspection sticker on the windshield was dated 1959 and had expired seven months earlier.

The ashtray overflowed with Pall Mall and Salem butts, while a couple of empty root beer bottles and peppermint gum wrappers lay strewn about the floor. I found three nickels and six pennies under the seat, along with a small, black, metallic canister. Nearby, a lonesome cap, made of the same material, was collecting crud. I recognized these last two items immediately; I had at least a hundred just like them in my refrigerator at that very moment: film canisters. I shimmied across the bench seat to exit on the driver's side and noticed the seat was in its rearmost position, far from the controls. Either little Jean Trent had been wrestling behind the wheel, or someone else had been driving the car.

I climbed out, closing the door gently, and crept to the rear of the Mohawk. Dipping into the bushes with my camera at the ready, I slipped along the wall to the center of the complex: Jean Trent's room. To my surprise, I found each louver secured on its hinge. The opaque glass thwarted any chance of seeing inside. I tried two other windows that had been loose the day before and found them closed tight. Afraid to press my luck any further, I pushed through the heavy brush and returned to the dirt road where I'd parked my car.

Once off Jean Trent's property, I stopped to put my camera back in its case. As I slid it inside, the lens cap popped off and fell to the ground. Bending over to pick it up, I came nose to nose with a triangular oil spot.

CHAPTER FIVE

Actually, there were two sets of triangular oil spots, a couple of feet apart. But the pattern was identical to the one I'd seen on the service road, though somewhat smaller. I snapped a few frames of the triangles, then returned to my car a little farther down the road. Heading back into town, I stopped at a corner phone booth to try the Boston number again. Still no answer. There was always Western Union, but that wasn't the fastest way to research a story.

☙

East Main Street was the hub of New Holland's barrio, if ever a barrio existed north of Spanish Harlem. Though counting barely thirty thousand souls, New Holland boasted a broad ethnic mix of English, Irish, Italian, and Polish. The Diaspora had cast a few Jewish families into New Holland's soup, and there was a smattering of Germanic names in the phonebook as well. Believe it or not, no Dutch. The Puerto Ricans were the last group to arrive on the shores of the Mohawk and, as such, enjoyed the distinction of low man on the totem pole.

Hawk Street ran about three hundred yards north and south, from East Main Street to the train tracks near the river. It had always been a working-class neighborhood, adjacent to the mills, railroad, and river. Even so, Hawk Street and the East End had seen better days. Clutter and disrepair marked the street like tar on a rag. The gray clapboard houses stood leaning, orphaned elders left to expire in a cold, miserable corner of a forsaken town. The street had the look of a neglected graveyard, and, if not for the parked cars, you'd think you'd stumbled into Hell's own vestibule.

I rapped on the door marked number 2, and flecks of cracking paint fell to the warped boards of the porch under my feet.

"What you want?" asked the man who answered the door. He was of medium height and weight, with wavy dark hair, a leathery face, and sharp, black eyes.

"My name is Ellie Stone. I'm a reporter for the *New Holland Republic.*" I knew I was unwanted. "I'm looking for . . ."

"I know why you're here," he said, joining me on the porch, closing the door behind him. He was wearing gray-green work clothes. The name "Miguelito" was stitched in cursive into a white oval tag on the right breast pocket of his shirt. "What you want with Julio?" he asked.

"Just some information," I said, stepping back.

"Don't know where he is."

"Listen," I said, steeling myself. "The sheriff is looking for him; you know that." The man did nothing to confirm or deny my statement. "I don't believe Julio had anything to do with this murder, but as long as he remains in hiding, people will assume he did. And that could be dangerous when he finally turns up. And he will turn up; they always do. So why don't you get word to him to talk to me now? I can present his side of the story in the paper. I won't give him away."

"Don't know where he is," repeated the man, staring coldly into my eyes.

"Just tell him what I said. The press has the right to protect its sources."

That wasn't exactly true. To be precise, the press had the right to go to jail for refusing to divulge its sources.

"Here's my number," I said, holding out a scrap of paper. "In case you see him."

The man took the number from me but said nothing. I could feel his eyes on my back as I returned to my car. When I reached my Belvedere, I looked up to see at least two dozen eyes watching me from neighboring porches. I climbed in behind the wheel and eased away from the curb.

My next stop was a phone booth on the corner of East Main and Broome. The dial was sticky with some brownish substance, and the receiver was no prize either, but it worked. It didn't matter anyway; there was still no answer at Ginny's number in Boston.

A few blocks away, on the north bank of the Mohawk, straddling the Cayunda, stood some of the old knitting mills—monuments to an era gone by. Only a few shops remained, among them was Fowler's Mill, where Pukey Boyle sewed fingers into gloves forty hours a week. The foreman wasn't pleased to have a reporter asking for one of his workers, and he told me so.

"He's working, girlie," he said, leaving me on the wrong side of the gate. "You can cool your heels till he breaks for lunch."

I waited outside, resisting the cold by drinking coffee and chatting with the sandwich truck guy, Manny.

"Do you know a fellow named Boyle?" I asked him. "Pukey Boyle?"

"What's he look like?" asked Manny.

I gave him what little description I had: a young greaser who smokes.

"There's gotta be fifty guys like that work here," he said, sticking a slice of bologna between two slices of Freihofer's bread. "I ain't got nothing to say to the young guys, anyways. Bunch of jerks, mostly. The older Joes are okay. Had good jobs till the mills packed up and left. They're stuck here 'cause they got families and mortgages, and this is what they done their whole life. The young ones are just losers. Smart folks know there's no future left in New Holland."

My father would have tipped Manny and slapped him on the back for that last remark.

Finally, when the noon whistle blew, a herd of working men spilled out of the gates and headed our way. As they reached the truck, I began asking for Pukey. A fat man with a two-day beard told me he'd be along soon. A second worker said he didn't know no Pukey Boyle, but he'd like to know me better. I edged away. As more men passed, I encountered indifference, wolfish leers, and outright hostility, but no Pukey Boyle. Then, after about twenty minutes, a tall, muscular young man with hair combed into a DA at least a couple of years out of style sidled up to me.

"You looking for me?" he asked, leaning against the fender of an old Ford behind me. He took a bite from his sandwich.

"Are you Pukey Boyle?" I asked, turning to look at him straight on. He was big, at least ten inches taller than I.

"Who are you, anyway?" he asked, squinting in my direction.

"Ellie Stone," I said, and my voice cracked. "I work at the paper. Can I ask you a few questions?"

"What about?"

Was he kidding? Surely he knew about Jordan Shaw's death; it was the biggest news in years. In fact, it was the only news in years, and she was a former girlfriend of his.

"I wanted to ask you about Jordan Shaw."

"What about her?"

"She's dead," I said, realizing that, indeed, Pukey Boyle lived under a rock.

"What?" He pushed himself off the fender and spat out a mouthful of his sandwich. It looked like egg salad.

"She was murdered Friday night."

He threw what was left of his sandwich to the blacktop and swore out loud. Then he laughed. Laughed!

"And people always said I'd get her into trouble. What happened anyway?"

"Someone broke her neck. Don't you read the papers?"

"You a comedian?" he said, towering over me. He wasn't laughing. I took a step back, and he chuckled.

"Don't sweat it, baby," he said, easing himself back onto the fender. "So tell me what happened."

"I take it you haven't seen her recently," I said, a little short of breath. He was intimidating.

"Not in two, two and a half years. And that was just running into her at Tedesco's Grill."

"Do you have any idea who would want to kill her?"

"What, are you writing a book?"

"No, just an article for the paper. Now, about my question."

Again Pukey chuckled, more to himself this time. "I'd bet any guy she ever went out with would be tempted to. CTs have a way of pissing guys off, know what I mean?"

"*CTs?*" I asked.

"Cockteasers. Sorry, I was trying to be polite."

I nodded. "I see. Have you ever been to the Mohawk Motel?"

"Is that an invitation?" He was looking me up and down without compunction.

"Where were you Friday night?" I asked, ignoring him. "Say, about eleven?"

Pukey stared at me with a quizzical smile, as if amused by my effrontery. He shook his head but gave no answer. He undressed me with his eyes one more time—I surely blushed—then he pushed off the car and trudged back to the mill. I watched him go, breathing more easily now that he'd left, and returned the favor of a thorough undressing.

Manny gave me a knowing look. "What'd I tell you? Jerks."

∂⃝

I phoned Judge Shaw from the booth at the bottom of Vrooman Avenue, on East Main Street. I half wished he would offer me lunch, but he never did. His tone remained cool and distant, despite the empathy I felt for him after our meeting. Perhaps he was reluctant to repeat the agonizing interview of the night before, or maybe he didn't want to feel close to me. Whatever it was, he stayed on script.

I described the difficulty I was having tracking down Ginny in Boston. He gave me her home address—109 Dudley Street in Brookline, near the reservoir—and her parents' phone number. I told him of the progress I'd made that day, and he listened patiently, painfully too, indicating his understanding from time to time with a soft grunt.

"How did you find out about Mr. Boyle," he asked when I had finished.

"I've been nosing around," I said, thinking "*Mr.* Boyle" a waste of formality on a man who called himself "Pukey."

"And what was your opinion of him?"

"A little rough around the edges," I said cagily, picturing his broad shoulders and handsome face. I didn't mention his mane of thick, shiny hair, though I remembered it. "He seemed genuinely surprised to hear the news. I didn't take him to be clever enough to pull off a convincing act, but you never know."

"Was there anything else about him that struck you?"

"He wasn't exactly broken up by the news, if you'll excuse my saying so."

"That doesn't surprise me," said the judge with a sniff. "He cursed me—and Jordan, incidentally—two years ago when I sentenced him to county jail for sixty days."

I choked into the phone. "You sent Pukey Boyle to jail?"

Perhaps I'd dismissed Pukey's involvement too quickly. According to Judge Shaw, he had been arrested for instigating a barroom brawl. The judge, who, at the time, was on the municipal-court bench, sentenced Pukey to thirty days and had only one regret: that he couldn't lock him away longer. At sentencing, Pukey uttered a few choice words for the judge and his daughter, though she'd had nothing to do with the matter. Indeed, she was in Boston at the time, unaware that Pukey had even been arrested. Mr. Boyle's outburst earned him thirty days more in the slammer for contempt.

I knew I'd have to talk to Pukey again, and the prospect intrigued me, despite the doubt in my mind. If Pukey was guilty, I'd prefer to meet him with Frank Olney's large self at my side. But if he was innocent, well . . . I can take care of myself. In the meantime I'd have to be content just to have a look under his car. First I had to find it.

I dialed Jordan and Ginny's Boston number again with the same result. Then I tried the White residence in Brookline and spoke to the housekeeper, Bernadette. She spoke rapidly in a high, tight voice and a strong Irish brogue as she told me Ginny had gone back to school Saturday afternoon, the same day her parents left for a Florida holiday. I made a note in my pad.

"Have you spoken to her since then?" I asked.

"Why would I be speakin' to her? I just saw her Friday, and she's got studyin' and boys to worry about before she bothers about me."

"Well, if you do hear from her, can you give her my name and number?"

"What's this all about anyway?" she asked.

Just then the operator broke in to ask for fifty-five cents more for the next three minutes, and I took advantage of the interruption to ring off.

಄

I was curious to know more about Jordan Shaw the girl. I'd heard good and bad and figured the truth probably lay somewhere in between. I wanted a picture more complete than a muddied corpse and an album of family photographs, so I drove to Walter T. Finch High School to find out.

My request to see Jordan's academic records was met with anger and indignant refusals, followed by threats to have me thrown out on my ear. But one phone call to Judge Shaw settled the question of propriety. The staff was surprised when the judge asked them to cooperate with me, but once he had, the principal—Herbert Keith—and his minions performed contortions to aid me in my task.

Jordan Shaw was born August 11, 1939, in New Holland, New York, and graduated third in her class of 412 in 1957. Her grade-point average over four years at W. T. Finch High was 3.96. Glowing reports of her intelligence, spirit, and promise filled the pages of her file.

Jordan's straight-toothed smile graced many pages of the 1957 yearbook, which a secretary provided for my perusal. Several of her more noteworthy activities were listed below her senior portrait. She had been a cheerleader, a yearbook editor, and a member of the drama, French, and photography clubs. Homecoming Queen, 1956; captain of the girls' field-hockey team, 1957; member of the National Honor Society, 1954–57; class vice president, 1956–57; recipient of the Joshua P. Wentworth scholarship for good citizenship; voted Miss NHHS, 1957 . . . For future plans, she made the bold prediction of "College."

She was pretty, hair brushed straight and curled at the shoulders, but she looked young and unsophisticated, like a high schooler in saddle shoes and a letterman's sweater. Not like the dead girl I'd photographed a couple of nights before. That was a young woman, and a beautiful one at that. Beneath her activities was a quote:

> *"A thing of beauty is a joy forever;*
> *Its loveliness increases; it will never*
> *Pass into nothingness." John Keats.*

I looked under the *H*s for Julio Hernandez, just to see if he was there. Fadge had told me Jean Trent's young buck was twenty-one, the same age as Jordan, but there was no portrait of him. Flipping toward the back, I stumbled across the only *Q* in the book: Thomas Quint. With his hair slicked down and a numb look in his eyes, as if he'd been doped, he looked awkward and dull in the studio portrait. I wondered how photographers did it. How did they manage to erase even the most ebullient personality with the push of a button? Tom's activities hardly matched Jordan's, but I remembered Fadge telling me he had worked at Fiorello's all through high school. Nevertheless, he had somehow found time to run track, play JV basketball, and captain the chess team. His quote was Samuel Johnson: "Hell is paved with good intentions." Marginalia for my investigation.

Glenda Whalen should have demanded her money back from the photographer, whose work was either a cruel joke or a dereliction of duty.

I took the yearbook with me. Maybe I'd get to know the victim better by a more relaxed study of the class of 1957. Or maybe I was just curious.

☙

Millicent Riley greeted me from her perch at the *Republic*'s receptionist's desk, smiling falsely from beneath her horn-rimmed glasses and mask of Woolworth's cosmetics.

"Mr. Short wants to see you," she said in her most severe voice.

"I just want to run some film first," I said.

"He said it was urgent, Miss Stone."

"Of course. Is Bobby in the lab?"

Millicent assured me that he was, but she insisted that Mr. Short was most eager to speak with me. I hoped to put off that meeting as long as possible.

Bobby Thompson—no relation to the New York Giant baseball great, though he did play in the Summer Twilight Softball League—was the head of the photo lab. In fact, he *was* the photo lab. If Bobby called in sick or took a day off, the photographers—all four of us—pitched in to replace him. I handed him two rolls: nothing more interesting than the triangular oil spots from behind the Mohawk Motel, which I wanted to match up against the one I'd shot on the service road Saturday night.

As I was giving Bobby the processing instructions, Artie Short goose-stepped into the lab with George Walsh on his heels.

"Miss Stone!" he barked, the special Monday-morning edition clutched in his hand. "Didn't Millicent tell you I wanted to see you?"

"Sorry, Mr. Short. I was on my way to your office. I just stopped to give Bobby my film."

"Damn it, young lady; I want an explanation for your piece in today's paper!"

I just stared at him.

"Well?" said Short. "I'm waiting."

"What exactly do you want me to explain?" I asked.

"Sources, Miss Stone. A journalist—a true journalist—checks his sources and gets confirmation of information before he publishes it. Especially on a sensitive case like this one."

"Yes?"

"You wrote that Jordan Shaw took a room at the Mohawk Motel, for God's sake!"

"I don't understand."

"You can't write that! George, here, didn't write that."

"George didn't know she'd taken a room at the Mohawk." I said, and the publisher's son-in-law winced.

"You can't write that, young lady. There's the girl's reputation to consider. This is a disaster! Why did I ever let Charlie hire a girl? In all my years, I've never seen such . . ."

"Mr. Short, please!" I interrupted. "They towed the judge's car from behind the motel on Saturday morning, her body was discovered less than a mile away that same afternoon, and the proprietress of the Mohawk identified her from a photograph I showed her. Jordan Shaw may not have spent the night at the motel, but she sure did check in."

Short scanned the paper, trying to find some fault somewhere in my carefully worded article. "What's your source on the car?" He was grasping at straws. "Who confirmed it was towed to Phil's Garage?"

I looked at him incredulously. "I did," I said. "I'm the source. While George was sharpening Frank Olney's pencils, I tracked down the car myself. The sheriff will tell you; he checked the registration. It's the judge's car."

"What about this bloody-tissue business? George says Olney never mentioned any tissue."

"That's because I found it. In a trash can at the Mohawk Motel."

Short glared at his son-in-law, burning a hole in his withering presence. I knew I'd won. Then he told me he wanted to see everything I wrote on the Shaw case before going to press. I agreed—didn't really have a choice—and he stomped out of the room with George Walsh trotting behind.

Bobby Thompson cringed at me in empathy. He liked the calm of the photo lab and didn't react well to raised voices.

"Are you all right?" he asked.

I shrugged. "At least I've still got my job. And scoring off Georgie Porgie is gravy."

After work, I returned home and lay down on the couch to think. I needed to have a look under Pukey Boyle's car, contact Ginny White, and find Julio Hernandez. And that was just for starters. I nodded off after a couple of drinks, and awoke only when the phone rang. It was Frank Olney asking if I wanted to go along on a raid of Jean Trent's place.

I rolled off the couch, slipped into my shoes, and pulled a brush through my unruly hair. Since it was Frank, I touched up my makeup; it couldn't hurt. Then I grabbed my Leica and took ten rolls of film from the refrigerator. Downstairs, I waited on the porch for the sheriff in the cold, evening air.

Mrs. Giannetti emerged from her door and joined me outside. A widow in her seventies, short and broad, with a loose bun of salt-and-pepper hair tied in the back, she pulled a sweater tight around her shoulders and sidled up to me.

"Hello, Eleonora," she began. "You're so busy. I never see you anymore."

I nodded and smiled politely. It wasn't a question.

"Of course I *hear* you from time to time. Wooden floors. And bottles. So many bottles."

"I try to walk around in slippers as you asked."

"Yes, dear, and thank you. Your shoes are quite quiet now. It's more the other noises. When you're entertaining." She looked at me expectantly.

"I see. Well, I'll be sure to ask my guests to remove their shoes."

"As long as they're removing clothing . . ."

Wow. That was bold even for Mrs. Giannetti. I tried not to give her her victory.

"You know, Mrs. Giannetti," I said, "some carpeting would dampen the noise. Remember you promised to look into it?"

That put her on her heels.

"Well, of course, dear," she said. "I've inquired at Dumart's over and over again, but they don't have the rugs I want. They tell me they'll have more come summertime."

"You'd think carpeting would be easy to find in this town."

"Yes, well, I always say it's because of the war."

The war?

"That reminds me, Eleonora," she said. "This ugly business of Judge Shaw's daughter. My friend Mrs. Isadora says that girl behaved shamelessly. I read your story in the paper. What can you tell me about it?"

"Nothing, I'm afraid," I said as Frank Olney pulled up to the curb in an unmarked Ford Fairlane. "Here's my ride. I must fly."

Mrs. Giannetti stooped to see into the car. She frowned, then adjusted her sweater again before slipping back inside.

Frank was alone. I climbed in, and he threw the car into gear as I closed the door. At Market Street, we turned north onto Route 40, and Frank hit the gas. He picked up the radio to alert his men that we were on our way.

"I'll be there in five minutes," he said, clicking the mike with his right hand as he steered with his left. "Nobody moves till I get there. You all follow me in, roger?"

Four cars acknowledged the sheriff's order, and he signed off.

"I don't want those guys tipping off Jean Trent," he said to me. "If Julio's there, we'll catch him with his pants down."

"That would be a first," I said. "Julio with an audience . . ."

Frank Olney laughed, his entire body shaking in the seat. I wondered how he fit behind the wheel.

We raced past Wilkens Corners, where four county prowlers crouched on the shoulder of the road. They jumped to life, one by one, first their headlamps blinked on, then the cherry tops began to spin.

The engines roared and tires spun on the loose gravel as they fishtailed onto Route 40 to join the chase. Gosh, cops are sexy!

We sped into the Mohawk with four cars on our tail, lights still spinning but sirens silent. I was impressed by the sheriff's timing and sense of the dramatic. The four prowlers skidded to a stop in front of the motel, headlights blazing against Jean Trent's door.

"Ready, Ellie?" asked Frank. I nodded, and he yanked his cap onto his head. "Say, you sure look pretty today."

I followed the sheriff to the front door, where Jean Trent was already waiting, barring the way.

"What do you want, Sheriff?" she scowled.

"I got a warrant, Jean. We're coming in."

Frank showed her the document through the storm door and explained he had the right to search her premises for a knife and any evidence of Julio Hernandez's presence. I understood the law well enough to know that such a document gave Frank carte blanche to snoop through everything in the motel. Jean tried to block the door just the same, and Deputy Brunello was summoned to remove her from the sheriff's path. She kicked and screamed, tried to scratch Brunello's eyes out, but a short moment later, Frank had won the first round without much fuss.

A couple of troopers from Albany were due within the hour to dust the entire motel for fingerprints, so Olney instructed his men to put on their gloves for the search. I churned through my purse, retrieved a pair of white gloves I'd bought a few years earlier at B. Altman in New York, and pulled them on. Pat Halvey was assigned to the office; Pulaski and Wycek to the guest rooms; Spagnola and Miller to comb the grounds, especially the area near the garbage enclosure. Vinnie Brunello drew the chore of keeping Jean Trent at bay while Frank and I went through her place.

Jean's inner sanctum was a cluttered nest of *True Police Cases* magazines, *TV Guides*, old newspapers, and half-eaten boxes of chocolate samplers. The stuffed couch, stained and brown, listed to the right, standing on three legs and a stack of dog-eared pulp novels. A coffee table, its veneer ringed and chipped, was moored on the dingy braided rug that stretched between the couch and the seventeen-inch, portable Zenith. On the walls, two yellowing landscapes, cut from a magazine, had curled out of their frames, showing cinderblock underneath. Atop a chest of drawers against the wall, Jean Trent's pale eyes stared across the room from a recent black-and-white photograph. The place smelled of menthol cigarettes, mildew, and hairspray.

Training his sights on the drawers, Frank Olney pulled a pair of leather gloves onto his bearish hands and invited me to help him turn the place upside down. I made a quick survey of the room while Frank rummaged. There was a heap of Pall Mall and Salem butts crammed together in the standing ashtray next to the lumpy couch, and five empty Rheingold bottles stood like duckpins on the floor. I pulled a couple of magazines from between the cushions of the couch, flipped through them absently, then tossed them back to where I'd found them. I lifted a corner of the rug, was frightened by what I saw, and dropped it. A close inspection of Jean's photograph convinced me it had been developed by an amateur—no quality judgment intended. I slid the back off the frame to look for a dedication or note, but the only words I found were "Kodak Paper."

"I'm going to have a look in the bedroom and bath," I told Frank, who interrupted his burrowing long enough to remind me to keep my gloves on.

Jean Trent's double bed, quilted satin cover and all, nearly filled her boudoir wall to wall. There was barely room for a wastebasket and a nightstand. I discovered her clothes in a small closet, hidden behind a crooked folding door. On the shelf inside, there was a shoebox filled with yellowing letters, creased snapshots, and memorabilia of what looked like a mostly forgettable life. Under the bed, dust colonies had long since prevailed over broom and mop, staking their claim to that netherworld. And there was a small strongbox amid the dirt. The lock was broken. Inside was a gun: a small, black Clerke revolver, unloaded but with a box of .22-caliber bullets. There was also an envelope with the gun's registration papers, made out in the name of Jean Marie Trent.

Everything looked in order, and Frank confirmed it when I showed him. He vaguely remembered having approved the permit a few years earlier.

"What should I do with it?" I asked.

"Leave it where you found it," he said. "Jordan Shaw wasn't killed with a gun."

The bathroom was easily the cleanest room in the place. I smelled the ammonia and soap, used liberally during a very recent cleaning frenzy. The sink was ordered and scrubbed to a shine. The dull linoleum countertop was spotless, though bleached and discolored in places. My heels scratched over the remnants of a gritty cleanser left on the tiled floor. The grimy porcelain of the toilet and the mildewed tub, however, revealed the same neglect Jean Trent displayed in the rest of her housekeeping. Why clean only half of the bathroom? The room smelled clean, all right, but the caustic detergents could scarcely cover the familiar odor of hypo underneath. I had lived with that smell for years. Someone had been developing photographs in Jean Trent's bathroom. And whoever it was didn't want anyone else to know.

I searched the medicine cabinet above the sink, hoping to find evidence of a man's presence, but the shelves were crammed exclusively with witch hazel, cold creams, depilatories, and other women's products. I went through the cabinets under the sink, looking for the chemicals, basins, clothespins, enlarger, or other photo-developing paraphernalia I had expected to find. But the place was clean, so to speak.

I rejoined Frank Olney in the other room. He looked at me with a satisfied grin, slapping an X-acto knife into the leather-gloved palm of his left hand.

"What's that?" I asked.

"Just might be the weapon Julio used to cut Jordan Shaw," he said.

The deputies gathered in the motel's office, gave Frank the rundown of their findings—nothing—and prepared to leave. Two men from

Albany arrived and started dusting room number 4 for prints. The sheriff sent his men back to the barracks, precious knife wrapped safely in an evidence bag.

"All right, Jean," said Frank, once we three were alone in the registration office. "Talk."

"Go suck an egg."

"Don't rile me, or I'll haul you in for complicity to murder." Frank's booming voice knocked Jean's insolence to the floor, and, knowing he had no grounds for arrest, I admired his convincing bluff.

"So ask me," she said, retreating into her parlor. "You've made up your mind I'm guilty, whether I am or not."

Frank winked at me, grabbed a folding chair, and dragged it into the next room. I followed, no furniture in tow.

Jean plopped herself down on the couch and lit a cigarette. She glared at Frank and me. The sheriff swung the chair around backward, planted it in front of her, and sat down. The aluminum legs squealed under his weight, and Jean snorted back the urge to laugh. Frank's face flushed red.

"Don't you know what kind of trouble you're in?" he yelled.

"I ain't done nothing."

"Accessory to murder, Jean." Frank stood and started to pace the room. "We've got the knife, and I'll have a warrant for Julio's arrest tomorrow afternoon, I promise you that. And I'll get an envelope with your name on it, too, if you don't start cooperating."

"Knife?" she croaked, puffing away. "What are you talking about?"

Frank lit himself a cigarette and took a deep drag. "The knife Julio cut her with," he said. "The pervert probably wanted a souvenir."

Jean spat two lungfuls of mentholated smoke, laughing, and jumped to her feet. "That kid wouldn't hurt a fly!"

"Where is he, Jean?"

"Who?" she asked, just to provoke him.

"We know he was living here. Where is he?"

"I don't know what you're talking about. Julio never lived here. Why don't you go look for him down on the East End?"

Frank's interrogation was getting nowhere fast, so I decided to try a different tack.

"Where do you do your laundry?" I asked, silencing both Jean and the sheriff. "I mean, do you have a washing machine or do you go to the Laundromat?"

Frank looked at me as if I were mad. Jean, too, was thrown.

"I do some washing by hand," she said, cautious, blushing, perhaps embarrassed to admit she didn't own a washing machine. "What's left I take to the Laundromat down at the shopping center on Route Forty."

"Where do you dry your things?" I continued. "When you wash your clothes here, where do you hang them?"

"I tie 'em to *Sputnik*," she sneered. "They dry in no time."

"Just answer her," Frank warned. He wanted to find out where I was going as much as Jean.

"In the bathroom, where do you think?"

"Do you have a clothesline?"

"Of course I do. How else am I supposed to hang my clothes? What is this, Sheriff?"

"And how do you keep your clothes from falling off the line?"

"Are you some kind of moron or something? I use the latest invention. It's called a clothespin. Ever hear of it?"

"What kind of clothespins do you use? The kind you push down on the line, or the kind with the spring clips?"

"Oh, I got only the best," she snipped.

By now, Frank was gaping at me in utter confusion.

"And where do you keep your clothespins?"

"In the bathroom, like any other God-fearing, anti-Communist American." She seemed to have no idea the pins and clothesline were gone, so I dropped it.

The men from Albany had finished dusting room 4 from top to bottom, including the louvered bathroom windows, and Frank gave up on pumping Jean Trent for information on Julio. I stood on the concrete walkway in front of the registration office, waiting for Frank to reappear from a trip to the toilet. I looked past the pay phone and Dr Pepper machine to where the trash can had once stood.

"You have any ideas on how the grave was dug?" I asked the sheriff once he'd joined me.

"I figure it was a shovel. Why?"

I stared at the rusty circle the garbage can had left, then looked at Frank. He was confused at first, but soon caught on.

◈

Frank's car heaved and pitched over the deep ruts of the service road, the throw of its headlights dancing against the gray trees. The woods were deathly quiet and looked like a graveyard. If Big Frank Olney hadn't been at my side, I would have been shivering from more than just the cold.

"Pull over here," I told him, and we both got out. Frank left the headlights burning. "Over here," I called once I'd found it.

"What the hell's that?" he asked, his breath billowing in the cold night air.

"I think it's Jean Trent's trash can."

◈

Frank dropped me off on Lincoln Avenue and headed back to his office with the flattened trash can in his trunk. He was sure now that it had been used to dig the hole in the woods, and that supported his theory that Julio was the killer. I reminded him that at least three other men had visited Jordan Shaw's room that night, and any one of them could have taken the garbage can. But Frank said he knew. Julio had been spying on Jordan, she caught him, and he killed her in a panic. And now he was on the lam.

It was after ten when I trudged up the stairs to my apartment. I kicked off my shoes, remembering Mrs. Giannetti below, poured myself a long Scotch, and sat down at the kitchen table to examine the 1957 yearbook. I pored over the whole thing, all 174 pages, not just where I might expect

to find Jordan Shaw, Glenda Whalen, or Tom Quint. Some people I'd
seen around town; others had surnames I recognized. Most rang no bells
nor drew any interest. Just forgettable souls in a fading town.

The list of Jordan's activities under her portrait led me to group
pictures near the back of the book. For the field-hockey team photo,
she knelt front and center in a plaid skirt. For the French Club, she
smiled brightly in the second row from underneath a beret. And for the
cheerleading squad her long, slim legs stretched into a full split on the
gym floor. Rah! She played Helena in a production of *All's Well That
Ends Well*. Her name and picture were everywhere, perhaps because she
had edited the book, perhaps because she had been so popular.

I spotted a pretty blonde in the photography club, but the picture
was out of focus—if you can believe it—and I wasn't sure it was her until I
checked the caption below. Jordan Shaw, treasurer. But what really opened
my eyes was the name next to hers. I checked it twice, then matched it to its
owner in the picture. Standing beside Jordan was a tall, skinny, dark-haired
boy who seemed to be more interested in her than in the birdie. His head
was turned to the side, and it looked like he was staring at the beautiful girl
to his right. The caption said it was Julio Hernandez.

I rechecked the *H*s for Julio's picture, but it still wasn't there. After
the *Z*s, however, I found a list of "camera-shy" students whose portraits
did not appear in the yearbook. In the middle, I found his name. No
activities, except the photography club; no quote; no future plans.

∂⟲

I repaired to the parlor, another tall, brown drink in hand, stacked
some records on the spindle of the hi-fi, and settled into an armchair
with a couple of crossword puzzles. The first long play was Beethoven
overtures: *Consecration of the House, Fidelio, Coriolan,* and a couple of
Lenores. The first puzzle, a reprint of the *Boston Globe*'s in the *Republic,*
was a breeze. I refreshed my drink and started in on the second: a
New York Times puzzle from the previous Friday's edition. The second
record dropped: Beethoven's Violin Concerto.

Seventeen years earlier. A Saturday night, and I was fast asleep in my bed. The door opened. Animated cocktail banter invaded the room along with a shaft of light thrown across the floor to my bed and onto my pillow. Cigarette smoke and perfume and spirits wafted in behind the noise and light.

"Abe, let her sleep!" whispered my mother.

"Nonsense, Libby," answered my father. "This will be fun. She loves to do this. Ellie, my dear. Come. Wake up."

Dragged from my warm bed, I was presented to a crowd of my parents' guests, pushed to the center of a wartime gathering in the parlor. Standing barefoot in my cotton pajamas, I rubbed my eyes, which were still smarting from the light, and recognized no friendly faces, despite the broad smiles beaming back at me. Then I saw Elijah in the corner, watching silently. He sent me a gritty nod of encouragement and support, and I looked to my father standing above me.

"Okay, Jack," my father called to the man in a plaid jacket and dark-green tie stationed next to the portable record player. "Play the first one."

Jack gave a thumbs-up and dropped the needle. The room fell silent as the music began to play.

"OK, Ellie," prompted my father. "What is it?"

"Schubert," I mumbled. "Unfinished Symphony."

The crowd cheered good-naturedly, but that was an easy one.

"Good girl, Ellie," said my father. "Next!"

Jack dropped the needle again, this time in the middle of a Bartók string quartet. I couldn't name which one, but the guests seemed impressed by my answer anyway.

"That's enough, Abe," said my mother. "Let the girl go back to bed."

"Just one more," he insisted. "Fire away, Jack."

This one was hard. I knew the music, the melody, so well, but I couldn't place it in the canon of orchestral piano music. Then I heard the voice behind the instruments. Not a human voice, but a musical one.

"Well, Ellie?" asked my father. "Don't make me wrong in front of everyone. I promised you'd get all three."

"Abe, don't pressure her like that!" whispered Mom.

"It's Beethoven's Violin Concerto," I said, and there was a collective gasp.

My father placed his hands firmly on my shoulders and turned me to look him in the eye. "Beethoven's Violin Concerto?" he asked as if to confirm. I nodded. "I hear a piano soloist, not a violin."

"I don't know why it's being played on the piano," I said tentatively, "but it's Beethoven's Violin Concerto."

"Are you sure?" he asked solemnly. "Don't embarrass me in front of my friends, Ellie."

I didn't answer. He asked again.

"Yes, it's Beethoven," I said finally. "The violin concerto. The third movement."

After a long, silent pause, my father burst into laughter.

"*Brava, Eleonora!*" he shouted, turning to the guests. "How do you like that?" he crowed as he joined his guests to accept congratulations.

"Tricky!" laughed Jack, slapping my father on the back. "I didn't even know there was a piano version of the violin concerto."

How do you do that, El?" Elijah asked me later. "How can you tell them apart? I just hear music."

"It's like a person's voice," I said. "I recognize the voice."

Now, before turning in, I listened to the late news from Albany and Schenectady. New Holland's murder was the lead story on WGY and WTRY. They quoted details from my stories and cited my byline. It was the last thing I had expected, and I was positively giddy, even if both radio stations referred to me as *Eleanor* Stone. As far as I knew, George Walsh had never had his name mentioned on the radio news. And in the midst of my gloating, I allowed myself a fleeting vision of my father catching the broadcast and beaming with pride, bragging to his colleagues and cocktail-party guests, and congratulating my mother for the fine job they'd both done raising me.

As I bedded down with yet another whiskey on my nightstand, I couldn't shake the Beethoven melody from my head. It just turned around and around without end, like a rondo, until I fell asleep.

CHAPTER SIX

Sleep is a funny state. Sometimes, when our minds are most preoccupied, it comes only after much tossing and turning. Other times, it washes over us easily, sweeping away the troubled thoughts of the day in order to replenish our physical and mental strength. But that night, my sleep was anything but refreshing. Once the music in my head had finally stopped, I found myself stuck in dreams of my father, my brother, and 1947. My childhood obsession.

> *"Tickets to the World Series, El," Elijah said, pointing a finger into my chest. "I don't know how he did it, but Dad got tickets to Game One."*
>
> *"No way," I said, sure Elijah was having a good laugh at my expense, playing dangerously with my Yankee emotions.*
>
> *"Don't believe me, then," he said, turning away. "I'll bring you back a program."*
>
> *I sought out my father in his study, interrupting his reading, to set the story straight.*
>
> *"As a matter of fact, Ellie, I do have tickets to the Series," he said, regarding me over his glasses.*
>
> *My heart stopped. Dad took note, and his expression darkened. He sat up in his chair and removed his glasses.*
>
> *"I'm sorry, Ellie," he said, leaning toward me. "You see, I could only get two tickets, and since Elijah is older, it's only fair to take him. You'll go next time."*

I lay awake, my gut churning, my mind working furiously to create fantasies to rectify the memory. It was September 30. The Yankees won that day, five to three. I watched it on television, and cried, resenting my dad and my brother, who was at best a lukewarm Giants fan. The Yanks took the series in seven games over Brooklyn. And there never was a next time.

I got up, lit a cigarette, and poured another Scotch I didn't want or need. The thing I had never understood was why my father didn't like me more. Why had he preferred Elijah, who shared few of his interests, none of his tastes, none of his goals? It was a fruitless exercise, especially at this late date, to blame either my father or my dead brother for the inadequacies of my relationship with my dad, but that's what I was thinking as I smoked that sour cigarette and washed it down with warm, watery Scotch. Too lazy to get up to wrestle more ice out of the tray in the freezer. I was the one who loved literature, the one who shared my father's love of classical music—witness my performance in the drop-the-needle test for his guests. I was the one who knocked off crossword puzzles like lint off my sleeve. Just like my father. I even looked like him, people said, while Elijah resembled Mom. Maybe it's like the horror you have at hearing your own voice in a recording. A form of self-loathing, I guess, only his self wasn't involved. Just me.

I finally dozed off after one thirty. I was hovering in that limbo of near sleep—about two—when the phone next to my bed woke me with two blasts. I knocked it over in the dark and bumped my head on the bedside table.

"You wanted to talk?" came a voice from the other end.

"What? Hello?"

"You were looking for me."

"Who is this?"

Nothing from the other end.

"Julio!" I gasped, almost in a whisper. "Where are you?"

"Meet me under the Mill Street Bridge, north side of the river. Alone. Be there in ten minutes."

I wanted to ask for more time, but he had thought of that and hung up the phone before I could say another word. Jumping from my warm bed, I pulled on the skirt and sweater I had taken off a short while before. I wrestled my way into my coat as I thundered down the stairs, surely waking Mrs. Giannetti. The Belvedere groaned but started after a few pumps of the gas pedal, and I was on my way. I rolled through a red light on Market Street after looking both ways for police—God, how much had I drunk?—and reached the river about seven minutes later. I was two minutes late.

A rusting steel-truss structure, the Mill Street Bridge was New Holland's only river crossing, straddling the Mohawk between downtown and the South Side. The Great Cayunda Creek, enema to the mills on the hill above, spilled into the Mohawk underneath the bridge, raising an acrid, yellowish foam. I waited on the west side of the creek, about forty feet wide at its end, sure I'd missed my chance to talk to Julio. Five minutes of shivering later, I was ready to leave; the black river, the biting cold, and the eerie underside of the bridge left me less than confident of my safety. Then a voice, nearly covered by the rushing water, called out in the dark, and I saw a young man in a light-weather jacket standing on the other side of the creek.

"Julio?"

"You that girl reporter?"

I nodded. "Did Jean Trent give you my message?" I figured it was worth a try.

He wasn't buying it. "My father said you were looking for me. What do you want?"

"I want to talk to you about the motel. About what happened Friday night. Can we talk in private? Someone will hear us out here."

Julio looked around, then shook his head. "No. I'll stay right here. If you want to ask me something, do it from there."

"You can trust me, Julio. I won't turn you in. Let's talk in my car. It's the yellow Plymouth right above us."

He hesitated, and I urged him again. He seemed to be considering me carefully from across the creek, weighing the risks, wondering what a young girl like me could possibly do to help him. Or harm him. Finally he nodded consent. I scrambled up the embankment above the Cayunda—not an easy feat in heels and with five Scotches under my belt. I reached my car and climbed in. A few moments later, a thin figure slipped into the passenger seat. He was a bony, dark-haired, handsome kid in rolled-up jeans and Chuck Taylors. He smelled of Vitalis, and he was scared.

"I don't have much time," he said.

"Were you at the motel Friday night?"

No answer.

"You're the number-one suspect, Julio. The only suspect. And nothing's going to change that until you talk to someone."

"I didn't do it!" he said, turning to look at me. "It had to be one of those men who visited her."

"Then you *were* there."

"I read your article."

Julio sat quietly for a minute, gazing at the South Side across the river, and I said nothing, hoping he wanted to talk.

"She was alive at eleven twenty," he said finally.

I turned to look at him. "What's that?"

"I know she was still alive at eleven twenty Friday night."

"Did you see her through the bathroom window?" I asked.

He dropped his head, rubbed his brow, and nodded yes. I could see the tension in his jaw. His skin burned red, and a vein stuck out on his forehead, just above his fingers that hid his eyes. He was crying silently.

"Did you see anyone in her room? What did the guy look like?"

"I don't know," he said, taking his hand away from his face. "I couldn't see him from the window." His voice shriveled to a whisper. "The bathroom door was closed most of the time he was there. But I heard him leave and start his car a few minutes after eleven."

"Did you see the others? The ones who came later?"

He shook his head.

"All right. What did you see at eleven twenty? Was she nude?"

He looked startled for a moment, then realized my question was only natural, considering what had been going on inside the room. He nodded, "Yeah."

"What was she doing?"

He shrugged. "Nothing. She came into the bathroom and brushed her hair. Then she went back to the other room."

I thought a moment, and Julio breathed heavily next to me.

"How long were you at the window?" I asked.

"You're not going to print this, are you?" he said, grabbing my right wrist and wrenching it toward him. "I swear I'll kill you if you do."

"No, Julio! Don't worry. I'm just trying to find out who killed her." My God, did I have a killer sitting next to me in my car? "You can trust me," I said, hoping I could trust *him*. "How long were you at the window?"

"I don't know," he said, dropping my arm gruffly and turning away. "Forty minutes, maybe."

"What was she doing when you left the window?" I asked, rubbing my wrist.

"The same. Stretched out on the bed. Nothing. I couldn't see much from that angle. Just her legs."

"Where are the pictures, Julio?"

His head jerked left, his eyes burning wildly at me. "What?"

"Where are the pictures you took of her? I want to see them."

"What? What are you talking about?"

"I know you took pictures, Julio, and you've got to show them to me."

"I didn't take any pictures! I just watched her!"

"I can't say I'm sure you're innocent, but I believe you are. And my opinion is based on the bathroom window and your camera. I know you were living with Jean Trent; I saw the chemical stains on the bathroom counter, and I smelled the hypo. You got rid of the equipment, even the clothespins you use to hang your prints, but I know when someone's been developing film. And Jean Trent doesn't own a Brownie, let alone a darkroom. You're a photographer, Julio, I know it. Come on; come clean."

"Why should I tell you anything?" he asked. "You're just a girl. And no older than me. What good can you do for me?"

Before I could answer, a pair of headlights lit the side of Julio's face, and we both jumped. He swore out loud, threw his door open, and bolted from the car. Before I could speak, he had disappeared down the embankment, toward the river. The car that had spooked him passed by, never even slowing down. I sighed, switched on the radio, and lit a cigarette. Connie Francis was singing "Lipstick on your Collar."

I drove around town, thinking, but no insights were forthcoming. Where could Julio be holed up? Somewhere in the Puerto Rican community, probably; surely he had friends who would shelter him, maybe even help him get away. Why hadn't he fled the area already? Or was he foolish enough to go back to Jean Trent's?

I circled the city, starting with the East End. The streets were deserted at three o'clock. Then I drove to Judge Shaw's home on Market Hill, finding all the windows dark, drapes drawn tightly. I sat idling in front of the house for several minutes, wondering which window had been Jordan's. And I thought of Judge Shaw. I wondered if he could sleep, if the wretched sorrow ever slipped from his mind, even for a moment, allowing a blithe respite from the pain. Could he permit himself the indulgence of oblivion? I knew the ache well. The emotional tug-of-war. But the mind can't grieve forever; it needs distraction or it will break. I still mourned the losses in my life, and I dealt with them as best I could. I wondered if Judge Shaw would do the same, in some other manner of his own choosing. Perhaps it was too soon for him. I wanted to ask him, but I didn't know if I had the courage.

The Mohawk Motel was deserted. All the lights were out. I gazed out over the steering wheel at room 4, conjuring a living, breathing Jordan Shaw behind its disreputable door. I didn't know what I was looking for or why I was there. Sometimes you just stare at things and search for inspiration.

My last destination was the rutted service road I had visited hours earlier with Frank Olney. The night was eerier than before; this time I was alone. A half-moon provided the only light in the sky, casting its washed-out rays on the high water tower and frosted ground in front of me. I scanned the woods from the road one more time, looking for something different. But nothing had changed. I turned my car around and drove home.

TUESDAY, NOVEMBER 29, 1960

At six thirty, I dragged myself out of bed and dialed Boston. No answer, and I was past annoyed. After a quick shower and a check of the local papers, I pulled out the slim New Holland phonebook to look for a name: Boyle. There were three, two at the same address, and one woman. None of them were named Pukey. I called the operator and ran up against another dead end. Frank Olney might know, but I didn't want to wait for him. Besides, he was busy tracking Julio. Julio! I cursed myself for having let him get away the night before. He had pictures of Jordan Shaw—I was sure of that—and I intended to find them.

My Belvedere barely coughed the first two times I turned the key, and it didn't start until I'd pumped the carburetor full of gas, almost flooding the engine. It was seven thirty, and I wanted to arrive at Fowler's Mill before Pukey Boyle.

Next to the mill, Fowler's tar parking lot covered about one hundred yards square. I positioned myself near the entrance where I could see every car coming in. From 7:50 on, the stream of vehicles and foot traffic was constant, and I had to look fast and hard to catch Pukey's witless face and mane of greased hair through the windshield. At 7:59 he squealed into the lot at the wheel of a maroon Hudson Hornet. The metallic paint was waxed and buffed to a sheen. He parked about twenty yards from me and ran for the gate to begin his eight hours of sewing fingers into gloves. Once the stragglers had disappeared inside, I climbed out of my car and made my way over to the Hudson. Pukey had parked it catercornered in two spaces so no other car could come near it. I ducked underneath and found the cleanest, best-maintained undercarriage I had ever seen. Certainly no oil leaking from this set of wheels. I stood up, surveyed the area for witnesses, then tried the door. Locked. Only a gearhead like Pukey Boyle would lock his car in New Holland. I took a close look at the wide tires, whose footprints were as distinctive as a signature. But I hadn't seen any tire tracks at the crime scene, let alone anything as unique as these.

At the *Republic's* offices, Tuesday afternoon's edition was already in at Composition, but I had some things to do in the photographers' room. I called Benny Arnold, a fellow I knew at the Department of Motor Vehicles, hoping for a little help. I wanted to know if Julio Hernandez of 2 Hawk Street had a car registered in Montgomery County, and, if by any chance, Jean Trent of R. D. 40 had a second car. Benny said his supervisor had been on the prowl all morning, but he would check and call me back at lunchtime.

"How come you never returned my calls, Ellie?" he asked before hanging up.

"I heard you had a new girl," I lied, trying to wriggle off the hook.

"No, I don't." He wasn't buying it. "I'll call you back anyway."

Charlie Reese dropped by to discuss my progress. I described the state of Pukey Boyle's car, and we both laughed. Then I told him about my late-night rendezvous with Julio Hernandez.

"He called you? Let's run the story as an exclusive interview with the chief suspect!"

"We'll never see him again if we do, Charlie. The kid's scared. And I'm sure he knows more than he told me last night. It's just a matter of gaining his confidence. He'll come across, I know it."

"Do you think he did it?"

"Who knows? He was there Friday night, peeping in her window. Had the opportunity and maybe the motive—if she saw him in the window."

"So what did he see?"

"He saw her alive at eleven twenty. And she was alone."

"Didn't see any of the men?" he asked, popping a cigarette into his mouth.

"I thought you'd quit again," I said.

"Yeah, well, I started up again. But what about this Puerto Rican kid? You sure he didn't see any of the men? Is he being straight with you?"

"I can't tell. I told you, he's scared. A car drove past us, and he bolted. If I'd only had some more time with him ... He was at her window for forty minutes Friday night, Charlie. He must know something more than what she looks like nude."

"Good luck. If you ask me, the next time he turns up, he'll be wanting to talk to a lawyer, not you."

"I'll get to him, sooner or later," I said. "And I'll get that film he shot of her, too."

Charlie nearly swallowed his cigarette. I smiled.

"Just a hunch."

Benny called at a quarter past twelve and told me there were no cars registered under the name Julio Hernandez. He had found, however, a red 1948 Chrysler that belonged to Miguel Hernandez of 2 Hawk Street. Julio's father, no doubt.

"As for Jean Trent," he said, rustling some papers, "she owns a 1948 Ford F-2 truck, three-quarters of a ton empty, registered as a commercial vehicle."

"Yes, I knew that," I said, already searching for an excuse to close the conversation. "Well, thanks anyway, Benny, I . . ."

"Wait a minute, Ellie. Don't you want to know about her other car?"

I had forgotten about the green Pontiac woody I'd seen parked behind the motel. Benny told me it was a 1946 station wagon, registration expired in April 1960. The title actually named Victor Trent of R. D. 40 as the owner, but he had been dead for several years. I had a feeling if I could find the wagon, I'd find Julio.

Tedesco's Grill served the best Italian bar food in the city. From standard fare, like ziti and meat sauce, to six-inch-thick meatball and roast-beef sandwiches, you got your money's worth. But more than anything else, Tedesco's was known for its pizza, and late Tuesday afternoon I was sitting at the dark bar in a gray skirt and a black jacket, waiting for a small mushroom-and-sausage pie.

"Look who's here," said Jimmy Tedesco, dropping a double Dewar's I hadn't ordered on the bar before me. "World-famous reporter Eleonora Stone." The crowd cheered and jeered me good-naturedly, and I blushed. "You're all over the news," he continued. "Now that you're a big shot, you tool around town all dolled up like this?"

"Going to a wake."

"Yeah? Who died?"

"Don't you read the papers?" I asked. "Oh, that's right, Jimmy, you can't read."

He laughed. "Yeah, I read the papers. How would you like some special garnish on your pizza?"

After twenty minutes and another Scotch, I called Jimmy over to ask a question: "Who's that guy over by the jukebox?"

"That's Greg something-or-other," he said. "Used to play quarterback for the high school team."

"He's been looking at me since I came in."

"It's a free country, Ellie," he said. "And by the way, every guy in here stares at you whenever you come in, including me." He winked and slapped a shot glass upside-down on the bar in front me, signifying I had a drink coming on the house.

Jimmy wiped his hands on his apron and called out to the young man by the jukebox: "Hey, you! Quit staring at the lady. You're making her nervous."

A few minutes later, once I'd recovered from the embarrassment, I felt a tap on my shoulder. A tall young woman in her early twenties stood before me in the dim light. She was wearing a sneer and a black dress.

"You're that girl from the paper, aren't you? Remember me?"

"Glenda Whalen," I said. "Hello . . ."

The next thing I remember was Jimmy Tedesco dabbing my swollen lip with a wet towel. The back of my head was pounding, and I realized I was on the floor amid a forest of barstool legs.

"What happened?" I stammered, my mouth sticky with the taste of blood.

"That girl decked you," said Jimmy, a touch more amused than I would have liked.

"What for?" I tried to get up, but Jimmy restrained me.

"Hold your horses, Ellie," he said. "You bumped your head pretty good on the bar. Just stay there for a few minutes till you get your wits back."

"But your floor's so dirty, Jimmy," I mumbled.

He laughed. "I guess you're feeling okay, then. But last night Billy Valicki puked right where you're resting your head."

"Why did she hit me?" I asked, trying to gather up my hair and keep it off the floor.

"I was just kidding about Billy Valicki puking on the floor," he said, brushing my hand away from my hair. "Relax and take it easy, I said. As for that girl, she said something about Jordan Shaw. Something about the Mohawk Motel."

"Where is she? I want to talk to her."

Jimmy laughed. "You better stay away from her, Ellie. We had to throw her out of here; she was going to beat you to a pulp. Best cat fight we've seen in here in years. Short, but good."

"What do you mean *was* going to beat me to a pulp? I'd say she did a pretty good job."

"Hell, she only hit you once. Like Khrushchev banging his shoe on the table, only the table was your face."

A couple of patrons helped Jimmy lift me to my feet, and a few minutes later I was steady enough to hold myself up. I washed down a couple of aspirins with some cold water and waited for my head to stop spinning. A New Holland police officer showed up and tried to convince me to press charges. There were plenty of witnesses, but I declined.

"Suit yourself," said the officer. "But when she comes back looking for you, don't blame the cops."

"I'll take my chances," I said, putting on my overcoat.

"And take your pizza while you're at it," said Jimmy, handing me a cardboard parcel.

I took the pizza—no charge—and drove to O'Connor's Funeral Home on Division Street. My altercation with Glenda Whalen had made me late, and, as a result, there were no convenient parking spots. The whole town had turned out for the wake, it seemed, and I had to leave my car three blocks away. Normally I wouldn't have minded, but I hadn't quite regained my land legs. Even worse was bending over to check for oil spots under every car around the funeral home. And I didn't know the first thing about engines and leaking oil. If the car was dripping slowly, there might not be any telltale spots for hours to come. But I had nothing else to go on, so I stooped. And stooped. I didn't find the one I was looking for.

The funeral parlor overflowed with New Holland's elite and curious, and it hummed with rumor and speculation about the girl in the open coffin. The mourners streamed in, signed the guestbook, and set their eyes on the shattered parents. The judge's wife, in a black silk dress, wore a veil to obscure her eyes. She was composed, indeed statuesque, to a point far beyond what I had been led to expect, and it was clear she was no longer under sedation. The judge sat straight and dignified next to his wife, but his stony expression warded off most people. Only the bravest approached the couple to offer condolences, and none got any response beyond a sober nod. After witnessing a few of these attempts, the funeral director stationed himself between the Shaws and the coffin to repel all but a select few friends and local VIPs.

I took up a discreet position near some flowers along the wall; I wanted to observe, but not at the cost of disrupting the solemnity of the occasion. The assembly represented a who's who of New Holland society, and I had to struggle to keep my foggy head clear to remember them all. Mayor Chester looked stiff in a black overcoat and matching fedora; Montgomery County DA Don Czerulniak, known affectionately to the boys in the newsroom as the Thin Man, was in somber consultation with Doc Peruso; Frank Olney stood against a pillar in the back, sweating puddles in a wrinkled shirt, short tie, and tight jacket. I compiled the list in my head: two dozen lawyers; seven judges, including three from the Third Appellate Division in Albany; all twelve city aldermen; the county supervisor, Gabe Fletcher; Herbert Keith, principal of W. T. Finch High; teachers; clergy—Lutheran, Episcopal, Presbyterian, Roman Catholic, and Jewish; doctors; restaurateurs; merchants; and on and on. Mrs. Lorraine Valeska, doyenne of New Holland's piano teachers, hobbled in behind a cane and took a place standing against the wall next to Artie Short, who'd found a chair he wasn't parting with. Eventually, a young man nearby offered her his seat.

New Holland's gentry was there, all right, but I was more interested in New Holland's rabble. Where was Pukey Boyle, for instance? There were many young people, former classmates and friends, I suspected, and I wondered if Tom Quint had made the trip back from Rochester. My lip throbbed again when I noticed Glenda Whalen glaring at me from across the hot room. Next to her was the same Greg fellow who had been ogling me at Tedesco's. He seemed to be undressing me with his eyes. At a wake.

I joined the DA in the adjacent parlor. I had met Don Czerulniak two years earlier when I covered his campaign, and we had remained friendly since, probably because I never once misspelled his name in print.

"Are you working?" he asked.

"Kind of," I said, looking over my shoulder for Glenda Whalen. "I'm trying to lie low, but I wouldn't be doing my job if I weren't here."

"I had a long meeting with Frank Olney today," said Don, nodding to a constituent across the room. "He wants a murder-one warrant for the Puerto Rican kid."

"Are you going to get it for him?"

"Not yet. We're treating him as a material witness for now. We issued a warrant, but I'm a bit more cautious than Frank. I like to go slow and see how things play out."

"What about the prints they took last night? Any luck?"

"Tomorrow morning," said Don. "And if his prints turn out to be on that X-acto knife, I'll have to go along with Frank on the murder-one charge."

"Do you even have his prints?" I asked.

"In spades. Apparently he painted a fence two days ago and left perfect prints all over the brush. Dried into the paint."

"Even if the prints match, what's that prove? His prints are bound to be on that knife just as they were on the paintbrush; he's Jean Trent's handyman."

"That's a question for a jury. I'm not saying we couldn't drop the charges later on, but you have to admit, it doesn't look good for the kid."

I concurred.

"What happened to your lip?"

"Fell off a barstool."

"You should take it easy, Ellie," he said. "I know you can hold your drink, but that doesn't mean you have to prove it every night."

"Listen to the pot calling the kettle black."

The crowd began to dwindle after eight, and I was thinking about leaving myself, when a girl of about twenty-one approached me. Short, with dark hair cut in a bob, she identified herself as Fran Bartolo, formerly Jordan Shaw's best friend.

"I've seen your stories in the paper," she said. "And I heard them talk about you on the radio. You might be interested in what I know about Jordan."

"I might," I said, unsure what to make of this girl. "Try me."

"Not here," she said, looking around the room. "I don't want her friends to see me talking to you."

So now I was a pariah. I made a quick visual inspection of the room and saw no Glenda Whalen. "Let's talk here," I said.

"No; meet me in Gem Cleaners' parking lot in twenty minutes," she said and disappeared.

I was in the cloakroom, retrieving my overcoat, when the funeral director's son, Tim O'Connor, asked me if I was Eleonora Stone. Judge Shaw wanted a word with me. O'Connor escorted me through two doors to a private room, where the judge and his wife were seated on a divan. Mrs. Shaw still looked remote, chin high, back straight, knees together. The judge rose when I came in, offering me no handshake but motioning for me to take a seat instead. O'Connor withdrew. Once we were alone, Judge Shaw mumbled an introduction to his wife, and I offered my condolences. She nodded coolly but said nothing.

"I've asked you here, Miss Stone, to share some information that has come to my attention," he began. "My wife, Audrey, suspects Jordan was involved with a professor from Tufts."

"What gives her that idea?" I asked.

"Phone calls, letters, bits of conversations overheard … Women seem to be more attuned to these signs."

"Do you know his name?" I asked Mrs. Shaw.

She shook her head and spoke for the first time. "Jordan never told me anything of this relationship," she said, her voice even and dry. "But last August I noticed Jordan was receiving letters posted in Medford, Massachusetts. The handwriting on the envelopes was always the same, and it was written by a man."

"No return address?"

"No, but the postage was metered. Tufts."

"Do you know where these letters are now?"

She shook her head. I stood up and crossed the room to the window. Cars were still pulling out of O'Connor's lot, but the one that caught my eye was parked on the street: a maroon Hudson Hornet.

"Jordan took an educational tour of India and Nepal in August of last year," said the judge. "We believe that this man accompanied her."

India? I thought of the man at the Dew Drop Inn the night Jordan died. I had put him out of my mind, but this was a coincidence. Or was it? A school trip to India a year and half earlier, and an out-of-place foreigner in a bar a quarter mile from her shallow grave.

"Is India where the kids are going these days?" I asked. "I thought coeds dreamt of visiting France or Italy."

"She'd already been to Europe," said the judge. "This was one of those organized tours, sponsored by Tufts alumni, a month with lectures and special speakers."

"Still, India. Not exactly a run-of-the-mill choice for a summer vacation."

"Jordan was not a run-of-the-mill girl," said Audrey Shaw, and I felt reproof in her tone. She didn't like me.

"And you think this man went along to India?" I asked, returning to the professor in question. "Why?"

"When Jordan returned from her trip, I noticed one fellow in particular in many of her snapshots," said Mrs. Shaw. "Nothing scandalous, of course. It just seemed he was always there next to her. There was a familiarity. And he was always smiling."

"What did he look like?"

"Judge for yourself, Miss Stone," she said, extending a four-by-five, black-and-white print to me. "You're a clever young woman. I'm sure you recognize handsome when you see it."

I took the photo from her. Three tourists in a bazaar somewhere in India, long garlands of marigolds hanging in a stall behind them. Jordan was in the middle—beautiful, I must say—flanked by two men: one in his twenties, thin with thick glasses and waxy skin; the other fortyish, handsome and tanned, with sandy hair blowing in a light breeze. They all wore big smiles, though the younger man seemed extraneous to the happiness of the other two. The older man looked like one of those easy globetrotters, equally at home on a camel in the Sahara or in a rickshaw in Peking. He was flat stomached, with taut skin and wiry muscles, and I could see how a young coed might find him terrifically romantic.

"I'll look into this," I said. "May I keep the photograph? Not for the paper, of course."

The judge nodded.

"I'd like to ask you about some of Jordan's friends," I said, feeling awkward. "Do you know a girl named Fran Bartolo?"

"Of course," said Mrs. Shaw. "What does Franny have to do with this?"

"She cornered me a few minutes ago and said she wanted to talk to me about Jordan. She said I'd be interested to know what she knows about her."

Audrey Shaw fidgeted and produced a cigarette.

"I doubt Franny Bartolo will have anything nice to say about Jordan," she said, inhaling deeply. "They were friendly a few years ago, but you know how teenage girls are. Franny was always jealous of Jordan because of boys."

"What about Glenda Whalen?"

"A devoted friend of Jordan's," said the judge. "I told you that the other night."

"A little too devoted, if you ask me," said Mrs. Shaw.

"Why do you ask about Glenda?" asked the judge.

"She knocked me unconscious at Tedesco's Grill about two hours ago," I said. "In case you hadn't noticed, she's the one who gave me the fat lip and the bump on my head."

"What a horrible story, Miss Stone," said Audrey Shaw, eyes well hidden behind the black veil. "You should see a doctor."

"I'll be all right, thanks. But I was wondering about Glenda. Why would she attack me?"

"Perhaps she didn't approve of what you wrote about Jordan," said Mrs. Shaw, arching a perfectly plucked and penciled eyebrow as she regarded me.

"The judge knew what I was going to write. I didn't betray any trust or print any surprises."

"Indeed, you did not," he said.

"Let me explain," said Mrs. Shaw. "I meant that Glenda Whalen may not have approved of what you wrote. I didn't approve either, but that's done now. You must realize that your article upset all those who loved Jordan. Myself, Glenda, Greg . . ."

"Enough, Audrey," said the judge, cutting her off.

"Who's Greg?" I asked, wondering if he was the same hungry young man I'd seen with Glenda. The one who'd unsettled me with his leer.

The name triggered a reaction from both, that much was clear. Their eyes met briefly, and some kind of silent communication took place. Judge Shaw squirmed in his seat, crossed and uncrossed his legs. Mrs. Shaw, ever more subtle, tightened the grip on her cigarette just enough to dislodge the ash, which fell into her lap. She brushed it away and recomposed herself before the ash had hit the floor.

"Greg Hewert," said the judge as the silence grew ponderous.

"Wasn't he once the quarterback?" I asked.

Again the look between them.

"Yes, that's him," said the judge. "Greg was a friend," he added simply, as if he wanted to close the subject. "But Jordan and he were not fast friends. As a matter of fact, Greg was more a friend of Tom Quint's."

"And Greg and Franny were going steady, of course," added Audrey Shaw.

I was beginning to reconsider the wisdom of meeting Fran Bartolo in a dark, empty parking lot.

"Anything else I should know about Greg Hewert?" I asked.

Both shook their heads.

Despite my sympathy for their loss, I couldn't quite shake the suspicion that they were holding out on me.

"What do you plan to do next, Miss Stone?" asked Mrs. Shaw.

"I need to talk to Jordan's roommate, Ginny," I said. "And I'm going to meet Fran Bartolo right now, along with Greg Hewert, I suspect. Or Glenda Whalen."

"Aren't you afraid for your safety?" she asked.

"Yes, I am."

Mrs. Shaw stubbed out her cigarette in the crystal ashtray on the end table. She rose, tall and slim.

"If Glenda gives you any trouble," she said, "tell her the judge and I disapprove of her bullying tactics."

"I'd rather have a restraining order and a bodyguard, but thanks."

Judge Shaw and his wife left the funeral parlor through a private door and were escorted home in O'Connor's black Cadillac limousine. I returned to the cloakroom for my coat, passing through the viewing room to get there. Three of O'Connor's sons were preparing to close the coffin and asked if I wanted to have a look before they did. I was taken aback at first but then realized that, indeed, I wanted to see her. I wanted to remember Jordan Shaw as something other than a muddied corpse. The O'Connor brothers retreated in deference and left the room.

Jordan Shaw, twenty-one, dead before my eyes. Just the two of us. Shrouded by a diaphanous chiffon, Jordan lay frozen in a white lace gown, head resting on a pearl silk pillow, blonde hair lustrous as if burnished by long strokes from caring hands. A bouquet of lilacs had been threaded through her willowy fingers. Where had they found lilacs in November? Her face was starchy white, matte through the sheer fabric with a hint of pink brushed over her lips. I was moved by the tranquility and beauty of the deceased, and never would have recognized her as the same body I'd photographed in the mud a few nights before. That body was human, if dead, while the one before me looked not of this world. Hers was an ethereal beauty, good and clean. Without realizing, I found my hand grazing the gauzy material draped over her body, as if I could communicate with the touch of my hand, and, for the first time, I was moved by her death. I felt sorry for her and wanted to find her killer for more than selfish reasons of my own.

Tim O'Connor cleared his throat and broke the spell. I didn't know how long I'd been standing there. I watched the three men arrange Jordan Shaw's finery, lower her head, and gently close the casket.

I trudged out into the gloom of the parking lot, my eyes cast downward in search of oil spots. Nothing. My lip throbbed in the cold as I walked away back to my car.

Gem's was New Holland's biggest dry cleaner, located in the heart of the city at the bottom of Market Hill. A recent demolition next door had provided a huge parking lot, and it was there that I was to meet Fran Bartolo. I arrived on time and noticed a solitary car, parked near the rear of the lot where Gem's and the back of the New Holland Savings Bank came together on either side of a dark alley. A subtle trap, I thought, and I was walking into it anyway.

Summoning the last shred of my common sense, I swung my car around and approached the alley in reverse; if things got bad, I'd gun the engine and make a run for it. I stopped about thirty feet in front of the other car, a dark-green sedan, and doused my lights. I left the engine running and stepped out onto the pavement.

"Fran?" I called. "Are you there?"

The door on the driver's side popped open, but no dome light went on inside. Fran Bartolo stepped out.

"Come over here," she said. "I'm afraid someone will see us."

"Where is he?" I asked.

She squinted at me through the dark. "What?"

"Where's Greg?"

She shrank, and I could see her apprehension grow. "I don't know what you're talking about."

"Tell Greg to come out," I said. "I want to talk to him."

"Are you crazy?"

"I came to ask Greg some questions," I said, my heart thumping.

Fran's eyes darted around the parking lot and back to me. She ran a hand over her hair, then inched closer to the car's open door.

"Look, I came alone. Greg isn't here."

I didn't speak or move during the tense silence that ensued. I was scared, at least as scared as Fran, but she seemed sincere.

"If he's not here, where is he?"

"How should I know?" she asked, very convincingly.

"He's your boyfriend, isn't he?"

She frowned; I'd touched a nerve. "Thanks, why don't you rub some salt in the wound? Greg dumped me. Who told you he was my boyfriend?"

"Audrey Shaw."

Fran threw her head back in frustration, and when she looked at me again, I could see the sparkle of tears in her eyes. "She probably told you that because she didn't want to say her precious Jordan stole him away from me."

I paused to consider her account. It was possible. I had sensed Judge and Mrs. Shaw were hiding something from me, why not that?

"Let's go somewhere private to talk," I suggested, and Fran agreed.

I took her to my apartment and gave her a bottle of beer. At another time and place in my life, I would have offered her a cocktail, but this was New Holland, and young people drank beer or nothing at all. Halfway through her second Genesee, she began to relax.

"It was our senior year in high school," she said, sitting cross-legged on my couch, the bottle of beer resting on her lap. "Greg was my steady, gave me his letterman's jacket, and pinned me. He'd always been the big man on campus, but as soon as Colgate offered him that scholarship, he changed, got real stuck on himself. I could tell things were changing between us, but you know how people try to hang on. I thought it was my fault, that I was doing something wrong. He wouldn't call for a week, and I'd apologize. He'd stand me up, and I'd call him. He'd flirt with other girls, and I'd take him back. He did that a lot. Kind of became obsessed with scoring. He even got into trouble once for not taking no for an answer from a girl who shot him down. Shot him down like Francis Gary Powers. Judge Shaw had to vouch for him, and the cops let him go. But that was long after we broke up. Long after I found out about him and Jordan."

"What happened?" I asked from my position on the other end of the couch.

"Jordan's parents had gone away for a week; I think it was when Judge Shaw's father was sick in New York, just a while before he died. Anyway, Jordan was home alone. She and Greg were seeing each other on the sly, but I never found out how long it had been going on."

"How did you figure they were seeing each other?"

She snickered. "By accident. Glenda Whalen was always stopping by unannounced to see Jordan. I used to call her 'Latch' for the way she latched onto her. Anyway, she was on her way to drop in on Jordan when she saw Greg's car in the driveway. It was pretty late. After ten,

JAMES W. ZISKIN   109

anyway. And then she ran to Tommy to tattle and phoned me too. I think she just liked to watch us suffer."

"I thought Tommy and Greg were friends," I said.

"They were. Before that happened. They're civil to each other now, but they haven't been close since. Greg still denies everything. He says nothing happened between them, that they were just talking about college. Jordan denied that he had ever even been there. But Tommy and I both know Greg. He's a liar. And Jordan was too."

"And you haven't dated Greg since?"

"No way. I may have been crazy in love with him in high school, but I got over it. Especially when I saw what a jerk he turned out to be. He bombed out as a football star at Colgate and enrolled at Mohawk Valley Community College. Couldn't make it there, either. Now he's just another ex-jock wishing he could relive his high school glory. It's sad."

"Was Tommy at the viewing tonight?" I asked, switching gears.

"Didn't you see him? He broke down over the casket when he went to view the body. It broke my heart. Poor fellow. She didn't deserve a boy like him."

I remembered my emotions upon viewing the exquisite girl, and I had never even spoken to her. For a moment, I lost my train of thought, forgot Fran was there.

"You said you knew things about Jordan that would interest me," I said finally, remembering how she had approached me at the funeral parlor. "Like what?"

"Well, you've probably guessed that boys really liked her. But not just boys her own age. Older men, too."

"Like professors, maybe?"

She looked at me dumbly. "How'd you know?"

"Her parents told me."

"Did they tell you she went to India with one of them?"

"I knew she had gone to India with a professor from Tufts, but what do you mean *one* of them? Are you saying there were others?"

"She went out with a few of them."

"How do you know this anyway?"

She looked away from me. "You know how some things are just known by everyone. It was common knowledge. Jordan dated older men in Boston, including her professors."

I couldn't tell if Fran was avoiding my eyes because she was lying or because she was ashamed for repeating malicious gossip.

"Why are you telling me this?" I asked. "What's in it for you?"

Fran took the question in stride: "She may have stolen my boyfriend, but that doesn't mean I'm happy to see her dead. She was my best friend once."

"And you think it was this professor from Boston who did it?"

She shrugged. "You're the hotshot reporter in the news. You figure it out."

I drove Fran back to her car at Gem Cleaners sometime after one, no longer worried Greg Hewert or Glenda Whalen would emerge from a shadow. We said nothing to each other except, "See you," and I drove away once she'd started her car.

The stillness of the night magnified the confusion in my head, and I wondered if I was nearing a solution or wading deeper into a labyrinth of false leads and rumors. Who killed Jordan Shaw? I didn't know. I had learned a little about her life but almost nothing about how she'd died. Three unknown men had visited her room at the Mohawk Motel within an hour or two of her death, and no one could tell me what they looked like. Perhaps Fred Peruso's faith in me was unjustified.

CHAPTER SEVEN

WEDNESDAY, NOVEMBER 30, 1960

I set out for Boston at four thirty in the morning Wednesday, packing my uneaten pizza and a Thermos of coffee for the drive on the new Massachusetts Turnpike. Eating proved difficult in the car; my swollen lip made it hard to chew. I thought of Fadge, who could steer and shift gears in traffic like Buck Baker while wolfing down a cheeseburger and guzzling a bottle of Coke. I dropped a slice of pizza upside down on my lap and nearly drove off the road.

I arrived in Boston a little before nine, stopped for fresh coffee at a Howard Johnson's, and tried Ginny's number. No answer. After a few inquiries for directions, I located Jordan and Ginny's apartment on Marlborough Street near Exeter in the Back Bay. The six-story brick building was a dignified prewar structure. According to the directory in front, Shaw and White occupied apartment 4E. I stood outside the locked lobby door looking in, marveling at the luxury two college girls were enjoying. Granite floors—square white tiles trimmed with green and gold borders; heavy, mahogany doors and thick, beveled glass, with delicate flowers and leaves etched in frosty designs; polished brass handles and mailboxes; oil paintings in gilded frames hanging from detailed moldings on the cream-colored wallpaper. I buzzed 4E and waited, buzzed it again and waited. Nothing. I tried the door, knowing full well it was locked, then climbed back down to the street. I paced back and forth, scanning the street for triangular oil spots and finding none. After a few minutes, an elderly woman, yanking a recalcitrant pug behind her, hobbled up the stoop, through the door, and into the lobby. I jumped into action and followed her in. She didn't notice me until after she'd picked up her dog. Then she threw me a suspicious scowl.

"Excuse me, ma'am," I said. "Just on my way up to four-E."

"Four-E? Are you a friend of theirs?" she asked.

"No," I said simply. She hadn't asked what I wanted, but continued giving me her opinions.

"Well, I don't approve. When I was a girl, we didn't allow men to call unchaperoned."

I tried to squeeze past her, and her dog nipped at my elbow.

"Oh, I knew they would end up making trouble," she continued. "I warned Dennis, our superintendent, when they moved in. Single girls playing rock-and-roll music, doing that twist dancing, and entertaining visitors at all hours!"

"Do you mean they throw late-night parties?"

"No, not parties! Intimate gatherings. Disgraceful, I told Dennis, scandalous. Two young girls—not out of college, mind you—keeping company with men, not boys . . ."

"Have you ever seen this man here?" I asked, showing her the photograph of Jordan and the two men in India.

She took the snapshot between her bony fingers and held it at arm's length to focus on the faces. "Oh, yes," she said. "He was here all right. I saw him a week ago yesterday. I remember exactly because it was the day poor little Leon was keeping poorly." The dog. "It was raining terribly, but little Leon still has to do his business, you know. I ran into that young man in the elevator and asked him if he would be so kind as to walk Leon to the curb and back. And he refused! Imagine!" She shook her head in woe. "He said his glasses would fog up again! Poor Leon," and she kissed the dog on the head.

She handed the photograph back to me. Jordan's handsome professor wasn't wearing glasses.

"Excuse me, ma'am," I said. "But which one of these men did you see here last Tuesday?"

"That one," she said, pointing to the waxy-skinned tagalong. "That's the one who refused to walk little Leon."

I rode the elevator to the fourth floor without a plan; I had no keys, and Ginny wasn't home. As I crept down the hallway, my heels muffled by the carpet runner, I knew I intended to break in, but how could a law-abiding person like me admit to that?

Apartment 4E was at the end of the hall, the last door on the southeast side. First I listened, and, hearing nothing, I buzzed the doorbell. No answer, so I tried the door. Locked. A noise from the far end of the hall sent me ducking for cover in the stairwell, but when nobody emerged, I returned to the door of 4E.

I pressed my ear to the solid oak again, and that's when I noticed the smell. Hypo? My first thought was that Ginny, too, had been developing photographs. But then the faint odor grew distinct, and a horrible realization crawled up my spine. Gas.

I rattled the doorknob, pushed hard at the door, but that was useless. Then I stepped back and surveyed the corridor, looking for help. Behind me on the wall was a glass case with a fire hose and an ax. I grabbed the ax, aimed it at the doorknob, and swung, missing my target by at least a foot. I chopped again and again, a fourth and fifth time in quick succession until the lock gave way to splinters. I was inside. That's when I realized how wrong I'd been. It wasn't gas I'd smelled, but rotting death.

Covering my nose, I checked each room, finally discovering Ginny in the bathroom. Fully clothed, she lay face down on the white tiles. To my inexpert eye, she looked at least a couple of days dead. I was overcome with a sudden revulsion and vomited into the sink next to the poor girl. Tears streaming down my cheeks, I found the wherewithal to throw open the bathroom window, then, with a wet washcloth over my nose and mouth, I knelt beside the body. Ginny hadn't died from a broken neck; that much was clear, even to a layman like me. The back of her head was bashed in, and there was blood everywhere. If there were any gashes sliced out of her skin, I couldn't see them.

I wanted to cover her, to comfort her somehow, to give her some dignity in her slumped, bloated death, but that was absurd. What did Ginny White care now? I was not there to pray over her or to weep for her; her family and friends would take care of those chores.

Pushing myself to my feet, I wiped my eyes and runny nose, and I fought back the urge to vomit again. I knew my time inside the apartment was limited, that the police would never let me see or use any evidence relevant to the case. So I decided to do the next best thing: copy everything with my camera. I pulled out my Leica and machine-gunned two rolls of film and a couple of frames of a third, capturing the body and bathroom from all angles. Then, five minutes after breaking down the door, I finally called the police.

Gloves on, I rifled through Jordan's room. Above her desk on a shelf, she had one of those portable Japanese record players and a pile of forty-fives. There was a French disc on the turntable, "T'aimer follement," by someone called Johnny Hallyday. She had been a French major, after all, even if the name Johnny Hallyday didn't sound very French to me. A standard, black Bell telephone sat on top of the desk; a tortoise-shell fountain pen, ink cartridges, and stationery in the top drawer. There was a checkbook, a calendar, a datebook, a bundle of letters, and a small photo album in the middle drawer, and school-work and telephone books in the bottom drawer. I wasn't interested in Jordan's finances or studies, so I plunged directly into her datebook, shooting page after page at a furious clip. I shuffled through the letters, sure I'd find plenty of metered mail from Tufts, but there was none. Many of the letters had come from her parents: weekly missives from home, as trivial as they were perfectly written. There were a few others signed *Jeffrey*, and I photographed them without even reading them. No time for that. Near the bottom of the pile, I found a resealed envelope posted July 15, 1958, from New Holland, New York. No return address. I tore it open and found a single sheet of paper with a brief message scrawled in pencil: "Fuck you, cunt! Rot in hell!" No need to photograph that; I was sure I'd remember. And I was sure Pukey Boyle had written it.

I glanced at my watch: 9:32. I took up the photo album next. Snapshots of Jordan alone, snapshots of Ginny alone, Jordan and Ginny together, Judge and Mrs. Shaw with Jordan ... A gallery of people above suspicion. No outsiders. No handsome travelers. I replaced her belongings and closed the drawer. That's when I noticed the purse on the floor beside the bed.

Inside, I found Jordan's keys, her wallet, her driver's license, some cash, and a Diners' Club card. I thought it curious she hadn't taken the purse to New Holland for Thanksgiving, but then I realized she had. Folded into a side pocket, a thin, white sheet of paper provided the proof. It was a receipt from the Mohawk Motel, dated Friday, November 25, 1960. How had her purse found its way back to Boston?

I sat on Jordan's bed and slid open the bedside-table drawer to examine its contents: empty except for a Bible, a box of Slim-pax tampons, and a compact with some kind of dark-green, aromatic powder inside. Nearby sat a crumpled icing cone with dark crust on its nozzle. I had no idea what that was. As I put my hand down to push off the bed, I felt the crackling of paper behind me. The pillow. I pulled back the covers, exposing a letter stashed beneath, written by a man and posted at Tufts University. Before I could open it, there was a noise in the hallway: the police. I didn't think; I just stuffed the envelope into my blouse.

I dashed from Jordan's bedroom and slid into an awkward seat on the couch in the parlor just as two patrolmen crept through the front door, service revolvers pointed at my chest and head, respectively.

∂⃝

After nearly blowing my brains out from the doorway, the police treated me quite nicely. Detective Sergeant Pat Morrissey arrived a few minutes after the patrolmen but didn't talk to me until his men had briefed him, chalked the body, and dusted the apartment for prints. A tall, strapping specimen, he wore his wavy hair slicked back like Robert Mitchum. I found him terribly handsome. He must have thought the patrolmen had searched me, because he never did.

"My boys tell me you discovered the body," he said, sitting next to me on the linen couch. He crossed his legs. "Mind telling me what you were doing in here?"

"Not at all, Detective," I said, a little short of breath, feeling the letter's sharp creases against my breast. "I write for the *New Holland Republic*, a local paper in upstate New York." I showed him my press card.

"Let's hear the punch line; I'm an impatient guy."

"I'm investigating the murder of Virginia White's roommate, Jordan Shaw. She's from New Holland."

"You're telling me her roommate was killed? That's a kick in the head. When?"

"Last Friday night. At first, it looked like one of those small-town murders that happen every so often: grisly, but run-of-the-mill, if you know what I mean."

Morrissey asked what the New Holland investigation had turned up.

"Not much," I said. "That's why I came to Boston. I was hoping to get some information from her roommate."

"Looks like you made the trip for nothing," he said.

I smiled sheepishly. I couldn't very well tell him I'd found the motel receipt in Jordan's purse; he'd arrest me for tampering with evidence. I'd just have to trust him to find the receipt on his own.

"By the way," he asked, "was that you who puked in the bathroom?" I blushed. "I could sure use a drink."

"Can't help you there. Sorry you had to find her that way, but that's why you call the police before breaking down a door. Nice job you did, though."

"Thanks," I said, and instantly felt like a fool. That probably wasn't a compliment. "Actually, I thought I smelled gas. Otherwise, I would have called the police right away."

Morrissey offered me a cigarette, then asked me when I was going back to New Holland.

"Maybe tomorrow. I still want to talk to some people here."

"Give me a call when you get a room," he said, standing up and offering me his card. "I'll want to talk to you later. Now go get yourself a stick of gum."

I rose from the couch and shook his hand. "I can go?" I asked, covering my mouth.

"It's a free country."

I drove to Medford and stopped at a drugstore on Broadway advertising fast film processing and dropped off one roll—the letters only. I would process the film of the body and datebook back in New Holland. For two dollars and a bit of flirting, the clerk put my film at the head of the line. My pictures would be ready in two hours. Back inside my car, I unfolded the letter I had stashed down my blouse.

Dear Jordan,   *14 November 1960*

There can be no more avoiding the difficult task. Since I believe you to be unwilling or unable to end our love affair, I must do it myself. I've explained to you time and again that our relationship depended on circumstances beyond our own wills and desires. I told you the day would come when we must part. Today is that day.

Your youthful zeal and guileless passion, which I so often urged you to restrain, ultimately destroyed the secrecy of our affair. My wife found one of the love notes you'd slipped into my jacket. She threatened to leave me and take my son with her. You must realise that we cannot go on, so I have no choice but to break off all contact with you.

My love for you will not fade, but as you know me to be a man of resolve, please accept my decision. I will never forget you; don't forget me.

The letter was unsigned. Whoever had written it didn't want to leave any footprints.

It was a little past two when I made the long climb up the steps from College Avenue to Miner Hall. The trees were bare, and a wet wind blew cold down my collar. I stepped into the lobby, grateful for the sweltering radiator heat, and checked the directory. The Romance

Languages Department was on the second floor. Past a frosted pane with black lettering, a lone secretary was typing away at a large, wooden desk. In her late twenties, her brown hair tied back in a tight bun, she was so intent on her task that she didn't notice me enter. I cleared my throat twice before she looked up from behind a pair of cat-eye glasses.

"Yes?" she asked with a bemused smile. She had one snaggled incisor on the left side, which she didn't seem to mind.

"I was hoping you could help me," I said.

"Who's your professor, miss?"

I smiled, noticed the nameplate on her desk: *Muriel Rosen.* "Actually, I'm not a student."

"Well, if you're not a student, you must be here about Jordan Shaw."

"You know about that?"

She shrugged. "The dean called our chairman yesterday to break the news. Who are you, then? You don't look like a cop, that's for sure."

"No, I'm not a cop," I said, wishing I could be. "I'm a reporter. Ellie Stone. I'm interested in her academics and social life."

Muriel shook her head. "You've come to the wrong place. She never spent much time here. At least not for the past year or so."

"I thought she studied French."

"Yes, but she finished most of her courses in her freshman and sophomore years."

"So you knew her?"

"Sure. Nice, smart, polite. She used to be a top student, active in department functions, mixers, and the like. Just kind of took a powder after her junior year."

"Any theories on why she disappeared?" I asked.

Muriel sized me up. She was an odd girl, and not afraid to make you feel uncomfortable. She shrugged.

"Found something better to do, I guess. No law against that."

"You said she was smart."

"She won a prize her sophomore year for best essay in French. She had great promise but seemed to lose interest after that summer."

"Which summer was that again?"

"Last year," she said. "After her trip to India."

"You keep track of these things, do you?" I asked.

"That's my job. Jordan Shaw was a star student. We were disappointed when she lit out."

"Did she have any friends here? Boyfriends? Suitors? Any professors interested in her?"

Muriel peered over her glasses at me. "So that's your game? Digging for dirt? Well, there was plenty of interest all around, but our faculty is very proper. This isn't France, after all. And you should be ashamed, Miss Stone."

"I am. But that's my job. What about the men in this photograph?" I asked, producing the snapshot Audrey Shaw had given me, the one of Jordan in a bazaar in India.

Muriel stood, smoothed her woolen skirt, and took the picture from my hand. She adjusted her glasses and took a quick look.

"Never seen them before in my life," she said simply. "Nice snap of Jordan, though. My, she was pretty."

⁂

I trudged back down the long sets of stairs to College Avenue, taking a seat on the bottom step, where I lit a cigarette. For a few minutes I just watched the students passing by, wondering what I should do next. The French Department had been a washout, and I still had a half hour before my film would be ready.

I reread the letter I'd swiped, trying to find clues between the lines, but there was little to go on. The fellow who had written it was married with a son. And he wrote well. Probably an academic. But if Muriel Rosen was to be believed, Jordan's French professors weren't the cheating kind. I folded the letter and looked up at the passersby. Most of them probably wrote well, too. This was a university town, after all.

Still, something about the letter nagged me. I was about to read it again when a young man in horn-rimmed glasses passed me and paused at the curb. He was waiting to cross College Avenue, not ten feet in front of me. I stood, stuffed the letter back into my purse, and approached him. He took notice and tried to edge away. I got a good look at him before he crossed the street. I'd seen him before, all right. Just to be sure, I fished the snapshot from my purse: two men with Jordan in a bazaar somewhere in India. I couldn't believe the coincidence, but the waxy-skinned man in the photo had just dodged a speeding taxi in the middle of College Avenue and legged it up the stairs of the large building on the other side.

I crossed the street and followed him into the building, Anderson Hall, and up to the fifth floor and the offices of the School of Engineering. There I found four young men leaning against the office mailboxes, discussing linear circuits as I might have talked about the weather with Bobby Thompson in the photo lab. An older gentleman—surely a professor—was stooped over a desk, giving instructions to the secretary, a thick woman in her forties. A dark young man with an Indian accent was engaged in conversation with another professor. No one seemed to take notice of my arrival. Finally, the secretary looked up from her desk and asked if she could help me. Her nameplate read *Phyllis Gorman*.

"I'd like to see the chairman," I said.

She looked at me queerly. "Are you a student?"

"No, I'm a reporter." I showed her my card. "Is the chairman in?"

"May I ask what this is in reference to?"

"It's in reference to a murder," I said, and the chatter around me stopped. I could feel several sets of eyes on me, waiting. "Is he in?" I repeated.

"One moment, Miss Stone," she said, handing me back my press card. She disappeared through a door behind her desk.

The four young men by the mailboxes resumed their discussion, but in low tones, and I knew they were talking about me. The foreign student and two professors just gaped at me, making no attempts to disguise their curiosity.

The secretary emerged from the door a few moments later, motioning for me to follow her. She ushered me into a dark office that smelled of chalk and old books. A stout, bald man in a brown suit rose from behind the desk—almost buried under a mountain of papers—at the rear of the office.

"Professor Benjamin; Miss Stone," said the secretary by way of introduction, and she left us.

"Have a seat, miss," he said. "You seem awfully young to be a reporter. Are you sure you don't work for the school paper?" He chuckled; I ignored.

His smile faded, and he motioned to a dusty cane chair in front of his desk. I took the seat.

"Now, what's all this about a murder?" he asked.

"Do you know a student named Jordan Shaw?"

He shook his head. "No, I don't know any student by that name. Who is this fellow?"

"It's a young lady," I corrected. "French major."

"You realize that this is the School of Engineering?"

"Yes, but I understood that she was interested in graduate work in engineering."

"That's possible, I suppose," he said. "I'm not aware of it, though. But tell me, what's this all about?"

"Jordan Shaw was murdered last Friday."

"Oh, dear."

"And her roommate, too."

I gave him the details, and, after a suitable pause to reflect on the tragedy, he asked how he might be of assistance.

"This is Jordan Shaw," I said, showing him the India photograph. "Do you know either of the men with her?"

"I know both of them," he said, frowning. "Are you implying that these two men are involved?"

"I don't know who's involved. I just want to talk to them. Who are they?"

"Well, I . . ." he adjusted himself in his leather chair. "I'm not sure I should be speaking to you without their consent. Or without my lawyer present."

"Off the record, if you like," I said. "I'm not a cop; you don't need a lawyer. I'm just trying to find people who knew Jordan Shaw so I can piece together what happened."

"Very well," he said, still hesitant, but broken. "The one on the left is an assistant professor here. His name is David Jerrold. He's up for tenure next month. The other is a lecturer, ABD in mechanical engineering, leads recitations and supervises the other teaching assistants. His name is D. J. Nichols."

"So the sandy-haired man is Jerrold?" I asked, writing the name on the back of the print. "And the younger one is Nichols?"

He nodded, watching my scribbling with interest. I chuckled to myself; Nichols was the one I'd seen outside, the one who'd refused to walk little Leon.

"What's ABD?" I asked.

Benjamin cleared his throat. "All but dissertation. It means Mr. Nichols has nearly finished his PhD."

Given my father's career in academia, I should have known that. Just another example of the gulf between us. I shook him from my mind and asked if Jerrold and Nichols had offices in the building, and Professor Benjamin told me they did.

"Is there anything else you can tell me about these two men?" I asked.

"Certainly not, Miss Stone. I'm sure I've said too much already. I don't know what makes you think someone from this department was involved in this murder, but I can vouch for the integrity of both men!"

"Then you know them well?"

Benjamin stammered an ineffective protest. He hardly knew them at all. I figured he spent most of his time playing with a slide rule in his cavernous office; he had little time or desire to rub elbows with junior colleagues.

I thanked him for his help and let myself out.

"Professor Jerrold is not in today," Phyllis Gorman, the secretary, informed me. "I haven't seen him in over a week. If you'd like to make an appointment, he holds office hours on Tuesdays from three to five."

"I'm afraid it's more urgent than that," I said. "Perhaps you could give me his home number?"

"I'm not allowed to do that, Miss Stone," she said. "Department policy. We can't release faculty members' home phone numbers to students."

"But I'm not a student." I smiled at her.

"Now, Miss Stone . . ." she smiled back.

"All right, Miss Gorman, let's try another tack. Is Professor Nichols in?"

"That's *Mister* Nichols, please. We're very careful about titles around here. And yes, I believe you'll find him in the graduate lounge, just past the library. I saw him go in there a few minutes ago."

The graduate lounge was a large room with a couple of couches, some chairs, and a silver coffee percolator resting on a Ping-Pong table. The net had long since been torn away, and there were no paddles or balls to be found. Some tinny music buzzed from a transistor radio on an end table across the room—Ricky Nelson singing "Poor Little Fool." A couple of students—Indian again, I think—relaxing on the institutional furniture along the wall, looked up at me expectantly, as if my arrival was an unwelcome interruption of their deep thoughts.

"I'm looking for D. J. Nichols," I said.

"In the loo," said one, and both students turned away and forgot I was there.

I heard a toilet flush, and a moment later, the waxy-skinned young man from the Indian bazaar emerged through a door behind the Ping-Pong table.

"Mr. Nichols?" I asked.

"Yes, that's me."

"My name's Ellie Stone, reporter for the *New Holland Republic*." I waited for a reaction. Nothing. "New Holland is a small town near Albany."

"And?" He was one of those arrogant wiseacres you'd like to slap silly.

"I've come to ask you some questions about a girl you know."

"I know a lot of girls. Which one?"

"Jordan Shaw."

"What about her?"

"She's dead."

His impudence melted away on the spot. He seemed truly surprised and devastated.

"How? Why?" he gasped, steadying himself on the Ping-Pong table, which wobbled under his weight.

"Murdered last Friday night," I said. "I'm investigating the story, and frankly I have very little to go on. That's why I've come to you for help. I was hoping you could tell me about Jordan. About the people she knew."

"I can't believe it," he muttered to himself. "It can't be true. No."

The two students across the room approached and helped Nichols into a chair. After they'd given him a glass of water and a few minutes to compose himself, I resumed my offensive. I thought it best—though not very kind—to pump him when he was most vulnerable.

"When was the last time you saw her?"

Nichols was woozy, floored by the news. "What?"

"When did you see her last?"

"I don't know," he said. "Two weeks ago? Before the holiday."

"What was your relationship with her?"

"Miss, please!" said one of the foreign students. "Can't you see he's had a shock? Give him a moment."

I ignored him. "How well did you know Jordan Shaw?"

"She was a friend," he said, holding his head. "I met her through her roommate, Ginny. She's an old friend of mine."

"I don't know of any other way to tell you this," I said. "Ginny's dead, too."

Nichols went limp and nearly slid off the chair. He began to hyperventilate, and the two students waved a notebook in his face to give him air.

"Do you own a car?"

He shook his head, struggling for air.

"He does not own a car. Why don't you clear off?" one of the students said to me. "Leave the poor man alone!"

When I left the graduate lounge, I nearly knocked over three more students—two of whom were Indian—who had been listening at the door. They smiled sheepishly and confessed their curiosity.

"We heard an undergraduate has been murdered," said one of the Indians, a tall, stocky man in a beard and a black turban.

"That's right," I said. "A pretty blonde girl named Jordan Shaw." I showed them the photograph from India. "Did you know her?"

"The name means nothing to me," he said. "But I've seen her around here."

"What can you tell me about her?"

"Not an engineering student, but the kind of girl one notices."

I nodded. "What about D. J. Nichols? He says he knew Jordan. Did anyone ever see them together?"

The three students looked at each other. "Sure," said the American. "They seemed to be friendly."

"But maybe she was friendlier with someone else?" I hinted. No reaction. "All right, tell me about Professor Jerrold. Did he know her?"

Again they looked at each other and shrugged their shoulders. "Casually, perhaps."

"He's in this photograph," I said, waving the evidence before them. "They look mighty friendly to me."

All three kept quiet. I asked if they knew of anyone who knew Jordan Shaw well, and they said they didn't, pointing out again that she was not an engineering student.

Phyllis was more helpful.

"You've caused quite a stir, Miss Stone," she said. "As soon as you left this office, the entire department started buzzing."

"What about Professor Jerrold?" I asked. "Can't you give me a hand?"

Phyllis glanced around the room. "Not now. Come back at five. This place empties out at four thirty. It'll be easier to talk then."

It was already after three; I could take a stroll on the campus, get a cup of coffee at the student union, or pick up my film. On my way out of the building, I heard a voice call my name. I recognized the tightly wound accent immediately: it was one of the students I'd caught eavesdropping, the tall Indian fellow with the turban.

"Miss Stone," he said, catching up to me. "May I have a word with you? Not here, though. Would you like to get some coffee?"

"Sure," I said, vaguely uneasy.

"My name is Prakash Singh," he said, once we were seated at a table in the student union, me with a cup of coffee, him with a cup of tea. "My American friends call me Roy."

"Okay, Roy. What do you want to talk to me about?" I asked.

"About Miss Shaw, of course."

"Go on."

"Well, it was very awkward when you asked about her in front of the others. You see, Jordan was well known to everyone in the department. D. J. Nichols was not the only one."

"What do you mean?" I asked. "Not the only one who knew her?"

"D. J. and Jordan were quite friendly. Involved. Intimate, I should say, and everyone knew it."

Roy's statement floored me. "Just a minute. You're telling me she was . . . *with* D. J. Nichols? What about Professor Jerrold?"

"Oh, no. The gossip was that D. J. and Jordan were seeing each other secretly. I've never heard a word about Professor Jerrold."

I rubbed my forehead, considering this news. "Jordan Shaw and D. J. Nichols?" I asked, as if challenging him to repeat his assertion. "Together? Excuse me, Roy, if I tell you that's hard to believe."

"No worries, Miss Stone. Sometimes you cannot account for taste, as I'm sure you've heard before."

"Yes, that sounds familiar, thanks. But, why were you reluctant to tell me this up at the department?"

"Though he is not a member of the faculty, Mr. Nichols is a very important man in the department. Very powerful. He is the graduate coordinator and, as such, wields great influence in deciding who receives fellowships and who does not. He's senior to all of us. The teaching assistants defer to him, and he has Professor Benjamin's ear."

"The man who nearly fainted away before my eyes is one of the most powerful men in the department?" I asked. "We are talking about the same D. J. Nichols, aren't we? The one whose mother never lets him go out into the sun?"

"The very one. Don't be fooled by appearances and stereotypes, Miss Stone. At least not in the sciences. Some of the world's most brilliant and strong-willed men have chosen science. What makes them great is their focused intelligence, and that can be found in the frailest of bodies."

"How long had Nichols and Jordan been seeing each other?"

"Just since very recently. Perhaps since the start of the semester."

"And had she ever dated anyone else in the department?"

"Why do you ask?"

"Something you said before. About Nichols not being the only one."

Roy cleared his throat and diverted his eyes. "I cannot say for sure, but there was talk about Jordan and others."

"Who?"

"It wouldn't be right to say. I don't like to spread gossip."

Where had this discretion been a moment before? "Just tell me what the rumors were. I won't take it as an endorsement on your part."

"I cannot say. Ask someone else if you must know, but you won't hear it from me."

"Two more questions, then," I said, conceding on that point. He wagged his head from side to side in a peculiar, waving manner, distracting me for a moment. Then I remembered Stosh Barczak's description of the Dew Drop Inn's late-night visitor: *Like one of those cat figurines with a wobbly head.* "Do you own a car?" I asked, finding my bearings again.

"I'm a modest student from a poor country. My parents have sacrificed greatly to send me here, and I'm living on a fellowship only. I cannot afford a car."

"Fair enough. Last question: Why did Nichols and Jordan keep their relationship secret? He wasn't her teacher, was he?"

"Oh, no. They kept it secret because Mr. Nichols is married."

My film was ready, and I could hardly wait to get into my car to examine the photographs of Jordan's letters. The first ones were from someone named Jeffrey, dated January 1959: greetings from Palo Alto, California. Well written and boringly platonic. A few months later he wrote to her from Ithaca, New York, where he was attending a symposium. No specifics. Then no letters for a year until September 1960. The tone now was completely different. While the first letters had been engaging, the last three read like a bad case of puppy love needing to be put down: endless professions of undying and unrequited love. The last letter was typical of the lot:

> *My dearest Jordan,*   *Boston, November 9, 1960*
>
> *Since my last letter, I have cursed my wretchedness. My words are inadequate, weak, lacking originality and spirit. The abstract is indescribable, except in trite, worn platitudes that are no more insightful today than when they were first coined. How can I communicate the exhilaration that swells my heart when I hear your name, your voice, or see your face? I realize that my words fall like stones as I try in vain to lay them gently on paper for you to read . . .*

You get the idea. Jeffrey's letters were so dull, in fact, that I could hardly finish them. I certainly didn't want to, but I thought there might be a reference to who Jeffrey was. In my haste in Jordan's bedroom, I had neglected to photograph the envelopes, so I didn't know Jeffrey's last name or where he lived.

At five, I returned to the Engineering Department. The fifth floor had indeed emptied out, and, as far as I could tell, Phyllis and I were alone. She locked the office door behind me and offered me the last cup of coffee from the communal urn.

"So what can you tell me about Professor Jerrold?" I asked.

"I can't give you his home phone number, if that's what you mean. But I can say that if you were to look up his name in the Boston telephone directory, you would certainly find a David Jerrold on Massachusetts Avenue."

I smiled. "What's he like, this Jerrold? No departmental rules against talking about a professor, are there?"

She pursed her lips in thought. "I suppose not. He's handsome, cultured, charming."

"Was he involved with Jordan Shaw?"

"Not that I know. He's happily married with a son. Did someone tell you they were seeing each other?"

I explained about Audrey Shaw's suspicions and showed her the photograph from India. Phyllis remarked that Mr. Nichols was in the picture as well—didn't I have any questions about him?

"I just can't believe that he and Jordan were lovers," I said, shaking my head. "How could I be so wrong about a man? He looks like Caspar Milquetoast. Then I'm told he's married, dating the prettiest coed in the school on the sly, and, as graduate coordinator, he's got the other students shaking in their boots."

"Shaking in their boots? Who fed you that load of malarkey?"

I watched her laugh, unsure of what to say.

"Mr. Nichols may be the graduate coordinator, Miss Stone, but he hardly commands respect. It's quite mean, actually, but the other students—even first-year plebes—walk all over him. And as for your rumor about him and Miss Shaw, that's the first time I've heard it."

Something was out of true in the Engineering Department, and someone or everyone was lying to me. At that moment, I was inclined to believe Phyllis's version; it did, after all, match my own suspicions. I was not, however, confident enough to take her entirely at her word.

"Any chance I might sneak a look at the student files?" I asked.

Phyllis frowned and shook her head. "You know I can't let you do that. What are you looking for anyway?"

"Is there a list of students and faculty somewhere?" I said, trying to avoid telling her what I really wanted. "That wouldn't break any rules, would it?"

"I suppose not," she answered, unsure.

She showed me a departmental directory that listed professors and graduate assistants, their campus phone numbers, and their office hours. I ran a finger down the list, looking not for a surname but for a first name: Jeffrey. None.

"Do you know anyone named Jeffrey?" I asked.

Phyllis shook her head. "My cousin's name is Jeffrey."

"What about Jerrold's son. What's his name?

"I don't recall what his name is, but it's not Jeffrey. He's just a toddler; never been in here before."

"And Nichols? Does he have a son?"

"I believe he does. Or is it a girl? You know, this is not a very social department. I'm embarrassed to know so little."

"I don't suppose you know if he has a car."

"Not Mr. Nichols, but Dr. Jerrold has," she said. "Everyone knows about his car. It's his pride and joy. A sporty English job, a Jaguar, and I've seen it, too. Fast and very sexy."

The undercarriage of Jerrold's car was probably cleaner than Pukey Boyle's.

"I was wondering about something," I said. "How many foreigners are there in this department? It seems everyone I meet is from India."

"Graduates? I think there are three Indians, two Germans, one Dutch, a Japanese, and several Taiwanese . . ."

"Only three from India?" I asked. "I've seen five already: one in here this afternoon, two in the hallway, and two in the graduate lounge."

"Oh, no, Miss Stone. Just three." Then she raised a finger in enlightenment. "You must be thinking of the Pakistanis. We have two of them as well. Of course, they don't get on very well with the Indians . . . Some kind of political or religious disagreement, I think. But don't get the wrong idea; we awarded twenty fellowships to graduate students this year, and all but three are Americans. Our foreign students are almost all supported by their own governments."

"What about the Indians and Pakistanis?"

"Without exception, supported by their governments."

"Why do you suppose that is?"

"I think they were sent here to learn how to make a hydrogen bomb." She tittered then grew serious. "But they really don't get along. Personally, I can't see much difference between them. Just what they wear on their heads."

"Thank you, Miss Gorman," I said, recalling descriptions of some of the more violent episodes that accompanied the Partition of India in 1947. (I'd taken a course in post–World War II geopolitics at Barnard.) "I may drop by to see you again."

"You're welcome. But don't tell anyone you spoke to me. You know how things are in an office."

The woman who answered Jerrold's phone asked who was calling. Somewhere inside me, a voice urged me to cut the handsome professor a break. I decided not to identify myself to his wife as a reporter investigating the murder of her husband's former lover—or so I believed. "It's Miss Gorman from the office, calling for Dr. Benjamin."

She asked me to wait, covered the receiver for a moment, and I got results. I heard a second phone pick up, and David Jerrold told his wife to hang up the extension.

"Yes, Phyllis, what is it?" English accent.

"Actually, I'm not Phyllis Gorman."

"Then who are you and what do you mean bothering me at home?"

"My name's Eleonora Stone," I said. "I write for a newspaper in New Holland, New York."

"I'm impressed. Now, please, what do you want?"

"I want to talk to you about Jordan Shaw."

"Who?"

I've never liked coy men, especially when they're talking to me. Personally, I go for the direct, take-charge types.

"Save the act for your wife," I said. "Unless you'd like me to explain it to her."

There was a long, dead pause down the line. He was thinking it over: How could he wriggle off this hook without me making things messy for him? Sure, I was playing hunches all the way down the line, assuming he had indeed been the author of the Dear Jordan letter and that the last thing he wanted was for his wife to be reminded of his infidelity. But it seemed to be working.

"Okay," he said finally. "I know who she is, but I can't talk to you now; my wife's in the next room. Ring me back later this evening, and perhaps I can meet you somewhere."

I didn't like giving him time to collect himself or sneak away, but I couldn't make him talk. "I'll call you in an hour," I said. "Be ready to meet me then."

Behold the motor lodge, rich relation of the lowly motel, recommended by the Automobile Club and the chamber of commerce. Anonymous, unsophisticated, and devoid of taste, the motor lodge thrives on the modern traveler's notion that he and his family are not good enough for a proper hotel. He resigns himself, and his station wagon, to paying a comparable price for an inferior room to match his worth. I'm no different; I took a room for $6.50 at the Paul Revere Motor Lodge in downtown Cambridge.

After checking the view from my room—a car wash and a White Castle—I phoned Jerrold. The conversation was short and sweet; we agreed to meet in an hour in the Minuteman Lounge downstairs at the Revere. That gave me enough time for a shower and a quick long-distance call to Charlie Reese back in New Holland.

"Looks like you picked the wrong time to leave town," he said. "Frank Olney arrested Julio Hernandez a couple of hours ago. They've charged him with first-degree murder."

"You got a pencil, Charlie?" I asked. "I'm going to dictate your lead story for tomorrow."

"Didn't you hear me, Ellie? The sheriff picked up Julio. His prints were all over the motel room and the knife. You'd better drive back tonight."

"I'm not driving back tonight. I've still got work to do here."

"You've got some crust, Ellie. George Walsh is stealing your story. Now, I want you back here!"

I was grinning ear to ear; this was too much fun.

"Tell me if George Walsh has this, Charlie: Jordan Shaw's roommate is dead, murdered in their shared apartment."

Nothing but white fuzz coming down the line from New Holland. Then I heard some fumbling, and finally Charlie spoke:

"Okay, Ellie. I've got a pencil. Speak slowly."

I made sure to arrive fifteen minutes before my appointment with Jerrold, intending to look around, but I ended up downing two White Labels while I waited. Jerrold was five minutes late. He looked relaxed in a jacket, open collar, and tan trousers, and I recognized him immediately as he stood in the Minuteman Lounge doorway. He was handsome all right. As he settled in at the bar and ordered a drink, I sneaked out to the parking lot. The silver Jaguar was hard to miss. I bent down to look for oil spots, still unsure of the utility of the exercise, but found nothing.

"Are you Dr. Jerrold?" I asked, taking the seat next to him at the bar. He already had a drink before him: a martini with three olives, pitted, no pimento. I notice these things.

"'Ello, 'ello," he said in his best cockney voice, looking me up and down in a most unwholesome way. He smiled and seemed relieved. "You're younger than I expected. Are you old enough to sit at the bar, Miss Stone?"

"I'm older than Jordan Shaw," I answered, throwing cold water on his flirting.

"Yes, now I see it," he said laconically, smile gone. "Would you like a drink?"

I ordered another Scotch. The bartender recognized me, looked back to where I had been sitting moments earlier, and raised his eyebrows. He said nothing, though, and fetched me my drink.

"Now what's this all about, Miss Stone?"

"Excuse my candor, Dr. Jerrold, but would you mind if we skipped the I-don't-know-what-you-want routine? What's next, a fainting spell when I tell you Jordan Shaw is dead?"

"I knew she was dead when I came in here."

"Who told you she was dead?"

"Please, Miss Stone. The entire Engineering Department knew she was dead inside of five minutes of your arrival. Lionel Benjamin rang me at home as soon as you left his office. He said you were asking questions about me and Mr. Nichols."

"That's right," I said. "May I ask you a question now?" He nodded. "Were you romantically involved with Jordan Shaw?"

Jerrold smiled, sipped his drink, then began. "Imagine for one minute that my relationship with Miss Shaw is any of your affair," he said, signaling to the bartender for a refill. He motioned to both our drinks, and the man raised his eyebrows again. "What makes you think I would know anything about her death? Furthermore, I assure you that Miss Shaw and I had no more than a nodding acquaintance."

I placed the Indian snapshot before him on the bar. "Was this taken when you were nodding your acquaintance to her?" I asked.

He considered the photograph for several seconds, surely vexed by its inopportune appearance, but too suave to let on.

"Nicely played, young lady," he said at last. "But this means nothing. I'm afraid you've misunderstood. We were in India together, but only by chance. There were twenty-five alumni, twelve of their spouses, and a smattering of children in our group as well. D. J. Nichols went along too, why don't you interview him? You know the rumors about him and Miss Shaw, after all."

Our refills arrived. Jerrold grabbed hold of the red plastic sword spearing his olives and drew it out like Excalibur from the stone.

"Garish things, these," he said, tossing the cocktail sword into an ashtray. "I'm sorry I can't help you, Miss Stone. You see, contrary to your suspicions, I was not trysting with this Miss Shaw. And although I feel saddened by her passing, I don't see how I can help you with your investigation."

Having your neck snapped and pelvis carved up didn't exactly qualify as *passing* in my book.

"Do you know anyone named Jeffrey?" I asked.

Jerrold shook his head and downed his drink. He turned to look me in the eye. "Afraid I've got to run, Miss Stone. Sorry I can't be of more help, but I barely knew Jordan Shaw." He paused, leaned in close—almost nose to nose—and said, "I don't want you phoning my home again."

He gazed deep into my eyes, and, despite myself, I felt both unsettled and drawn in by his charm at the same time.

"But if you'll give me your number," he said, suddenly all smiles, "I'll be happy to phone you once this has all blown over."

"But . . ."

"The drinks are on me," he said with a smile, and he slapped five dollars on the bar. "Good night."

CHAPTER EIGHT

A hotel is a lonely place. A motor lodge is a depressing, lonely place. I had already met with Jerrold and spoken to my editor in New Holland. By eight fifteen, the excitement in the Minuteman Lounge had leveled off, and last call seemed not far off. I wasn't looking forward to an evening with the Gideons Bible and the television set in my room. Knowing no one in Boston, I decided to call Bernadette, the White family housekeeper.

She had spent the afternoon talking to the police, so at least I was spared the unpleasantness of breaking the news to her. She remembered me from my phone call on Monday, and, from the sound of it, she was stunned by Ginny's death and frightened to stay in the White's big, empty house by herself. I asked her if I could come see her to ask a few questions. She agreed and gave me directions.

I paid my tab at the bar and dropped off my key at the front desk. On my way out the door, I spied D. J. Nichols standing behind a plastic plant near the exit. He was sweating, looking at me over his glasses as if to implore my help.

"What are you doing here?" I asked.

"I've got to talk to you." He glanced around the room. "But not here. Can we go up to your room?"

"I'm on my way to an appointment," I said, not sure I wanted a strange man in my room. Not this strange man anyway. "Can't it wait till tomorrow?"

"No!" His eyes jumped about, and he snorted back a runny nose. "I'm afraid for my life!" He was whispering. "Please!"

I asked if he'd like to talk in the bar, but he said he didn't drink. Reluctantly, I retrieved my key and led him to my room on the third and top floor, locking the door behind us.

"They want to frame me," he stammered once he was seated on a chair in my room.

"Who's they?"

"Whoever killed Jordan and Ginny. They must think I know something."

"What do you know?"

"Nothing—I swear it!"

"Then why did you lie to me this afternoon?"

Nichols stopped panting long enough to look at me with the expression of a confused dog. "Lied to you? What do you mean?"

"You said the last time you'd seen Jordan was two weeks before Thanksgiving. Around the fifteenth."

"That's right," he said, wiping his brow. "That's the truth, I tell you."

"One of Jordan's neighbors identified you as the man she saw in the elevator last Tuesday, two days before the holiday."

"Well, yes, of course. I was there all right, but I didn't see Jordan. She wasn't in. I had a cup of tea with Ginny."

"Where was Jordan?"

He shrugged his shoulders, breathing easier now. "I suppose she was out with *him*."

"Who's *him*?"

"Didn't you get the dirt this afternoon at the department? Surely someone told you. They're such nasty gossips."

"Why don't you tell me?"

"Everyone knows Jordan and David were an item. Don't tell me you didn't hear that."

I took a seat on the corner of the bed and considered Nichols carefully. Studying his eyes in the dim room was no easy task. I leaned forward and delivered my carefully worded answer:

"What I heard was that *you* and Jordan were an item. I asked several people about Jerrold, and they all said no one had ever heard such a rumor."

"Then they were lying to implicate me. They've been together for the past year and a half. They went to India together."

"A trip you made with them." I added. He hadn't expected me to know that.

"Yes, that's true, but totally irrelevant. Jordan and I were friends, nothing more, and everyone at the department knows that."

"Are you married?" I asked.

"Yes, why?"

"Any kids?"

"One," he said. "A boy, Ned. Why?"

I said it didn't matter and reminded him I had to leave. His panic returned, and he grabbed my arm, begging me to give him some useful counsel.

"Relax and take it easy," I said simply.

"Thanks loads," he said. "I'll be sure to remember that if you ever need help."

Bernadette was about thirty-five, small and round. Her skin was porcelain white, and she wore her wavy auburn hair short. The line of her lower teeth twisted a bit behind her full lips, and her pale eyes and pug nose were rimmed with red from hours of crying.

I introduced myself, though she was expecting me, and she invited me in. The clapboard house's cold gentility made an immediate impression on me, and I could see how an outsider like Bernadette, far from home, would feel lost and afraid when left alone inside its polite walls. She took my coat and led me past the parlor and dining room to the kitchen, where she offered me a cup of coffee. I looked around the room as she busied herself at the stove. Nothing out of place, everything polished and in perfect order. The house gave me the same unsettled feeling as had Judge Shaw's perfect home.

Bernadette, or Bernie, as she liked to be called, had last seen Ginny the previous Friday evening, around ten. Bernie was washing up the dinner dishes when the phone rang. Ginny answered and took the call in her bedroom. Bernie didn't know who had phoned.

I asked if Ginny had seemed nervous at all, but Bernie said she was the same as always: spirited, worried about her approaching exams, but happy. Ginny had lots of male admirers, but Bernie couldn't give me any names. I asked her about Ginny's roommate, but she had never met Jordan.

We pored over Ginny's habits for two hours, from the most insignificant everyday routines to where she had vacationed in the past two years: Palm Beach, Los Angeles, and Bermuda, all with her parents. Ginny used Johnson & Johnson swabs and cotton balls, Gleem toothpaste, and Listerine mouthwash. She washed with Lux soap, shampooed with Breck, powdered with a variety of talcs, and wore Emeraude spray mist. She liked books, music, and horses, and she owned her own car: a red-and-white Buick Century, which she kept in the lot behind her Back Bay apartment. Ginny was studying English literature at Tufts.

I asked if the police had contacted Ginny's parents in Florida, and Bernie said they were returning home on the first flight in the morning with Ginny's eleven-year-old sister, Nora. Ginny hadn't accompanied them this time because of a busy schedule at school, studying for upcoming finals, and working long hours in the library stacks.

I thought about Virginia White and Jordan Shaw. Two young women of privilege, coming of age in an atmosphere free of parental supervision, answering to no one but themselves: atypical of girls of their age and generation. Were they wrong to live the way they did? To invite grown men in until all hours for "intimate gatherings"? Who was I to judge them? I could give lessons.

Other questions consumed me. Why had they been murdered, both of them, a state apart? According to Doc Peruso, Jordan was killed late Friday night. I figured Ginny died sometime Saturday afternoon or evening upon her return from the Thanksgiving holiday. It seemed her killer had been waiting for her. Or maybe she had surprised him rummaging through Jordan's belongings? Had her assailant stolen anything? If so, what? Was Ginny killed as an afterthought, by accident, or for the same obscure reasons as Jordan? Had they both known their killer? I was certain that, at the very least, Jordan had known hers.

Ginny may have been the unlucky friend, a remainder in the equation, but my gut feeling told me it was her close relationship with Jordan that had marked her for death. She knew her murderer all right.

I asked Bernie if I could have a look at Ginny's room. She agreed on the condition that I not disturb anything.

The room was neat, cleaned by Bernie herself after the police had pawed through every corner that afternoon. It was a bedroom typical of a teenage girl, I supposed, though I was sure Ginny had outgrown the stuffed tiger on the bed and the teen-magazine cutouts plastered on the walls. This was the world of a thirteen-year-old Virginia White, before she'd shipped out to Dana Hall, then Tufts. I paused to admire the lovingly prepared collages of Tab Hunter and Montgomery Clift memorabilia under glass on her desk. Nearly all the artifacts were datable to the early- to mid-1950s, with few exceptions. One caught my eye from across the room. Above her desk, pinned to a barren bulletin board, a colorful postcard and an airmail envelope stood out. I crossed the room and plucked them from the board.

The letter was addressed to Ginny, written in a neat hand, with colorful Indian stamps on it. I put that aside and examined the postcard.

"What is that?" asked Bernie, joining me at the desk.

"That's the Taj Mahal," I said, showing her the card. Then I turned it over:

Agra, August 17th, 1959

Dear G. W.,

Having loads of fun! I had a touch of Delhi-belly from the water, but D. J. took me to a clinic run by a friend of his. He knows India like the back of his hand! He's so wonderful! And I got it! I feel as bright as a new penny! (wink) I'll tell you all about it when I get back.

Yesterday we went to a beautiful Hindu wedding. Friends of D. J.'s. I got mehndi painted on my hands and feet. So beautiful! I took snaps of it to show you.

Got to run. Taj Mahal tomorrow then Jaipur and Nepal after
that!

    Love, J. S.

What was *mehndi*? Sounded like some Indian wedding ritual. I wondered if Jordan had ever shown Ginny the photos. I snapped a picture of the postcard and took up the letter. I didn't ask Bernie for permission to open it, figuring she might say no. In fact, she twitched a bit as I fished the letter out, but she said nothing.

             Fatehpur Sikri, August 19th, 1959

Dear G. W.,

Yesterday D. J. and I spent the most wonderful night together! We had a free afternoon and evening from the tour and managed to slip away from the group unnoticed. We drove over bumpy roads to Fatehpur Sikri, an abandoned palace city near Agra. Beautiful Mughal architecture, all red sandstone, quiet—almost like a ghost town—and very romantic! We took a lovely bungalow for the night in a nearby guesthouse, completely private and anonymous. We were invisible and safe, hidden from the world and its prying eyes, if only for one night. It was even better than Istanbul, because this time there wasn't a soul we knew or who knew us. There was no sneaking around. It felt like we were married, and I didn't want it to end!

    We drove back to join the group in Agra early the next morning and arrived just before they left for Jaipur. Close call!

    Love, J. S.

It was late—after midnight—and Bernadette was not happy to see me leave. I reassured her she'd be all right, that the Whites would be back the next day. I said goodnight and stepped out into the cold air. Bernadette closed the door behind me and bolted it shut. As I drove away, I could see she'd left all the lights on.

Back at the Revere, I threw myself onto the bed around one thirty. Not much of a sleeper to begin with, I couldn't nod off at all and ended up staring at the ceiling in a very empty bed.

To pass the hours and to distract myself, I parsed the postcard from India, word by word. Were Phyllis and Nichols the liars after all? I had found the proof, it seemed, in Jordan's own handwriting. "D. J." was wonderful. "D. J." took her to the hospital when she was sick. No, not hospital, clinic. Did the difference matter? How would a white-bread bookworm subject to hyperventilation manage to know India like the back of his hand? What was the significance of highlighting the word penny? Obviously a private joke between the two girls, but what did it mean? D. J., J. S., G. W. . . . Why initials? Just a personal quirk, or more subtle signaling across oceans? I, too, wrote notes for articles in the same manner, using initials as shorthand whenever possible. Then I remembered a note I had scribbled in my book earlier that afternoon. "Does D. J. have a child?" David Jerrold: D. J.? Ginny White: G. W.; Jordan Shaw: J. S.; D. J. Nichols: D. J. N. . . .

I climbed out of bed and retrieved a pencil and paper from my purse. I plotted out the initials of everyone I'd met who'd known Jordan. Tom Quint: T. Q.; Julio Hernandez: J. H.; Pukey Boyle: P. B.; Ginny White: G. W.; Glenda Whalen: G. W.; Greg Hewert: G. H.; Franny Bartolo: F. B. None matched, none made any sense. And now I had two G. W.s, though there was no confusion on that score in the postcard. D. J. had to be Jerrold or Nichols, but what was the penny?

THURSDAY, DECEMBER 1, 1960

Thursday morning, I was awakened by a banging on my door. I had hung the Do Not Disturb sign the night before and cursed the idiot who couldn't read plain English. I pulled on a robe and shuffled to open the door. Detective Morrissey was leaning against the jam. Why did he always show up when I was looking my worst?

I invited him in and took a seat on my bed. He pulled up a chair and sat down before me.

"You were supposed to call me when you found a room," he said. "Where were you last night?"

Face-to-face with the handsome detective, I tried to arrange my unruly hair, which was always a battle in the morning.

"I was at Virginia White's house," I said.

"But there's no one there but the housekeeper."

"Do you have something against domestics?" I asked.

"My mother was a domestic," he said, shutting me up. "When did you get back here?"

"About a quarter past one. But you didn't come here to ask me that."

"Smart girl. So why do you have a sudden interest in the School of Engineering?" he asked. "Your girl studied languages, didn't she?"

"That's right. How did you know about the Engineering Department?"

"We got around to it eventually," he said. "No thanks to you. Jordan Shaw's dean told us she was interested in studying engineering after graduation. Said she was spending a lot of time over there."

"Good work, Morrissey."

"Thanks, but I don't need a girl reporter to keep my score. My question for you is how did you beat me to the punch by more than twelve hours?"

"Her father mentioned she wanted to study engineering, but I never would have followed up on it if I hadn't seen this fellow walk right past me on College Avenue yesterday."

I handed the well-traveled snapshot to the detective and pointed out D. J. Nichols.

Morrissey grunted. "Funny, I was just going to ask you about this guy, Nichols."

"You know him?"

"I saw his picture just before I came over here. He's gone missing."

"What happened?" I asked, my mouth suddenly dry.

"One of my men went to talk to him last night, only someone broke into his digs. Trashed the place like they were looking for something."

"What about his wife and kid?"

"In New York visiting her folks," he said. "We can't find Nichols anywhere. Either someone was looking for him and found him, or he's in hiding."

I described the unexpected visit the evening before, Nichols's fears, and my own frustrations at dealing with the Tufts Engineering Department. Someone had tried to set up Nichols the day before, making him out to be a Don Juan to the ladies and a galley overseer to his fellow graduate students. Now he was missing—apparently—and I began to reconsider the indifferent advice I'd given him the night before.

Morrissey filled me in on the results of Ginny White's autopsy—killed by at least three sharp blows to the back of the head—and the five sets of fingerprints collected in her apartment: Ginny's, Jordan's, and three unknowns. No other wounds on her body, and nothing missing from her effects. He said the coroner had fixed the time of death somewhere between late Saturday night and Sunday noon.

"We'll check the unknown prints against Nichols's," he said. "Any idea who the others might belong to?"

"How about David Jerrold?"

"Him? He hasn't moved from his apartment since just after Thanksgiving."

"How do you know that?" I asked.

"He's been under police protection for almost a week," said the cop. "Filed a complaint about harassing phone calls and threats last Saturday night."

This was news to me. "Who threatened him?"

Morrissey pursed his lips in a mocking grimace. "If we knew that, we'd arrest the guy, wouldn't we, and Jerrold could go feed the ducks in the Common."

I told him of my suspicions that Jerrold and Jordan had been having an affair, possibly until the very night of her death: Friday. I told him about the letter and postcard I'd read at Ginny's house but made no mention of the one I'd stolen from Jordan's room.

"I need to know more about Jerrold," I said. "He wouldn't talk to me yesterday."

"Why don't you get yourself prettied up and come with me to Medford?" asked Morrissey. "I got a warrant to look through some records at Tufts. I don't mind if you tag along."

"I'd love to. Would you be kind enough to wait outside while I dress?"

He looked me up and down, smiled a bit hungrily, which I liked, and said he didn't mind waiting here. I pushed him to the door, and he complied.

⁂

I would have preferred to dig through Jordan's file, but Morrissey didn't have a warrant for that. He was more interested in the engineers. I found D. J. Nichols's file first and perused it for ten minutes. He was born in Los Angeles, matriculated into Stanford at fifteen, had perfect scores on all boards, and was admitted as a PhD candidate at Tufts in 1954. His transcript was blanketed with top scores and special mentions. I came across academic evaluation forms, nearly all of which sang Nichols's praises as the most highly motivated and competent graduate in recent memory. His mathematical skills qualified as genius, according to Professor Benjamin. The only sour note in the file was sounded by David Jerrold, who wrote that Nichols, although talented and superbly trained, lacked the vision to become a great chemical engineer.

I moved on to Jerrold's file, which overflowed with vouchers and reimbursement forms. The receipts left a trail of dinners with visiting professors, honoraria for lectures, and lab supplies. My antipathy for him aside, I still figured he was taking the university for an extra ten bucks at every turn. But what caught my eye was one receipt on thin, brownish paper, stamped three times in different colors, detailing an expenditure of 232 Indian rupees ($48.52, quite a large sum) for treatment at the P. R. Varma Medical Clinic in Delhi, India. The date was August 14, 1959.

There was no information about a wife or a son in the file, but why should there have been? Among the papers, I found a copy of a letter from the Immigration and Naturalization Service, confirming his status as a permanent resident alien. It was dated April 1959. I jotted down the permit number and made a note to make some inquiries.

I spotted the name Prakash Singh on a folder near the back. The file was thin, though he'd been in the country more than two years. There was a mention of an unofficial reprimand for leveling an accusation against another student. There were no details. His academic evaluations were as dismal as Nichols's were brilliant. I gathered that Professor Benjamin had decided to terminate him when David Jerrold intervened on his behalf. In fact, the lone dissenting opinion on Roy was provided by Jerrold, who acknowledged Singh was a poor student, but one who showed flashes of brilliance. From what I gathered, only Jerrold's review—dated September 5, 1960—had saved Roy from being sent home.

The police raid on the department's files caused a great stir. When Morrissey and I surfaced from the records room, a crowd of students and faculty was waiting for us. Most were curious, but others were downright offended we had nosed through their files. I noticed the absence of David Jerrold, Roy, and the other foreign students I had seen the day before.

While Morrissey interviewed Benjamin, I asked anyone who would stand still about Jordan Shaw. One young man said he knew her, but the hostile eyes trained on us convinced him to shut up. No one would talk about D. J. Nichols either, except one chubby student who implied that I'd had something to do with his disappearance. When I asked where Roy was, all I got were icy glares. This was a spooky place.

Morrissey and I chatted on the steps outside the Engineering Department, and I asked him if he wanted to come with me to New Holland to pursue the case; I was planning on leaving later that afternoon.

"I'll take a rain check," he said, and I felt a twinge of disappointment. "It looks like our killer is here in Boston."

"Could be," I said. "If there's only one."

"You think there's two?"

"Could be. Different MO on each murder."

"Different circumstances might explain that, but I'll keep an open mind. I'll let you know if there's news. You do the same."

He offered me his rough hand, and I took it in mine. He held on for a moment when I tried to let go and looked at me from the corner of an eye.

"You were in that apartment quite a while before we got there," he said. "What'd you do to keep busy?"

"I threw up," I offered meekly, not sure he'd swallow it.

Morrissey stared into my eyes a little longer, and I didn't know where to look or what to say. Then, finally, he released my hand, turned slowly, and trudged across the green. I drew a breath and watched him go.

"Miss Stone." A familiar voice interrupted my thoughts.

"Hello, Roy," I said.

"I've just heard about Mr. Nichols. What happened?"

He walked with me toward my car as I filled him in on the latest. I found his surprise and grief ironic. He had, after all, tried to lead me in all the wrong directions the day before. I wanted to see where he might take me this day. He asked if the police had any theories on why someone would want to ransack Nichols's flat. I shrugged my shoulders, and we walked on.

"I've got a question for you, Roy," I said as we reached my car. "Your friend Jerrold: Do you have any idea why he would want police protection?"

"He must be afraid for his family after these murders."

"But the police have been protecting him since last Saturday, when he didn't even know about the first murder."

"I'm afraid I can't help you there," he said, wagging his head again in that strange way. I opened the car door and climbed in. "Unless . . ."

I waited. I didn't trust him, but he obviously wanted me to ask.

"Unless what?"

"Well, there is a student you may wish to talk to. His name is Hakim Mohammed."

"What will he tell me?"

"That I can't say. Just talk to him, but don't mention my name. Hakim is Pakistani, you see, and we are not friendly."

He smiled at me, wagged his head, then sauntered away, leaving me to ponder this new information.

Before searching out Hakim, I phoned the local INS office. Two referrals and one transfer later, I was connected to Gloria, a functionary in the records bureau in Boston. It's remarkable how much information is available over the phone, if you just ask nicely. After a brief search through some files, Gloria told me she had Mr. Jerrold's dossier in front of her.

"British subject," she began. "First came to the United States in 1946, immigrated in 1952, permanent alien status . . ."

"Yes, I know he's English," I said.

"Yes and no, Miss Stone. Mr. Jerrold is a British subject, but he's never lived in England."

"Where did he come from, then?"

"According to my records, he was born January 12, 1918, in Calcutta, India, and lived there until the war, when he served in the Corps of Royal Engineers in Burma. Then in 1946 he obtained a visa to study at the University of Chicago."

"India, you say?"

"That's correct. His father was with the British colonial administration, according to this. And they stayed on after Independence."

"What about his family here? Is there any mention of a wife and son?"

Gloria ruffled some pages. "Married Diana Reynolds, American citizen, on June 21, 1952. No record of children here."

I found Hakim Mohammed in the graduate lounge and recognized him as one of the students who had helped Nichols the day before. He didn't seem to like me any better this day.

"I want to ask you about Professor Jerrold," I said. "Do you know any reason why someone would want to do him harm?"

"No," he said, staring out the window, smoking a cigarette. "Dr. Jerrold is liked by all."

"Someone suggested you might know why he needed police protection."

Hakim chuckled, still not caring to look at me. "I don't suppose it was Prakash Singh who suggested that?" I didn't answer. "It's curious that he should point to me, since he and Dr. Jerrold have their own differences."

"My impression was that Jerrold was his benefactor here in the department. What differences do they have?"

"I don't know what tricks he's up to, but their friendship has enjoyed a recent improvement. Since the start of the semester. Before that, the bloody *Sardar* was on very thin ice."

I begged his pardon.

"*Sardar* means 'Sikh.' Prakash Singh is a Sikh. Turban, beard, and kirpan." He'd lost me again. "The dagger," he explained. "It's called a kirpan. All the bloody *Sardars* carry them."

"I think I've heard lies from just about everyone in this place, Mr. Mohammed. No story matches the last. Why should I believe what you're telling me?"

He looked at me for the first time. "Believe whom you will, Miss Stone. I've told you the truth."

I stared him in the eye: "Do you own a car?"

"I am a student. I share rooms and meals, and I have books to buy. I can't afford a car."

I had just one more stop before leaving: Jordan and Ginny's apartment building, where I looked underneath Ginny's two-toned Buick for oil spots. None. Ditto for the cars in the other parking spaces. A search of the immediate area on Marlborough Street yielded no triangular oil drippings either, but it appeared the street sweeper had passed recently, so that didn't prove anything.

At four o'clock Thursday afternoon, I got onto the Mass Turnpike and headed west. I stopped for gas at Framingham and called Charlie Reese collect from a phone booth while the attendant filled the tank and checked the oil.

"I'm driving back now," I said. "I'll be there in about three hours, and I want to run some film right away. Can you wait for me at the paper?"

"I'll be here. They've just arrested Jean Trent as an accessory, and we're working on that story," he sighed. "We've got to redo the front page."

⁂

You have ample opportunity to think while staring at the lines in the road for three hours. My thoughts bounced from New Holland and Jordan's murder to Medford, Ginny White's death, and D. J. Nichols's disappearance. The responsible party had to be one of the people I'd met at the Engineering Department, but who? And why? Nichols wasn't the Mohawk Murderer or the Boston Basher, I felt sure of that. I also eliminated the secretary, Phyllis, and Professor Benjamin from my short list. I suspected Jerrold most of all, because I believed he was closest to Jordan. And because he had charmed me with his slippery appeal. Roy had been a little too helpful to be trusted, but could a man I'd shared coffee with, a man who smiled so broadly, actually have killed two young women with his bare hands? Hakim seemed the perfect suspect—somehow sinister and churlish—but I believed he was telling the truth.

Or was it possible I hadn't met the murderer at all? I considered my movements in Boston. I had only scratched the surface of two recently ended lives, and there was no shortage of possible avenues of investigation. I hadn't managed to talk to Dennis, the superintendent of Jordan's building; I had interviewed only a handful of students and faculty from the Engineering Department; I'd had no time to search out Jordan's academic advisor, roommates from previous years, or Ginny's parents. On one hand, I felt my investigation slipping away; it was unfurling too rapidly, growing exponentially. And George Walsh was encroaching by the minute. On the other hand . . . Well, on the other hand, nothing. I had nothing. This was an opportunity to make something of my three years in New Holland. But I was stuck.

I also thought about Jordan's Boston bedroom. The order didn't surprise me, but the dearth of personal touches did. Aside from the one letter under her pillow, I'd found only generic articles among her belongings, no intriguing faces in her photo album, nothing to suggest the emancipated behavior I had come to discover. Her room looked like one of those model homes, furnished with conventional, inoffensive trappings, right down to the bland framed photographs on the shelves. Could her sentimental side be so cool, so removed from the passions of her conduct, that she left no evidence? Was she capable of switching off her emotions when it came to cataloguing her love life? And if so, why had she kept the Dear Jordan letter under her pillow? And how could I forget the mushy love paean she'd written to Ginny about her night in Fatehpur Sikri with D. J.? The questions spun around in my head, but I kept arriving at the same two answers: either she had hidden the memorabilia of her love life elsewhere, or Ginny's murderer had made off with some of Jordan's belongings. If so, he'd missed the letter under her pillow.

⟋⟍

On my return to New Holland, I took a few minutes to make a phone call I'd been neglecting for days: Greg Hewert. I found his name in the phone book; he was living at home with his folks.

"You're that girl reporter, aren't you?" he asked when I identified myself.

"That's right. I wanted to ask you some questions about Jordan Shaw, if you don't mind."

"Are you planning to twist what I say and make her look bad? Because if you are, you're barking up the wrong tree."

"Not at all, I promise. Judge Shaw has asked me to help investigate Jordan's murder for her sake. I can have him call you, if you like."

"Never mind," he said. "I saw you talking to the judge and Mrs. Shaw the other night at the wake. What do you want to know?"

"For starters, can you tell me where you were last Friday night?"

There was a long silence on the line. Finally, Greg spoke.

"So it's like that?" he chuckled. "This is about me, not Jordan. Well, I don't have anything to hide. I was out at Blue Diamond Bar Friday from about nine thirty till one thirty when I went home to bed."

"Did anyone see you there?" I asked.

He laughed. "About hundred and fifty people, I guess. And I woke my ma when I got home, so she can vouch for me."

"You're quite well prepared. Like a Boy Scout," I said, flirting a little. I figured it might put him at ease. "If only everyone were as cooperative as you."

"Any time you'd like to question me personally, I'm game."

Okay, maybe I had gone too far.

"Can you tell me about Jordan?" I asked. "How well did you know her?"

"We were old friends. I've known her since grammar school," he said, more sober now that the subject had turned back to Jordan Shaw. "Whoever did this to her should fry in the electric chair and then rot in hell. If I get my hands on him, I'll kill him myself."

"Did you ever date Jordan?" I asked abruptly, and I got a dial tone as an answer.

My film of Ginny's body turned out to be grislier than I had remembered. In my haste to photograph the scene, I had paid little attention to the lighting, and the result was a grainy, ghostly look. Charlie Reese shook his head.

"How do you manage to focus a camera on a dead body?"

"It's not like I make a habit of it," I said. "And it wasn't easy. I was sick in the sink."

"Looks like a still life," he said, though not as a joke.

"Do you know what the French call still lifes?" I asked. "*Nature morte*. Dead nature."

"And that's apropos of what?" he asked.

"Nothing. Just feeling philosophical."

"Just showing off is more like it. So who do you think painted this scene?"

"I don't know," I said. "I met a couple of men in Boston who might fit the bill, but I just don't know."

"What are you looking for?" asked Charlie. "What would wrap this up for you?"

"A car," I said slowly, staring at Ginny White's bloated body. "A poorly maintained car."

CHAPTER NINE

FRIDAY, DECEMBER 2, 1960

"You've got to let me see Julio, Frank."

"Forget it, Ellie. His lawyer doesn't want anyone talking to him."

"Please, Frank," I said, using all my feminine wiles on my new chum. "I've played straight with you. Just give me ten minutes alone with him."

"I appreciate the way you've written this thing, but I can't. If our case against him gets thrown out because of some monkeyshines like this, I'm the one who's got to answer to the public. And to Judge Shaw."

"That's not it. You're afraid maybe the kid's innocent and you'll have to start over. Come on, Frank, you know there was another murder in Boston. Doesn't that clear Julio?"

"Hell, no," he said. "From what I understand, the White girl was killed Saturday evening or Sunday morning. That would have given Julio plenty of time to drive to Boston and back before I picked him up. Don't forget, he disappeared for four days."

"The kid trusts me. Maybe he'll tell me what he saw that night."

"What he saw was Jordan Shaw undressing. And when she caught him, he broke her neck and buried her body in the woods."

"You're burying your head in the sand, Frank. There are too many questions here. Don't you think it's important to know who those three men were who visited her that night?"

"I know who one of them was, and he's cooling his heels in a cell downstairs right now. It's a free country, Ellie. People have the right to

JAMES W. ZISKIN 155

go where they please, visit who they want. I don't care if the Shriners threw a party in her room that night; I know I got the right man."

I fought to maintain my calm, remembering Charlie Reese's admonition on estranging the goodwill of the sheriff.

"Why don't you talk to Jean Trent?" he offered. "We brought her in for accessory to murder, harboring a fugitive, and obstruction of justice."

"She doesn't know anything. Please, Frank. I promise you I won't print a word of what he tells me."

The sheriff thought about it, probably weighing the damage I could do to him with a negative article.

"Joe Murray is his lawyer," he said finally, glaring at me. "You know what a pain in the neck he is. He'd get the Israelis to release Eichmann if they put too much starch in his shorts. I don't want him to know I let you talk to Hernandez. Tell you what I'll do: I'll let you go downstairs to talk to Halvey—he's sitting suicide watch in the cell next to the kid's. See if you can stand five minutes with Halvey, then I'll call him out of there and give you ten minutes with Julio."

⁂

The Montgomery County Administration Building straddled the line between the Town of New Holland and the Town of Poole, northwest of the river, on Route 22. A three-story brick building, it housed jail cells in the basement, sheriff's office on the ground floor, courtrooms on the second, and administrative offices on the third. I had cut my teeth in the old building when I began working for the *Republic* a couple of years before. From family court to county board meetings, I had spent my share of meaningless evenings doodling into my notepad. The local judges were known for leniency and an inclination toward probation. The accused's families got to keep their husbands and sons, while the county probation officers surrendered gradually to the inconsequence of their efforts. The jail's population consisted of Saturday-night brawlers, wife beaters, drunken drivers, and petty thieves. Once, an accused child molester tried to hang himself from a water pipe and was knocked unconscious when the pipe broke and clocked him on the head. He succeeded in flooding the cell and was roughed up in the yard by the other inmates for forcing them to evacuate the building on a cold day.

Julio was the most notorious criminal the Montgomery County Jail had seen in recent memory, and as such he occupied the VIP suite—the center cell in the block. Pat Halvey, a finger in his ear, was sitting in the next cell, leaning back against the wall on two legs of his chair, and didn't hear me coming. When I called his name, the chair slid out from under him, and he crashed to the floor.

"Darn it, Ellie," he said, picking himself up. "Why don't you make some noise when you come into a room?"

A gale of laughter rose from the cellblock.

"What do you want, anyway?"

I glanced at Julio, who'd sat up on his bed in the next cell. He stared at me with dark, miserable eyes. I turned back to Halvey and asked him how his bowling game was coming along. That was all it took; he treated me to a dissertation on the new spin he'd been working on.

"What do you say we go bowling sometime, Ellie?" he asked. "I could teach you."

"I don't know, Pat. I've never seen your picture in the High Rollers' column of the paper. Do I want to be seen bowling with a guy who's never made the High Rollers?"

"You will soon, don't worry about that. I'm saving up for a new Brunswick Black Beauty, and with the spin I'm working on . . ."

Frank Olney left me twisting for at least ten minutes before calling Halvey away.

"How are they treating you, Julio?" I asked the shadowy figure, once we were alone.

He didn't speak. He just stared at me.

Invisible voices called out from the other dark cells: "Hey, spic, we're gonna get you! You killed a white girl, spic. We're gonna cut you into little Puerto Rican pieces!"

"Tell me what I can do for you," I whispered, once the taunts had died down.

His head dropped into his hands, and I could tell he was sobbing.

"Tell me, Julio," I said. "I know you didn't do this. Let me help. What can I do for you?"

"You would help?" he asked finally, lifting his head and wiping his nose on his sleeve. He rose from the bed and approached the bars that separated us. "Would you talk to my mother?"

"Of course," I said. "What do you want me to tell her?"

"Just tell her I'm okay. And . . ." He brought his face to the bars. "Tell her I'm innocent."

"All right," I said. "But I can do even more to help you. If you'd tell me where you hid the film, I could get you out of here."

"I told you there isn't any film!" he snapped, and turned away from the bars.

The voices returned, this time threatening me, the *spic lover*, with unspeakable acts of wickedness.

"The sheriff's determined to hang this on you," I said, still whispering. "And if I were in your shoes, I wouldn't want to try my luck in front of a jury. You heard those guys," I threw my head back to indicate the other inmates. "You can expect the same enlightened attitudes at your trial. They're going to want someone to pay for what happened to Jordan, and you're handy. So, please, tell me where the film is."

"There is no film," he repeated, more softly this time. Then he returned to his bed, lay down, and turned his back to me. I could see his shoulders shaking silently in the semidarkness.

⁂

"He tell you what you wanted to know?" asked the sheriff when I came out. I shook my head. "That doesn't surprise me. He's not going to help you, because he killed her."

"Tell me, Frank," I said, ignoring his gloating. "Did you ever find Jordan's effects? What happened to her clothes? Her purse? Her keys?"

"No, we haven't found any of that. My idea is Julio buried them somewhere or burned the whole lot. Why?"

"I don't know. I've been thinking about her keys. Maybe her killer used them to get into her apartment in Boston."

"Say, I'll bet you're right," said Olney, leaning forward in his swivel chair. "Hernandez grabbed the keys, drove to Boston, and bashed in the roommate's head."

"Why, Frank? There's no reason for him to go to Boston. And why would he cut that gash in Jordan's pelvis?"

The sheriff's eyes narrowed and grew dark. "I think it's voodoo. *Santoría*, they call it in the islands. I've been studying up on it, Ellie, down to the library. And I think that's the answer."

I just stared at the sheriff dumbly, turned slowly, and walked out to my car.

I was stopped at a red light on Market Street just inside the city limits when I happened to glance in my rearview mirror. Idling behind me, purring a soft rumble, was Pukey Boyle's maroon Hudson Hornet.

The sensation was an unsettling one, as I recalled my encounter with Glenda Whalen. When the light changed, I turned left to see if he would follow. I shifted my eyes from the road to the mirror and saw the shiny car swing into view. I tried a few more side streets, and the Hudson marked me at every turn, hanging back about thirty yards. As I approached the intersection of Franklin and Van Der Meer, the traffic light blinked to yellow. I eased up on the accelerator, letting the amber ripen, then gunned through a fresh red light, leaving Pukey Boyle and the maroon Hudson behind.

In late 1957, Don Czerulniak had used his influence—not to say his weight—to move the DA's office to the top floor of the New Holland Bank Building. Erected in 1899, the ten-story edifice was remarkable for its height, one of the earliest "skyscrapers" in upstate New York. The bank had been half-empty, in disrepair, and the first choice of eight city aldermen for a new parking lot. Within a year of the DA's move, however, the New Holland Bank Building was filled with city and county offices, and the owner, Harvey Richards, had drawn up plans for a complete renovation due to begin in January 1961. The DA had saved the historic building from demolition and saved county taxpayers a couple hundred thousand dollars at the same time.

Don had chosen the southwest corner of the top floor for his own office because, he claimed, he worked late, and the setting sun made his day seem longer. But I knew he liked to have a cocktail at twilight. He was just hanging up the phone when his secretary showed me in.

"Have a seat, Miss Stone," he said playfully, pointing to the chair in front of his desk. "I want to talk to you about your trip. But first, how about a thimbleful?"

I looked at my watch: 12:21 p.m. "Friday afternoon—why not?"

He poured us each a Scotch, then settled into the leather chair behind his desk.

"So what's this I hear about a murder in Boston?"

I explained how I had found Jordan's roommate dead in their apartment, and I told him that some enterprising soul had redecorated D. J. Nichols's digs and frightened him into hiding. Or perhaps worse.

"Boston police think he'll resurface soon; I'm just hoping it won't be in the Charles River. I was a little dismissive when he asked me for help."

"He'll be fine," said Don, a little dismissive himself. "Who do you think killed the roommate?"

"Not sure, but I've got some candidates. Nichols told me someone was trying to set him up for the murders, though he couldn't say why. What about on your end?" I asked. "You're still going with murder one against Julio Hernandez?"

The DA took a sip of his Scotch and ran a hand absently through his blond hair. "I don't know," he droned in his nasal whine. "I'm inclined to agree with you, but I don't want to drop the charge just yet. The kid might crack and admit to the whole thing. Busting the charge down to voyeurism and invasion of privacy won't exactly persuade him to talk."

"Why should he admit to something he didn't do?" I asked. "Look, he may have been getting his jollies peeping through Jordan's window, but the murder in Boston kind of lets him off the hook, doesn't it?"

"Maybe. But he was on the run for four days after the first murder. Maybe he killed Jordan's friend, too."

"There are two hitches in that theory, Don," I said. "First, *why* would he kill Ginny White? It's a long way to go just to peep. And second, how could Julio have ransacked Nichols's apartment? He was posing for a mug shot at the time."

"Maybe the burglary was a coincidence," he offered. "And maybe Julio had a reason for going to Boston."

"You don't believe that," I said. "That's Frank Olney talking."

"Well, there's no rush to drop the charges. Hernandez is still a few days away from the electric chair."

I left the DA's office a little lightheaded and crossed the street to the paper, where I developed enlarged prints of Jordan's datebook. In the months before her death, Jordan had written down many of her comings and goings in the diary, but it was far from a comprehensive record. I began my search more than a year earlier, in June 1959:

Jun 4	G. W. @ library 2:00 p.m.		
Jun 7	Phone Mom & Dad	My Fair Lady 8:00 p.m. @ Beacon (D. J.)	
Jun 15	OK	Hair appt. 3:00 p.m.	Dr. Meltzer 4:45 p.m.
Jun 18	*		
Jun 22	OK	Vacc. Dr. Garvey 11:00 a.m.	

Jun 25	NO		
Jul 3	Train to New Holland 9:12 a.m.		
Jul 8	Train to Boston 3:45 p.m.		
Jul 12	OK	D. J. dinner 7:00 p.m.	
Jul 15	*	Pick up tickets @ travel agent	
Jul 18	OK	Symphony/ dinner D. J.	
Jul 22	NO		

The entries continued in the same cryptic fashion through August, with notes from her journey to India. I found it curious she had marked the visit to the clinic in her book; one doesn't usually plan on emergency dysentery treatment or note down appointments after they've taken place.

Breaking from her routine, Jordan had made detailed entries about her India adventure in the datebook. She described the excitement of the arduous, seven-day string of flights to reach Bombay. Aboard a BOAC DC-7, she and a dozen fellow travelers left Idlewild for London Airport North. Jordan traveled de Luxe class, while D. J. had to settle for tourist. After a night in London, which included a ! with D. J. in his room, the group took off for Rome, then Istanbul on a Super G Constellation. They stopped for two days in Istanbul to rest and to take in the sights. Jordan and D. J. managed a !* in the Istanbul Hilton while the others undoubtedly slept unawares in their rooms under their mosquito nets.

From Istanbul, the group hopped to Cairo, then Karachi, before finally reaching Bombay, where they spent two nights at the magnificent Taj Mahal Hotel near the Gateway of India. Two more !*s in her room there.

Jordan described in gushing detail exchanging dollars for pounds sterling, then liras, then rupees. Long lines at museums, wrestling with Italian and Turkish and Hindi in restaurants, bazaars, and hotels. Nearly fifty hours in the air, and stolen moments of whirlwind romance on the ground in European and Near Eastern capitals. It sounded terrifically romantic, and I was more than a little curious about D. J.'s punctuation prowess.

After her return from India, there were several mentions of someone named J. N., mostly for dinner, movies, coffee, and study breaks. I groaned at the appearance of another unknown. Who the hell was J. N.? I pushed on. In September, the asterisks, OKs, and NOs disappeared, and I was sure I knew why. A year later, closer to the date of her death, I found phone numbers, appointments, class schedules, and many references to D. J. Whoever J. N. was, he hadn't completely displaced D. J.

November 1960 posed its own mysteries:

Nov 1	Calc. midterm 8:00 a.m.
Nov 5	D. J. 9:30 p.m.—511 Ritz-Carl.
Nov 7	Physics paper due
Nov 11	G. W. & J. N. @ boathouse noon
Nov 12	Dinner D. J. and . . .
Nov 16	Heartbroken!
Nov 23	Train to New Holland 5:25 p.m.
Nov 25	M. M. 9:00 p.m.—OK!!!

It was almost as if Jordan had known someone would try to decipher her datebook. Maybe she was having fun, or maybe it was a habit she'd learned over time to cover her tracks. Some of the initials still stumped me, but her secret codes and winks, intended to be known only by her, hadn't fooled me. She hadn't counted on a sister in crime finding them. I only hoped her cipher would point me to her killer. But with Julio in jail and quite unwilling to cooperate, I needed help. I had an idea to stir the pot and decided to start a rumor.

Fran Bartolo lived with her parents near the public golf course. I called and arranged to pick her up at three for a drive out to McAllister Road—a quiet thoroughfare by day, desolate lovers' lane by night—which cut across several farms overlooking the valley. It was the perfect spot for an uninterrupted chat.

"So, what did you want to talk about?" asked Fran, once I'd thrown the car into park.

"I wanted to ask you about Glenda Whalen."

"Glenda the Whale?" she asked, fiddling with the radio dial. "Tutti Frutti" came on. "Oh, I love this song!"

"Really?" I asked, the horror surely visible on my face. "Pat Boone?"

I remembered my brother, Elijah, railing against the travesty a few years earlier. He couldn't understand how people preferred the soulless Pat Boone version to Little Richard's original. Elijah cared about everything, from music to politics, and he was always on the right side, though that was always pretty far left. That assured him of butting heads with my willful father on a daily basis. They seemed to disagree on everything *except* politics. And yet, neither harbored any ill will toward the other, at least not after a few minutes had passed. Where I was concerned, however, a disagreement over the weather could incur my father's rancor for weeks.

"What's wrong, Ellie?" asked Franny, rousing me from my thoughts. "You look sad."

"Nothing," I said, chasing Elijah and Dad from my thoughts. They'd be back later, I was sure, once my guard was down, once I fell asleep.

"Anyway, what do you want to know about the Whale?"

"That's not nice, Fran," I said.

"Well, Glenda's not very nice," she said as a matter of fact. "A horrible creature, who doesn't know how to act in civilized society."

"Jordan liked her, didn't she?"

Fran shrugged her shoulders. "Some hero-worship thing, I suppose. Maybe Jordan enjoyed the devotion. But Glenda is a weirdo, unpleasant, and a bully. She didn't want anyone near Jordan, acted like

Jordan was her property. And even when you tried to treat her nice, she'd do something rotten, like talk behind your back or spread a rumor. Everybody hates her."

"She punched me in the mouth," I said after a pause. "Knocked me cold."

"There, what did I tell you? She's a bully."

"Maybe she's just unhappy."

"Unhappy is right. She never could get what she really wanted: Jordan. Fat lesbian."

We sat quietly for a while, then she provided the opening I needed to play my hand.

"So you're no closer to finding who killed Jordan?"

"Not yet," I said, turning down the music a bit. "But I will be, once I find those photos."

Fran switched off the radio altogether and looked at me. "What photos?"

"The ones that Julio Hernandez shot through the window at the motel. The film's lost, but he got the murderer, I'm sure of that."

"You're saying he took pictures of the murderer? How do you know that?"

I switched the radio back on—Bobby Darin, "Beyond the Sea"— and surveyed the view of the valley. "Julio told me."

I dropped off Fran, watched her run inside—surely to make a series of phone calls with the news—and slipped the shift into drive. Checking the mirror before pulling away from the curb, I spotted the maroon Hudson Hornet about fifty yards back, behind another car. Pukey was changing his tactics. I wound through the looping streets of the golf-course district and regained Route 40 via a seldom-used gravel road. As I pushed my Belvedere to speed, I could see the Hudson turning into traffic behind me. With a couple hundred yards' lead, I took to the side streets, hoping to lose Pukey. Seven turns in alternating directions took me back to Route 40, inside city limits, and I proceeded downtown, mindful of every vehicle that appeared in my rearview mirror.

At the office, I spent two hours hammering out my copy for Saturday's paper. The Boston murder and burglary dominated my story, which stressed the times and dates of the crimes. While not directly accusing the sheriff and the DA of blindness to the obvious, I suggested that the man they had arrested could not have burgled D. J. Nichols's apartment.

I phoned Judge Shaw from the photographers' room to discuss what I had learned in Boston and to ask him a few questions pertaining to the datebook.

"Do you know of any friend of Jordan's in Boston whose initials were J. N.?" I asked.

"Not that I recall," he said. "But I don't know all her friends' surnames. There was a Judy, I think, and a Jeffrey she mentioned a few times."

Jeffrey. I'd read his letters to Jordan and had put him out of my mind. J. N. could well be Jeffrey, but who exactly was Jeffrey?

"Where did you come up with J. N.?" he asked while I was thinking.

I didn't want to tell him about the datebook, didn't see how the judge could benefit from reading about her trysts in fancy hotels with a married man. My father had suffered greatly from too much knowledge of *his* daughter's behavior, and I wanted to spare the judge that.

"I don't remember where I heard it," I said. One of my weaker lies.

I was sure D. J. was Jerrold and that the Dear Jordan letter was from him, the heel. But just who was J. N.? The answer was not far off.

CHAPTER TEN

My handsome detective Morrissey phoned me from Boston to report that none of the fresh bodies in the morgue were Nichols's. He asked if I had anything new.

"I'm at a dead end," I said. "There's a new set of initials I can't identify. Have you come across any J. N.s or Jeffreys?"

"You're kidding me, right?" he said. "Your boy Nichols's name is Jeffrey. Duane Jeffrey Nichols. Goes by D. J. at school, but his wife calls him Jeffrey. She's been whining at us for two days about her poor Jeffrey."

"I can't believe I missed that."

"You're welcome."

That was sure to clear up a few items on my list. It made perfect sense now. Jordan had been consistent and particular in her notations and abbreviations. First name initial, surname initial. If she knew Nichols as Jeffrey, then J. N. had to be him. The pathetic love letters from Jeffrey fit Nichols's profile better than the lady-killer described by Roy. And suddenly, what had nagged me about the Dear Jordan letter came into focus. There was no signature, but there was spelling.

Before ringing off with Morrissey, I told him of my suspicions that Julio had taken pictures through the window at the Mohawk Motel. I asked him to help me play my gambit on the Boston end, to spread the word that both photos and a witness to the murder existed. Morrissey said I was crazy, but, since he had nothing else to go on, he agreed to give it a try.

It was after five thirty when I left the *Republic*'s offices. I climbed into my car, turned the key, and adjusted my mirrors, still on the lookout for Pukey Boyle. The coast was clear, and I drew a sigh of relief. But as I eased away from the curb, my eyes caught sight of a young man loitering on the sidewalk across the street. He was just standing there, staring at me. It was Greg Hewert.

I gunned the engine and headed east on Main Street. I couldn't be sure if Greg's presence was a coincidence or if he'd been waiting for me to leave the office, but his glare had unsettled me. I cranked down the window for some cold air and shook the vision of him out of my head.

I didn't relish the prospect of calling on the Hernandez family, especially with the light falling, but I told myself that unpleasantries were part of any job, and reporters sometimes had to knock on doors where they weren't wanted. As it turned out, my visit was doubly unwelcome because the family was just about to sit down to supper.

"What you want now?" asked Hernandez, padre, through the door.

"I saw Julio today," I said. "He asked me to give a message to his mother."

"What's the message?"

"He wanted me to speak to her personally."

He closed the door, and I heard a high-pitched voice on the other side, answered by the father's baritone. Another exchange, and the woman won. The door opened, and *Señora* Hernandez invited me in.

"Please sit," she said, gesturing nervously to an armchair in the dark parlor. I was sure it was the place of honor. She smoothed her apron and asked if I would like some coffee. I said yes.

She turned to the teenage girl watching from the kitchen door and rattled off in Spanish some instructions to her, I believe to fetch me coffee. The girl disappeared into the kitchen.

The house was neat, in contrast to the ragged appearance of the exterior. A thin, worn rug covered most of the dark, wooden floor, and the only light in the room was a floor lamp in the corner. A dull fluorescent spilled from the kitchen into the parlor, and I could smell something spicy cooking.

Hernandez, padre, still didn't like my being there, and he watched me intently from a wooden chair across the room. Three small children—a girl and two boys—streaked in and out of the room, excited by my presence. The older girl brought me a cup of coffee from the kitchen.

"What Julio say?" asked Mrs. Hernandez, pulling a small armchair closer to mine. She sat down as if bracing for the worst. "He okay?"

"He says they're treating him fine, that he misses you."

"*¡Ay, Dios mío! ¡Pobrecito!*" Tears flowed down her cheeks. She crossed herself, then wrung her hands to God. "What else he say?"

"He insisted that I tell you one thing," I said, fixing my eyes on hers. "He wants you to know that he's innocent."

"*¡Lo sabía! ¡Lo sabía!*" She crossed herself a few more times, held her hands close to her heart in a tight fist, and cried. Then she asked me when he would go free.

"Not yet," I said. She seemed surprised then confused. Her older daughter explained to her in Spanish, and she looked at me as if I'd pierced her heart willfully. "I can help Julio," I insisted. "But I need his cooperation, his help. I need to see his cameras, his film equipment. Do you know where he keeps them?"

The father made a clicking noise with his tongue and shook his head. "He never keep no camera here." I looked across the darkened room, barely able to see his eyes. "Try that lady's place. The motel."

"He's a good boy," said Mrs. Hernandez, reaching out to take my hands. "Please help us, Miss Stone. Don't let them kill my son."

I smiled at her, but I worried she would hold me accountable if the unthinkable ever came to pass. "I'll do my best," I said. "If the sheriff lets you see him, tell him to trust me, to tell me everything. Otherwise, I can't help him."

Mrs. Hernandez swore she would tell him, crossed herself again, and kissed my hand. I was embarrassed and politely excused myself to leave. But at some point during my five-minute visit, I had earned the family's gratitude. The father wasn't exactly ready to slap me on the back, but his gold-toothed smile betrayed a thawing in relations. They compelled me to stay for a supper of rice and beans. When I left an hour later, I no longer feared the dark on Hawk Street.

I did, however, fear the maroon Hudson Hornet I noticed in my rearview mirror as I headed west on Main. By instinct, I resorted to the evasive tactics I had learned in my two previous encounters with Pukey Boyle. I slowed for yellow lights, then sped through reds; zigzagged through side streets and crowded parking lots; and even cut across the high school practice fields. But the Hudson clung to my heels. Finally, in desperation, I decided to drive home and face whatever awaited me. I pulled over to the curb across from Fiorello's, expecting the worst, but the Hudson zoomed past me and down the street before I could throw the car into park. I shrugged my shoulders, climbed out, and went upstairs. A couple of hours later, after a call with Charlie and a drink, I crossed the street to see Fadge.

The store was jammed with teenagers sipping cherry Cokes and playing the jukebox. It was a little after ten, and the youngsters were trying to pack in a few last minutes of flirting—the girls preened and giggled; the boys strutted and postured—before having to head home for curfew. A booth in the back freed up suddenly, and I grabbed it for myself. It took Fadge twenty minutes to get around to asking for my order. When busy, he always left his regulars to wait long beyond their turn, well aware that they would suffer the slight out of loyalty. I didn't mind; he was mixing fountain drinks and scooping ice cream furiously, sweating like a horse, and breathing through his mouth, as was his wont. And I enjoyed watching the rituals of teenagers anyway, as if I were an anthropologist living in their midst.

One pretty girl was being courted by two boys in the next booth. The males may not have realized it, but they were locked in an epic battle for dominance, the prize for which was the female across the table from them. Their competition did not devolve into blows, clattering of antlers, or beating of chests—at least not literally—but the affections of the female were at stake. Solicitous and mature one moment, juvenile and boastful the next, the two males sought success through an instinctually heuristic strategy, a shotgun method of "try everything and see what works." This was the desperation of the innocent.

As they jostled for advantage, an older male approached, slid into the booth next to the female, who was receptive to his advances, and he began his own confident mating dance. The adolescents made one attempt to rally and hold their ground, cracking some inane joke or other, but the older male was physically intimidating and soon grew tired of their irritation. At length, he chased them away with a grunt and a sneer.

I watched the girl and her champion. They were cozy in the booth, clearly well acquainted and probably going steady. At least three years out of school, he was probably five years older than she. He looked to be a goon, what Fadge called a greaser, unsuited to the girl-next-door with him. I thought of Pukey Boyle and Jordan Shaw just as Fadge appeared before them to take the young man's order.

"What can I get you?" he asked.

"Nothin'," answered the young man.

I braced myself. If there was one thing Fadge couldn't abide, it was a greaser who didn't buy anything.

"This ain't a waiting room," he said. "Out."

The boy disengaged himself slowly from his seat as his girl sat frozen in fear and embarrassment. He sauntered across the store toward the door, trying to salvage a scrap of his honor by feigning indifference to the ejection and grinning at the onlookers. The girl made a dash after him, just as the jukebox started playing Paul Anka's "Puppy Love." Fadge looked sideways at the machine, bent over behind it, and pressed the reset button.

"I hate that song," he said to me. No one protested, though I noticed one girl who seemed crushed that the song—probably her selection—had been scratched from the program.

About an hour later, the place had emptied out, and Fadge and I were alone. He joined me in the booth and slid a coffee mug of ice cream and hot fudge across the table to me. This was the hip way to have a sundae, reserved for after-hours habitués in good standing.

"Thanks," I said. "I'm going to get fat."

"Fat's where it's at," he said. "Look at me."

"You're not going to throw me out for dawdling in the booth?"

He looked a little sheepish and didn't have a witty comeback. Then he asked what I was working on.

"This is a datebook," I said, motioning to the photographs in front of me. I'd pulled them out of my purse once the last of the kids had cleared out.

"Mind if I have a look?" he asked.

I hesitated. He noticed, assured me he was trustworthy and wouldn't tell a soul, but if I didn't want him to ... Fadge had helped me through the darkest days after my father's death, cheering me with his humor, flattering me with his attention, and plying me with alcohol in hopes of taking advantage of me. At least that's what he used to say. We'd grown very close over the months, and, unless I was up to no good in the arms of some rogue, my days began and ended in his company. I loved that fat guy like a brother, so I let him see.

He shuffled the photos around for a minute, then asked for my help.

"Very simple," I said. "These asterisks are her period."

"How do you know that?" he asked.

"Look: June 18, asterisk; July 15, asterisk; August 12, asterisk ... Twenty-eight days each time. I'd say Jordan Shaw was as regular as clockwork. And that explains these other entries: OK means she's safe and won't get pregnant, NO means behave."

Fadge gaped at me. "You figured all that out, just like that?"

"You should see my datebook." I mumbled. "This Jordan Shaw knew her rhythm. She was careful."

"Wait a minute," he said, taking up one of the photographs. "If the OKs and NOs refer to her rhythm, why is August of last year the last time she marked them down?"

I smiled knowingly. "She found a better method of birth control."

A customer came in, and Fadge got up. As I sat in the booth, I focused on the evening of November 25. Jordan had arranged to meet D. J.—David Jerrold—at the Mohawk Motel at 9:00 p.m. I couldn't be sure how she had convinced him, given the Dear Jordan letter he'd sent her about twelve days earlier, but I doubted any man could resist an invitation to love from such a pretty young thing. I figured Jean Trent was right; Jordan had slept with the first man—Jerrold—somewhere between 9:30 and 11:00 p.m. Julio had given me further details, and I consulted my notes to be sure: Jordan was alive when he stopped watching her through the window at 11:20. Jerrold had left shortly before then.

So much for the first act. That left me with the problem of finding the other two visitors. There was no shortage of prospects, from Pukey Boyle to Greg Hewert, and no one was fessing up to having seen anyone. Julio would have to open up to me, or I would remain stuck.

As things turned out, it wasn't Julio who unblocked the impasse, but a midnight caller. Having left Fiorello's around eleven thirty, I crossed the street and took up the three days of crossword puzzles I'd been neglecting and another glass of White Label. The distraction swept the cobwebs from my head and relaxed me besides. By the time I'd finished the first puzzle, I was nodding off. The last clue I remember was "Policeman in slang, six letters." The surrounding boxes made *copper* the only possibility. The next thing I knew, the telephone was pealing.

"Butt out!" A hoarse, sluggish whisper, right out of a B movie.

"What? I beg your pardon?"

"Quit nosing around."

"I think you have the wrong number."

"Stone!" The voice called out to stop me from hanging up. "You heard me."

My heart was pumping. I said nothing, hoping my silence would solicit more information from my caller. For several seconds, he said nothing, then he spoke in the same eerie, torpid whisper he had begun with.

"Remember those girls; you don't want to end up like them," and the phone clicked in my ear.

The voice bore no distinguishing characteristics, besides the whisper, and I knew I would never be able to recognize it in normal conversation. If there was an accent, I didn't hear it. I tried to decide whether the call had been local or long distance, but there was no way to be certain. It didn't matter anyway; I was easy enough to find.

I tried to sleep, but the haunting whisper kept me awake, taunting me to guess its identity. It seemed logical to assume that the caller was part of the Boston crowd, since he had alluded to *girls*, plural. But then again, by now everyone in New Holland knew of the Boston murder, thanks to my article, and I had given up assuming things I could not prove. I stared at the ceiling for hours, sitting up every now and then to jot down a note or an idea on the pad next to my bed. Alone in the dark, I thought with horror that I didn't want to end up like Jordan Shaw, neck broken, body desecrated. And poor Ginny, like my father, clubbed to death in her own home. I tried to distract myself, think of something else, but, like a magnet, my thoughts were drawn to the events I least wanted to recall. My father had been murdered ten months earlier, but I still turned the bloody details over and over in my head.

⌀

SATURDAY, DECEMBER 3, 1960

When I awoke at half past six, I couldn't remember having fallen asleep. I glanced down at the newspapers and the crossword on the floor, and the idea came to me like a bolt.

"Copper," I said with a knowing smile, thinking back to Jordan's datebook.

Of course I had known since the autopsy about the IUD, but this was Jordan herself telling me something in her own words. I wasn't any closer to solving the murder, but the minor revelation yielded my first glimmer of understanding. I felt triumphant. I could trust her for the truth where others had lied, exaggerated, or just plain misunderstood.

⌀

Ron Fiorello opened the store at eight, collected the odd change left for newspapers on his stoop, and set the day's first pot of coffee to brew. I climbed onto a stool and laid the envelope with prints of Jordan's datebook on the counter.

"How's it going?" asked Fadge, tying a chocolate-spattered apron around his waist.

Indeed, how? The late-night phone call hadn't told me much—just that somebody somewhere didn't appreciate my snooping and considered killing me for it.

"A little progress, but no breakthrough," I said, fiddling with the envelope. "One moment, I feel completely lost; then Glenda Whalen knocks me cold at Tedesco's. I think the trail's gone cold, and I get a threatening phone call last night. And then there's Pukey Boyle, who's been shadowing me all over town . . . I can't figure why so many people want to stop me from poking around. Where's my coffee?"

"A threatening call?" He stared with his bulging eyes. "Jesus, Ellie, what are you getting yourself into?"

Fadge glared at me for a long moment, then snatched a cup, filled it, and set it down before me. "Be careful, will you?"

"I'll be okay," I said and sipped my coffee. "I'm sure it was one of the three men who visited Jordan's motel room last Friday night, but I only know who one of them was. A professor, David Jerrold. Married and unwilling to cooperate for fear of scandal."

"You think it was him?"

"Could be. But according to Julio, Jerrold left Jordan alive and well in the room a little past eleven Friday night. At least I'm convinced it was Jerrold. Julio didn't see him. I've been trying to plot out what happened after that."

I pulled the prints from the envelope and spread them on the counter. Then I flipped open my notepad for reference.

"Listen to this, Fadge: My only two sources so far are Julio and Jean Trent, and each has filled in different holes. Jean told me Jordan arrived at eight thirty, and that matches what Jordan wrote in her datebook, right here," and I pointed to November 25: "M. M. 9:00 p.m.—OK!!!"

"What's that mean?" he asked, cranking his head to see.

"Mohawk Motel, 9:00 p.m.," I said. "Her rendezvous with Jerrold." Fadge studied the photographs with me.

"Remember last night I said she had found a new form of birth control?" I asked.

"Yeah, so what was it?"

"Jordan went to India last summer, where she visited a private health clinic in Delhi. In a postcard to her roommate, she described the procedure as treatment for dysentery. But she added some cryptic hints about the care she'd received. She wrote something to the effect that she came out of the clinic feeling like a bright, new penny."

"Yeah, so what's that got to do with dysentery?" asked Fadge, still leaning over the photos of Jordan's datebook on the counter.

"Nothing. Jordan didn't have dysentery; she wasn't even sick. She had arranged an appointment at that clinic before she left for India."

"I know," said Fadge, lifting his weight off the counter. "She was pregnant and had it taken care of."

"Wrong. Now, what I'm about to tell you stays right here," I said. Fadge nodded. "When Doc Peruso performed the autopsy on Jordan, he found an IUD."

"What's that?" he asked.

"The IUD is the latest in birth control. It's a small metallic coil that is implanted in the girl's uterus, and it prevents pregnancy. Kind of tricks the body into thinking it's already pregnant."

"Get outta here," said Fadge, doubtful.

"It's true. The device is safe and very effective. Anyway, I'm sure now that Jordan had one implanted on August 14th, right there." And I pointed to the datebook: "Varma Medical Clinic 10:00 a.m.—D. J."

"What makes you so sure she got this thing over there? If you drink the water in India, your shit flows like the Ganges."

I was startled by the imagery.

"Sorry," he said, "but maybe she did have dysentery and got the coil thing in Boston."

"No. They've been testing them in the Third World for a few years, and they're not common here. Besides, the postcard clinched it. Jordan said she felt like a bright, new penny. Pennies are made of copper, just like her IUD."

"Good work," he said. "But it all sounds like science fiction to me. If I'm lucky enough to get lucky, I still use a rubber."

"Let's put that to one side for now," I smiled.

"What about these three exclamation points after the OK on November 25th?" he asked. "If she had the PUD, she wouldn't need to write OK, would she?"

"IUD," I corrected. "Jerrold had given her the brush a week or two before. I'd say she missed her man and was excited to get him back. She obviously still had the IUD; it was found in the autopsy. So she had no worries that night."

"If this Jerrold guy had broken it off with her, how did she convince him to come all the way to New Holland?"

I gave Fadge a knowing look, and he figured it out for himself.

"What is it about a pretty woman that'll make a man stand on his head?" he asked, pouring himself a cup of coffee.

"And it was safer here," I said. "No accidental discovery at a Boston hotel, no risk of being recognized. It's ironic, too. Jerrold held all the cards; he made this great show of strength and resolve, told her it was over between them. Then, when that pretty young thing crooked her finger, he came running two hundred miles."

"With his crank in his hand."

"You should be ashamed of yourself and your gender," I said, unable to suppress a grin. "But to get back to the night of November 25th," I said, closing my extended parentheses. "We know Jordan arrived alone at eight thirty and parked her father's car out back, because it wouldn't do for an Appellate Division judge's car to be seen at the most notorious love lounge in the county. Jean Trent checked her in and heard Jerrold arrive around nine fifteen."

"And that's where Julio comes in?"

"That's right. You don't think an accomplished voyeur like Julio would fail to notice a treat like Jordan Shaw, do you? Plus, he knew her from high school. So he sets up surveillance at the window, misses the main event, I believe, because the bathroom door is closed, but gets his reward watching Jordan shower off afterward."

"Not an ugly sight, I'd wager. But did he see Jerrold?"

"If he did, he's not admitting to it."

"So then what?"

No need to check my notes; I had the timeline memorized by now. "Jerrold leaves Jordan a little after eleven. About quarter past midnight, Jean Trent hears a car pull into the parking lot. She's curious, peeks out the window, and sees another man go into Jordan's room. There's no scream, so she goes back to her movie. Afterward, she looks out the window again. The second car's gone and a different one is parked outside. A third man is leaving Jordan's room."

"Okay, that's nothing new; I read that in your article last week. But what does it mean?"

"First of all, it means the third man—the one Jean saw leaving after her movie—didn't take the body out. Whether the second man, or someone else, removed Jordan earlier, I can only guess right now; apparently Jerrold didn't, since Julio heard him leave. But I'm wondering what happened to our voyeur that night. Did he leave after watching Jordan through the window, or did he go to Jean Trent's room? I have the feeling Julio's scared because he has evidence."

"Now that's news," said Fadge. "What kind of evidence?"

"It's just a hunch, but I think he took pictures through Jordan's window and got more than he bargained for."

Fadge shook his head. "If he did take pictures, and if he did shoot something that scared him into shutting up, wouldn't he simply destroy the film?"

"I don't think so," I said, sliding my photographs back inside their envelope. "If worse comes to worst, that film will save his neck."

❧

The possibility that Julio had shot film of Jordan Shaw through the bathroom window aroused my interest and, and at the same time, dampened any hopes that I would ever solve the murder and save my sinking career. If the photos existed, they could be hidden anywhere. And Julio might well have destroyed them. Or maybe they had never existed at all, which sent me back to square one. I was poised to invest considerable time and effort to prove my hunch, and if there was no film, I feared I might lose the trail for good.

Did Julio shoot photographs of a naked Jordan Shaw? I turned the question over and over, trying to climb inside his mind. What would I have done in his shoes that night? Would a voyeur have squandered such an opportunity? A voyeur who was a fair hand with a camera and a darkroom? The answer, of course, was no. On Friday, November 25, Julio had shot some of the hottest film he'd ever cranked through a camera. I was sure of it. And I was going to find it.

Frank Olney was slurping coffee from his mug when I entered his office. He offered me a cup, but I declined.

"I just want to ask you a few questions, Frank," I said. "And maybe have a minute with Julio."

"Forget it, Ellie. I've already gone out on a limb for you. The other prisoners might open their fat mouths. And if Joe Murray finds out I let a reporter talk to his client without him present, we'll have a dismissal on our hands faster than you can say *habeas corpus*."

"What about his family? Have a heart, Frank. Let them see the poor kid."

Frank chuckled with irony. "*Poor kid*. What about Jordan Shaw? That *poor kid* in there should have thought about the consequences before he snapped her neck."

I shook my head but didn't argue; Frank knew where I stood on Julio. Instead, I turned to the subject of Jean Trent.

"I've been thinking maybe I should ask her a few questions. Can I see her?"

Frank shook his head. "She also hired Joe Murray, who told me Jean won't talk to anyone, especially—quote, unquote—'that little shit of a reporter Ellie Stone.'"

"She specifically said she wouldn't talk to me?" I asked.

Frank nodded. "She thinks you got her involved in something she had nothing to do with. She's off-limits. Should have talked to her last time I offered."

"All right," I granted, not too worried about the long-term effects of the chill in my friendship with Jean Trent. "What do you know about her?"

The sheriff shrugged, then downed the last swig of his coffee. "What's to know? She's been at the Mohawk for as long as I can remember."

"What about her husband? When did he die? What kind of money did he leave her?"

"He died about seven years ago. Some kind of cancer. He was a small guy, quiet but kind of mean. He didn't like people very much and kept to himself. I don't know what money he left Jean, but she manages somehow. I'll tell you one thing: what she makes from that motel couldn't support a refugee."

I jotted down some notes as the sheriff spoke. "I've got an idea, Frank," I said, putting away my book. "It's Saturday; the offices upstairs are closed. Let's take a quick look at Victor Trent's will."

"Why are you so interested in Jean Trent?" he asked. "You're not going to tell me she killed Jordan Shaw."

"No. But I've been wondering about her second car. Have your boys located it yet?"

Frank shook his head. "Nothing to locate. Jean says the wagon died somewhere in Rensselaer County about six months ago. She junked it and hasn't seen it since. End of story."

"That's not true, Frank. I saw that green wagon parked behind the Mohawk just last week."

"Can't be, Ellie. I checked with Motor Vehicles—registration expired several months back, and Jean never renewed it."

"I know it was her car," I said, "because I checked with Motor Vehicles, too. The registration has expired all right, but someone's been driving it here in Montgomery County very recently."

The sheriff scratched the back of his neck, considering the significance of the lie Jean Trent had spooned him.

"Well, it doesn't change anything," he said finally. "Half the slobs I pull over for speeding are driving with expired registrations. She probably lied to save herself a ticket."

"So, do I get a look at Victor Trent's will or not?"

Frank and I climbed the stairs to the third floor, where the Montgomery County Administration shared a cramped space with the Department of Motor Vehicles. Had it not been a Saturday afternoon, I would have had to duck Benny Arnold, who had given me the dope on Jean Trent's second car.

These were the catacombs of New Holland's legal patrimony, crumbling under the weight of time, moisture, and munching insects. We wound around a bulwark of high shelves and dusty files, traveling backward through time, searching for 1953, the year of Victor Trent's death.

"Why do you want to snoop through Victor Trent's meager bequests?" asked Frank as we scanned the dates.

"I'm interested in the will, what he left and to whom."

"I'd wager he didn't leave a pot to piss in, unless you count the Mohawk," and he roared with laughter, raising a cloud of dust from some folios on the shelf before him.

"Here it is," I said, hoisting a file box from its resting place. "Probate wills, 1953–1954."

Frank lugged the heavy box to the clerk's counter up front. Flipping through the official stamps and, yes, even some red tape, we found Victor Trent's will in short order. He had left his wife the Mohawk Motel and all his personal possessions, including $12,130 in a savings account, a coin collection appraised at $6,200 when the will was in probate, a garage full of furniture-refinishing equipment, and a life-insurance policy worth $15,000. But the document didn't end there. Victor Trent owned seven acres of land on Winandauga Lake, about twelve miles north of New Holland, as well as a house his sister occupied in Johnston's Mill, just west of the city limits, along the river. He left the house to his sister, Reba, with an executory devise that the property pass to Jean upon Reba's death. The will stipulated further that the land on Winandauga Lake would remain in trust, to be shared equally by Reba and Jean, until the death of one or the other. At such time, the survivor could dispose of the property as she saw fit. Frank informed me that Reba had died two years earlier.

Victor Trent's estate was an impressive show of wealth for a small-town innkeeper. But it wasn't all that unusual in New Holland; the mills had been good to a great number of sensible, hard-working Joes who had saved their money, bought land whenever they could afford it, and ended up retiring to their Social Security checks and rental incomes. Most failed to take any personal advantage of their relative wealth, sticking to the habits of a lifetime of honest toil and moderation, and left it all to their children instead. What I found puzzling, however, was Jean Trent's situation. Why would she continue to live in the gloom and squalor of the Mohawk Motel when she had inherited enough money to see her comfortably through her last days?

⑽

I backed my car away from the Montgomery County Jail, swinging to face Route 22, and saw the deep-maroon, metallic paint half-hidden by some trees. I swore to myself, straining to make sure it was Pukey Boyle's Hudson Hornet. It was. I sat at the wheel of my car for several moments, considering my options. I could barrel out of the parking lot and take my chances, or I could leave my car at the jail and sneak away through the woods on foot. The first choice seemed dangerous, the second was downright cowardly, which was okay; I am a girl, after all. Then I noticed a third option: if I was willing to risk a few scratches on my company car, I could squeeze through a narrow break in the shrubs leading to the rear of the building and a small dirt road. Convincing myself that this was a brilliant feint, I eased my car through the brush and gained the back road unnoticed. I turned south on 22 and drove right past Pukey, whose eyes, I could see, were glued on the county jail.

⑽

Charlie Reese insisted that I cover the New Holland high school basketball game Saturday night because his regular sports photographer had the day off for his daughter's Confirmation.

"Short won't let you work just one story," he said. "He's making noises again about handing the murder case to Walsh. Now I'm ready to make allowances for you, but you've got to help me out on nights like tonight. It'll keep Artie off our backs."

I agreed, figuring a basketball game was better than a VFW Ladies' Auxiliary meeting or some other such event I might have landed. So, at eight o'clock, I was courtside to watch the Falcons of Albany High crush the New Holland Bucks, 85 to 63.

On my way back to the paper, I stopped at Korky's Liquors and bought a fifth of Scotch for later on. Hot time in the old town tonight. I left the bottle on the front seat and let myself into the office to develop my film.

For Monday's edition, Ralphie Fisher, the *Republic's* sports editor, chose a tight shot of a grimly determined New Holland player defending against a much taller opponent from Albany.

"By the way," said Ralphie, "Bobby left a lens adapter for you. It's in the lab."

I'd been meaning to try a longer lens I'd bought years earlier for a different camera, and needed the adapter to attach it.

"Thanks, I'll grab it before I leave."

After I'd captioned the film, I sat in front of the typewriter and tapped out two articles related to the Shaw murder. One examined the links between the two murders and Tufts's Engineering Department, while the other concentrated on the medical and physical evidence in the two cases: blood, fingerprints, and autopsies.

By the time I dropped the stories on Charlie Reese's desk, it was after midnight. I walked out into the brisk night air, yawned, and stretched. I hadn't forgotten about Pukey Boyle, whose constant presence in my rearview mirror had not endeared him to me, and I wondered if he might be waiting for me. A quick inspection of Main Street allayed my fears.

I drove up Market Hill, heading home, then realized I'd forgotten to take the lens adapter from the lab. I turned around at Summit Avenue, the crest of Market Hill, and headed back down the incline. As I neared Division Street at the bottom, I pumped the brake pedal lightly and felt the car slow. On the second pump, the brakes responded momentarily and then released, and the pedal hit the floor. The car began to accelerate down the hill, pulled by gravity and its own weight. The brakes were gone. I shifted to low, slowing the rate of acceleration, but not the acceleration itself. The grade of the hill seemed to grow steeper as the car's transmission screamed against the speed. The last reading I remember on the speedometer was thirty-four miles per hour. I saw pedestrians ahead and instinctively steered the car directly into a large elm tree just beyond the sidewalk. It was the only impediment in sight. The crash propelled the car several feet straight up into the air, and only a fortuitous quirk of physics prevented it from somersaulting down the street into even more mayhem. Instead, the car bounced to rest a few feet from where it had hit the tree. Glass rained down about me after impact, and some dislodged parts of my Plymouth, including three of the four hubcaps, rolled away from the scene of the accident, clattering in the quiet night. The fifth of Scotch I'd left in the car smashed to pieces against the dashboard, splattering whiskey everywhere. I slumped over in the driver's seat, stars in my eyes and a lump growing on my forehead. I heard dogs barking and voices calling out to each other.

Ten minutes later, two firemen pulled me from the wreck. I ignored their advice to lie down and, instead, leaned on the unscathed left rear fender of my demolished car.

After they'd stopped my bloody nose with gauze and I was able to identify the correct number of fingers held up for my inspection, the patrolman investigating the crash asked me to walk a straight line.

"You've got to be kidding," I mumbled. "I can hardly stand up."

"It's either that or a blood test," he said.

I assured him that I hadn't been drinking, that the whiskey had been unopened before the crash. But he wasn't buying it, and the ambulance took me to the hospital for observation and a blood test.

Sam Belson, the young doctor on ER duty at St. Joseph's, siphoned some blood out of my arm at the insistence of Patrolman William Trevor, badge 479, who was undoubtedly hoping for the first collar of his career.

"Look officer," said Sam. "I don't want to tell you how to do your job, but any fool can see that this woman hasn't had a drink all day."

"She sure smells like booze," said the cop.

"Her clothes, yes, but there's nothing on her breath."

"We'll let the blood test determine that," answered Trevor, though I could see he was beginning to doubt his conviction.

"Do you know this is a respected writer from the paper?" Belson warned the cop, who ignored us both.

I asked an orderly to call Charlie Reese to tell him what had happened. He arrived fifteen minutes later and, with threats of a nasty lawsuit, convinced the police officer to accept the good doctor's professional opinion.

Sam Belson and Officer Trevor left Charlie and me alone in the ER waiting room. Charlie wanted to know exactly what had happened. After I explained that my brakes had failed, he chewed me out for neglecting my car maintenance.

"I had the brakes checked two months ago when the car passed inspection at Ornuti's Garage," I argued. "And you know Dom Ornuti; he wouldn't give his own mother a sticker if her tire pressure was low."

The ER doors swung open, and Big Frank Olney strode in.

"Who invited you?" I asked, holding an ice pack to my forehead.

"I just wanted to shake hands with the human cannonball," he said, swallowing a growing smile. "Actually, I heard what happened on the scanner about a half hour ago. I went over to Market Street to check out the damage you did. Something about that tree you didn't like?"

"Where's my car now?" I asked.

"New Holland police towed it to Phil's. But you're not driving that heap again; it's totaled."

"I don't want to drive it, Frank," I said, pulling the ice away from my cold head. "I want Dom Ornuti to have a look at the brakes."

"What for?"

"I want to know how they were cut."

CHAPTER ELEVEN

I went home and climbed into bed, nursing a terrific headache. Charlie Reese ordered me to take a few days off to recuperate. The sick leave was opportune, freeing me of all editorial responsibilities except those I wanted to take on. No more NHHS basketball games or VFW meetings to interfere with the Shaw murder.

SUNDAY, DECEMBER 4, 1960

Despite a banging head and some dizziness, I had no time for bed on Sunday morning. At eight, I called Frank Olney, who had arranged for Dom Ornuti to meet us at Phil's Garage at ten. After a cup of coffee, four aspirins, and a warm bath, I dressed and headed to Fiorello's to borrow Fadge's car, a '57 Nash Ambassador.

Never stoic where pain was concerned, Fadge winced at the bandage over my nose and my blackening eyes. Not a good look for a girl. I said it was nothing and sat down in a booth to do the Sunday crossword puzzle over another cup of coffee. As I passed the time waiting for my appointment at Phil's Garage, Tommy Quint walked in.

"Hey, Tom," smiled Fadge. "I didn't know you were in town."

"I came home for the funeral Monday and stayed. I'm going back to Rochester this afternoon."

I lifted myself out of the booth and joined them at the counter. "Hi, Tom. Remember me?"

The young man recoiled when he saw me, and I couldn't be sure if it was my face or my presence that troubled him. He nodded hello and took a stool at the counter.

"What time are you going back?" asked Fadge.

"Later. I'm not in any hurry."

"Taking the bus?" I asked.

Tommy turned on his stool to face me, still looking horrified at the sight. "I've got a car."

I remembered that he had taken the bus the weekend before, two days after Jordan's murder.

"Don't you usually take the bus?" I asked.

"What business is it of yours?" he said, his discomfort turning hostile. "I don't take the bus to Rochester because it stops a million times."

"What about last weekend? You took the bus then, didn't you?"

He glared at me, sweating. "Yeah, my car was in the garage. I picked it up at Ornuti's Thursday. Go ask Vinnie Donati if you don't believe me."

"I'm meeting Dom Ornuti about a half hour from now," I said. "I can check your story very easily."

"Leave him alone, Ellie," said Fadge in a low voice.

"I don't know why you don't believe me," said Tommy, suddenly at the point of tears. "I told you I loved Jordan. Everyone in town knew I did."

He wiped his left sleeve across his wet nose and caught his lip on his watchband. It must have hurt like the devil, because he hopped around swearing for about thirty seconds. I thought it was pretty funny, but Fadge frowned and shook his head disapprovingly at me. Then he handed Tommy a napkin and put his arm around him.

When I left Fiorello's a few minutes later, I bent over and examined the ground under Tommy Quint's dented, white Plymouth. Piece of junk, but clean. I wondered, though, if it had been leaking oil the Friday before.

॰

I had met Dom Ornuti only once: the time two months before when he inspected my Belvedere. He wore a thin mustache over his long mouth and bluish lips. His skin color betrayed a liver problem (due to heavy drinking, according to rumor), and he smoked like a Turk: Lucky Strikes. A lean, sullen type, Dom was no conversationalist.

Frank had invited him to Phil's, a competing garage, to assess the damage and give an opinion on the brakes he had so recently pronounced fit for the road.

This day at Phil's Garage, he grunted hello to me. He dropped to the pavement, scooted beneath the twisted chassis, and loosed a satisfied hoot a few seconds later. Shimmying back out from under the car, he popped to his feet and beamed smiles at the sheriff and me.

"You thought I missed something, didn't you?" he accused me, now gloating and cocky. "Well, think again. Someone did a job on your brakes."

"Shit," said Frank in frustration. He was tired, I could see that. But then he took a deep breath and rejoined the game. "All right," he continued. "Let's get a winch under that thing and lift it up so I can see."

At first glimpse, the damage was hardly evident to Frank and me. But Dom explained, pointing a flashlight toward one of the brakes.

"You see the line leading to the drum?" he asked, and, after taking turns, Frank and I answered yes. "That's how your man cut your brakes," he continued. "This guy knew what he was doing. And there she is," he announced, pointing to a pinhole with a grease-stained finger.

Now the damage was plain to see, even for a nonmechanic. The blackened hydraulic tube had been punctured cleanly.

"What do you make of that?" asked Dom, as if to bait me.

"I'd say someone wanted to let the fluid drip out slowly. So the brakes wouldn't fail before I'd picked up a good head of steam."

"That's right," said Dom. "It was a cold night, and brake fluid thickens up in the cold. But after the car had a chance to warm up, the fluid just ran out, and so did your brakes."

"Couldn't it be rust?" asked Frank.

"Not a chance. See the way the hole is formed? Sharp, clean. Probably used a little nail. Whoever did this did a good job; the leaking brakes were strong enough to stop the car in ordinary conditions, but coming down Market Street . . ." he chuckled. "You just pumped the last of the fluid onto the pavement! You're lucky you didn't flip over and kill yourself."

Dom Ornuti seemed amused by my brush with death. Frank Olney was baffled.

"Who the hell would want to cut your brakes?" he demanded.

I shook my head and said I didn't know, but I told Frank about the threatening phone call I'd received late Friday night. He scolded me for not having reported it. I told him Pukey Boyle had been following me around for several days. And how could I forget Glenda Whalen—she of the bad temper and bruising fists?

"You've sure made yourself popular," he said, shaking his head. "Why don't you just back off this story? Let a man handle it. George Walsh."

"I'll be fine," I said. "And I don't need Georgie Porgie stealing my story."

"Suit yourself. Much as I'd like to, Ellie, I can't guarantee your safety if you decide to stay on this story."

I looked up at the blackened brake lines again and groaned. My head hurt. This was becoming more than a minor annoyance, more than a sock in the mouth or a car in my rearview mirror. Whoever it was who wanted me dead was brazen and able.

⁂

Dom Ornuti didn't know anything about Tommy Quint's car, but he referred me to Vinnie Donati, the mechanic who had worked on it. Over the phone, Vinnie told me he had started on Tommy's car the previous Saturday afternoon, two days after Thanksgiving, and Tommy picked it up late in the week—Thursday or Friday. I asked him if the car had been leaking oil.

"No, that wasn't it. The car's a rust bucket, full of problems. Me, I wouldn't have bothered fixing it. The timing was all screwed up, and one of the valves is cracked. But it runs."

"Are you're sure there was no oil leak?" I asked.

"Surprising, ain't it? But the car didn't lose a drop of oil in the five days I had it in the shop. The floor under that bomb was so clean, I'd let my two-year-old eat off it."

"You're a regular Father of the Year, aren't you, Vinnie? So how come Tommy Quint drives such a jalopy?"

Vinnie chuckled. "His old man ain't Nelson Rockefeller."

⁂

Before leaving Phil's Garage, I knelt down, my backside in the air, and took a long look at the brakes under Fadge's car. I felt silly, especially since I could hardly have recognized sabotage without Dom Ornuti's blackened index finger pointing the way. When I rose to get into the car, I noticed Billy Jenkins and two mechanics leaning against the wall, coolly contemplating my form. They had watched the entire show and were grinning broadly at me. I ducked into the front seat, no more confident of my safety, and drove home without incident.

I sensed something was off beam as soon as I entered the stairway leading up to my flat. The doorknob twirled uselessly on its spindle, clearly stripped by force. There was no one in the apartment, but someone had recently finished ransacking my humble home. The floor was strewn with things that had once sat on tables, counters, and bookshelves. The cleaning closet and dresser drawers had been turned inside out. Even the refrigerator was empty, its contents spoiling on the kitchen floor. Among the smashed beer bottles, in the puddles of spilled milk and melted butter, and underneath the ripening cold cuts, dozens of rolls of film—all ruined—had been pulled out of their canisters and exposed to the light. But the saddest sight of all was the bathroom. Most of my expensive developing equipment had been destroyed, chemicals poured on the tiles, photographic paper burned in the tub. I brought a hand to my aching head and went to lie down on the couch. I called Frank to tell him what had happened. He lectured me again, then said he'd ask the city police to look in on me. Why did I have to start that rumor about Julio's film?

⁂

MONDAY, DECEMBER 5, 1960

As a rule, I am not easy to find when off duty. When I began working at the *Republic*, I would call in at least ten times a day to let them know where I could be found, even on my days off. But after a few weeks, I realized that the emergency phone call and big story weren't coming. So I had a police scanner installed in my car to know what was going on. The system had worked for me on occasion; I had gotten the jump on a couple of stories listening to the scanner instead of the hit parade. But nothing compared to the dispatch I'd picked up Saturday, November 26.

Now, with my company car dead, I was deaf to the world. But at least I was mobile again; Charlie Reese provided a new set of wheels. By eight thirty Monday morning, I was tooling around town in a nifty red-and-black Dodge Royal Lancer. There was the hint of a mildew smell I couldn't quite locate, but it was a swell car.

I stopped at Fiorello's for a cup of coffee and a look at the crossword, but I never got the chance. Fadge met me at the door.

"Frank Olney's looking for you. He's at the Mohawk Motel and wants you there right away."

"What happened?" I asked, heading back to my car.

"Someone broke into the motel and tore the place apart."

The Mohawk Motel parking lot was clogged with police vehicles for the second time in a week. Stan Pulaski waved me through the cordon, and I parked my Dodge next to the sheriff's unmarked cruiser. Big Frank, arms crossed over his chest, was leaning against the Dr Pepper machine as he talked to the Thin Man, Don Czerulniak. We exchanged good mornings, news about my black eyes and bandaged nose, then we all went inside.

The sheriff led the way, through the office to Jean's plundered parlor. Furniture had been upset, drawers emptied, and carpet pulled up. Her bedroom had suffered a similar fate, with Jean's clothes and possessions scattered everywhere.

"What do you think they were looking for?" I asked, certain I knew.

"It's hard to say what all is missing," said Frank, "seeing as it ain't my stuff. But one thing's sure: they took Jean's revolver."

"Just a routine robbery?" I asked.

"Looks like it to me. Some local kids, maybe, read that Jean was in jail, so they took advantage. Probably looking for money, jewels, what have you."

We stepped outside for a smoke.

"Your robbery scenario seems possible," I said. "Except a girl was murdered here last week; her roommate in Boston, ditto; and someone tried to kill me the other night. My place was ransacked yesterday, too."

"Well, what do you make of this, then?"

"From the looks of this place, there's nothing to steal but a few towels."

"So what are you saying?" asked the DA.

"It was robbery, all right. But not like you think. The burglar was looking for something in particular, the same thing he'd been looking for in my house. Film."

"What?" chimed Frank and Don.

"I haven't said anything till now because I figured people would think I was crazy. But I believe Julio shot some photos the night Jordan was killed."

"Goddamn it, Ellie! Did he tell you that?" asked Frank, ready to erupt.

"Of course not," I said. "He denied it. But I've had this suspicion since we searched this place. We all believe Julio was living here, right? Well, Jean's bathroom had been used as a darkroom up until a day or two before we searched it. I know photo-developing chemicals, and someone had been using them in there, trust me. Remember those strange questions I asked Jean Trent about clothespins, Frank? That's what I was driving at."

"I was wondering about that," he said, relieved. "I thought maybe it was your time of the month."

"Frank!"

"Sorry, but it was kind of out of left field."

"Well, you can still see where the countertop was discolored by spills," I said, glaring at the sheriff.

"What makes you think it was Julio and not Jean?" asked the DA.

"Jean doesn't know the first thing about photography. Doesn't even own a camera."

"And you're sure Julio does?"

"He was in the photo club in high school." I paused for effect. "Along with Jordan Shaw."

The two exchanged looks.

"So what's on the film?" asked the sheriff.

"I don't know. The murderer perhaps. Some other clues. Something worth killing for."

The two men weighed the plausibility of my theory. Frank was struggling with the idea. The DA was hard to read.

"What makes you so sure Julio took any pictures at all?" asked Frank. "And if he did, why would he go on rotting in jail when the pictures could prove his innocence?"

"Julio is a voyeur, a serious one, if we are to believe the stories. Jordan Shaw was too good to pass up. And, furthermore, why lose the moment forever? Julio is a good amateur photographer, with a darkroom of his own to develop the racy pictures. As a matter of fact, I'd wager he's been shooting the action through these windows for as long as he's worked here."

"So where's the collection?" asked the DA.

"I don't know. But the darkroom was dismantled and is stashed somewhere. My guess is that the candid photos are as precious to Julio as the processing equipment. I can't believe he'd throw any of it away. If we can find his camera gear, we'll find the pictures."

"Maybe he took out a safety deposit box," said the sheriff, finally dismissing my theory. "This kid's in hot water, charged with murder.

You really think he's going to worry about saving some dirty pictures he'll never see again?"

"Who knows?"

The three of us pondered that for a while.

"Can I buy you a drink?" asked the DA, fishing in his pockets for change. Nobody. He deposited three nickels in the Dr Pepper machine and pulled a bottle through one of the refrigerated holes.

"If I can locate Jean Trent's woody," I continued, "I think I'll find more than a tire jack in the trunk."

"You still going off on that?" asked Frank, throwing his hands in the air. "I told you that car was junked six months ago in Rensselaer County."

"And I saw it a week ago, right out back here."

"Go ahead and waste your time looking," said Frank. "I've got a murderer locked up already. As for this two-bit burglary, I couldn't care less. Let Jean's insurance company handle it," and he stomped off to confer with some of his deputies.

"How about you, Don?" I asked the DA.

He sipped his Dr Pepper. "First thing I'm going to do," he said, squinting into the mild December sun, "is drop murder charges against Julio Hernandez."

CHAPTER TWELVE

Just a few hundred yards from the Mohawk River, I found the house Victor Trent had left to his sister Reba. The ground floor of the brick building had been a furniture warehouse: Johnston's Mill Refinishing, according to the faded lettering painted on the side. Upstairs was an apartment. The building stood alone amid the elm trees, forgotten, abandoned. A shallow creek, no more than a trickle of cold, clear water in wintertime, skirted the house and emptied into the river below. From the crumbling concrete sidewalk, the view consisted of overgrown shrubs and weeds and a dirt pathway to the front of the building. A weathered wooden staircase clung to the east side of the structure, leading unevenly to the upstairs. By all appearances, the shop had lain fallow for much longer than the home above it. The doors were padlocked and the windows boarded up, but around back, I found a loose two-by-four and a way inside.

My idea, of course, was that Julio had hidden his film equipment here, but there wasn't the slightest indication of his or Jean's presence anywhere. Someone had been inside, but it looked more like mischievous teenagers than amateur photographers. Beer cans, cigarette butts, and a hot rod magazine lay in the dust. Some creative soul had scrawled obscenities on the dirty windowpanes, complete with primitive representations of male and female anatomies.

The workshop itself was nothing more than a shell. Unidentifiable instruments, tools, and pieces of broken furniture cluttered the floor. Rusty hinges, boxes full of bent nails and screws, one jaw of a vice, cans of solidified lacquers, and dried-up stains ... An insurance calendar from 1946 still hung on the wall above a caved-in worktable. Julio couldn't have hidden his things in the shop without leaving a trail of footprints in the thick dust on the floor. Besides, no self-respecting photographer would store his equipment in such a filthy place. I pushed past the two-by-four and stepped back outside.

The upstairs was locked tight, having been vacated two years earlier, and there was little sign of life. I trusted my instincts and decided it would be a waste of time and effort to get inside; this had been Reba Trent's place, not Jean's.

Driving back to town, I stopped at a red light at the bottom of Windsor Street. Up the hill and a few streets over, Judge Shaw's proper home sat on two-and-a-half acres of manicured landscape. When the light turned, I shifted into low and headed up the steep incline.

⌘

"Miss Stone," said Audrey Shaw, in her cool manner. "I'm afraid the judge is not in."

"I didn't come to see him," I said. "I wanted to talk to you."

"What about?"

"Jordan's boyfriends. You seem to have been more in touch with her personal life than your husband was."

"I was on my way out, but I suppose I have a few minutes. Come in."

Audrey Shaw led me down the hall in silence, her slim hips swaying easily under the tapered navy skirt. She was an attractive woman, no matter her age, and she knew it. She invited me to sit in the parlor, then offered me a cigarette from a box on the cherrywood coffee table between us. Not my brand, but I didn't quibble.

"What happened to your face?" she asked. I'd tried to hide the black eyes and bruises under makeup with mixed results.

"Just a car accident," I said. "I'm fine."

"So, how can I help you?" she asked.

"I've spoken to the judge about some of Jordan's boyfriends, but I'm interested in your opinion." She lit her cigarette, and I lit mine. She stared at me, composed, waiting for me to explain myself. "If you could tell me about them—her boyfriends, I mean—I might learn something."

"All of them?"

"Yes, I think that would be best. We could start with Tommy Quint."

Audrey Shaw crossed her nylons and set about thinking. "Tommy was like an annoying puppy dog. He was an average boy in love with an extraordinary girl. They began going steady in the ninth grade," she said, inhaling from her cigarette. "He was nice looking, and serious, too. He started working at that ice cream parlor at fourteen and never acted like a typical teenager. While the other kids were loitering on street corners, experimenting with their first beer, stealing their first kisses, Tommy was scooping ice cream and drawing Cokes."

"Not a good deal for a teenager."

"I don't know if I'd go that far. Tommy enjoyed a privileged position at that place."

"Fiorello's," I prompted, sure she knew the name. "Privileged how?"

"Privileged because every boy and girl in high school wanted a part-time job at that place, Fiorello's. Even Jordan asked that fat man for a job one summer, but he said he didn't need any more help. She went to Europe instead." She smiled to herself. "Strange, isn't it? Jerking sodas in a small-town ice cream shop like Fiorello's qualifies as status . . ."

"You're not from around here, are you?" I asked with a conspiratorial smile.

"Baltimore," she said simply. "Neither are you. I know you're from New York, and I'll bet not Brooklyn or Queens."

She smiled sadly, probably thinking of her daughter. "Yes, I'm a snob, Miss Stone. But don't kid yourself. You're as big a snob as I, but you're a liberal and won't admit it to yourself. You probably voted for Kennedy."

"What about Tommy Quint?" I asked, ignoring her remark. I didn't want to offend her with my politics; I'd seen the Nixon bumper sticker outside, after all.

"Oh, yes," she said, remembering herself. "The girls liked Tommy very much in junior high school; he was handsome and polite. But that job marooned him outside the circle of his peers. I suspect he was considered somewhat different, and I'm sure *you* know what an impairment that can be for a teenager."

"You say that as if my peers might have considered me different in high school," I said.

"Of course they did."

I nodded. "Maybe Tommy enjoyed being different."

"I can't say. But I know he was crazy for Jordan. Every so often, she tired of him and went out with other boys. For Tommy, it was the end of the world. He moped, whined, cried, and when she'd had her fill of the excitement of someone new, she'd take him back. Jordan was kinder than I would have been. Just as she was with Glenda Whalen. I never understood how she could stand that girl. Just an unhappy, unlikeable soul. As for Tommy, his delicate nature turned my stomach, to be quite frank. No woman likes that in a man, I'm sure you'll agree."

"I'll bet Pukey Boyle never shed a tear in his life," I said and waited for an answer.

"Ah, the charming Mr. Boyle . . . Well, that was another mess."

"Did you ever meet him?"

"Yes, several times. Jordan took up with him about four years ago, the summer before she went to college."

"How did they meet?"

Audrey Shaw took a last puff on her cigarette and stubbed it out in the ashtray before her. She leaned forward, eyes bright, lips parted just so: the pose she'd perfected at mixers and cocktail parties in Baltimore to capture the complete attention of her interlocutor.

"Jordan went to Winandauga Lake to a summertime bash at the camp of a friend. She was to spend the weekend with the others but came back unexpectedly that first night. When her father and I asked who had brought her home, she said Henry Boyle." She sniffed. "It wasn't until later that we found out that he was known as Pukey."

"Did she ever talk to you about him?"

"Not much, but she shared some things. Most of the information we got on Mr. Boyle came from Jordan's friends, who were justifiably concerned."

"Tommy Quint?"

"For one."

"And Glenda Whalen?"

"For another. You're a clever girl, Miss Stone, but I'm not sure I like that. I can't figure your angle in all this."

"How do you mean?"

"What are you after? Why do you care about Jordan and Ginny? Why aren't you married? Why do you chase after murderers?"

"That's a lot of questions."

"Well, why *do* you care?"

"I believe in justice," I said, defensive. "And I do care about Jordan. I feel . . . an affinity with her."

Audrey Shaw seemed horrified. "Indeed? How?"

"In ways you might not understand. We're nearly the same age, and . . ."

"With all respect, young lady," she announced, "I think that that's where the resemblance ends. I thought your motivation might have something to do with you, with your own life."

"So you know about my father?" I asked, staring her down. I think she enjoyed transferring some of her pain to me.

"Yes, Harrison told me all about it. He'd got it from Fred Peruso and Sheriff Olney. I wonder if that's why you're playing detective. From what I understand, you performed brilliantly in that investigation."

"That has nothing to do with your daughter," I said. "And this is my job as well. I don't have any other income, and I need it."

"But you enjoy this a little too much, I think," she said. "Never mind. Let's continue."

"Were any other friends concerned about Jordan and Pukey Boyle?"

"Are you referring to Greg Hewert?"

"I'll get to him in a minute. Anyone else?"

"Not that I know of."

"Did you or the judge discourage Jordan from seeing Pukey Boyle? Was he good to her?"

"My husband and I let Jordan make her own decisions when it came to boys. In general, she used good judgment. Mr. Boyle was an aberration, of course. As for how he treated her, Jordan never complained nor showed any reasons to."

"I spoke with him last week," I said. "And he said some things that may offend you, Mrs. Shaw. If you prefer, I won't tell you."

"Then why bring it up at all?"

"Because I'm curious to know if he was typical or, as you put it, an aberration."

"You can't say anything to hurt Jordan now, Miss Stone. Ask me what you will."

"He seemed bitter about their relationship, but that could be just so much bruised male pride talking. He did imply, however, that Jordan led boys on only to leave them disappointed."

Audrey Shaw bowed her head, and I couldn't exactly read her thoughts. After a pause, she looked me straight in the eye. "I think I know the expression," she said. "It's nicer than some other names a boy might call a girl."

"Oh, he used some of those as well," I said. "In Boston I came across a letter he'd sent to Jordan a couple of years ago. It was short and sweet: he told her to rot in hell and called her a rather ugly name."

Audrey Shaw straightened up and frowned. "Henry Boyle wrote Jordan a letter?" she asked.

"Yes. At least I assumed he'd written it. It wasn't signed."

"Ah," she said, leaning forward again, reasserting her composure. "That wasn't Henry Boyle. Tommy Quint wrote that letter."

"Really?" I asked. "It was so . . . unexpectedly violent."

Audrey Shaw shrugged.

I asked her how Jordan and Pukey had broken off, and she explained that Jordan had simply tired of the novelty.

"She once told me his reputation was exaggerated," she said. "That he was a good person deep down. Misunderstood. But, ultimately, she wasn't interested in molding him into something better. She was no Pygmalion," and she looked doubtfully at me, as if she had overestimated me.

"And he's no Galatea," I answered.

She smiled touché. "Oh, but that's right, your father was a famous professor of literature."

I felt a sharp pain stab me in the right temple. "Could we please not talk about him?" I asked.

"As you wish," she sniffed. "Of course, you don't have the same qualms about discussing my murdered daughter."

"Mrs. Shaw, I'm very sorry for Jordan and your loss, but this is not a lark for me. Nor is it some mixed-up attempt to come to grips with my father's murder or my personal bereavement. I'm here to help find Jordan's killer."

Audrey Shaw smiled knowingly at me. It was a cruel, wicked smile, approaching delight. "Miss Stone, you don't need to explain anything to me. Only you can know your true motivations."

"May we continue?" I asked, terrified to move a muscle, lest the swollen tear in my left eye overflow the lower lid. I resisted, didn't blink for nearly a half minute before she looked away and stood to pour herself a drink.

"Something for you?" she asked. "I've heard you do well with whiskey. Or is that an off-limits topic as well?"

"My drinking is fair game," I said, relishing the prospect of a short one.

For all the practiced tricks and affectations, Audrey Shaw was a shattered woman. Sharp and cunning, to be sure, but damaged and in desperate need to compensate for the death of her daughter. Wounding others must have given her some kind of wicked respite from her pain. She acted the ice queen, but under the façade, a deep, aching agony lurked, and it showed each time she forgot herself.

"This Greg Hewert," I began, savoring the first sting of the judge's Chivas Regal, "Franny Bartolo told me that he and Jordan saw each other during their senior year in high school."

"That's a lie," she said adamantly. "Jordan and Greg were fast friends. Nothing more, I assure you."

"Franny and Tommy felt otherwise."

"That's because they have small minds. Typical of this place. Those two were like brother and sister. I don't know where Tommy and Franny ever got such an idea."

"They said it began when the judge's father was sick, and you and your husband went to New York to visit him. Glenda Whalen saw Greg's car here late one night."

"That's ridiculous," she huffed. "Harrison went alone on that trip. I stayed home with Jordan. Don't you think I would have known if she had seen him here? In this very house?"

I didn't know what to believe. Could I be duped by a dimwit like Franny Bartolo? I doubted it. She obviously believed what she told me about Greg and Jordan. Was Audrey Shaw lying, then? Or just ignorant of her daughter's scrimmages with the quarterback?

"What about David Jerrold?" I asked. "Did you ever meet him?"

"No, but I knew of him."

"Why did you tell me you didn't know his name?"

"I didn't want my husband to know that I'd concealed Jordan's behavior from him. Besides, I figured you would find him easily enough. Why else would I have given you that photograph?"

"But the judge said Jordan planned on studying engineering after graduation. Wouldn't that have been awkward?"

"I assure you it would never have come to that. I work slowly and deliberately, Miss Stone, and I wasn't about to let that happen."

"So, what can you tell me about David Jerrold?"

"I discovered their liaison by accident on my last trip to Boston," she said. The alcohol was loosening her tongue, if not her geniality. "Jordan and I had planned a girls' weekend, just the two of us. I arrived late Friday afternoon, and after tea at the Ritz-Carlton, we walked to her apartment on Marlborough Street. When I went to hang a skirt and blouse in her closet, I came across two pairs of men's slacks and three button-down shirts. I confronted Jordan, and we had it out."

"What did she say?"

"She couldn't very well deny it, and in the end she told me all about him."

I fixed my stare on Audrey Shaw, urging her silently to tell me more. Perhaps it was the Scotch talking, but she told me more about her daughter's relationship with David Jerrold than I ever would have expected from her.

"Jordan explained how they had met: at an orientation meeting for the India trip. He was some kind of expert, it seems. She said he charmed her with his good looks and posh English accent. I was concerned, of course, but she said he was the man she was going to marry."

"Didn't you know he was married already?"

Audrey Shaw's nostrils flared. "Jordan didn't mention it that day. I found out the following afternoon when her friend Jeffrey met us for lunch. While Jordan was away from the table, he told me Jerrold was married and had a son."

Audrey Shaw took a taste of her Scotch and slipped another cigarette between her lips. "I decided to handle the matter myself, without Jordan's knowledge, since she'd already misled me once. It was obvious that this man was abusing his position of authority to take advantage of the romantic inclinations of a young girl."

"What did you do?"

"I phoned him and told him to break it off with Jordan. I threatened to tell his wife."

"Did that work?" I asked, remembering the letter I'd stolen.

"He put on a fine performance, protesting his innocence. He said he had no idea what I was talking about, that Jordan was just a student he had seen around the department. I didn't believe him, of course, and promised to go through with my threat if he ever saw Jordan again."

"What date was that?"

"Saturday. It must have been the 29th of October," she said.

"But Jerrold didn't break off with Jordan until two weeks later."

"I wonder how you find out these things," she said. "I received a phone call from Jeffrey Nichols about two weeks later, on November 12th. I remember the date because it was Harrison's birthday, and we were having drinks, right where we're sitting now, before leaving for dinner with Dr. Terrell and his wife, next door. Jeffrey thought I might be interested to know that David Jerrold and Jordan were having a romantic dinner in a little restaurant in the North End."

"I see."

"It took all my strength to contain my fury. I couldn't very well make a scene that night; we were expected at the Terrells'. But first thing in the morning I phoned Jerrold's wife and told her everything, except Jordan's name of course. I didn't want to blacken my own daughter's name."

"How did the wife react?"

"She was speechless."

I knew how she'd reacted: she'd flown into a jealous rage, searched her husband's belongings for clues, and found the love note from Jordan in his jacket. Then she threatened to leave Jerrold and take their son with her. He broke things off with Jordan, but like a greedy weasel scared off by the barnyard dog, he couldn't resist raiding the chicken coop after a couple of weeks had passed. Jerrold had never wanted to dump Jordan; my bet was that he was in love, or obsessed with her, up until the very night she was murdered. And that obsession may have played a part in her death.

When I finally stood to take my leave of Audrey Shaw, it was nearly five thirty. We had polished off the better part of a bottle of Chivas, so I was feeling no pain. Mrs. Shaw didn't get out of her chair. She stared off at the wall at nothing in particular and ignored my farewell. She slumped into a deep melancholy, the one she'd been so expert in hiding, and I went to let myself out.

"Miss Stone?" It was Judge Shaw in the foyer, hanging his hat and coat in the closet. "What are you doing here? What's going on?"

"I was talking with your wife," I said, feeling quite unwelcome.

"Have you been drinking?" he asked. "Already?" When I didn't answer, he shook his head. "What happened to your face? You look terrible."

I explained. Car accident.

"Were you drinking then, too?"

"No, sir," I said softly.

"Well?" he asked. "Do you have any news for me? How is your investigation coming along?"

"I've hit a roadblock, sir."

He ran a peevish hand through his silver hair. "Perhaps if you put in the same effort as you did for your father's case . . ."

That was a haymaker. I put my head down and walked purposefully out of his house. I had just yanked open the car door when he caught up to me.

"Miss Stone, stop! You can't run off like that."

"Why not?" I shrieked, and he slammed the car door shut. I huffed and puffed in the cold night air, fed up with the digs he and his wife had doled out concerning my father. "What do I owe you?"

The judge was surprised to see my anger, and he stammered some words of apology. I glared at him, and he turned away from my prying stare. Then he sighed and continued in a measured voice.

"You must understand my disappointment, Miss Stone. I was hoping for better results by now."

I circled around him to fix my eyes on his. Mine, blackened and bloodshot; his, steely gray in silent, lonely agony.

He seemed to be weighing a difficult question.

"Are you Jewish?" he asked finally.

"What?"

My wife said that you are Jewish," he said. "Is that true? Are you Jewish?"

I didn't know what to say and uttered something incredibly stupid: "Not so you'd notice."

"What does that mean?"

"Well, I don't go to temple," I said. "Why would you ask me that? Does it matter?"

He shook his head and looked away. "No, it doesn't matter. I just wanted to know."

"Know what?"

"Does your religion give you any . . . solace, comfort?"

I shook my head. "No."

"Neither does mine," he mumbled.

"Do you want to talk about it, sir?" I asked.

"No," he said. "This is something I must cope with by myself. Alone."

"But . . ."

"No!" he shouted.

I fumbled through my notes in the phone booth at Fiorello's, searching for David Jerrold's phone number. His wife answered, and I identified myself as a reporter investigating the Tufts murders.

"My husband isn't home," she said, though I knew she was lying.

"Actually, I wanted to speak to you, Mrs. Jerrold," I said, still a little drunk from my cocktails with Audrey Shaw.

"Me?" she asked. "I don't know anything about those murders; I never even met those girls."

"True enough," I said. "But one of them knew your husband."

There was an icy pause. "What are you implying?"

"You may not have known Jordan Shaw, Mrs. Jerrold, but I believe you spoke to her mother about three weeks ago."

More silence.

"What do you want?"

"I'm trying to find a killer."

"Are you saying that my husband is involved in these killings?"

Before I could answer, David Jerrold wrenched the phone from his wife's hand.

"Damn you! What's the meaning of phoning my wife and spreading your despicable accusations?"

"I asked you for help once, and you stonewalled me," I said, emboldened by the whiskey. "I called your wife because I have new information that you concealed from me."

"What are you talking about?"

"First of all, you denied being involved with Jordan Shaw."

Jerrold hesitated a moment; his wife was surely standing beside him, hanging on his every word. He spoke carefully: "What else could I have done?"

"All right," I conceded. "But Audrey Shaw threatened to tell your wife everything if you didn't break it off with Jordan, and ultimately she did. Why were you afraid of your wife finding out about Jordan from me when she already knew?"

Again Jerrold chose his words wisely. "It's only natural to avoid reminders of such unpleasant topics," he said, and I could hear him sweating. "Listen, Miss Stone. Why can't you just leave us alone?"

"That would suit you just fine," I said. "Jordan Shaw and Virginia White are dead. Tragic, sure, but the end of the story. Well, not exactly. You see, while you've been holed up at home, somebody's tried to kill me, too. Cut my brakes and ransacked my apartment."

"What do you want from me, damn it!"

I borrowed a line from my midnight caller: "Does *butt out* mean anything to you?"

There was a pause, then he cleared his throat. "Look," he whispered, "I don't know what your cryptic message means, but I did not try to kill you. I'm sorry for your trouble, but can't you leave me be? I know nothing of this affair."

"Someone is trying to kill me," I said. "Give me a hand, here."

"If you fear for your life, Miss Stone, I suggest you follow your own advice and butt out. You'll soon be left alone," and he hung up.

Next, I called Morrissey to fill him in on the burglary at the Mohawk. He thought it might be local kids, but the coincidence was troubling. Then I told him about the threatening phone call and the brake job someone had done on my car.

"I just spoke to Jerrold," I said. "He refuses to help me. Can you squeeze him a little? And while you're at it, could you check if he owns a second car?"

"I'll go see him tomorrow," said Morrissey. "And by the way, you'll be happy to know that Nichols turned up a couple of hours ago in Worcester. He's fine, but his prints were among those in the girls' apart-

ment. State police are bringing him back in now. I've got other trou-
bles. A couple of other students from the department have dropped out
of sight. A guy named Singh and another named Mohammed."

"Dead or guilty?"

"Maybe both. At any rate, I've been dropping hints at the Engineering Department that some photographs of the Shaw murder might
exist. Maybe that's why they've gone underground."

"Then I'll have to beat some bushes to flush them out. I'm going to
put it in the paper."

"Put what in the paper?"

"That pictures of the murder exist, of course."

"I think you're crazy," he laughed. "You're asking for trouble."

※

I was just drunk enough to pull the stunt I had in mind. I cajoled Fadge
into helping me. He didn't want to at first but soon got into the spirit
of the proceedings. I dropped a dime into the phone and dialed George
Walsh's home number. Walsh answered in his affected gentrified
manner, voice rising and dipping over the phonemes of a simple *hello*. I
handed the phone to Fadge for his big performance.

"Don't say a word," whispered Fadge, doing his best imitation of my
own midnight caller. I'd coached him beforehand but was impressed by
his flair. He was great! "Keep your mouth shut and listen," he continued,
"or you'll never solve the Shaw murder. The case has been botched by
the police, and fouled up by your stupid paper from the start. Evidence
was stolen. There are photos of the murder. The Puerto Rican kid shot
pictures through the bathroom window, but someone grabbed the film
when they searched the motel. That's your tip, Bozo, don't blow it," and
he hung up before Georgie could utter a syllable.

Fadge took me to Tedesco's for a pizza after closing, then dropped
me home around two. The wheels were in motion.

※

Monday night brought a black sky and freezing temperatures, the coldest of the season. I pulled a second quilt out of the closet and threw it over the bed, but I still didn't sleep well. A half pizza, washed down with several Scotches, doesn't agree with me, no matter how nice the company.

⌘

TUESDAY, DECEMBER 6, 1960

Monday morning, I rolled out of my warm bed around eight and shuffled into the bath. I felt lousy, but the memory of Fadge's performance the night before cheered me. I stopped by Fiorello's for a coffee and a poppy-seed roll. Feeling my oats after breakfast, I had an idea of where to find Julio's stash.

"Wish me luck, Fadge," I said, heading for my car. The Royal Lancer roared to a start on the first turn of the key, and I blessed Charlie Reese.

⌘

Lake Winandauga. Its name suggests a quiet waterway nestled amid tall pines; a place where Indians in their canoes once sliced through cool, clear water; a miracle of nature, discovered and settled millennia ago by the natives. Actually, the Army Corps of Engineers built the lake in 1936 when they stopped up a dripping stream known as Winandauga Creek. It was a WPA project, part of a larger plan to control the Hudson River's water levels and stabilize the reservoirs downstate. The dam also provided a modest source of electricity for the surrounding area, and the leisure preserve was gravy.

The farmland in the valley above Winandauga Creek became lakebed, and cheap, sleepy forest was transformed into valuable beachfront. Victor Trent had bought some of the land in the early '30s, a few years before the lake project was announced, and he hit the jackpot. As Frank Olney put it: "Third-class fellow, first-class luck." Later,

Trent built an enchanting cottage beneath a canopy of thick, verdant trees, about forty yards from the water. The view from the porch was a sublime panorama of rolling hills, blue water, and lazy skies. I wondered how I could ever afford such bliss on my meager salary. Assuming I could hold onto my job at all . . .

The house was closed for the winter, padlocked and deserted. I got through a window easily enough, though, and found myself in a small parlor. There were a few books—old furniture-repair manuals and *Reader's Digest* condensed novels—and piles of movie and crime magazines. A black-and-white print of Jean Trent in a wistful pose dominated the room from the brick fireplace's mantelpiece. I peeked into a few drawers, finding nothing but pencils, a yellowing pad of paper, candles, and a box of kitchen matches. In the bedroom, two dusty twin mattresses were rolled up on top of a narrow double bed. A warping chest of drawers against the wall was empty except for two bags of mothballs and more candles. My search of the closets produced no cameras or film. There was no basement or attic. I squeezed back through the window I'd jimmied and explored the grounds.

The property fronted the lake on the north side. A sloping grass lawn led to the water, where a wooden dock reached thirty feet into the lake. Along the shore, a clean, stony beach broke the gentle waves. Foraging into the woods near the shore, I came across a rusting corrugated-tin shed. The lock didn't hold for long, but there was nothing worth seeing inside—an old outboard motor, two splintering oars, faded orange life-jackets, and some fishing gear. I tramped through the woods flanking the lawn, pushed through a thicket of weed trees, and there it was. In the small clearing before me sat the weathered Pontiac station wagon.

A glance through the windows showed nothing inside. I was discouraged and, had I not searched so long, probably would have given up there. But I decided to break a window and have a closer look. Nothing under the seats, still nothing in the glove compartment. Then I looked in the back and spotted the spare-tire well. There was no tire inside. Hidden in the belly of the car was my trove.

A Kodak Pony 135, about ten years old; a dozen or so rolls of film; a

medium zoom; jars marked *silver nitrate*, *hypo*, and *fixer*; clothes pins—
the kind with spring jaws; twenty feet of clothes line; an enlarger; and
a box of Kodak photosensitive paper. At the bottom, sealed in a protec-
tive envelope, I found about a hundred black-and-white negatives. My
skin crawled. These were the fruits of Julio's long hours spent spying
through bathroom windows. But after twenty minutes of squinting at
negative images of rumpled beds and naked bodies, I gave up. As far as
I could see, there were no pictures of Jordan (or of me, for that matter)
anywhere in the bunch.

I put the negatives back, covered Julio's equipment in the tire well,
then searched the rest of the car. I ran my hand along the floors, dug
into the crevasses of the fraying thatch of seat fabric, and inspected
the engine and undercarriage of the car. No exposed film or negatives
hidden anywhere.

As I clapped my hands clean, wondering if I'd neglected some
clever hiding spot in or on the car, I heard a twig snap behind me.

I reeled around to locate the source of the noise, but it was a gray
day in thick woods. An eerie silence followed. Nothing stirred.

"Who's there?" I asked. No answer. "Who's there?"

Still no answer. I turned slowly, scanning the dense trees for some
color, some human life. Then a figure stepped up behind me.

I recognized him at first sight: the creepy guy who'd watched me
from across the room at Tedesco's the night of Jordan Shaw's wake.
Greg Hewert. I was actually relieved; at least it wasn't Pukey Boyle.

"Greg, you scared me," I panted. "What are you doing here?"

He said nothing, just took a step toward me. His mouth hung open
slightly on one side in a strange, lopsided smile, as he stared at me with
hungry, blank eyes. He took another step. I recoiled, backed up into a
tree, and froze.

"What are you doing, Greg?" I asked more insistently.

"Come on, Ellie," he said. "I've asked around. It's not all work for
you, is it? You like a good time, don't you?"

"Get out of my way," I said and tried to push past him. He barred
the path and forced me back against the tree.

"Come on, don't go rushing off. We're just getting to know each other."

"What do you want?"

"The same as you. I saw the way you looked at me at Tedesco's and at the funeral parlor. Then you called me to flirt, didn't you?"

"Are you sick?" I asked, sneering at him. "I was looking at everyone. And I was doing my job when I called you."

"You don't have to act. I know when a girl's interested, and you're not exactly saving yourself for Mr. Right, are you?"

He took another step toward me.

"Wait a minute, Greg," I stammered, holding my hands out. "Don't touch me! I know karate." No effect, and a lie to boot. He continued his menacing approach.

I made another dash to get by him, but he grabbed my arm and wrenched it, yanking me toward him.

"Let me go, you creep!" I yelled. "Take your hands off me!"

I pulled and tried to run, but he held fast, and I slapped him hard on the cheek. His eyes ran bloodred, and he reeled me back in, wrapping his other arm around my shoulders, crushing my face against his chest. I squirmed and fought, thrashed legs and arms, losing both my shoes, but he only squeezed tighter, now cutting off my breathing. As the struggle went on, as the air became scarcer, I was seized with the panic that I would suffocate. I dug my nails deep into his arm and raked them over his skin. He roared, and his determination turned instantly to a violent anger. He threw me to the ground like a ragdoll and fell on top of me, knocking what little wind I had left out of me. My chest burned for air, and I thought I would lose consciousness. Then he pushed up off me, and I gasped for breath, but my lungs wouldn't fill.

Greg slobbered on me, saliva bubbling and dripping from his mouth as he struggled to immobilize my flailing arms. He yanked my coat off my shoulders and clutched the neck of my blouse. For the first time in my life, I doubted my knack of wriggling out of tight situations with persistent men. I'd done it so many times, always able to avoid the worst. But this time was different. He was going to rape me.

I screamed. He clamped one hand over my mouth and clawed at my blouse with the other, tearing the fabric and my brassiere and scratching my chest in the process. I continued to thrash about beneath him, twisting, kicking, and spitting. Then he took me by the shoulders, hoisted me roughly off my back, and slammed me back down, bouncing my head off the muddy ground. And he did it again, and a third and a fourth and a fifth time, until I went limp, dazed, gasping for air as my addled head swam. Now he positioned himself atop of me, straddling me on the wet ground, and pinned my arms over my head. I wasn't moving, could no longer fight back. Then he pulled my blouse up over my face. He was breathing hard; I could hear it, feel it on my bare torso, as he reached under my skirt and began to rip and pull the fabric.

Then he fell forward onto my head, into the mud, relinquishing his hold on my clothing and on my body. He crawled off me, and I heard a grunting and commotion. I rolled to my left and pushed the torn blouse out of my face. Looking back over my shoulder, panting like a drowned man rescued on the shore, I saw a large man in a black pea jacket throttling Greg Hewert, punching him repeatedly in the head, reducing him to a whimpering, semiconscious, curled mass within mere seconds.

The man in black hovered over his defeated opponent like a gladiator in victory, huffing in the cold air, relishing his dominance before the coup de grâce. Then he planted a heavy boot broadside into his prostrate victim, driving a deep, heaving grunt from his belly, over his diaphragm, and out his lungs. Greg lay on the ground, bleeding from the nose and mouth, and gasping for breath. I watched, transfixed, unable to move, trying to regain my own wind. Then, realizing too late I'd lost my chance to flee, I remembered the man in the black peacoat.

His adversary humbled and down for the count, he turned to me. That's when I saw it was Pukey Boyle, as tall as a mountain and twice as strong as the man who'd tried to rape me.

Pukey hiked up his collar and slapped some imaginary dirt from his hands. "I don't like that guy," he muttered sullenly as he approached me.

I retreated, crab-walked backward in the mud, trying to escape him. I caught sight of his shoes: heavy, black biker's boots, not good for running. Then I looked up at him again, weighing my chances for a successful run for it, and I saw the insult and offense in his hard eyes, as if my fear had wounded him to the core. I stopped. After a moment, he took a step forward and offered his hand.

"You all right?"

I took his hand. He tried to help me up, but I wasn't ready. Sitting in the mud, my skirt still hiked up around my waist, I dissolved into hysterical sobbing. Pukey knelt in the mud and wrapped his arms around me.

I wept wildly into his chest, shaking with terrors, just now realizing the horror I had dodged. In that moment, I wanted only to cleave to the man who'd saved me from such an unspeakable fate. I gasped and choked, as much from the near asphyxiation I'd suffered as for the rape I'd narrowly escaped. My head pounded, and my arm ached where Greg had twisted it near the tree.

Pukey patted my back and soothed me as a mother would. He folded my skirt back to its intended length, adjusted my blouse, and buttoned my coat over it, restoring my modesty to me. At length, my breathing slowed, my sinews slackened, and a sense of numbness overcame me.

"Come on," he said finally. "You need to see a doctor."

I stared at him, blinking slowly, my pupils surely dilated from the pounding my head had taken. I think I looked over at Greg Hewert, still flat on the ground.

"No cops," said Pukey, shaking his head. "They'll ruin your reputation. I'll take care of him later. He won't bother you again. Trust me."

I was groggy, unaware of where I was or the day of the week, but I seem to recall hearing Buddy Holly singing "True Love Ways" as we raced down Route 5 toward New Holland. Then Sam Belson was holding up several fingers for me to count, and I vomited in the emergency room.

Hours later, I sat up in my hospital bed and wondered where I was. Fadge touched my arm and told me I was okay.

"Where's Pukey?" I asked.

"He left," said Fadge. "He said him and a buddy had some business to take care of. But what I don't get is how you fell down a hill and hit your head. What were you doing, anyway?"

"Fell down a hill? What are you talking about?" I asked.

"Boyle said you fell down a hill and hit your head. You probably don't remember anything."

I turned away on the pillow and said nothing.

⚬

I had suffered scratches, bruises, and a concussion, but no broken bones. By evening, I felt better. The nausea had passed, and the Darvon had dulled the pain in my head and back. Dr. Williston, a tall, avuncular man of seventy or seventy-five, insisted I spend the night for observation, but he was confident I could leave in the morning.

"Just one thing, young lady," he said to me when we were alone. He peered at me through his black, horn-rimmed glasses, as if trying to read my mind. "I've spoken to Dr. Belson about your injuries, and we both have come to the same conclusion. Is there something you want to tell me about what happened to you?"

I gulped, looked away, and shook my head as vigorously as I dared.

"You have scratches on your chest and upper thighs," he continued softly and slowly. "Your mouth and wrists show signs of contusions, and your underclothing was torn." He paused to give more weight to his statement. "That young man who brought you here, did he do this to you?"

"No! I fell down a hill," I said. "I just fell down a hill."

He touched my hand softly, still gazing into my eyes, still searching for the truth. "Would you rather speak to a nurse about this?"

"I fell down a hill."

⚬

I lay in the low light, staring out the hospital window, when I became aware of a presence in the room. Without looking, I knew it was Pukey Boyle.

"Why?" I asked.

"That's my business," he said, sitting on an aluminum chair, leaning forward, elbows resting on his knees.

"You were following me," I said. "But then I hadn't seen you for a few days."

"That's because a guy's got to take a number to tail you."

"What do you mean?"

"I mean between Joe Varsity and the other guy, I was so far behind you, you couldn't have seen me."

"Other guy?"

CHAPTER THIRTEEN

WEDNESDAY, DECEMBER 7, 1960

Next morning I was discharged from St. Joseph's, and Fadge came to take me home. He tucked me into my bed, boiled me some tea, and served me biscuits. He was so sweet, indulgent, and gentle, that it nearly broke my heart to wish he'd leave. When he finally did, I threw back the covers and jumped out of bed. My head still hurt, but a couple of aspirins would help that. Pukey honked a couple of minutes later, and I slipped down the stairs and into the Maroon Hudson Hornet that had so unsettled me just days before. I prayed Fadge wasn't watching from across the street.

Like embarrassed lovers, we didn't say much at first beyond hello. Pukey roared down Market Hill, over East Main Street, and onto Route 5. More than anything, I wanted to ask him why he had been following me, why he had wanted to help me. But I was afraid of what the answer would be. If what I suspected was true, I didn't know how to reject a man who'd saved me from the horror of rape. So I kept my question to myself.

The Hudson hummed along the river at seventy miles per hour, and we spoke about Greg Hewert.

"Why do you think he did what he did to me?" I asked.

He shrugged. "Maybe he doesn't like what you wrote about Jordan. Or maybe he's just got blue balls. You're a nice piece of action, Ellie. Who wouldn't want to have a roll with you?"

"Do you think he loved her?" I asked, ignoring his inelegant compliment. "Do you think he loved Jordan?"

Pukey laughed, glanced at me and then back to the road. "What gave you that idea?"

"Fran Bartolo. She said Greg and Jordan had a thing about four years ago. Did Jordan ever mention it to you?"

Pukey shook his head, not by way of an answer, but in amused disbelief. "Four years ago, you say?" and he threw back his head in laughter.

"Fran Bartolo said Glenda Whalen caught the two of them sneaking around."

"Tell me what the Whale saw, and we'll put your brain power to work, Nancy Drew."

I thought a second, my memory still foggy from the concussion, but still managed to be impressed that Pukey had heard of Nancy Drew. "Franny said that Glenda had seen Greg's car there, and that the judge and his wife were out of town."

"Can you be sure of that information?" asked Pukey. "Did you check on that story? A good reporter should be sure."

"Audrey Shaw contradicted Fran's version," I said. "Quite vehemently, in fact. She swore she didn't go with the judge on that trip."

"So, can you think of any other possible explanation for why Greg's car was in their driveway?"

Pukey's drift was unmistakable; he'd practically spelled it out for me.

"You're not suggesting that Greg Hewert and Audrey Shaw . . ."

Pukey just stared down the road, swallowing a mushrooming grin.

"Why should I believe that?" I asked. "To be honest with you, it seems unlikely."

"Mrs. Shaw is a pretty lady, right? Not my style, but I can't say it wouldn't be a gas to screw an ex-girlfriend's mother. And the wife of a state judge to boot."

One who had sent him to jail.

"But we're talking about Greg Hewert," I said. "Suppose he was interested in her. What makes you think she'd go for him?"

Pukey took his eyes off the road and looked at me. "Women like strong types. Don't judge Joe Varsity by yesterday at the lake; he's no creampuff. Just no match for me. And I suppose some women think he's good looking."

"Do you know this firsthand? I mean, did you ever see them together?"

"No, but I knew what was going on. And Jordan knew it, too, though she never admitted it."

"And the judge?" I asked, recalling the tense exchange I'd witnessed between the Shaws at the funeral home.

"Maybe. I can't say for sure."

About ten miles east of New Holland, Pukey swung off Route 5 into a long drive that cut through the high grass near the river: the Leatherstocking Motel.

"This is the place," he said, rolling to a stop about twenty yards from the registration office. "And that's the car I followed here." He pointed to a late-model, light-blue Chevrolet Impala parked at the end of the lot.

"Let's take a closer look," I said, and we popped open our doors in unison.

The blue sedan had New York diplomatic plates, which baffled me, and the engine was cold; it hadn't moved in hours.

"You two looking for something?" A frail, gray-haired man in a faded flannel shirt and rumpled fishing vest peered across the lot at us. The manager.

"We're looking for the man who owns that car," I said, walking toward the office. "My name is Ellie Stone. I write for the *Republic*."

"And who's that with you, the paperboy?"

Pukey's eyes turned red, and I thought he was going to punch the old guy's lights out. I grabbed him by the arm and restrained him.

"He's with me," I said. "Who belongs to the car?"

"It's mine," called another voice, this one with a familiar foreign accent. I knew it was Roy before I'd even turned to look.

He was standing in the doorway of one of the rooms, smiling and relaxed. Instead of his usual turban, he was wearing a sort of sheer black cloth wrapped tightly around his head and knotted on the top in front. He motioned for me to join him.

"What a pleasant surprise, Miss Stone," he said with his unflappable cordiality.

"Surprise?" I asked. "You didn't expect to see me?"

"Please come inside, and I'll explain everything."

I took a step toward him and felt Pukey on my heels. (God, I thought, not entirely displeased, he really has it bad for me.) Roy seemed alarmed and insisted that he wanted to talk to me alone. I agreed, provided the paperboy stand guard outside the door.

"Have a seat," said Roy once we were alone in his dark, musty room. I sat on a slat-backed chair—the only one in the room. "Now, how can I help you today?"

Was he kidding?

"I'm here for two reasons, Roy," I said, noticing the latest edition of the *Republic* on the dresser. I could read the headline from my seat: "PHOTOS OF THE MURDER?"—the story I'd had Fadge plant in George Walsh's ear two nights before. Another item caught my eye: "DA RELEASES HERNANDEZ." "First, I want to find out who killed Jordan Shaw. I assume that discovery will clear up another recent murder, a couple of burglaries, and some creative automobile maintenance. Second, I'd like to know why you've been following me the past few days."

Roy's dark eyes sparkled in the low light, as if he was laughing. He thought for a moment, then took a seat on the bed.

"I'll speak candidly with you in this room, Miss Stone, then deny whatever I choose when we walk back outside."

"Fair enough," I said.

"As for your first question, I cannot say who killed Jordan Shaw because I don't know."

"But you were in her motel room that night."

"Why do you say that?"

"Because you stopped for a beer at a local tavern the night Jordan Shaw was murdered. And now you're holidaying here in lovely New Holland, New York."

"Perhaps I have other business here."

"For instance?"

"I've come to retrieve some property. I have reason to believe that it is here."

"At the Mohawk Motel?" I asked. "Or in my flat?"

Roy smiled again. "It could be anywhere."

"What exactly is this property of yours?"

"I didn't say it was mine. It doesn't belong to me, in fact, but I have an interest in recovering it."

"Maybe I can help," I said.

"You know very well what I'm looking for, don't you, Miss Stone? And you know where it is."

"I may admit to something here in this room," I said. "Something that I'll deny once we walk back outside."

He nodded; well played. "Perhaps we can do business."

"Fine by me. But first, I want to know about November 25th. If you didn't kill Jordan, what did you see in her room?"

"I've already told you I was not there. But if, for the sake of an intellectual exercise, you would like to assume I was, then let's do a proof of it." He leaned back on his elbows and waited.

"Okay," I said. "Who do you think would have reason to kill Jordan?"

"It could be anybody. Perhaps a local. Why do you insist I know?"

"Come on, Roy. What did you see in that room? Was Jerrold there? Was Jordan already dead, or did you talk to her?"

"What has Dr. Jerrold to do with this?"

"I know the story you fed me in Boston was a pack of lies," I said, leaning forward, toward him. "You told me Jordan and D. J. Nichols were an item, when everyone in the department knew that was bunk. Why did you tell me such an obvious lie? Didn't you think I would check on it?"

"I told you what I had heard through the grapevine."

"You were protecting Jerrold. He was your benefactor in the department, at least of late. Isn't it only since August that you two have shared a common interest?"

Roy stood up, circled the room, then answered.

"You're right; I did lie to you in Boston. When you first appeared at Tufts, I was surprised. How had you traced Jordan Shaw to the Engineering Department? I couldn't figure it. I was impressed, but then I thought, she's just a girl, and so young. I thought I could be rid of you with that story. I underestimated you. Now I know better. Yes, I was shielding Jerrold. He's married, as you know, and I was sure the scandal would hurt his family. Jordan was already dead, so what was the harm?"

"How does Nichols fit in, then? Why point the finger at him?"

"He was the only alternative. Jordan was not easily approached. Of all the men who courted her, only Dr. Jerrold and D. J. Nichols had any luck. And with D. J., it was clearly a friendship only. Still, he was the only man I knew who saw her socially. So I lied about the rumors."

"You're still lying," I said. "But we'll leave that for now. What about my second question? Why have you been following me?"

Roy smiled. "Quite simple. I thought you might have picked up the trail of what I'm looking for. And you almost had me convinced a moment ago. But I doubt you have any idea where it is. You're too coy, Miss Stone. You've made some clever guesses, to be sure, but you don't know where it is, do you? Or perhaps it doesn't exist at all."

I said nothing.

"I am planning to drive back to Boston today itself," he announced.

I stood to leave, and, since I was holding nothing, played my hand accordingly: I bluffed.

"Take a good look at that article on the front page of today's paper," I said. "Read it carefully and see if you still think I can't put my hands on what you want."

"You don't expect me to believe you, do you?" he asked, nearly laughing.

"It's all the same to me," I said, opening the door. "You're not the only person looking for it," and I left.

Outside, Pukey was leaning against a wall, picking at the grease under his fingernails. As we walked back to his car, I ducked underneath Roy's blue Chevrolet to look for oil spots. Nothing. Then I wrote down the plate number and made a note to check with Motor Vehicles.

Perhaps Roy had a vested interest in protecting Jerrold, but I couldn't be sure he was the killer. To pin the murders on him, I needed three little oil drippings, arranged in a neat isosceles triangle.

Pukey dropped me off at home, where I phoned Benny Arnold at Motor Vehicles. I needed some information and, so, had to brave the awkwardness. If he knew I wasn't interested in him, did he have to mention it each time? Does it help one's self esteem to draw attention to one's failings with the opposite sex? For my part, I can verify that it does not improve one's odds of success.

I asked Benny to check on Roy's license plate for me.

"Sure," he said. "Maybe if I do this for you, you'll agree to go on a date someday."

"We'll see," I said.

He took down the number and promised an answer soon.

A few minutes after ringing off with Benny, Morrissey called from Boston.

"Here's an interesting tidbit for you," he said. "We know whoever killed Jordan Shaw brought her purse back to her apartment in Boston. That ought to erase any lingering doubts that Ginny White was murdered by anyone other than Jordan Shaw's killer."

"How do you know Jordan had the purse in New Holland?" I asked, relieved that they had finally found the motel receipt.

"We came across a dated receipt from the Mohawk Motel. The way I figure it, the killer grabbed her purse and brought it to Boston. He used her keys to get into the apartment and kill Ginny. That leads me to believe our man is one of the Boston crowd."

"Why's that?"

"Why would he kill the two roommates unless he knew them both? What motive would one of your locals have to drive four hours to Boston to kill Ginny White? She obviously wasn't a witness. He'd be running a terrific risk of getting caught with Jordan's stuff."

Morrissey had a point there. Was I wasting my time on the New Holland end? Then I told him that Roy had turned up in New Holland.

"What's he doing over there?" he asked.

"He's trying to recover the photographs. He says he wants to protect Jerrold. Blackmail is more likely."

"Makes sense."

"What about Jerrold?" I asked. "Did you find out if he owns a second car?"

"We found one registered to his wife: a 1958 Pontiac Bonneville, cream color."

Then, before hanging up, he told me he was going to call Frank Olney.

"What do you want with him?" I asked.

"I'm going to ask him to pick up Singh. He's a suspect and, at the least, a material witness. I don't want him disappearing again. Besides, I think you might be in danger."

If he only knew.

About an hour later, I phoned Frank Olney, who had already spoken to Morrissey.

"I'm going out to the Leatherstocking to pick up that Indian guy now," he said. "You want to meet me out there?"

"No, my car's in the shop again," I lied. In fact, it was still parked on Jean Trent's property on Winandauga Lake, but I didn't want Frank to know that. For one thing, there wasn't a hill for me to fall down anywhere near there. "I was hoping to go out to the Mohawk while Jean Trent is still locked up," I said. "I'd like to poke around one last time, if you don't mind."

"I suppose there's no harm. I'll send Halvey over with the keys to the motel. He'll give you a lift."

While I waited for my ride, I phoned Dom Ornuti. I asked him to tow my car back from the lake and inspect it for tampering. Who knew if someone still had it in for my brakes? This way, I could get my car back and feel safe at the same time.

Pat Halvey pulled to a stop in the gravel parking lot of the Mohawk Motel, but he didn't switch off the ignition.

"You're not coming in with me?" I asked.

"No way. We've turned this place upside down at least ten times. If you want to hang around this dump, go ahead. I'm going up the road to Carmen's for some coffee. I'll pick you up in an hour."

"An hour for coffee?" I asked.

Halvey blushed. "I was kind of hoping to make some time with Carmen."

"Carmen? What about me?" I asked. "I thought you wanted to take me bowling."

He grinned. "You're too late. Carmen bowls a one fifty-seven average."

"See you later," I said, climbing out of the car. "Don't leave me stranded out here, Pat. One hour, okay?"

"If I don't get lucky," and he threw the cruiser into reverse and spun his wheels through the gravel. Then he roared out onto Route 40 and turned north, leaving me alone at the ghostly motel.

The Mohawk Motel will be the stuff of legend in twenty years. Its place in local lore is assured, having hosted New Holland's most infamous murder. Old folks will recall with a shudder the gruesome Thanksgiving of 1960; raconteurs will pepper the story with suitable hyperbole; and Boy Scouts will share the chilling story of the haunted Mohawk Motel around the campfire. I stared at the cracked concrete and gray glass. By summer, the motel would be swallowed by the relentless overgrowth around it. Within weeks, all the windows would be smashed by strong-armed, sharp-eyed kids toting rocks and BB guns.

I decided to have a good look around while the locks and windows were still intact. I stood outside Jean's door, wondering where to start. I hadn't had a coffee for hours and my caffeine levels were low. Plus my head ached, compliments of Greg Hewert, and I still felt a little queasy. I shuddered as I thought of the creep and wondered what Pukey had done to him. As there was no coffee in sight, I deposited three nickels into the Dr Pepper machine and pulled out a soda.

There were three keys on the chain Halvey had given me: a passkey for the guest rooms, another for the registration office, and the third for

Jean Trent's rooms. Beginning in room 4, where Jordan had been murdered, I found little to go on. The police had turned the room inside out several times. There was surely nothing left worth finding. The only thing I had to go on was the physical layout of the room. The walls, doors, and windows hadn't moved since November 25. The murderer had walked into this room, seen things from the same perspective as I, navigated around the same furniture, considered the same angles. Did any of that help me? Who knew? In fact, I knew nothing. The fruits of my investigation were, for the most part, hunches, guesses, and conjecture. I had nothing concrete.

I put my soda down on the counter in the bathroom and promptly knocked it over into the sink. At least the bottle didn't break. I rinsed the soda down the drain, opened the bathroom door wide, then went around back to put Julio's statements to the test. Could what he had described truly be seen from that window? He hadn't lied; I could see the bathroom, the lower third of the bed, but not the outside door. If Jordan had been murdered on the bed, as I suspected, then Julio's camera probably wouldn't have captured it, presuming he had placed it on the sill and pointed it through the louvered bathroom window in the first place. Even if the film existed, even if I found it, what would it show: Jordan's bare legs kicking as someone off camera broke her neck and sliced a piece of skin out of her pelvis?

I came back around to the front of the motel and closed room 4. Drawing a deep sigh, I scanned the grounds, wondering if there might not be some forgotten corner we had all missed. I slid three more nickels into the machine and retrieved another soda before setting out into the woods in search of Jordan's clothes, the postulated film shot by Julio, anything.

There were millions of wet leaves well on their way to decomposition, and there was mud, but little else. I tramped through the northern extreme of Wentworth's Woods for about twenty minutes and was circling back toward the motel when I heard a car rolling over the gravel in the parking lot. I picked up my pace, careful, however, not to make any noise. My caution slowed me down, and I didn't emerge from the brush until it was too late. But I did see Julio Hernandez at the wheel of an old, red Chrysler, burning rubber as he raced from the parking lot onto Route 40.

I made a brief and vain effort to run after him, giving up well before I had reached the huge, wooden Indian. I returned at a gallop to the motel and examined the tire tracks in the gravel. It was clear Julio had pulled into the space just in front of the registration office, and he hadn't stayed long. He had left the engine running; I could see the sooty smudge left in the gravel by the belching exhaust pipe. I crawled on my hands and knees for several minutes, combing the gravel for an oil spot below where the engine had been idling. Nothing. It was uncanny. I had looked under every car I had come across for the past week and a half and had found no oil spots anywhere. The leaking crankcase was a phantom.

I brushed off my hands and checked the registration-office door. Julio hadn't opened it, that much was sure, since the seal Frank Olney had placed on the door after the burglary was intact. By all appearances, the other doors hadn't been touched, either, since the scuff marks left by Julio's shoes were all bunched together in the vicinity of the office door.

I stepped back to think. What had Julio been looking for? The only explanation I could imagine was that he had hoped to get inside, saw the seal, and thought better of it.

As I considered Julio's strange visit, I heard a car approach. It was Halvey, but he wasn't alone. Surly-faced, slumping handcuffed against the door in the backseat, sat Julio Hernandez.

"I was coming back to get you when I saw him pull out of here like a bat out of hell," explained the deputy. "I knew the sheriff didn't want anyone snooping around up here, so I chased him down. Imagine my surprise to find the Puerto Rican at the wheel."

"Did he have anything on him?" I asked, peering past the deputy at the youth in the cruiser.

"Naw. Just his keys."

"Nothing else?"

Halvey shrugged. "Seventy-five cents."

"Can I see the keys?" I asked.

"Have a look," he said, pulling a key ring out of his pocket. "Two for his car, and this other one." He showed me a long, thin, silver key unlike any one I'd ever seen. "I don't know what it fits."

"Obviously not any of these doors," I said, handing the keys back to Halvey. "You radio Frank?"

"He's on his way. He wanted you to wait here for him; says that guy he went to pick up checked out of the motel. He ain't found him yet."

Frank Olney arrived a few minutes later with two county cruisers on his tail. He climbed out of his car, hitched up his belt, and sauntered over to Halvey and me.

"What do you say, now, Ellie?" he asked. "Maybe the DA was a little too quick to spring Julio? Good thing we held Jean Trent on the obstruction charge. Course that won't stick, but she busted my chops a little too hard and deserved it."

"He was looking for something, Frank," I said. "That doesn't mean he's guilty of murder."

The sheriff waved a dismissive hand at me. "Halvey tell you that Indian guy checked out? I talked to the manager, and he told me what his car looks like. We'll find him."

Frank Olney questioned Julio for the next hour, trying to grill a confession out of him, while his deputies went through every room of the motel looking for evidence of tampering. The DA arrived a little later, interrogated the suspect, then held a private powwow with the sheriff.

"What do you think, Ellie?" asked the Thin Man, once he and the sheriff had finished. "You saw him tear out of here, right?"

"He couldn't have been here for more than thirty, forty-five seconds, Don. I was off in the woods, over there," I pointed for their benefit. "Then I heard a car, so I ran back. By the time I got to the parking lot, he was pulling out onto Route Forty."

"Your boys find anything on him or in the car?" the DA asked Frank.

"Nothing."

"I don't think we can hold him, Frank," said the DA. "In fact, I'd advise you to let him go and put a tail on him. He seems nervous about something. Maybe Ellie's right; maybe he came up here to find something of value."

"Pictures?" asked the sheriff. "Come off it, Don. There's no pictures. Besides, we know he didn't go inside. Maybe he was pining for the old days with Jean Trent."

"I advise you not to arrest him, Frank. Take him in for questioning, but face it: he didn't break the law here. He didn't even break the seal on the door."

The DA offered me a ride back to town, and I accepted without volunteering to return the motel keys to Frank Olney or Pat Halvey. No one asked. The Thin Man dropped me off at Ornuti's, where my car was up on the lift.

"How does it look?" I asked. "Brakes still work?"

Vinnie Donati pulled his black hands from underneath the Dodge and wiped his sweaty brow.

"It ain't your brakes, Ellie," he said. "Alternator's busted. I'm waiting for a rebuilt one from Freeman's Auto Supply, so I don't know if I'll finish this today."

I have the worst luck with cars.

"Don't you have a new alternator you can put in there?" I asked.

"Nope. But keep your shirt on; I'll give you a loaner in the meantime. Give me a couple of minutes."

While Vinnie disappeared inside, I phoned Benny Arnold again from the phone booth outside.

"What's this all about, Ellie?" he asked eagerly. "Some kind of international intrigue? The car is registered to the Indian consulate," he explained. "I made some calls to a guy I know in the lower Manhattan DMV, and he helped me out. Said the car is assigned to the New York Consul General—a guy named P. V. Singh. Ring a bell?"

"Loud and clear," I said, sure it was Roy's father.

"So do you still find me too unattractive for a date?"

A few minutes later, Vinnie handed me a set of keys and pointed to an old, green Studebaker across the lot. It started, and I drove away happily. I stopped by Fiorello's and found Fadge gazing up at the television. The after-school run on penny candy had subsided, and business was in its usual late-afternoon lull. I asked for an aspirin and washed it down with some carbonated water.

"At least your black eyes are fading," he said.

"Makeup," I explained.

He asked me how the investigation was going, and I described the day's events: Roy and Julio.

"I thought you promised to take it easy."

"I lied."

"So who do you think did it? My vote's for the Indian guy."

"Maybe," I said. "But if it is Roy, how do I prove it?"

CHAPTER FOURTEEN

When Roy disappeared from the Leatherstocking, I could only hope he would fall for my bluff, that he believed I had what he was looking for. I spent Wednesday evening at home. Nothing to drink. Something about the concussion had put a damper on my thirst. Instead, I hand washed some unmentionables, polished off several crossword puzzles, and waited for a phone call. Roy knew where to find me.

Charlie Reese called a little past eight to see how I was feeling. It was plain by his tone that there was something else on his mind, and I pinned him down on it.

"It's Artie Short," he said finally. "He wants to know when you're coming back to work."

"I was hoping to finish up this Shaw murder first."

"Artie says it's George's story now. He got a big scoop the other night, you know. Someone called and gave him that big tip about missing evidence and pictures of the murder. You had a hunch about that, but he broke the story. He's the golden boy again."

I kept my mouth shut; despite my friendship with Charlie Reese, I couldn't admit that I was the source of George Walsh's phony information.

"Then why does Artie care if I come back tomorrow or next Monday?" I asked.

"Because we've got other news to cover, Ellie. He gave me an ultimatum. He said either you're in the saddle Friday morning or you're fired."

"Doesn't he know I just fell down a hill?" I asked, ashamed of myself, but in for a penny . . .

"He doesn't know and wouldn't care if he did."

"Can't you fix it for me, Charlie? Just a couple of days more."

"Not this time. He means it."

"I don't have much of anything else besides this job, and I want to keep it. I like it. But I've got to see this Shaw story through to the end."

"So what do I tell him?"

I thought a moment. "Tell him he'll have his answer Friday morning."

There was no time to wait around for a phone call from Roy. If he was still in the area, I would have to find him in one of the twenty or so motels in the valley. I grabbed the Yellow Pages and headed out into the cool, December night.

The AAA Motor Lodge, the Valley View, and the Sleepy Dutchman were inside city limits. The Pale Moon, the Half Moon, the Traveler's Inn, and Georgette's Lodge were west of town. The most fertile area was north and east of New Holland, where I quizzed a dozen innkeepers at such establishments as the Hayseed, the Route 5 Motel, the Adirondack Inn, and the Poole Hotel and Grill. No foreigners, no diplomatic plates.

It was after ten thirty when I threw the Studebaker into park in front of Fiorello's. Fadge was alone inside, broom in hand, sitting on a stool and watching a werewolf movie on television.

"Say, Ellie, what am I, your social secretary?" he asked. "Your editor leaves messages, your boyfriends, the sheriff . . . And now some guy was looking for you about an hour ago."

"An Indian guy?" I asked. "Beard and turban?"

"No, he sounded English, I think. I asked if he wanted to leave a message, but he said he'd find you later."

"What did he look like?"

"I don't know. Slim, about forty, forty-five. He was driving a light-colored car."

"Is this him?" I asked, producing the photo of Jordan in India.

"How did you manage that?" he asked in wonder. "You're like a magician."

At eleven, the phone rang. It was not the eerie whisper I expected, but David Jerrold in normal tones.

"I'm ready to do business with you, Miss Stone," he said. "Can we meet tonight?"

"What kind of business?"

"I'm interested in buying some film."

"Planning a vacation?" I asked.

"Funny. How does five hundred dollars tickle you? Meet me in thirty minutes at the Mohawk Motel. Come alone." And the line went dead.

I questioned the wisdom of driving out to the Mohawk Motel by myself at such a late hour, but what else could I do? Artie Short's ultimatum might have had something to do with my reckless decision, but deep down I knew that my desire to solve the case and show up George Walsh was too strong to resist. And there was my car—I had really liked that yellow Belvedere—my ransacked apartment, and the assault I'd suffered at the hands of a brute. I wanted to get to the bottom of the whole mess and put it behind me.

Route 40 was deathly still on that December night. The stars sparkled in an icy black sky. My borrowed Studebaker rumbled north, its bouncy tires holding onto the asphalt for dear life, and I didn't pass a single motorist on the way. Then the huge, wooden Indian rose from the dark landscape like a sentry. I slowed to a stop and looked up at him, his painted face blistered by years of weather and neglect. Last chance to turn around. I released the brake, and the car lurched forward.

The parking lot was empty and dark. I stopped in front of the registration office, my headlights shining on the Dr Pepper machine and the pay phone. I climbed out of the car and looked around. The night was still, as if holding its breath, and the only sound was the clicking growl of the Studebaker's engine.

"Are you alone?" Jerrold's voice called out from somewhere in the dark trees.

"Yes," I answered, trembling from the cold and my nerves. "Why don't you show yourself?"

A moment passed, then he stepped from the woods and into my sight.

"There is no film, is there?" he asked.

The abrupt change in subject took me aback. Jerrold came toward me, the gravel crunching beneath his feet. "Prakash is looking for film," he said. "He had no reason to suspect that it existed until you planted that phony story in your paper. And now I've come here to tell you to stop this game."

"But you said you wanted to buy . . ."

"How else was I to convince you to meet me?"

"And the five hundred dollars?"

"It's yours," he lit a cigarette and drew deeply on it. "Provided you quit this investigation and stop calling my home."

"What makes you believe there is no film?"

Jerrold laughed, albeit on edge. "I've played some poker in my day. It doesn't exist."

I thought a moment, watching him in the dark. He just stood there with a small parcel under his arm.

"So what happened that night in number four?" I asked.

"What do you suppose?" he said. "We had a roll, and that was it. Jolly good one, too. If you're game sometime, I'd be happy to show you how it's done."

"That's it?" I asked, ignoring his remark.

"How was I to know Prakash would show up afterward and kill her?"

"Do you know that for sure?"

He didn't answer.

"So he's blackmailing you?" I asked.

I thought he fidgeted, but I couldn't be sure in the dark. "Do you want the money or don't you?"

"You're a coward," I said. "You don't care about anyone but yourself. Including the beautiful young girl who loved you."

"You paint such a wretched picture of me. I loved her, you know. I never dreamed any harm would come to her." He stopped short, perhaps because he was afraid to say too much. Then he began again. "It was Prakash who dragged her into this. God, I nearly died myself when I heard he'd killed her."

"Who visited her after you that night?"

"Well, *Sardarji*, for one—Prakash. And after him, I don't know. When I left her room, she was alone and preparing to leave."

"What time was that?" I asked, hoping perhaps to catch him in a lie.

"About eleven, a few minutes past. I'm not sure. I felt vile as it was, sneaking around, cheating on my wife, leading on a wonderful girl like Jordan. But I couldn't easily resist her, you know. She was a jewel— warm, sincere, loving. And as a man, I can tell you she was a champion in bed. Raw spirit and physicality."

"She was in love with you," I said to accuse.

"As was I with her! I was powerless to resist her, don't you see?"

"Powerless but not impotent."

"For God's sake, just take the money, Miss Stone. I didn't kill Jordan, and if you persist, you'll only ruin my marriage. Diana is ready to leave me as it is, and she'll take my son with her. She's had it with police and reporters calling. She's only stood by me this long for our son."

"Roy's in town," I said. "Why don't you offer him the five hundred dollars in addition to the good notices in his academic file?"

Jerrold perked up at the mention of Roy's name. "You've seen him?" he asked. "Prakash is here?"

"He's been following me for a couple of days. I'm fairly certain he's the one who ransacked my apartment and cut the brakes on my car."

"Following you?" he stammered. "Good God, he may have followed you here! He'll kill us both."

"He doesn't know you're here," I said, afraid he was about to run for the woods.

Jerrold wasn't listening. He charged for the end of the concrete walkway and the path to the rear of the motel. And I remembered his car: the cream-colored Bonneville, not the Jaguar. It was the only car I hadn't checked for oil leaks. It had to be the one.

Jerrold was a pathetic coward, incapable of any decisive action, let alone murder. But I sensed that the car he was running to was the one that had leaked the oil. As I chased after him through the bushes, an image flashed through my head: Diana Jerrold cracking Jordan's neck in a jealous fit. I saw it well. The deranged wife, driven to a blind rage against the girl who threatened to destroy her family by stealing her man, the father of her child. It seemed perfect. She had learned of the tryst, raced to New Holland for the confrontation, then killed her once her husband had pulled up his trousers and slithered away.

Jerrold scrambled through the brittle sprigs of the thicket, and I followed close behind. Breaking into the clearing, he made a dash for the car, parked next to the trash enclosure, where I had first spied Jean Trent's green Pontiac woody. I called to him to wait, but he had tucked back both ears and wasn't about to stop. He gunned the engine and threw the car into reverse just as I reached him. Holding onto the door, I appealed to him to stop, but once he'd wheeled the Bonneville around, he was gone. I let go and watched the tail lights recede down the dark back road.

"Damn!" I said, though not too disappointed. If there was oil in the dirt, Diana Jerrold would be easy to find.

I hurried back to the trash enclosure and bent down where Jerrold's car had been, my fingers almost too impatient to strike the match. One, two strokes, then a spark. The match flared, and I could see the colors of the ground. I inspected the dirt with my light until it burned my fingers. A second and third match yielded no better results. There was nothing but dirt.

I shuffled back to my car on the other side of the motel, dejected, pondering the baffling absence of oil drops. It had been folly to think Diana Jerrold had murdered Jordan Shaw; I doubted she had the requisite strength to snap a neck, and, besides, no one had mentioned a woman in Jordan's room that night.

By the time I'd reached the registration office, I was laughing at myself. After nearly two weeks of snooping, bumps, and bruises, I was losing my good sense. Diana Jerrold, murderess? If so, how did Ginny figure into the equation? I had been hoping for a simple way out before 9:00 a.m. Friday morning, when I'd have to give up my self-esteem or my job. I shook the last of the ridiculous notion from my head and drew a restorative breath of resolve.

The tension of the meeting with Jerrold and the exertion of the chase had left me a little dizzy. My headache throbbed less with every passing hour, but my pounding heart intensified the pain. I wanted a cool drink. I fished through my purse for some change, and produced a quarter. Reaching to deposit the money in the Dr Pepper machine, I noticed the little, illuminated message next to the coin slot: *EXACT CHANGE ONLY*. Fine by me; I could spare a dime. I dropped the coin in and pulled out an ice-cold bottle. But then I stopped. Strange that the machine had no change; I myself had pumped six nickels into it that very afternoon. And Don Czerulniak had deposited three as well on Monday morning. Jean Trent had said that the man from Gloversville came down every Thursday to collect the empties and cash from the soda machine. Maybe the indicator was broken.

I took a healthy gulp of Dr Pepper, wiped my lips in the cold air, then pulled the motel keys from my purse. I examined them in the night, thinking what a dullard Pat Halvey was to have left them with me. He probably hadn't even realized they were missing yet. I took another sip, then figured I might as well make use of the keys while I had them. The crime-scene seal would have to be broken, but I reasoned that I had tacit permission, since Frank had told Halvey to give me the keys.

The registration office was cold and dark. The lights worked when I flicked the switch, but there had been no heat since Jean Trent's arrest. I looked around the room, unsure where to start, wondering if it would do any good anyhow; the sheriff and his men had been through the office at least a dozen times since the murder. And then there was the burglary.

I stepped behind the registration desk and flipped through some bills Jean had impaled on a spindle: Niagara-Mohawk, Bell Telephone, Kyber's Heating Oil, laundry, and a monthly statement of deliveries from Chicken-Lickin'. I moved on, sliding open the center drawer under the counter. Pencils; preprinted bills and carbon paper; three rubber stamps: *PAID*, *AMOUNT DUE*, and *RECEIVED OF*; paper clips and cellophane tape; and a ring of twelve keys, each of which was clearly marked with a black number on white adhesive tape. The brass keys were nearly identical, aside from the indistinguishable variations in their cut. They opened the ten guest rooms and the office's front door.

The twelfth key was the odd one. Unlike its sisters, it bore no number. But I never would have given it a second look if it hadn't been a different color and shape altogether. I closed my fingers around the unmatched key and lifted it from the drawer. A long, silver key, unlike any I'd ever seen—except one. Julio had been carrying a twin key that morning.

I lowered my head in concentration, trying to imagine a hole for the key. I stepped outside and stood facing the door, my eyes scanning the face of the building, looking for another keyhole. There was nothing but cinderblock, the phone, and the damn Dr Pepper machine.

The Dr Pepper machine.

I took a step to my left and considered the glowing hunk of metal and glass. There, on the right, about halfway down the side, was a small, round, silver keyhole. My heart climbed over two ribs, hoisted itself over my collar bone, and lodged itself in my throat. I'd found Julio's hiding spot.

Once I'd opened the refrigerated machine, it didn't take long to find what I was looking for. Nestled out of view in one of the structural cavities of the steel, a black, metallic cylinder rested against the cold walls: Kodak Tri-X, thirty-six exposures.

CHAPTER FIFTEEN

I mprovising with what was left of my damaged equipment, I processed the film myself, rolling the strips of celluloid in my seldom-used developer. My hands were shaking in anticipation as I set about making a contact sheet. I could always make individual prints later, but I wanted to see Julio's photographs in sequence immediately.

I swished the tongs in the chemical bath, squinting through the low, red light as the black-and-white images spread across the paper. Of the thirty-six frames shot by Julio, four were blank. The other thirty-two were sharp, well-exposed, beautifully composed candid nudes of Jordan Shaw. I swallowed hard, with no saliva, examining the frames under a loupe, and I understood why Julio had been so reluctant to admit to the existence of the film. She was genuine, without shame, so casual and full of grace in her nudity that it seemed perverse to find her provocative. Yet I knew she was. The photographs were intensely erotic: the tall, lean, blonde, captured in the intimacy of her bath, unapproachable but powerfully seductive. In my ten years as a photographer, I had never made such gripping photographs.

I made one set of eight-by-tens, then found myself obsessed. Like a novice hobbyist, I reprinted the set, experimenting with exposures and grains, searching for the look I liked best. Hours wasted for nothing more than furtive voyeurism. But then I enlarged the photographs and I saw it. A dark smudge on her pelvis—just above her pubic hair.

"Good God," I mumbled to myself, examining the photograph under the loupe. "It's a tattoo."

It was some kind of scribbling, possibly writing, but that's all I could discern.

Julio had played his hand close to the vest, thinking he had a sound hiding place. He thought he could wait it out and reclaim his treasure once the heat was off. His only mistake, in fact, was doubting the integrity of his cache. Not even the Dr Pepper man would have found the hidden film, unless he'd known where to look. But Julio couldn't resist running to the Mohawk as soon as he had been released from jail. He checked to see that the film was safe and swiped the small change from the soda machine as a bonus.

∂⃝

"I need your help, Ellie."

 "You? What are you doing here?"

 "Help me. Don't let me die without justice."

 "I'm not up to it. I'm not that clever."

 "You're a lot like me, Ellie. You and I would have been friends; I sense it. Please find my killer."

 "Can't you give me a hint?"

The phone pealed, and I bolted up in my bed. I'd taken a Darvon and must have nodded off.

"Hello," I said, rubbing my eyes and cursing the rude awakening. God, had I really asked the murdered girl in my dream for a hint? And yet I found myself wishing the phone hadn't rung; now I'd never know what Jordan might have said to me.

"I have to see you, Miss Stone," said the voice over the phone, thick with what sounded like an Indian accent. It wasn't Roy.

"Who's there?" I asked.

"This is Hakim Mohammed. I'm across the street in the ice cream shop. I must see you tonight itself."

"I'll be right down," I said, and he hung up.

For safe keeping, I placed Julio's photographs and negatives into a large folio of Curtis prints (one of my mother's) on my bookshelf. No one would ever look there.

Hakim was sitting in a booth in the back, a glass of carbonated water in front of him on the table. Fadge gave me a what-the-hell's-going-on look when I came in.

"Take this envelope," said Hakim, once I'd slid into the booth across from him. "Use it any way you deem fit."

"What is this?" I asked, starting to open it.

"Not here," he said, stilling my hand with his. He was wearing a mean little green onyx ring on his pinkie finger. "You'll know what to do when you see it."

"Why are you helping me?" I asked. "For Jordan?"

"I never even met Jordan Shaw. Goodbye, Miss Stone."

With that, Hakim slid over to get out of the booth, but he didn't make it that far. As large as a house, Fadge stood above us, blocking his escape.

"Please, sir," said Hakim, craning his neck to look up at Fadge. "Let me pass."

"First you tell the lady what she wants to know, then you can drag yourself out of here."

Hakim inched back across the seat until he was in front of his half-empty glass of water again.

"I would go to the bloody police to file a complaint," he muttered, "but I'm sure they would treat me even worse than you."

"She's worked hard on this story," said Fadge, leaning over the table, inches from Hakim's face. "Tell her what she wants to know."

Fadge straightened up and backed off a step. I gave him a nod to indicate thanks and that he'd done his job. He stared down at Hakim for another moment, then left us. Seconds later, he switched off the front lights, and I could hear him lock the door. Hakim settled back against the wall of the booth and cleared his throat. We sat quietly for almost a minute, Hakim glaring at his water glass, struggling to control his temper. I don't think he appreciated having to answer to a woman, even if a six foot two, three-hundred-pound beast was the muscle behind her.

"So you want to know why I want to help you?" He said, fiddling with the little onyx ring. "It has nothing to do with you or that *randi*, Jordan Shaw."

"I beg your pardon?" I asked.

He looked pleased for having surprised me and insulted Jordan Shaw with one simple word.

"It means 'whore,'" he said simply.

"Oh! Well, let's put that to one side, shall we? Why are you trying to help me if not for me or her?"

"Prakash Singh is a bloody Indian," he began. "Do you understand what that means to a Pakistani?"

I shrugged. "I know you're not friendly with Indians, but this seems like a lot of trouble to take."

"What do you know of trouble? Was your father murdered?"

That stung hard. I bit my lip but said nothing. After a moment, Hakim resumed.

"Does the year 1947 mean anything to you?"

"That was the year of India's independence," I said, grateful the subject had turned away from my father.

"And Pakistan's," he said as if to scold me. "I was ten years old in 1947, the year of Partition and Independence. My family was from the Punjab. East Punjab. Jullundur. That's inside India today. My father, *abbaji*, was a doctor, a learned man. I had three brothers and two sisters. I was the youngest. My father was not interested in politics. He did not hate the British or the Hindus. He was a peaceful man."

Hakim paused, shifted in his seat, refusing to look me in the eye. He seemed to weigh his words, deliver them slowly. His closed mouth, twisted into a snarl, tried to subdue the violent emotion just inside.

"As Independence neared, there were rumors and threats against Muslims. Slaughter, rape, and settling of old scores by the bloody Hindus. Many Muslims decided to leave for the new Pakistan. My father did not believe the worst. He wanted us to stay in this new India. He had his practice, his friends, his brothers and cousins. Our family had been in Jullundur for generations.

"My mother's family was from Lahore. She had five brothers. They begged my father to shift from Jullundur to Lahore before Independence. But he was determined to stay." Hakim drew a sigh. "Until his brother Asif and his family were attacked by a mob of Hindus. They barely escaped alive and fled to Lahore."

"So you all moved to Pakistan?" I asked.

"Not quite. There were many horrible tales of rioting, violence, and strife. More than a million died in the bloody days before and after Independence. Unspeakable atrocities were committed by the Hindu dogs and their Sikh partners."

"Didn't a lot of Hindus die as well?"

He pounded his fist on the red, linoleum tabletop. Fadge appeared from the front to investigate, but, seeing that I was in no danger, he withdrew again.

"I don't care about the Hindus or Sikhs or Jains or Parsees or even the other Muslims," he said. "I care that my family was murdered."

"I'm so sorry," I blurted out. "I didn't realize."

Hakim went quiet, breathing deeply, looking mournfully at his ring. I could see the tears in his hard eyes, though they never fell.

"We boarded the train at Jullundur on August 20th," he resumed in a soft voice. "All of us. My father and mother, three brothers and two sisters, just two days after Eid, with all the possessions we could carry. *Abbaji* was sure he would be able to return later to collect the rest of our belongings and the items from his small clinic.

"It was a short distance to Lahore. Perhaps 350 kilometers. We settled in and watched the hot countryside pass by. Everything seemed fine." He closed his eyes and drew another breath. "And then we reached Amritsar, where the train stopped to take on passengers. That's when a mob of Hindus began stoning the train. *Abbaji* and my older brothers told my mother and sisters and me to lie flat on the floor. They covered us with our baggage to hide us. Then some men stormed the train with knives, rifles, and *lathis*. The police stood by on the platform as the marauders ran through the train, beating and stabbing anyone in a kufi or a turban. Anyone wearing a beard. A group of ten Hindus burst into our car, swinging *lathis* and machetes. My brothers, Yusuf and Faroukh, threw themselves at the mob and tried to defend us. I watched in horror from under our baggage as they were cut down with machetes. They died on the floor before us. Then the Hindus took my fourteen-year-old brother Zahid and *abbaji* and dragged them off the train. They beat them and stabbed them to death on the platform."

I felt sick. Hakim's soft voice narrated the horrors so calmly, almost in a whisper, like a prayer. I didn't have anything to say. No words of comfort or solace came to me. I just sat there, frozen in my seat, waiting for him to close his tale. But he wasn't finished.

"The men took my sister Rehena away. She was thirteen, the sweetest child that ever lived. The last I saw of her was her foot, still colored from her Eid celebration *mehndi*."

"Oh, my God," I croaked, my throat too dry to gasp.

"We never learned her fate," said Hakim, shrugging sadly.

"I'm very sorry," I offered. "So very sorry."

He finally looked at me. "My mother and my sister Kamaliya and I survived the attack. My *chachaji*, my father's brother Asif, took us in, raised us, and cared for my mother."

Hakim grunted a small, bitter laugh. "You know, only fifteen men and boys were murdered that day. And a handful of girls abducted. A minor incident in the greater tragedy of Partition. There were no headlines. No international outrage. No monuments to the dead ... That makes it harder for me somehow. As if they died and no one took notice."

His story was over now, I was sure.

"So that is why I help you, Miss Stone," he said. "I don't hate all Indians. Just certain ones like Prakash Singh, who smirk at me for my heritage and my country. Who believe in India over Pakistan and shrug their shoulders indifferently at the misery they gave to us."

"But Prakash wasn't there," I said. "He didn't murder your family. Why do you blame him more than others?"

"Prakash Singh is from Amritsar," he said. "That's why I hate him a little more than the rest."

"You mentioned *mehndi*," I said. "What exactly is *mehndi*?"

"Is this a joke to you?"

"No, I've heard of it once before. Jordan mentioned it in a postcard."

Hakim thought on it a moment, then answered. "It's henna. A dye used for celebrations. A tattoo. It fades away after a few weeks."

"One last thing," I said. "How did you end up in Jordan's motel room that night and what did you see?"

Hakim took my question in his stride. He didn't deny, feign innocence, or lose his temper. He just answered.

"I hired a car and followed Prakash Singh here," he said. "I knew he was up to no good, and I wanted to catch him at it."

"That still seems like a lot of trouble to me," I said. "With nothing personal against him, why drive two hundred miles on the off chance he might be doing something underhanded?"

"It *was* personal, Miss Stone. Prakash Singh filed a grievance against me. Tried to have me dismissed from the program. He accused me of cheating. He said I copied a paper from a journal and presented it as my own work."

"Was it true?" I asked.

That riled him.

"No! The faculty and dean investigated the charge and found nothing. Instead, they reprimanded that bloody *Sardar* for filing a false report. Prakash Singh engages in this harassing behavior just to make my life difficult, and all the while with a smile on his lying lips."

"What did you see in Jordan's room?"

He sneered and shook his head. "Nothing. I was too late. That bloody *Sardar* had already killed her and removed the body. There was nothing in the room but some blood on the bed. Her clothes and possessions were gone. I cleared out fast. I didn't kill that girl, Miss Stone, if that's what you're suggesting."

"I'm just trying to tie up the loose ends," I said. "A witness said three men visited the room. You were the last one."

"But not the one who killed her."

Hakim pushed out of the booth and stood up. Fadge made no move to stop him this time. Hakim nodded curtly in lieu of a good-bye and then strode purposefully to the door. He grabbed the handle and gave it a yank. The door refused to open. He rattled it two more times, then turned sheepishly to Fadge, who was watching from a stool at the counter.

"Would you unlock the door, please?"

Fadge pushed off his stool, shuffled over to the door, and fished a key ring from his pocket. To Hakim, it must have seemed like five minutes for the big man to locate the correct key, though it was probably more like twenty seconds. When Fadge finally unlocked the door, Hakim slipped past him into the cold night. I followed him out, intent on having a look under his car. But a taxi was waiting, and he climbed in. Then he was gone.

Inside the envelope, I found four color snapshots of Jordan and Jerrold, taken somewhere in India almost a year and a half earlier. In two pictures, they were holding hands. From a distance, it appeared Jordan was wearing some dark lace gloves reaching halfway up her forearms. In the third and fourth, Jordan and Jerrold were wrapped in a tight embrace, nose to nose like lovers, standing in the courtyard of some kind of palace. The buildings were beautiful—with intricate, carved detail—deep red in color and nearly deserted. The last photograph was taken with a long zoom, a little bit grainy, but I could see the lace gloves were not gloves at all. They were actually magnificent henna tattoos. *Mehndi.*

The pictures had been taken from a distance of about fifty or sixty feet. They almost passed for simple tourist shots, but there was an unsettling feel of voyeurism about them, and I was sure they were stolen photographs, surreptitiously taken by someone who didn't want to be seen. I thought back to Jordan's letter to Ginny, the one gushing about the perfect night in Fatehpur Sikri with David Jerrold, and I wondered if perhaps the lovers hadn't escaped the prying eyes of the world after all.

And there was more. Two letters at the bottom of the envelope, both written in Jordan's hand, made most interesting reading. The first was dated September 1, 1960, addressed to Jeffrey Nichols. After some small talk about the boredom of New Holland, Jordan Shaw gave me what I wanted.

> *I've been thinking of the time we spent together in India and realize that David and I were perhaps indiscreet. I know that I can rely on your tact and friendship. As far as I'm concerned, it makes no difference. I don't care if people gossip about me because I love David so much. His position is very delicate, though, at least until he gets his divorce and his tenure case is decided. I know people wouldn't understand, but this is not a frivolous affair for us. We're planning to marry as soon as possible . . .*

I wasn't so sure Jerrold ever intended to divorce for Jordan, but she seemed convinced.

The second letter was dated November 16, 1960, and was a stream of consciousness narrative of her heartbreak. She had just received the Dear Jordan letter and was pouring her heart out to her friend Jeffrey Nichols.

> *He led me on. He told me he loved me, and now he's tossing me aside. I called him after I got his letter, and he said my mother had phoned his wife and told her everything. I suppose that's my fault, but that liar had said he'd already told his wife! He promised me that he was leaving her, that we'd be together by Christmas, but he was just stringing me along. Ginny warned me about getting involved with a professor, but I fell in love with him anyway. And you were right about him, too: David Jerrold is a liar and a cheat. I want to forget him forever, but I know I can't. I can't because I'm still in love with him.*

Less than two weeks later, Jordan welcomed the cheating liar back into her bed, this time for the last time, at the Mohawk Motel.

THURSDAY, DECEMBER 8, 1960

"Ellie, it's Frank Olney," came the voice over the line. "You better get over to my office right away. We picked up that Indian guy after midnight, but there's a snag."

"I'll be there in twenty minutes," I said, rolling out of bed with great difficulty.

George Walsh was waiting outside Frank Olney's office when I arrived. He glared at me, inspecting my fading bruises, and wrote something on his pad.

"This is my story, Stone. You can't see the sheriff; I was here first."

I smiled, then Pat Halvey entered from the sheriff's office. "Is Frank in?" I asked.

"Sure, Ellie. Go right in, he's expecting you."

I turned to George Walsh and shrugged.

"That does it!" he said, rising to leave. "I'm calling Mr. Short."

"Get me some coffee first, will you?" I said as he stormed out.

Frank Olney was lodged behind his steel desk, and the DA was staring out the window when I came in.

"We got trouble here," said the sheriff.

"The guy claims he's with the Indian consulate," said Don. "Produced a diplomatic passport. He demanded his one phone call right away, and when we finally let him make it at about three a.m., he called New York. He spoke for a couple of minutes in Hindi or some such language, then handed the phone to Frank."

"A man named P. V. Singh was on the line," said Frank, reading from some notes. "Said he was the consul general of India, for God's sake. He was hooting that we had no right to hold his son, and we'd better let him go immediately if we didn't want an international incident right here in New Holland. He said his son was protected by a diplomatic passport, and he was calling the State Department!"

"So what did you tell him?"

"Don talked to him," said the sheriff, motioning to the DA.

"I told him he could call the State Department if he wanted, but we were going to hold his son regardless. A diplomatic passport doesn't mean we can't detain him. We've got the right to process him and check his status, like anybody else we bring in. Then the Indians called back and hollered a little more, said they were sending a representative immediately to fish him out of jail."

"What's the bottom line?"

"We're going to release him. I've been on the phone to Washington, Boston, the state police, and J. Edgar Hoover. His papers are in order."

"How much longer can you hold him?"

"Not long. They're due within the hour."

"So, that's it," said Frank, standing up to circle his desk. "I don't want to risk an international incident over this damn turbanhead. I want that guy out of my jail before George Walsh finds out he's here. That's all I need, the whole town knowing I had Jordan Shaw's murderer locked up, then let him go. I promised Pat Halvey I'd rip his tongue out of his mouth if he breathed a word. So nobody knows but us: Don, Halvey, you, and me. And that's the way it stays."

"Can I talk to him?" I asked. "Maybe we can get some answers without an international incident."

"Go ahead," he said in disgust. "But that damn Indian is leaving when his paisans come to fetch him."

Roy was not in a cell. The sheriff had locked him in a holding room used for prisoners awaiting arraignment. How ironic, I thought; Judge Shaw had passed sentence so many times on men who had waited in that room. Frank let me in alone.

"Miss Stone, yet again a pleasant surprise!" said the jolly prisoner, rising to greet me.

"Hello, Prakash," I said, opting for his given name. "Or is it good-bye?"

"I'm afraid so."

"Will you answer a couple of questions for me?" I asked.

"Of course."

"Tell me about November 25th."

"Don't blame me, Miss Stone. It's indeed unfortunate that any harm came to Jordan; I rather liked her, actually."

"But you didn't want to flunk out of Tufts, right? So you killed her regardless of your affection for her."

"I did not kill her."

"But you cut out a piece of her skin."

Roy smiled again, but didn't answer yes or no. "Dr. Jerrold put himself in great jeopardy with his indiscretion. He's up for tenure and would be of little use to me if he were sent away. An affair with an undergraduate could be fatal to his career. And mine. After Monday, the question will be settled once and for all; the faculty are meeting to take their final decision. With no scandal, he's a sure bet for tenure."

"Jerrold says you killed her."

"Not true," he said. "He's been imagining conspiracies ever since I ran into them in Delhi last August. He was horrified, of course; he assumed he was safe from scrutiny so far from home."

"So you don't want to leave Tufts?" I asked. "Is flunking out so bad? Worth blackmail?"

"I don't believe there is any proof I have blackmailed Professor Jerrold. Has he lodged a complaint with the police?"

"You know he hasn't," I said, and Roy smiled.

"As for my studies, you don't know my father. He would send me back to Delhi. I've grown accustomed to this country; I like it. What would I have in India? A government job, an arranged marriage to the daughter of some backwater *babu*, and the attentions of my overbearing mother. I like to smoke, enjoy a beer or whiskey in the evening. I can't do that there. No, I want to stay here."

"Even if it means exerting a little influence over a randy professor? A couple of innocent girls die, but so what? So long as Jerrold walks away unscathed and in your debt."

"It is not as heartless as you make it sound. I told you I didn't kill Jordan."

"But you did remove all evidence of Jerrold's presence in her room that night, tampered with evidence, and probably jeopardized the investigation."

He smiled but said nothing.

"And maybe you palmed Jordan's things, too. Her purse, for instance?"

"I've read the papers and know that the purse was discovered in her Boston flat. Perhaps she neglected to take it with her for the Thanksgiving break."

"She took it with her, all right," I corrected. "The police found a receipt from the Mohawk Motel inside, dated November 25th."

Roy's eyebrow inched up his forehead, but there was no other sign of concern. "I'm sure the Boston police tested the purse for fingerprints?"

"Wiped clean."

"I see. Did you expect anything else?"

I confessed that I had not.

"Just a few more questions, then," I said. "To satisfy my own curiosity, you understand."

"As many as you like, Miss Stone. You've worked long and hard on this investigation; your curiosity is understandable."

"Who do you think killed Ginny White?"

Roy frowned. "Why do you think I would know that?"

"Because I went through Jordan's apartment before the police did," I said. "I believe someone removed incriminating evidence against Jerrold. That leads me to think of you."

"But I've admitted to nothing of the kind. You present interesting theories, but all are conjecture."

"I think you removed all of Jerrold's effects from the apartment: clothing, letters, photographs ... You couldn't risk having the police link him to the deceased, or the scandal would sink his tenure bid. But I'll wager you've saved every last item you took. How better to hold a threat over Jerrold's head? It was a thorough job, to be sure. But you missed something."

"Obviously," said Roy. "Otherwise, you would never have pursued Dr. Jerrold with such zeal. Tell me, Miss Stone, what did you find?"

"The brush-off letter he'd sent Jordan," I said. "It was under her pillow."

"And you're sure it was from Jerrold? He actually signed the letter?" asked Roy.

"No, there was no signature," I conceded.

"Then how can you be sure it was Jerrold and not someone else who wrote it?"

"He spelled *realize* the British way."

Roy's eyes sparkled, and he granted me my small victory with a smile. I couldn't figure him; it was just a game, nothing personal at all, and he enjoyed the friendly contest.

"Your burglar clearly underestimated her romantic side. He should have checked the pillow."

I was ready to turn up the heat. "What about the tattoo?" I asked.

Now Roy was surprised; his smile faded. "What?"

"Jordan had a tattoo," I said. "At least when she arrived at the Mohawk Motel."

"Are American girls in the habit of getting tattooed?" he asked after giving it some thought. "I've never seen one in this country."

Neither had I, at least not outside a carnival sideshow.

"Did the police find a tattoo on her body?" asked Roy.

"You know they didn't. Someone cut it out of her skin with a large knife. Maybe something like a kirpan?"

Again the smile. "That's an interesting theory, but difficult to prove."

"Not so difficult." I paused for effect. "Wasn't there something in the paper about pictures shot through the window?"

"That was just your bluff," he said, unnerved just the same.

"Do you think so? How else would I have known about the tattoo?"

I had him there. He had been forthcoming with a lot of information, as long as he thought I was holding nothing. Now his attitude changed. He couldn't risk talking to me about the tattoo; only a select few could have seen or known about it, and he didn't want to be on that list.

"If she had a tattoo, it's news to me," he said coolly. "I don't like them anyway. You see them on villagers and *junglees* in India, but what respectable Western girl wears a tattoo?"

"Jordan Shaw," I said. "At least for a couple of weeks."

Roy screwed up his face. "What do you mean by that?"

"Her tattoo was temporary," I said. "Just some henna. It would have faded away in a couple of weeks."

Roy seemed genuinely surprised, impressed even, but he said nothing. This was dangerous territory for him.

"I wouldn't know anything about that," he mumbled.

"Jordan had some henna powder in her room in Boston. And an icing cone to apply it. She must have learned how when she went to that wedding in India. Still," I said, "it would have looked awfully bad for Jerrold if that tattoo had been seen by the police. Henna or no, that tattoo had to go."

I felt I had all the information he was willing to share. I stood to leave and noticed Roy's troubled expression. He wanted to say something but couldn't get it out.

"Maybe you have a question or two for me?" I asked.

"One thing has made me curious," he said. "You've been very thorough in your questioning, but there's one thing you haven't asked me."

"What's that?"

"Who ransacked Nichols's apartment?"

He was right. There seemed little utility in asking him that, since I was sure Hakim Mohammed had carried out that sloppy job. That's where he got the letters and photographs of Jordan and Jerrold in India. Poor D. J. Nichols was obsessed with Jordan and must have followed her to Fatehpur Sikri and taken the photos of the lovers. Thinking back on Roy's ordered searches of Jordan's room at the Mohawk Motel and her apartment in Boston, I was pretty sure Hakim had also trashed my place and Jean Trent's digs, probably looking for Julio's film. But I wasn't about to share this information with Prakash Singh.

"So?" I said, retaking my seat. "Did you break into his place?"

He shook his head and said he had assumed I was responsible for the burglary.

"Really? How exciting you make me sound."

"I know that reporters sometimes get carried away," he said. "I figured you were looking for something—pictures from last summer's Indian tour, perhaps? Letters from Jordan?"

"Sorry, it wasn't me," I said.

Roy grinned one last smile at me. "I suppose if something of the sort turns up, I'll know you were lying."

We stared into each other's eyes for a long moment. I had nothing more to ask him, and he had nothing more to tell me.

"Your ride will be here soon," I said. "Good luck."

"Luck is for the unprepared," he said, taking my hand. "Good planning is the better strategy."

☙

"So, did he kill Jordan Shaw?" asked Frank.

"I don't think so."

"Bull!" said Frank Olney, slapping his hand down on the desk. "He's lying. He killed Jordan Shaw and Virginia White, and that's that. You never want to give up, do you? 'The Case That Never Ended,' by Eleonora Stone," he proclaimed, framing headlines in the air. "Well, I'm satisfied he's guilty; and the voters'll just have to accept that we couldn't hold him because of his immunity."

"Why don't you think Roy killed Jordan Shaw?" the DA asked me. "Just because he denied it?"

"That's part of it," I said. "He was pretty straight with me in there because he thought he had nothing to fear. Even so, he was careful; he's not rash enough to brag about breaking the law. But what really convinces me he didn't kill them is his car."

"What about it?"

"Jean Trent saw three cars in the parking lot that night. The first belonged to Jerrold, Jordan's lover, probably driving his wife's cream-colored Bonneville. The second, I believe, was Roy's. Finally, a third car of unknown ownership showed up. I think it was driven by a Pakistani from Tufts, Hakim Mohammed, but it's a moot point since Jordan was already dead when Roy arrived."

"So what about the car convinces you he didn't kill her?" repeated the DA.

"No oil drippings," I said, and Frank screwed on his most incredulous expression.

"What are you talking about, Ellie? Oil drippings? What's next, a Ouija board and tea leaves?"

"The morning after you found Jordan Shaw's body in the woods, I came across a distinctive pattern of oil drippings on the water-tower service road, not fifty yards from her grave. The next day, I found the same pattern on that little dirt road behind the Mohawk Motel. The person who drove the car that left those spots killed Jordan Shaw. The killer never parked in the lot. Jean Trent never saw his car."

"So who do you think dripped the oil?" asked the Thin Man.

I shook my head. "I just don't know. For the past ten days I've been bending over, looking for oil under every car that's not moving. It's just not there."

"What about Julio?" asked Frank, hopefully. "Or that hood, Pukey Boyle?"

I shook my head. "Frank, when I said every car, I meant *every* car. I'm wearing out the knees in my stockings. The spots are gone."

CHAPTER SIXTEEN

Thursday afternoon: barely twelve hours to go before I had to give Artie Short my answer. My head was pounding. I felt as if I had fought a grueling game, outplayed my opponent at every turn, but still lost, striking out with the bases full in the ninth. I shuddered at the idea of looking underneath one more car, of postulating one more theory of how the oil spots had come to be near the grave and behind the motel. I was tired, yearning for a long sleep with nothing more momentous to worry about than my fuzzy television reception. I lay down on the couch with a Scotch and tried to empty my head.

My thoughts drifted from the insipid to the banal, without ever truly freeing themselves from undercarriages, crankcases, and motor oil. Worse still, nightmares of Greg Hewert infected my dreams of cars and greasy pavement.

I remembered my dream of Jordan Shaw and felt I had let her down, along with my father and myself. That beautiful young girl was dead, and her killer had gone unpunished. All for want of a triangular oil spot. The clock was running out, and I was failing. I sensed I would be covering basketball games and VFW meetings very soon.

❧

"Is it ready, Vinnie?" I asked as the mechanic scrubbed some of the day's grime off his hands.

"Your Dodge is out back," he said. "Good as new. How'd you like the loaner?"

"Greased lightning?" I said. "Good thing you're at the bottom of a hill; I was tired of pushing that thing around."

"Yeah, but I don't hear you complaining about the price. Which reminds me: it'll cost you thirty-six fifty for the miracle I performed on your car."

"I'll call her Lazarus," I said, but Vinnie had forgotten his catechism.

I wrote a check, hoping the paper would reimburse me, hoping I'd still have a job tomorrow, and reclaimed my keys. I went around back to get the car, but it was the heap next to mine that caught my attention: a rusty, white Plymouth. I returned to the garage and corralled Vinnie Donati.

"Isn't that Tommy Quint's car over there?" I asked.

Vinnie looked out the window over his shoulder. "Yeah, that thing's always breaking down."

"Two times in ten days?" I asked.

"I wouldn't talk if I were you," said Vinnie with a grin.

"When did he bring it in this time?"

"This morning. We had to tow it from his old man's driveway."

"He's not in Rochester?"

"He rode with me in the cab of Dom's wrecker."

I went back to the lot and stared at the Plymouth. Something about its presence bothered me. I bent over and examined the ground beneath it, though I was sure I'd find nothing. I found nothing. Two times in ten days. The last time the Plymouth had given out was the day after Jordan's murder. Or was it?

"Vinnie?" I called, having circled around to the garage yet again. "What day did you say Tommy Quint brought that car in the first time?"

"I don't remember," he said. "A week ago, maybe two."

"Can you look it up?"

Vinnie shrugged his shoulders and threw open the ledger lying on the counter. His permanently blackened fingers slid over the names and numbers. He turned a page, then another.

"Here it is," he said, spinning the oversized book around so I could see. "Saturday, November 26th, one p.m. Why do you want to know?"

I shook my head. "Nothing. I thought maybe . . . Nothing."

It was half past six, and Vinnie was closing up. I walked back to my car for the last time. I stared at the white Plymouth. Its headlights looked back at me, but I couldn't read their secrets.

"What a bomb." A voice behind me.

I turned to see Al Ornuti, Dom's son, in coveralls. I nodded silently.

"Those Plymouths are okay, though this particular job's in bad shape," he continued, joining me in solemn contemplation of the car. "But that's the owner's fault."

"Uh-huh." I'd eaten cars for the previous ten days, and I wasn't eager to pass the time talking about them with a grease monkey.

"This one's a perfect example of poor maintenance," he said, motioning to Tommy's Plymouth. "The kid that owns her called in a couple of weeks ago to ask for a tow. Dom's wrecker was getting a paint job, so I told him we couldn't hook him up until it dried. He calls again the next morning, Saturday, mind you, and wants to know if the tow truck's ready. I tell him not before Monday. So guess what he does."

"I have no idea," I said, ready to nod off.

"He gets his old man to push it down here with the family car. And the killer is, he forgets to release the emergency brake! That poor car. It's a wonder she still runs at all."

The image of Tommy Quint's father nudging the white Plymouth along flushed all the tedium and frustration from my mind. Something new to concentrate on. My headache vanished; I knew. I knew!

"Good evening, Mrs. Quint, my name is Eleonora Stone. I'm a reporter with . . ."

"I know who you are," she said, barring my path with the front door. "What do you want?"

"I was wondering if I might speak to Tommy."

"What for? He hasn't done anything. Why don't you leave him alone? The poor boy. He's been in such a state since Jordan died. And he's getting worse; won't go back to school, mopes around, refuses to eat. I won't have you making matters worse by tormenting him with this mess."

"I'm sorry, ma'am, but I've got a job to do. Your son saw Jordan Shaw hours before she was killed, and, like it or not, he has a responsibility to cooperate. A beautiful girl with a promising future was murdered. We owe it to her to find her killer."

Mrs. Quint wrinkled her nose. "She was asking for it, if you want my opinion. Imagine, a young girl like that meeting men in a motel room. She was not a proper young lady, Miss Stone."

"No one's life looks pristine under a microscope, Mrs. Quint. We all should remember that."

"My son has gone out. I hope you won't be offended if I don't invite you in." And she closed the door.

I cruised the city, following the rise and fall of New Holland's hills, stopping at every watering hole I knew—and I knew them all—in search of Tommy Quint. The night was cooling off fast, making for a chilly ride. At eleven, I pulled up in front of Fiorello's and went inside for some hot coffee.

"Where have you been?" asked Fadge, reading the *New York Post* at the counter. The place was deserted.

"I'm trying to find Tommy Quint," I said. "You know where he might be?"

"Try Rochester. Isn't he at school?"

"No, he's been in town since the funeral. I went to his house, but he wasn't there."

Fadge shrugged. "He hasn't been in here since Sunday when you saw him. I didn't even know he was in town."

"His mother says he's very upset by this whole thing."

"I believe it; he was crazy about Jordan. Tell you the truth, I'm worried about him. I wouldn't be surprised if he did something stupid, like Romeo and Juliet. He was just plain nuts about her."

I considered the thought: Romeo and Juliet. I had an idea.

"Thanks, Fadge," I said, and ran out to my car.

Jordan Shaw was buried in Maple Hill Cemetery, east of town about halfway down Widow Sarah Road. It was a dark, deserted neck of the woods, perfect for a cemetery around midnight. I cut the motor at the entrance, and glided to a stop near the first headstones. I climbed out of the Dodge and set off toward Monument Bluff, a quarter mile away, where Jordan's grave was located. Moving quickly, I crackled over broken twigs and dry leaves. A December breeze ran down the hill, muffling my approach and chilling my uncovered ears.

Monument Bluff was a bald mound that protruded high over the surrounding hills, dominating the valley below. By moonlight it was one of the prettiest vistas in the state, and people paid fortunes for the right to inter their departed loved ones there.

Jordan Shaw's final resting place was a shaded plot near a towering maple. Beside her grave, as still as a statue, sat a solitary figure. At first, I thought it was another tombstone, but as I came closer, I recognized it as a human form.

"Hello, Tom," I said, just a few yards behind him.

He nearly jumped out of his skin, scrambling to his feet and taking a defensive position behind a tree.

"It's me, Tom," I called. "Ellie Stone."

"What do you want?" he panted. "Why can't you leave me alone? I'm not hurting anyone here."

"No, you're not hurting anyone *here*," I said. "But I've come because of what you've already done."

"What are you talking about?" he asked, stepping away from the tree.

"I'm talking about Jordan Shaw and Ginny White."

He stared at me in the dark. "What?"

"You killed them both."

"That's a lie! Why would I want to kill Jordan? I loved her with all my heart!"

"Exactly," I said. "You didn't *want* to kill Jordan. It just happened."

"Liar! I didn't kill Jordan or Ginny."

"Let it go, Tom. This is tearing you apart."

"I loved her, damn it! I didn't kill her."

"You killed her, Tom. You followed her to the Mohawk Motel that Friday night and waited to see who was meeting her. You stewed for an hour or two until the guy left. Then you went inside, and things got complicated, a little rough, maybe."

"No! How could I have followed her that night? My car broke down that afternoon."

"Oh, I know that . . . now. It took me a long while to figure it out, but once I did, I knew it was you."

"You're making this up as you go along! How does my car breaking down prove I killed Jordan?"

"Because you followed her to the motel in your father's car."

Tommy stared at me, jaw slackened. "You can't prove that."

"Oh, yes, I can. You see, Tom, bad habits are learned, usually from our parents. Good and bad habits. You might learn good manners and bad penmanship from the same parent. It's not a value judgment; it's just the way things are."

"What are you saying about my dad?"

"I'm saying he doesn't take good care of his car."

"You're nuts!"

"And you've taken after him. I can prove you were at the Mohawk Motel on Friday, November 25th, because your father's car leaks oil."

"What? So do a million other cars."

"Not like your dad's. It drips these perfect little triangles. I know you killed Jordan, Tom. Then you took her body from the room and put her in the car. You had an idea where you could bury her, a place you thought would be safe. But you didn't have anything to dig a hole with, so you swiped the garbage can from the Mohawk Motel and drove out to the water tower. You carried her about fifty yards into the woods and scraped a hole in the ground with the garbage can."

"It's all lies."

"No, Tom. There was an oil spot on the water-tower service road, and two more behind the Mohawk. They're identical to the last detail."

"Your imaginary oil spots have surely disappeared by now," he said, posturing like a savvy tough. "What proof do you have?"

"I've got the proof," I said. "I took pictures. And good ones, too. I can place you behind the Mohawk and on the service road on the night of the murder. I can prove it, Tom."

"I've got Jean Trent's gun, you know," he said, his voice beginning to tremble.

My knees began shaking about the same time. I had assumed Hakim had rifled through Jean Trent's place, but if Tommy had the gun, I'd have to rethink that theory. Then it hit me. The film. Tommy had ransacked my place, too, in search of Julio's photos.

"What were you looking for?" I said carefully. "Was it the pictures?"

Tommy pulled something from his coat pocket: something that flashed in the moonlight. He didn't point it at me, though. It just sort of hung from his limp hand.

"Yes," I said, drawing strength from Tommy's wavering. "It must have been the pictures you were looking for. Afraid maybe Julio caught you in the act with his handy camera. Or maybe you just couldn't stomach the idea that someone else might look upon Jordan's naked body. You'd kill for that, wouldn't you, Tom? You'd kill again, I'll bet."

"No!"

"Another man, looking at Jordan's smooth skin, possessing her with his eyes. You couldn't bear that, could you? I've seen her, Tom. I saw the pictures, and she was beautiful."

Tommy lifted the gun and pointed it at my chest. Damn, I was hitting him a little too hard. I straightened up, trying to still my quivering legs.

"Give me the gun, Tom. You don't want to kill again."

The gun flickered in the moonlight, and I could tell he was shaking. I took a step toward him and saw that he was sobbing. His eyes were clenched shut, tears streaming down his cheeks. I wanted to jump him, but my nerve didn't go that far.

"It's true, isn't it, Tom?" I asked gently. "Everything I've said is true."

His arm fell back to his side, and his body shook from his weeping.

He turned around and dropped to his knees on Jordan's grave. I saw the metal flash again in the night, and this time I found the courage to move. I dived at him and deflected his arm just as the gun went off. The bullet sailed past his right temple and disappeared into the night. In his weakened state, Tommy was no match for me. I pried the gun from his hand with little trouble, and he collapsed on the fresh dirt of Jordan's grave, wailing from deep inside his lungs.

I put a soft hand on his heaving shoulder, but I doubt he even knew I was there. "Eyes, look your last," I mumbled.

⁂

Tommy Quint's father's car was parked on one of the nearby pathways, dripping the prettiest isosceles triangles you've ever seen. Not that I had any real doubts by that time, but it was satisfying to see them just the same. I promised myself I would never again look under a car. Never again.

CHAPTER SEVENTEEN

Tommy Quint gave Frank Olney a full confession about an hour later. He explained that he had parked his father's car on the dirt road behind the motel at about 9:30, where it dripped the first set of spots into the dirt. Frank asked if he'd seen Julio peeping through the window, but Tommy said it was dark and the heavy brush would have hidden him anyway. Tommy waited for Jerrold to leave around 11:15, then agonized for nearly an hour over what to do. Unable to contain his jealousy any longer, he slipped into Jordan's room. She was bending over next to the bed, naked, drying off her legs with a towel after her shower. She didn't hear him enter. Julio must have run out of film or had his fill, because he wasn't at the window when Tommy let himself into the room. Retching from jealousy and desire, Tom watched as Jordan dried the body she had just given to David Jerrold, the body she'd never given to him. Then she stood up straight, turned to face Tom, her head wrapped in another towel, and he noticed she was holding the telephone receiver in the crook of her neck. According to Tommy, she jumped a little when she saw him, but smoothed the ruffles out of her surprise in short order. She seethed but didn't scream.

"Oh, my God, Ginny. I've got to go," she said into the phone. "Tommy Quint just walked into my room. Can you believe it? Pathetic! I'll see you Sunday."

She hung up the phone and then, to take her revenge, just stood before him, her skin radiant, and made no move to cover herself. Then she said something along the lines of "You wanted to see? Well go ahead," and lifted her arms to display her nudity better. He saw the tattoo, could read the name, *David*, scrawled awkwardly into the most intimate part of her anatomy, a place she had just shared with another man. She was ruined forever. Even if he could win her back, the tattoo would always remind him of the man who'd sullied her: David. The name swirled in his head, taunting him, sickening him. Tommy crumbled to the floor and wept uncontrollably.

Finally, in disgust, Jordan unwrapped the towel from her head and stormed into the bathroom to dry her hair. She railed at him from behind the half-closed door, emasculated him, ridiculed him, mimicked his sobbing. How dare he follow her? How dare he intrude into her personal life? How dare he walk into her room without knocking? She told him she never wanted to see him again, that he was a despicable crybaby and a Peeping Tom besides. Rubbing the towel through her hair, she never heard him approach from behind.

The sheriff told me he had listened with a dry mouth as Tommy described Jordan's naked back, her perfect buttocks, her willowy legs—the last image he had of her alive, before his eyes filled with blood, and he grabbed her around the neck. The next thing he remembered was laying her dead body on the bed.

He ran scared, drove up to the lake, and wandered through the woods for about an hour. Then his mind went to work, and he decided he had to move the body before someone discovered it. He drove back to the motel, parked the car a few feet from where it had dripped oil the first time, and returned to Jordan's room to find the bloody mess. Roy had already been there, and Jordan's pelvis bore the grizzly wound. Her clothes and purse were gone; things had been rearranged. Tommy was too confused to know exactly what had happened, but he was lucid enough to realize someone had sliced out a piece of Jordan's flesh.

The sight of her bloodied pelvis sickened Tommy, and, later on, in an irrational state of mind, he convinced himself that someone else had actually murdered her. But at that moment, he hoisted her over his shoulder and carried her out back to his car. Then he returned to snatch the garbage can. Twenty minutes later, he smeared the last of the mud and leaves over her body in Wentworth's Woods.

Frank asked him about Ginny White, and Tommy gave an economical description of what had happened: Ginny knew he had barged into Jordan's motel room and would tell the police everything she'd heard on the phone. He took his father's car to Boston on Saturday afternoon, went to the girls' apartment, and rang the bell. Ginny felt funny letting him in after the phone conversation with Jordan the night before, but she thought he needed some compassion. When she turned her back, he clubbed her to death with a tire iron he'd grabbed from his father's trunk. Then he returned home late Saturday night and boarded a bus for Rochester the following morning, arriving at school just hours before I phoned him.

Tommy completed his statement, closed his mouth, and didn't open it again. He just stared into space. Pat Halvey led him downstairs, shut him in the middle cell, and took up the suicide watch. Frank just shook his head, saddened and numb.

FRIDAY, DECEMBER 9, 1960

I used the remaining three hours before dawn to write the final story on the Shaw-White murders. When I arrived at the paper at eight o'clock, I strode into Artie Short's office and handed my copy to the publisher himself. I watched him read it. His expression did nothing to betray his thoughts as his eyes ranged across the lines, one by one. Finally, when he had finished, he tossed the pages back across his desk without even looking at me.

"Print it."

EPILOGUE

Two weeks after Tommy Quint's arrest, Judge Shaw invited me to his law office on Main Street for a late-afternoon meeting. He thanked me on behalf of himself and his wife, who was not present.

"In truth, I doubted you from the first moment I heard about you," he said. "Fred Peruso assured me you were my best bet, but I was skeptical."

I didn't know what to say. Not exactly a ringing endorsement.

"But," he said, pausing for several beats, "you, of course, proved me and my wife wrong. For that, I am grateful to you."

"You're welcome."

"It's the hardest thing I've ever known, Miss Stone. And it's not gone away. It never will. I suppose you could have told me that the first night we met."

I watched him, without a word, breathing slowly and deeply. He wouldn't look at me, just stared at something on the floor somewhere across the room.

"I take no satisfaction that Tommy Quint will pay for this crime. It's a horrible tragedy in these modern times. Of course I'm relieved that there is a resolution, an end to the . . ." he searched for a word, apparently failed. "An end to the not knowing," he managed finally. "Now I can mourn my daughter without the added torture of simply not knowing."

He stopped, looked at me pointedly, and asked if I felt that way about my father. Now it was my turn to look away at nothing in particular.

"It was different with my father," I said. "I let him down, disappointed him till the day he died, alone in that hospital bed. You didn't let Jordan down."

"I suppose it's not quite the same," he granted, then fell silent for a long while. "What about that ... man? That professor?" he asked, uncomfortable with the question and, perhaps, the eventual answer.

"I hope you won't mind a little indiscretion on my part," I said, looking up at him again. "I came into possession of a couple of letters Jordan had written to a friend. And there were a couple of snapshots of Jordan and Jerrold holding hands in India."

The judge stiffened.

"In the letters, Jordan described her love affair with Jerrold." I paused. "I sent photostatic copies of the letters and prints to Professor Lionel Benjamin, chairman of the Engineering Department and Jerrold's tenure committee." I licked my dry lips to moisten them. "And I dispatched copies to Jerrold's wife, too."

"And?" asked the judge.

"I'm sorry, but I got word yesterday from the department secretary that Jerrold got his tenure despite the information I sent. I'm afraid my ploy failed."

Judge Shaw stared blankly at me, and I couldn't be sure if he was annoyed or not.

"His wife is standing by him, too," I said. "I can't imagine why."

He coughed lightly, but showed no outward emotion at the news.

"What about that Indian fellow?" he asked in a hoarse voice. "You said he was the one who ... mutilated my poor Jordan."

"Even if the letters I sent didn't sink Jerrold, they finished off Roy," I said. "Jerrold doesn't protect him anymore and, in fact, blamed him for the embarrassing appearance of the letters. Singh must have assured him that he had collected all incriminating evidence from Jordan's apartment the day after the murder, so when the letters and photographs surfaced at the tenure meeting, Jerrold assumed he'd been double-crossed. Singh's father shipped him off to India three days ago."

I don't think any of this pleased Judge Harrison Shaw. The cavernous sorrow left by Jordan's death would remain forever, of course, perhaps becoming familiar with time, but the heartbreak and the cruel sting would surely dog him all his days.

Now, there was only one thorn left to pull. The judge put the question to me with great discomfort: "We read in your paper that there might be . . . film. Photographs of Jordan."

"Oh," I said, feeling the sweat on my brow. "Don't let that trouble you. I invented that story and fed it to George Walsh."

His dumb expression begged for an explanation.

"I thought the story might flush out the killer."

"Then you're sure no photographs of her exist?" asked the judge. "I would choke on my rage if any pictures of her ever turned up."

"There is no film of her, Judge," I said, my mouth sticky dry. "You have my word of honor. My promise."

We talked a while longer, reviewed the last niggling details until there was nothing more to say. Once we'd covered everything, all that was left was an awkward ending. I thought I might be able to help him cope and suggested another meeting if he wanted, anytime he wanted.

Judge Shaw looked embarrassed. "I'm sorry, Miss Stone," he said. "I appreciate your fine work on this case, all your efforts. But I see no reason for us to see each other again."

I was stunned.

"You must understand," he explained. "This does not establish a social bond between us." He paused. "In fact, just the opposite."

If he had gutted me with a knife, I could not have felt more hollow. I left his office sobered, humbled, and filled with self-reproach. What had I been thinking? Harrison Shaw was no father of mine, and I was not his Jordan. I should have wished him well on my way out the door, but I couldn't do it. I had my own demons to wrestle. The judge and his wife had no monopoly on grief.

I returned home and pulled the heavy Curtis folio off its shelf. I hadn't looked at the haunting photographs since I'd first developed them, and I didn't want to see them now. I burned them and their negatives in a metal wastebasket in my bathroom. Mrs. Giannetti banged on the door, wanting to know what the smell was.

About two months later, I ran into Pukey Boyle at the Dew Drop Inn—I had become something of a regular. When I first caught sight of him across the room, I thought, "God, that is a lot of man!" Not my type, perhaps, but a lot of man just the same. It was the first time I'd seen him since that day at the Leatherstocking Motel. Now, in the dim light of the bar, we had several drinks and a couple of pickled eggs together. We talked late into the night, and he asked me if I'd ever heard from Julio Hernandez.

"His mother sent me a thank-you note, but that's it," I answered. "I don't get down to the East End much these days."

Pukey grunted a chuckle. "The East End? Your boy's moved up in the world. He's shacked up with Jean Trent and got himself a brand-new Corvette. I heard they're getting married. Can you imagine? That old hag?"

I sipped my drink and smiled inside, happy to see Victor Trent's nest egg finally being put to use.

It was hours later when I found the courage to ask Pukey the question I had tried to ask him in the hospital.

"Why were you following me? Why did you want to protect me?"

"I knew you were on top of things, and I didn't want anyone getting in your way," he said with a shrug.

I was flattered. I thought how sweet it was that he'd been carrying a torch for me. He'd probably been too shy to tell me his true feelings. Then he smiled, a little sadly, and looked into his beer.

"You might not understand this, Ellie, coming from a guy like me," he said. He shook his head slowly, then looked away. "I loved her. I loved her like you can't imagine."

And, yes, I felt like a chump. I laughed silently at myself and thought what a great guy Pukey Boyle had turned out to be. I touched his hand to comfort him and to convey that I understood. Our eyes met, and I shared a smile in the dark with my hero, my paperboy.

ACKNOWLEDGMENTS

A book is made by a lot of people. My books have been made better by the great team at Seventh Street Books. I am grateful in particular to Dan Mayer, editorial director, who tears apart my plots, looking for holes to plug and logic to correct; Mariel Bard, editor, who ferrets out the buried errors in my manuscripts and polishes my words; Meghan Quinn, publicist, who works so hard and cheerfully to get my books seen and read; and Jackie Cooke, senior graphics designer, who produced the beautifully evocative covers for *Styx & Stone* and *No Stone Unturned*.

Some wonderful friends have provided me with invaluable feedback and support: Lynne Raimondo, Kay Kendall, Raik Sabeel, and Dr. Kunda. Thank you, all.

Special thanks to my agent, William Reiss of John Hawkins & Associates, for his advice, for his efforts, and for Ellie Stone herself.

ABOUT THE AUTHOR

J ames W. Ziskin lives in the Hollywood Hills with his wife, Lakshmi, and cats, Bobbie and Tinker.

He is the author of Styx & Stone. A linguist by training, James earned a bachelor of arts and a master of arts in Romance languages and literature from the University of Pennsylvania. He is currently working on the next Ellie Stone Mystery.